BOUND

THE SPIDER'S MATE #3

TIFFANY ROBERTS

BLURB

Ketahn will protect his mate at any cost.

Queen Zurvashi will not rest until everything Ketahn cares about is gone and he belongs to her.

His sweet, compassionate Ivy, his sister, his friends, his new tribe of humans—all are in danger. He fears nowhere is far enough away to escape the queen's wrath.

But Ketahn will see the whole jungle burn before he lets any harm befall his mate. Even if he must stand against Zurvashi and her army, even if he must face every beast in the Tangle, even if he must defy the gods themselves, he will not surrender his female.

Ketahn and Ivy are bound, and no force in the universe will sever the threads that connect them.

For you, the one to whom I am bound.

CHAPTER 1

DARKNESS DOMINATED THE CHAMBER. It filled the space down to the tiniest cracks in the cold, damp stone. It enveloped Ketahn, seeping into his core, and made his every thought heavy and black. But it could not snuff out his rage.

The fire within him blazed stronger than ever. Though it could not emit light, it radiated terrible heat.

He could not see the silk ropes binding him, but he struggled against them. His muscles strained to tear the strands apart, to create even the slightest slack, to find any spot along the coils he could reach with his claws. His snarls, growls, and ragged breaths bounced off the chamber walls; they were hollower and more impotent in their echoes.

For all his rage, he was being thwarted by simple rope.

His upper arms were lashed together over his head, and his lower arms were pulled back behind him. His right and left legs had been tied into tight bundles and pulled to either side with only their very tips touching the floor. More rope was wrapped around his middle, and another coil—only barely looser than the rest—was around his neck.

All those silk bindings were anchored to points on the

ceiling and walls that were masked in the darkness. The rope bit into his hide, and each of his movements sharpened that bite, producing new sparks of pain that added to his existing agony.

Faces flashed through his mind's eye. His sweet, beautiful mate, Ivy. His friends. His broodsister.

Somehow, the chamber's already impenetrable darkness thickened.

He saw Korahla, concerned and unsteady. He saw little Ella, so innocent, so confused, so frightened.

He saw Zurvashi.

The surrounding shadows took on a bloody hue.

Ketahn roared. It was the sound of a wounded beast; ragged, raw, defiant.

Meaningless.

He threw his weight against the ropes. His body swayed forward, and the coils tightened around his limbs, creaking with tension. His right legs shifted forward by not even a handspan, striking debris on the floor—bones.

The images in his mind intensified.

Ella's broken, bloody form pieced itself back together in his imagination. The damage wrought by the queen's merciless hands was slowly undone, but the blood remained. The blood would not go away. That vision of Ella turned her head toward Ketahn.

But those eyes were the vibrant blue of a clear sky instead of green, and that blood-matted hair was golden instead of brown; it was Ivy looking at him. It was Ivy in Zurvashi's clutches. And Ketahn could only watch as the queen squeezed and tore, as bone shattered, and veins burst. As everything he cared about, everything he *loved*, was crushed.

Ketahn's struggles faltered. He sagged in the bindings, his arm and leg joints crying out in desperation as they were forced to take his weight without the aid of his muscles. All the while, his mind repeated that dreadful vision. All the while, he watched Ivy die at the queen's hands. Over and over.

That sorrow and despair was enough to pierce his fury when nothing else could have.

The Fangs and Claws who'd dragged Ketahn down here had been no more than shades through the eyes of his rage. He could not recall their faces. They'd rained blows upon him the entire way, had beaten him before restraining him in this dark chamber. They'd left his body battered. But the pain they'd inflicted could never compare to the agony in his hearts.

Ahnset had brought Ella to Takarahl despite Ketahn forbidding it. Now Ella was dead, and Ketahn was Zurvashi's prisoner, cast into the deep, dark place where the queen sent her enemies to wither and die.

My mate. My Ivy. My everything.

Zurvashi's words rose from his memory, dripping with venom and the promise of suffering.

She is going to lead my Claws to the rest of these creatures.

"No." Ketahn seized his fury and forced his legs onto the floor, relieving some of the strain on his arms. He flexed and stretched his fingers, seeking even the slightest brush with the silk strands no matter how awkward the angle.

Ella was gone; Ivy was not. His mate was out there waiting for him, and the queen's servants were searching. Ivy was in danger. Ketahn's entire tribe was in danger.

He needed to escape this chamber. To escape Takarahl. He needed the Eight to sweep him up upon a vengeful wind and hasten him to the pit so he could protect everyone who was left.

"Release me!" He pushed his arms in opposite directions, battling the restrictive rope. His limbs trembled with the exertion. He succeeded only in causing himself more pain.

If he had to tear them apart one thread at a time, he would break these bonds. He would get through that door. He would return to his mate and lead his tribe to safety.

Zurvashi would take *nothing* else from him.

Darkness, agony, and rage were all he had as he thrashed within his bindings. The pounding of his hearts marked the passing time, but time meant nothing to him; he did not know how long he'd been locked in the chamber, only that it had been far too long since he'd left the human ship in pursuit of his broodsister.

And that each moment brought Zurvashi's forces another step closer to the pit.

My nyleea. My Ivy.

"Blood for blood, Zurvashi," he snarled, his words rough and feral.

The claws of his forelegs touched the floor, and he raked them across the stone, searching for something to latch onto. The scrape of rock against his claws reverberated into his bones and made him clench his teeth, but he would not relent. His need to be with his mate would outlast every accursed stone in Takarahl.

Faint vibrations coursed through the floor.

Ketahn stilled, fine hairs standing on end. Something heavy had moved out in the tunnel. His body thrummed with discomfort, anticipation, and the boundless energy of his rage. A cold, unsettling weight churned in his gut.

A gentle, brief air current flowed around his legs. The entrance to the corridor beyond this chamber had been opened.

Despite his discomfort, Ketahn held his position, planting the tips of his legs as firmly as possible on the floor. Moments passed, and he felt nothing—nothing but the same cold, unyielding stone that had been beneath him since he'd been dragged into this chamber.

Ketahn drew in a deep breath. The silence that followed was nearly total. In such dark and quiet, it would have been easy to lose himself, to became nothing more than a seething cloud of pure rage and hatred floating in the impenetrable blackness between the stars.

But he was more than his fury. He still had love to hold him in the present. He still had Ivy.

He felt new vibrations through his legs, so faint at first that he might have missed them had he not been holding his breath. The vibrations gradually grew more distinct. The steady steps of approaching vrix—at least two of them by the feel.

There were only three sorts of visitors he could expect here —Fangs, Claws, or the queen herself.

Ketahn tipped his head back, trying to hook a mandible fang under the rope around his upper arms. He'd attempted such at least a hundred times already, and the result was no different now. Failure. His arms were drawn too tightly together, leaving him unable to turn his head to the right angle. The coils were just out of reach.

He growled and tugged on the strands, making his body shake, and causing fresh pain as the ropes rubbed his already irritated hide.

All he needed was a single hand free. By the Eight, all he needed was a damned chance!

The clinking of metal adornments drifted to him, just audible through the tiny gap under the door. That same gap was soon lit by a faint, bluish glow, so weak that it only deepened the darkness within the chamber.

The approaching group of vrix halted on the other side of the stone door.

Ketahn clenched his teeth and pulled hard on his bindings. His legs rose off the floor, and the ropes creaked as they reached their limits. The outer curve of his mandible fang brushed a silken coil.

Wood scraped stone on the outside of the door. The bars were being lifted out of place.

My Ivy... My mate.

Using every muscle in his body, he pulled his upper arms down while drawing everything else up. The haze of his fury could no longer dull the aches wracking him; from head to hindquarters, from fingertips to the ends of his legs, he throbbed. Yet he refused to give up.

Zurvashi had captured him, but she was not yet the victor.

Another scrape of wood, this one accompanied by a grunt. The door shuddered, and the strip of light at its base grew.

Ketahn's fang caught on the lowermost coil of rope. His hearts fluttered, and his eyes widened. Just a moment longer. Just a moment longer and—

Stone grated as the door opened. That blue light, which had seemed so weak, struck Ketahn fully. Compared to the darkness that had become his world, the light was dazzling. It was blinding.

Ketahn snapped his eyes shut and turned his face away from the light. His fang tore free, fraying the rope but not breaking it.

Hope, that precious, delicate thing he'd cradled in his hearts through every challenge, cracked. His fury blazed into a firestorm, swirling around that fragile core as though it could act as a shield. As though it could act as a replacement.

He slitted his eyes open. The blue glow flooded the chamber, still overpowering to his unadjusted vision, but now he could make out the doorway and the shadowy figures stepping through it. The light gleamed upon the figures' gold adornments with a sickly hue.

Ketahn dropped his legs again. They'd scarce touched the floor before he kicked away from it, swinging himself forward with claws turned toward his visitors. His hands didn't come within even a few segments of the closest figure; his body had barely moved at all.

"Such fury," Zurvashi said. Her voice crept through the small chamber like a jungle vine seeking another plant to strangle. "Would that you had chosen to turn it against my enemies."

"You are the sole focus of my fury," Ketahn growled, gnashing his mandibles. "My hatred is all you shall ever have of me."

The queen became more distinct as Ketahn's vision adjusted. She stood at the center of the newly arrived group with a Fang positioned to either side of her. Her eyes reflected the light of the glowing blue crystals the Fangs held high, staining their usual amber a pale green. The color did nothing to soften her gaze.

She chittered. The sound was as full of malice as it was humor, and it sent a chill through Ketahn despite the heat of his rage.

"Even now you are too great a fool to see what is plain." Zurvashi stepped closer, a long swath of purple silk trailing behind her.

The Fangs hung back, keeping their crystal shards raised. As the queen advanced, the shadows on her face thickened, giving Ketahn the fleeting impression that her eyes were spiteful spirits glowing eerie green in the dark of the Tangle.

Ketahn's instincts were torn between the urge to attack and the urge to recoil—not in fear, but in disgust. He spread his mandibles wide and strained toward her despite those conflicting instincts. He could no longer hide his thirst for her blood. Zurvashi's death would be the closest thing to justice Takarahl had seen since Ketahn was a broodling.

He snapped his mandibles closed once she was before him. His fangs clacked together on empty air, sending a jolt through his skull.

The queen did not flinch. She held Ketahn with her gaze, his fangs no more than a finger's width from her chest. Voice becoming low and raspy, she said, "You are already mine, little Ketahn. Your fury and hatred, your joy and sorrow, your arms, legs, and hide. Your past, present, and future. All mine. And soon, I will have your seed—and your broodlings."

Those inner flames flared, their heat blazing up from Ketahn's core and scorching his chest and throat as they emerged in a thunderous roar. "Never!"

He strained toward the queen, envisioning himself shredding her flesh with his claws, tearing out her eyes, ravaging her throat with his mandibles. Envisioning a thousand bloody deaths for Zurvashi, none of which was punishment enough.

Her hand darted out and caught him by the throat. Despite the dim lighting, he swore that hand was covered in blood. Glistening, crimson, human blood.

Zurvashi leaned closer. Her fingers tightened around his neck, one of them pressing hard into the soft spot beneath his mandible to render it motionless; her thumb did the same to his other mandible.

Her scent filled his nose holes, heady and overwhelming even though it did not possess the fullness of her lust.

"You deserve only death," she growled, "and yet here you are, lingering. Clinging to the warrior's spirit that has carried you through so many trials. You exist because it is my will. And despite your dishonor, despite your betrayal, you remain the only male worthy of siring my brood."

Ketahn answered her with a growl of his own; it was the only sound he could make given her hold on his throat. His fists were clenched, his claws digging into his palms, and the fire in his chest had only intensified.

He would return to his tribe, to his *nyleea*. Zurvashi could not stop him. She would not get what she wanted.

"You behave like a wild beast," Zurvashi continued. Her mandibles twitched, making the shadows on her face tremble. "The best male Takarahl can offer. Disloyal, disrespectful, and incapable of achieving his true potential. Such a waste." She shoved Ketahn's head back hard, releasing his throat. "I had hoped for so much more from you."

He gritted his teeth and sucked in a breath that burned into his lungs. "I will give you more. Your death."

"Oh?" Zurvashi chittered again and threw her arms out to the sides. "Do you mean to claim Takarahl as your own? Does my little hunter think he can succeed where so many females have failed?"

The queen's scent strengthened; the tang of her desire sharpened. Ketahn's insides twisted against the influence of that fragrance. He fought to draw Ivy's scent from memory so its sweetness could comfort him, so its potency could ward him from the queen. But only one smell surfaced—that of human blood.

"You have never found your equal because you are beneath every other vrix in the Tangle," Ketahn said.

Those hard, piercing eyes remained on Ketahn, their light intensifying.

"Your cruelty is not strength," Ketahn continued, holding her gaze. "The fear you instill in those under your rule is not strength. For all the might in your body, Zurvashi, you are the weakest vrix in Takarahl."

True strength was found not in muscle and bone, but in hearts and spirit. True strength was in staring at a world so much larger than oneself, a world determined to crush you, and fighting on even when there seemed to be no hope of success.

True strength was Ivy.

The queen could never match Ketahn's mate. There was no comparison to be made.

Zurvashi did not move, but menace radiated from her, wave after wave of it slamming into Ketahn. He had not succumbed to her scent. He would not succumb to her withering wrath, either.

"Leave us," she finally said, her words low and measured.

The Fangs behind her exchanged a hesitant glance.

"Now." Though she'd spoken no louder, there was command in the queen's tone.

One of the Fangs stepped forward, offering the queen her glowing crystal. Zurvashi did not accept it. She'd not even looked at the Fangs; apart from her order, she had not acknowledged their presence.

The Fang withdrew her extended hand, made a quick gesture of apology, and retreated from the chamber with her companion. Darkness gripped the space again, combated only by a faint glow from the corridor that turned Zurvashi into a looming shadow, a mass of darkness that would surely swallow up everything—even the light.

But the blue crystal glow died when the door was pushed shut, leaving Ketahn only with Zurvashi's cloying scent, with the stifling heat radiating from her body, with his roiling rage. He exerted force against the bindings on his upper arms— against the rope that had been damaged by his fang.

He knew that even were it to break, it would not do so quickly enough to matter.

"The offspring of a weaver thinks to tell me what strength is?" Zurvashi's voice seemed to emanate from the walls all around, the echoes making its true source impossible to determine.

Ketahn's fine hairs bristled, and his hide tingled with unsettled heat. He could feel her nearby, but he was helpless—blind and bound. The resurgence of rage in his chest could not help him.

"Do you know anything of my bloodline, Ketahn?"

The faintest clink of gold drew his attention to the left of the doorway, where there was only more darkness to be seen. His head snapped aside when cloth rustled from the same direction, even closer than the first sound.

Ketahn clenched his fists harder. Warm droplets of blood

oozed from the wounds his claws had inflicted upon his palms. "Only that it will end with you."

"It will not."

Something hard and thick rubbed against Ketahn's left legs, and he felt the queen's fine hairs brush his. Her scent assaulted him anew, made bolder and more powerful through that contact. The bindings allowed him no slack to pull away from her touch.

"My broodmother was a Queen's Fang"—Zurvashi withdrew her leg—"and her mother before her. For generations, my ancestors served Takarahl by protecting the queens and enforcing their will. For generations, my ancestors fought and bled. Thornskulls from beyond the mire, spiritstriders from the Great Dark, fireeyes from the rock lands where the sun crests. My ancestors battled any vrix that threatened our home, and Takari's heirs claimed all the glory."

Ketahn grunted and opened his hands. Blood trickled down his wrists as he curled his fingers, straining to reach the ropes. "So you slew your queen instead."

A large fist struck his abdomen, the blow forcing the air out of his lungs.

"I took what should have been mine by right!" Zurvashi's thunderous words vibrated into Ketahn, enhancing the pain she'd just caused. "I spent my youngest years in service, fighting Azunai's battles for her. Crushing her enemies. My body bore the scars, not hers. My blood was the price paid, and yet hers was the name shouted by Takarahl in reverence. My victories were claimed by her."

Ketahn drew in a ragged breath. That shallow inhalation made his chest ache further, and it wasn't nearly enough to fill his lungs.

Zurvashi flattened her hand on Ketahn's abdomen, pressing the tips of her claws against his hide. She raked them downward slowly, and he drew his claspers in, firmly closing his slit. Her lust-laden scent was entirely at odds with the rage she emitted.

Whenever Ivy grazed Ketahn's hide with her nails, it sparked a thrill in him. It roused his hunger, his desire, made him yearn to have her hands all over his body, caressing, teasing, and exploring.

The feel of Zurvashi's claws made him want to tear off his own flesh so she could never touch it again.

The press of the queen's claws grew firmer as they trailed lower. "Too long had my mothers and sisters gone without their due. Too long was my prowess overlooked."

"She made you her Prime Fang," Ketahn rasped.

Her hand stilled, with those huge, sharp claws far too close to Ketahn's slit. His hearts raced, and liquid fire flowed through his veins, but he could not get hold of the rope. Even with his wrists bent harshly enough that they felt likely to snap, he could not get hold of the rope.

The queen was right in front of him. One bite of his mandibles could've ended this. One bite could've meant his friends, his mate, his tribe, would be safe.

"Not enough," Zurvashi hissed. She flexed her fingers, and her claws pricked Ketahn's hide. "Especially when she lacked the strength and will to see our enemies truly defeated. How many of my spear sisters died only for that coward to order us back?"

"You have never acted for anyone but yourself." One of Ketahn's claws brushed a coil of rope, scraping the outer threads. "You do not care for your spear sisters or Takarahl."

"What chance you might have had to know me, little Ketahn, has long since passed." She sank her claws in deeper and moved her head close enough for him to feel her breath on his face. "I am Takarahl. Takarahl is mighty because of me."

He gnashed his mandibles, but they found only empty air.

Zurvashi's hand caught his throat again, and she slid a foreleg along all three of Ketahn's bound left legs. He strained against his bindings, a bestial growl rumbling in his chest. Her scent assailed him, but that tang of human blood, whether imagined or not, prevented Ketahn from wavering.

The queen had killed Ella. The queen wanted to kill Ivy.

Zurvashi's thumb claw sliced a tiny cut on Ketahn's jaw. "My line will continue on forever. My brood will be rulers of Takarahl, and my legacy will eclipse that of Takari and her weak descendants. All the Tangle will know of Zurvashi, and they will speak my name in awe and terror for all time."

Her hold on his throat prevented Ketahn from speaking, but he stared at her unblinkingly; Zurvashi was the deepest darkness, impenetrable and terrible. Not a monster of legend—she was much, much worse.

"You will sire my brood, Ketahn, and fulfill your every duty as my mate while I craft my legacy with our offspring. But first you will watch as I slaughter all the rest of your little creatures"—her hold on him strengthened, drawing out fresh blood—"and everyone you care about, your broodsister included. You will learn your lesson, but it will be much too late to help you."

Another of her hands came up, and she stroked the outside of his mandible with the pad of her finger. The darkness grew fuller, and her smell crashed against his willpower, reaching into him to rouse the instinctual reactions he'd fought so hard to resist. She was everywhere, all around him, a ravenous cloud, a hungry mire from which there was no escape.

No.

There would be escape. So long as blood flowed in Ketahn's veins, so long as breath filled his lungs, so long as his hearts beat, he was for Ivy. The light with which she'd instilled his heartsthread could never be overcome by the queen's darkness.

Through Zurvashi's relentless grip on his throat, Ketahn chittered.

The queen roared and yanked him closer. The ropes pulled agonizingly taut, especially the one around his neck—but the strand coiled around his upper arms loosened, if only barely. Her fingers locked his mandibles open even as her fangs dug into the sides of his face.

"Each time you utter a sound, you encourage me to devise a new punishment for you," Zurvashi snarled. As she continued, her voice stretched into a purr. "But you will not be granted the release of death. It will be much more satisfying to know you are suffering for all the wrongs you have done me."

The queen released him and withdrew. The bindings pulled Ketahn back slightly, reclaiming the bit of length the queen had forced out of them. The coils around his upper arms loosened further still.

He sucked in a labored breath.

Ketahn's hide pulsed painfully everywhere she'd touched him, and blood trickled from the small, stinging wounds she'd opened on his abdomen, neck, and face.

Nearby, the queen moved, the sounds of her clinking gold and rustling cloth dominant in the silent shadows.

Ketahn grasped at his inner fire, desperate to flood his limbs with a surge of strength—the queen's back was turned toward him, he could sense it, and this was the moment to strike, to end her with all the honor and respect she deserved. But his lungs and throat were ablaze, and the pain was more intense and pervasive than ever. He strained for a few heartbeats before his body sagged in the bindings.

The door opened with a scraping that made it feel like all Takarahl was quaking. Ethereal blue light crept in through the doorway, turning Zurvashi into a hulking shadow-beast with dully gleaming scales.

"I will visit you again soon, my little Ketahn," Zurvashi said. "Our next encounter will be far more pleasurable...at least for me."

The door slammed shut with deafening boom; Ketahn's hearing was still recovering when the wooden bars slid into place on the other side. There were no words venomous enough, no curses vile enough, nothing brief and firm enough to fit the situation but a simple human term.

Fuck.

He would not allow his body to fail. He would not allow weakness to steal this opportunity. Even if he'd missed his chance to strike the queen, he still had a chance to free himself. He still had every reason to keep fighting.

Growling, Ketahn tipped his head back, pulled his body up, and hooked the damaged rope with his fang again, twisting his arms back and forth as much as the restraints allowed to put more stress on the strand. He ignored the thrumming aches in his shoulders and wrists.

Between his harsh breaths, he thought he heard the faint but distinct sound of silk threads breaking, one by one.

Soon, Ivy. I will be with you soon.

CHAPTER 2

KETAHN LET OUT a labored breath and relaxed his muscles. The rope pulled tighter around his throat, putting pressure on flesh already made tender by the queen's rough hold. He inhaled slowly and deeply; it hurt to fill his lungs, but it was just different enough from the rest of his pain to sharpen his focus.

He squeezed his eyes shut. Somehow, the darkness had seemed more complete while his eyes were open.

With a thin, strained growl, he pulled himself up again. Rage still burned inside him, but it was a cold fire now, low and steady. That was what he needed—a constant source of strength for his battered body.

Twisting his head, he probed his forearm with a mandible fang. He'd caught the rope with that fang a few times since the queen had departed. Each time, he'd managed to tear a few more fibers before his fang had slipped free or exhaustion had forced him to ease his limbs.

Thread by thread, he would free himself. Just as thread by thread he had woven his words into a bond with Ivy. Into a promise.

A short line of searing pain flared on his forearm as his fang

17

caught his hide, but he ignored it. That same fang hooked the silk rope an instant later.

Ketahn jerked his head away from the rope in tiny, measured movements, dragging the tip of his fang across the threads.

Zurvashi would not have her way. No matter what opposition he would have to face, Ketahn would return to his mate.

He stilled and took another breath to steady himself against the crippling weariness in his muscles. Carefully, he worked his fang back under the strand. It brushed over hide that was raw and slick with blood.

Most vrix bore their scars with pride, seeing them as symbols of the dangers they'd overcome and the bravery they'd demonstrated. Any marks left on Ketahn's body today would serve only as reminders of his failure.

He'd failed Ella. He would not fail the others. He could not.

The trembling of his upper arms warned that they'd not last beyond a few more heartbeats. He grunted and stretched his neck, working that fang as firmly under the rope as he could.

"I *will* return to you, my *nyleea*," he rasped.

Ketahn whipped his head aside. His fang remained caught on the rope briefly, pulling hard on his mandible joint before ripping free, severing many of the woven threads.

His weight tugged down on the strand as his upper arms lost their strength. The tearing sound echoed off the walls, and the coils around Ketahn's wrists loosened significantly. Jumbled emotions erupted in his chest, filling him with new heat. He drew upon it without hesitation.

Using his entire body, Ketahn bucked and twisted in his restraints, placing as much strain upon the damaged strand as possible. Much too soon, his newfound energy was fading. Ketahn's hearts quickened.

No, he couldn't falter. Not yet, not here. Not until his mate was safe.

A roar burst from his throat as he threw all his weight and

strength downward, trying to swing his upper arms as though to bring an axe down upon wood. The silken coils offered an instant's more resistance and then snapped, unwinding from his upper arms with speed enough to burn his flesh.

Ketahn's torso pitched forward until its momentum was halted by the rope around his neck.

With a choked grunt, he lifted his freed hands to his neck. His fingers fumbled for a hold on the rope, claws scratching his hide, as he struggled to draw breath. Finally, they found purchase toward the back of his neck.

He sliced through the rope.

His torso bent farther down, head hanging, as he drew in a ragged breath, most of his weight now supported by his lower arms. Though his lower shoulders felt like they'd be torn off by the pressure, he remained in that position for several heartbeats.

Ketahn's body cried out in protest; in his mind, he roared back at it.

Gritting his teeth, he curled forward, bending at his middle in a way that felt like it would crack his spine. But his blindly groping hands found what they sought—the ropes securing his legs.

He cut them away. The strain on his lower arms increased eightfold before he unfolded his stiff legs and planted them on the floor. The bindings around his lower arms didn't last another heartbeat against his claws.

His legs were unsteady, his body overly heavy, his muscles stiff. Ketahn couldn't even begin to count all the individual points of pain and soreness comprising his being. They didn't matter. His heartsthread remained, strong as ever, and it was all he needed.

Ivy's name echoed through his mind, through his spirit, as he stumbled forward with arms outstretched before him. The darkness looked thick enough to touch, but his hands struck nothing until they met the wall. His palms rasped over the cool, roughhewn stone in his search for the door. The many grooves and gouges he felt beneath his fingertips had not been left by the chisels and picks of stoneshapers, but the claws of former captives.

Ketahn let out a victorious growl when one of his hands encountered the tiny gap that marked one edge of the door. Its surface was gouged even more deeply than the walls. Determining its boundaries by feel, he braced all four palms against it and pushed.

The door did not yield. Snarling, Ketahn shifted his legs to better make use of their strength in his efforts. This time the door moved, but only by a thread's width before the bars on the other side stopped it.

No. If all the black space between the stars and more than a hundred years had not been able to keep Ketahn and Ivy apart, this door certainly would not prevent their reunion.

He threw himself against the door again and again, barely aware of the pain it caused, barely aware of the guttural sounds escaping him. He'd taken the rope apart thread by thread; he would destroy this door one speck of stone dust at a time if that was what it took.

A door opened out in the corridor. He felt the vibrations of its movement far more clearly now, and the flow of air around his legs was more pronounced.

The queen. It had to be her, returning to taunt him, to torment him, to take him.

Mandibles gnashing, Ketahn eased back from the door and set his spinnerets to work, feeding a thick silk strand into his hands.

Faint vibrations coursed through the floor at a rapid but steady rhythm. Was the queen coming by herself?

His fingers flexed, and his muscles tensed. If Zurvashi was alone, that would allow him to finish it. To end her. No interference, no interruptions, nothing but her blood running over his claws and pooling on the floor.

Ketahn moved to a side of the room that had remained shrouded in darkness when the door had opened earlier. He drew out more silk, winding it around his hands and pulling the strand taut between them. It was no spear, but it would serve as a weapon all the same.

Zurvashi would know how it felt to have her throat crushed.

In the silence, Ketahn heard the queen stop on the other side of the door, separated from him only by a stone slab and a few segments of distance. Far too much more than that separated him from his mate.

Weak blue crystal light glowed along the bottom of the door. The queen began lifting the bars.

A hundred curses and a thousand sounds of bestial fury threatened to burst from his mouth. Ketahn held them all in. He willed the rage at his core to expand and spread through him like flames across dried kindling, slowing his breathing. His muscles coiled in readiness for the imminent battle.

As the door opened, Ketahn retreated deeper into the shadows. A single thought repeated in his mind.

I will be with you soon, my Ivy.

A large figure stood in the doorway with a glowing crystal in one uplifted hand.

He knew immediately she was not Zurvashi—her stance made that clear enough—and that knowledge speared him with relief and bitter frustration.

The female wore a heavy, hooded shroud that hid her head and shoulders, but it did not mask the glint of the golden adornments on her belt and arms. She didn't have to be in the full attire for Ketahn to know she was a Fang.

The Fang stepped through the doorway, crystal held forward. "Keta—"

Ketahn lunged at her, lashing the silk strand around her

outstretched forearm. Before she could get out as much as a startled grunt, Ketahn pulled the strand taut and threw himself into a roll, using all his weight and strength to drag the larger female down with him.

Her body landed on Ketahn, but his momentum carried her smoothly over him. She fell on her back with a heavy thump and the clanking of dozens of gold pieces. Growling, Ketahn scrambled atop the female, his hands working swiftly to catch her limbs with his rope.

This was not Zurvashi, but all he could see was the queen's face. All he could see was blood on her hands—Ella's blood. Human blood.

He needed vengeance. Ella deserved justice.

His claws sought hide to rend, and his mandibles spread wide, their fangs gleaming in the crystal's light.

"Ketahn!" The Fang threw her arms up to defend herself despite them being tangled in the strand, grabbing at his hands. She sounded distantly familiar. Recognition teased at the edges of his awareness, but it was beaten back by rage.

Ivy. He needed to return to Ivy. Anything in his path was an obstacle, anyone in his path was an enemy.

He growled and caught another of the Fang's arms with the rope, tugging it aside. She shifted beneath him, and he felt her legs move, but his opportunity had nearly come—she was angling her head back to avoid his slashing claws, and she was about to expose her throat.

"I have not come to fight you!" The female braced two hands against Ketahn's abdomen. She arched her back and pressed her hindquarters down, bucking Ketahn up—and pitching his torso down as she did so.

Ketahn's hand darted forward, claws aimed at her vulnerable neck.

The instant before his claws would have met flesh, the Fang

heaved Ketahn off. Despite her limbs being restrained by his strand, she put immense strength behind it.

He was cast up and aside; the rope drew tight around his hands and halted his flight. The lower half of his body swung outward and came down hard on the floor, and his lower left shoulder struck a half-moment later. Pain flared through his fury, but it was fleeting. Dragging on the rope, he pulled himself back toward the female.

She'd propped herself up with her lower arms. Using the upper pair, she tugged on the strand, yanking Ketahn's arms out from beneath him. His chin hit the floor.

Ivy's face flashed in his mind, bloody and broken.

Ketahn hissed. He braced his palms on the floor and leapt atop the Fang like a pouncing xiskal. One of her big hands caught him by the throat, but he only growled, snapped his mandibles, and attacked with his claws. The muscles of her arm bulged with the exertion of holding him back.

"By their eightfold eyes, it is I," she said hurriedly, reaching up to tug her hood fully back. Light glinted off a gold ring around her left mandible.

His cold rage burst outward, making that inner flame sputter. In a ragged rasp he said, "Korahla?"

Her fingers flexed around his throat, and she let out a ragged breath. "Yes. Now release these bindings."

Ketahn growled and pulled harder on the strand, forcing her arms closer to each other. Korahla was his broodsister's mate, but she was also the Prime Fang. She'd been the queen's second for nearly a decade, bound by loyalty, duty, and a sense of purpose which Ketahn had once envied.

"I have not come to fight you," she said, stiffening her arms to halt the tightening of the silk strand.

He rotated his wrist, coiling the rope around his hand more securely. "Then why are you here?"

Korahla's mandibles twitched apart, and a brief, barely perceptible tremor coursed through her. "To free you."

"Do not lie to me!"

"By their eightfold eyes, Ketahn, listen to me."

Throwing his weight forward, Ketahn gnashed his mandibles at her face. They strained for something to grab—for flesh to tear or bone to crush.

Korahla hissed. "Curse this day." She shoved him by his throat, releasing her hold as she did so.

Ketahn fell back onto the floor, his hindquarters suffering the brunt of the impact. Cold stone scraped his hide.

He and Korahla scrambled upright simultaneously. She'd hooked a thumb under the silk strand, which offered only an instant's resistance before her claw sliced it apart.

Ketahn's muscles tensed for another leap even as he adjusted his hold on the remaining rope.

"Your broodsister bade me free you," Korahla said, her green eyes gleaming wildly in the dim light.

Everything within Ketahn stilled. He stumbled forward a step as his body abandoned the jump he'd intended, and his hearts went silent.

Korahla took a heavy step forward. The silk rope fell away from her arms as she hunched her shoulders to place her head closer to Ketahn's eye level. "We had little time to speak, but she begged me to free you."

Narrowing his eyes, Ketahn regarded Korahla closely, his instincts torn. Was she ally or enemy? She had always been honest, but could he trust her?

"You would betray your queen?" Ketahn asked.

"I..." She released a huff and dropped her gaze, her firm posture crumbling. "I gave Ahnset my word as her mate."

Somewhere within the torrent of rage and desperation swirling inside Ketahn, something softened. He felt it along his heartsthread, in the most delicate threads of his being, and he could not stop it despite himself.

Because it was enough. Enough for him to trust this female, though she was Zurvashi's Prime Fang.

"Then release yourself from further involvement and stand aside," Ketahn said, gentling his tone.

Korahla lifted her gaze. The light in her eyes was brighter now, but it was hard, it was purposeful. "First you must listen."

A growl rolled from Ketahn's core. The humans awaited him. His friends awaited him. *Ivy* awaited him. And with every beat of his hearts, with every lungful he took in of this cool air, the danger to his tribe increased. "Speak."

"The guards in this area are being changed. I ensured there was a delay between that change, so the way is clear as long as you are swift. Hasten to the burial chambers, and you will be met by a spiritspeaker near the Queens' Tomb. She will guide you to a passage that leads to the surface."

"A spiritspeaker?"

"Archspeaker Valkai was unsettled by today's events. She offered aid."

"And it will be gladly accepted."

Releasing another heavy breath, Korahla glanced over her shoulder. "The queen forced Ahnset out of Takarahl with a group of Claws and Fangs, commanding her to lead them to the rest of your creatures. Your sister said she would take them to somewhere she called Needle's Point. That she would delay them long enough to allow you to escape with the others."

His voice sounded thin even to himself. "Does she lead them as a Fang?"

Korahla's mandibles drew together haltingly. "No."

Knots twisted in his gut, making everything taut and heavy.

The Prime Fang shifted on her legs, making the cloth of her shroud rustle and her metal adornments clink softly. "Ahnset is deeply sorry for—"

"I do not want to hear her apologies," Ketahn said with a snap of his fangs. He could not shake the feeling of betrayal. He could not simply extinguish his anger at his broodsister...but neither could he leave her to whatever fate the queen had chosen for her.

"You will listen all the same," Korahla snarled, clacking her fangs together in response. "Ahnset is sorry for what happened. She is...broken. I have never seen her like this in all the years I have known her, Ketahn."

"*Ella* is broken," he replied, his words low and strained. "Ahnset should have done as I said. She should not have brought Ella here."

Korahla's mandibles twitched uneasily. "Ella...that was the creature's name?"

"The human's name."

"She was...your mate?"

"No, she was my friend."

"She was Ahnset's friend also."

Those words—or perhaps just their terrible truth—were more painful than any physical punishment Ketahn had received. He curled his hands into fists. The bite of his claws against his palms was lost amidst the other pains already wracking his body.

Ketahn tossed down the rope and strode up to Korahla, holding her gaze. "I must keep the others safe. I must keep my mate safe. I must go now."

Korahla tensed, chest and shoulders swelling as she drew in a slow, deep breath. "You must give me your word, Ketahn."

"What do you ask of me?"

"Find Ahnset. Take her far away from Takarahl and see that she never returns."

A thought flickered through Ketahn's mind, seizing his hearts and pulling hard on his heartsthread despite not even being fully formed—the thought of never seeing his mate again.

So long as he lived, he would do all in his power to ensure that never became a reality.

"Come with me, Korahla."

Her mandibles twitched, and her gaze faltered. "I cannot. My place is here."

"What loyalty can you have to Zurvashi?" Ketahn demanded.

"What loyalty does she deserve?"

"The Fangs are splintering, Ketahn. If I leave, those who may yet have the courage to stand against the queen will be without a leader...and Zurvashi will discover them all one by one and make examples of them."

"Ahnset needs you."

Korahla growled and stomped a leg on the floor. "Ahnset needs to *live*. Now give me your word."

Ketahn crossed his forearms and bowed his head. "Beneath the gaze of their eightfold eyes, Korahla, I vow I will find Ahnset and take her far from Takarahl."

She closed her eyes and bowed her head, releasing a long, slow breath. The tension seemed to seep out of her. "Thank you."

"I must thank you, Korahla." Ketahn lifted a hand and tapped his knuckle against his headcrest.

"Thank me by safeguarding my mate. May the Protector shield you both."

"And you."

Korahla tugged something from her belt—a folded piece of cloth—and held it up. She shifted aside, opening a path to the doorway, which was a patch of utter blackness at the center of a stone wall cast in weak, eerie light. Ketahn stepped forward to take the offered cloth, but Korahla did not release it.

"As far as you can go, Ketahn. For if ever I lay eyes upon you again, I will kill you. It is the only way you will find mercy."

He nodded. "It will not come to that."

She let go of the cloth, and Ketahn took it and hurried into the corridor without a backward glance. The way forward was marked by a distant light—another crystal set on the wall dozens of segments ahead.

He unfurled the cloth. It was a black silk shroud, sized for a female. He whipped it over his shoulders and tugged the hood over his head as he strode along the corridor. Stone doors secured by thick wooden bars flitted past him on either side, all just like the door to the chamber in which he'd been held, all bathed in shadow.

When he reached the end of the corridor, he slipped through an open stone door larger than all the rest and found himself in a wider tunnel with crystals mounted along the walls. As Korahla had said, no one else was there.

Soon, Ivy.

The steady, rapid thumping of his hearts set his pace as he traversed those deep tunnels. Fortunately, there was only one way to go. He sensed the strands of fate beneath his legs, laid in place by the Weaver, leading him onward.

Behind him, stone scraped and slammed, echoing along the still corridors; Korahla closing the heavy stone door again.

He emerged in a passageway that spiraled up and down. The only such passageways he was aware of in Takarahl all led down to the burial chambers. He turned and began his descent.

Blood filled Ketahn's mind again. Blood and Ella's agonized, terrified scream. A shudder wracked him.

"No," he rasped, pulling the dark shroud more snugly around him. He had to cast those memories away, had to keep them out of his mind, had to continue forward. Had to ignore his failure until there was time to stop. Time to breathe.

Ivy needed him. They all needed him. And he...he needed them, too. But most of all, he needed his mate.

Yet it was difficult to forget death as he entered the dark, deserted tunnels connecting the burial chambers, where the only light was cast by flickering blue-green flames. It was difficult to disregard the feeling that he was simply burrowing ever deeper into a trap—that he would never leave this place again.

His rage answered those misgivings with fire and ferocity. He would fight his way of out Takarahl if necessary. He would wade through a river of blood to return to his mate.

He slowed as he reached the tunnel leading to the Queens' Tomb. The last time he'd come down here, the queen had...

No. The past is past. It cannot hold me.

Pressing himself against the corner wall, he peered around it into the tunnel. It was better lit than the others—which still left it dim compared to the rest of Takarahl—allowing him a glimpse of a white-clad figure near the entrance of the Queens' Tomb. Had he not seen the horror on Archspeaker Valkai's face as Zurvashi committed her unforgivable act, Ketahn would not have trusted her promise of aid.

Entering the corridor, he strode silently toward the waiting speaker. When he'd closed half the distance between them, she turned her head to scan the tunnel, and her eyes fell upon him, glinting with reflected light. Her face was lost in the shadows beneath her raised hood. She lifted a hand and beckoned him.

Ketahn sped his pace. Even as he reached the speaker, he could not see her face, but he knew her voice when she spoke.

"Come, Ketahn. We must make haste. I fear the Claws will be hunting you much too soon."

He shook his head, not even considering that the gesture was alien to his kind. "Archspeaker, I cannot ask this of you. You risk too much."

"You have not asked it, and I will not be dissuaded. Would that it had all gone differently, that the Eight had judged differently the day Zurvashi challenged Queen Azunai..." Her mandibles sagged, and she seemed suddenly smaller. "But now is no time for such thoughts. We must away."

Ketahn's insides twisted again; he feared they would never right themselves, that he would never feel normal. "Archspeaker, I must ask. Ella, the female Ahnset brought to the Den of Spirits…"

Valkai slid a leg out from beneath her shroud, settling it against Ketahn's gently. "My sisters tend to her remains, Ketahn. Though it would not please Zurvashi, your Ella will be laid to rest with all the respect we would afford any vrix, and we will pray that her spirit finds the peace she assuredly deserved."

That could not undo what had been done, could not eliminate the horror that had been wrought upon the innocent human…but it was *something*. It had to be enough.

Ketahn bowed and crossed his forearms in the sign of the Eight; all the reverence with which he instilled the pose was not for the gods, but for the kind female standing before him. "Thank you."

"Thank me by making good on your escape, Ketahn." She looked past him, down the long corridor, and then turned, waving him along again. "Come. There is not a moment to spare."

He strode behind her with fire flowing through his veins, more aware of the truth of her words than she could ever know.

I am coming, Ivy.

I am coming, Ahnset.

CHAPTER 3

Ivy stood staring at the chamber's door. It'd been all she'd done since Ketahn left to find Ahnset and Ella, taking her heart with him. So much time had passed—*too* much time. The stasis chamber's lights had long ago automatically dimmed for their night cycle. Some of the tribe had slept, in her case due to sheer exhaustion, but Ivy doubted anyone got more than a few hours of fitful rest. The lights had come back up not long ago, marking another morning.

The dread she'd felt the moment that door had closed behind Ketahn had only grown in all that time, becoming an ugly, vicious thing that threatened to drown her.

Ketahn was going back to *her*—the queen. And if all had gone well, he would've been back yesterday.

Ivy's belly clenched, and she swallowed hard to keep her nausea at bay. She dug her nails deeper into the flesh of her forearm, dragging them to her wrist and back, again and again. Her throat was tight, her breath was shallow, and her eyes were watery with stinging tears she refused to cry.

He will come back to me. He promised he would come back.

But every horrible thing the queen could possibly do to Ketahn and Ella played through her mind.

A warm, rough hand covered hers, stopping its restless motion. With a start, Ivy looked up, meeting Rekosh's crimson gaze.

"You are harming yourself," he said in vrix, cocking his head. "Why?"

"I…" Ivy looked down as Rekosh lifted his hand, and it was only then that she realized what she'd done. Her nails had left several long, red scratches on her skin, some of which were deep enough that tiny drops of blood had begun welling from them. "I did not mean to. I just…"

She looked back up, her bottom lip trembling. Those tears lingered on the verge of spilling. "Where is he, Rekosh? Why has he not come back yet?"

"I cannot say, Ivy." He reached into the pouch hanging at his side, pulled out a small piece of pristine white cloth, and gently laid it on her arm, deftly tying two corners together to hold it in place. Miniscule spots of crimson bloomed on the fabric. "But Ketahn said he will return, and so he will. It is no short journey to Takarahl, especially in a storm."

"But what about the queen? What will—"

"Do not concern yourself with her." Though his tone was as smooth as always, his mandibles twitched down. "Soon we will be far out of her reach."

Ivy covered the cloth with her palm and closed her eyes. "I just want him back."

"He will come," said Telok, drawing her attention toward him. He'd stepped outside several times since Ketahn's departure, always returning to his spot beside the stasis chamber door. Droplets of water glistened on his hide, reflecting the white overhead light, and his hand absently flexed and relaxed on the shaft of his spear. "Even if I must go and find him."

"We must remain here, Telok," Urkot rumbled. He was

lowered on the floor beside one of the covered pods, bouncing and rolling a pebble in one hand. "We are the protectors of this tribe."

Telok snapped his mandibles. "Nothing will come in my absence."

"Ketahn came. Others might also, especially with the signs of our presence outside," said Rekosh.

A low vibration rolled through the chamber, rattling the ceiling. Ivy's skin prickled with unease. She knew it was the thunder, but that knowledge didn't make it any less unsettling than the first time it had happened—though at least she didn't jump every time the room shuddered anymore.

"What are they talking about?" Cole asked. He was leaning against his cryochamber with his arms folded across his chest, fingers drumming his bicep. His bag, already packed and ready to go, sat on the floor beside him. Like Telok, he'd been restless, and must've paced around the room at least forty times.

"Telok is thinking about going after Ketahn. Rekosh and Urkot told him that he needs to stay," Ivy said. As much as she wanted Ketahn back, as tempted as she was to ask Telok to go find him, she knew the others were right. Telok didn't need to put himself in danger, and everyone who was left needed to stay together.

If the worst had come to pass, and Ketahn was—

No, damn it. Ketahn will come back to me.

Cole thrust a finger toward the door. "We should be going after him! We can't just abandon one of our own to..." He waved his hands vaguely in frustration. "To all that!"

"We're not abandoning Ella, Cole." Ivy scrubbed her hands over her face and dropped her arms to her sides. "There's nothing we can do. Even if there wasn't a violent thunderstorm raging out there, we'd never catch up to him. He has a full day head start."

"I agree that we need to stay here, together," Callie said. She was sitting on the floor with her back against the wall, her knees drawn up, and her arms folded across them. "It'd be stupid to split up any more than we already have."

"And all we would accomplish is getting someone hurt," Diego added. He was one of the few who'd been relatively still through all this, having posted himself beside Ella's empty cryochamber.

Cole pushed away from his pod to face the others. "We need to do *something*! Are we just supposed to sit around and wait forever? It's already been a whole fucking twenty-eight hours or however the fuck long a day is on this planet!"

Lacey, who was sitting against the wall near her cryochamber, lifted her head to look at Cole. "We'll wait for as long as we need to. We're a tribe now."

Cole growled. "I can't stand this. I just... I need to do something."

Will shook his head and let out a bitter laugh. He sat beside Lacey, wrists resting atop his knees. "You think the rest of us don't feel the same way? I would've rushed out that door right behind him if I thought it would've done even a little good."

"How do you know it wouldn't have?" Cole asked. "How the hell can you all just sit around acting so calm?"

"We're not calm," Will replied. "I'm not calm. But I am trying to be realistic, Cole. I'm a fucking IT guy. Five days of playing with spears and going on nature walks doesn't change that! You saw how big Ahnset is. Do you really think we'd stand a chance against another vrix her size or bigger? A *queen*?"

"If we work together—"

"If we work together, we can survive out here," said Diego. "And we all know by now, even you, that together means *with* these vrix. It means trusting them, man. It means deferring to them as the experts in cases like this, even if it feels like we're having to take a big bite out of a shit sandwich."

Ahmya, who was sitting in her pod near Ivy, wrinkled her nose and muttered, "That's a disgusting mental image."

"We all deal with stress differently." Lacey let her head tip back against the wall. "We're all scared and worried, but ranting and raging isn't going to help."

"The best thing we can do right now is conserve our energy so we're ready to leave when they come back," said Ivy.

Cole flopped back into his pod. Its cushion creaked beneath his weight. "Yeah, I get it."

Ivy turned back to Rekosh, Telok, and Urkot. They were silent observers, undoubtedly not understanding more than a few words here and there. But Ivy knew they were learning.

Not for the first time, she wished there'd been more of a chance for everyone to learn from each other, to ease into the relationships they'd been forced to build. And not for the first time, she cast that wish aside. It did no good. She knew from experience that no matter how much you wanted something, the universe did what it was going to do—which usually meant kicking you to the gutter and stomping all over your dreams.

Ivy folded her arms across her middle, and it was only as her fingers touched the cloth tied to her forearm that she realized she'd been about to scratch herself again. She curled her fingers around her arm and held them still. The sickness in her belly hadn't fully subsided, but now it was accompanied by a cramp in her pelvis.

Wonderful.

Looking up at Rekosh, she frowned. "If Ahnset reached Takarahl...what will the queen do to Ella?"

His eyes softened. "Do not worry over such things. You will only allow what you do not know to devour you from within."

"You would do better to tell her not to breathe," said Telok gruffly. "We all worry over such things, and she knows already what is likely. If Ella is discovered by the queen, we will never see her again."

35

That quickly, Ivy's vision blurred with the tears she'd fought for so long, and her stomach twisted in revolt. Of course she'd known. How could she not have? But she'd hoped for a different answer, for something more. "The queen will…"

Kill her.

Ivy shook her head. "No."

"By the Eight." Urkot rose and strode to Telok, his steps heavy. "Of what help are such words, Telok?"

"They are true," the green marked vrix responded.

Urkot huffed and clacked his fangs. "And if the others could understand, you would have crushed the spirit of every human in this chamber."

"What, then?" Telok turned to face Urkot. "You would have me lie?"

Urkot's foreleg shifted forward, and his leg joint rapped hard against Telok's. Telok growled and drew his leg back.

"I would have you think," Urkot said. "We are their protectors. There is more to shield them from than the jungle's dangers or the queen's wrath." He turned to Ivy and brought his upper forearms together, side by side, holding his lower right arm in a straight line with them. That was a vrix gesture of apology. He eased into a bow. "He speaks true, but his words are hard as stone. Unnecessarily so."

A damnable tear slid down Ivy's cheek, and she quickly wiped it away. She didn't know what else to say. All she could do was pray Ketahn found Ahnset in time.

Rekosh chittered softly. "I cannot recall ever saying this before, but…well said, Urkot."

Telok's mandibles fell, and his eyes darkened. He made his own apologetic gesture. "I have allowed my own worries to consume me. I ask your forgi—"

His head jerked toward the entrance, and he was already raising his spear into a fighting grip when the door released its usual hiss and slid open. Urkot too was in motion, half a second behind Telok. But they both froze when their eyes fell upon the figure in the doorway.

"Ketahn," Ivy breathed. The relief flowing through her was so strong that it took all her willpower to remain standing.

His eyes met hers; pain flashed in their violet depths, but it was lit by a spark of rage. Were that not enough to tell her something was wrong, he averted his gaze after a single heartbeat.

Ketahn rushed through the doorway, and Telok and Urkot stepped back to allow him space. Water dripped from his hide, pooling beneath him on the floor, and the black cloak draped over his shoulders was soaked through. There was also a new cut upon the side of his face.

He tore the cloak off, tossed it into the corner, and reached past Telok to grab one of the spears standing against the wall. "Telok, Rekosh, Urkot, with me," he said in vrix. "Bring your weapons."

Where was Ketahn's spear? Where was his backpack?

Where were Ahnset and Ella?

All Ivy could manage to get out was, "Ketahn?"

He looked at her again and released a heavy breath. Her brow furrowed; he shook his head, the miniscule movement barely perceptible. Still, it was enough to make her heart crack and sink.

"What is wrong, Ketahn?" asked Urkot.

"What's going on?" Cole asked at the same time.

"A hunt," Ketahn growled in English. With one leg, he guided Telok farther aside, and then he stepped to Ivy. He hooked a finger under her chin, angling her face up toward his, and leaned down to tip his forehead against hers. Closing his eyes, he quietly rasped, "I am sorry, my *nyleea*."

Ivy squeezed her eyes shut and shook her head. "No." She raised her hands and cradled his jaw between them. "No."

"What the hell happened out there?" Lacey asked.

"Where are the others?" Though her voice was soft, Ahmya's question carried throughout the room. The crack in Ivy's heart widened.

"I will return soon," Ketahn said in his native tongue. His thumb trembled as he brushed it over Ivy's cheek, wiping away her tears. "They must be ready to travel, Ivy. You must see to it."

Ivy opened her eyes and searched his gaze. "Ketahn, what's happening?"

"I will come back to you, my heartsthread. I will *always* come back." He lowered his hand, lifted his head, and stepped away from her, facing the other humans. He switched to English. "Keep your spears in hand. Do not leave this room. We will be back in small time."

The other vrix were staring at him, what further questions they might have had hidden behind hard, grave masks. Ketahn glanced at them briefly and said in vrix, "Come, brothers. Quickly."

He did not look at Ivy again before exiting the chamber. Telok followed immediately behind him. Urkot lingered a moment, giving Ivy a look that almost spoke of some deeper sorrow, but then he left too.

Rekosh paused in the doorway, meeting Ivy's gaze. His mandibles twitched, and his mouth opened, but he did not immediately speak. "He will explain. I will ensure that when he returns, he will explain."

And then he too was gone.

The only sign of Ketahn having come back was the water puddled on the floor, mixed with the mud that must've been clinging to his legs, and the sopping cloak lying in a wad in the corner.

Ivy stared after the vrix, heartbroken and numb as the others spoke around her, but she registered none of their words. All she could hear was one voice, echoing in her head.

I am sorry, my nyleea.

CHAPTER 4

THUNDER BOOMED over the jungle as Ketahn pulled himself up onto the crest of the pit. The scant gray light filtered through the storm made it hard to judge the time of day, but his instincts said it was late morning.

By the Eight, had he lost a full day in Takarahl?

Rain hammered his hide, mud clung to his hands and legs, and his hearts beat furiously; they hadn't eased since he'd left to pursue Ahnset yesterday morning. He didn't stop to clean off the muck, didn't allow himself even a backward glance.

To look back would have been more than he could bear. Were he to did so, he'd be helpless but to return to Ivy...

But his sister needed him now. However angry he was with her, however betrayed he felt, Ahnset needed him.

Growling, Ketahn rushed forward.

"Ketahn, wait," someone called from behind him.

Telok or Rekosh, perhaps. It was difficult to tell when the storm sounds—drumming rain, thrashing boughs and leaves, and howling wind—were so strong.

Ketahn gritted his teeth. His every instinct demanded he continue onward. His sister was in danger, and his mate was alone again. This needed to be brought to a swift end. But he halted all the same, twisting his torso to look back.

Telok, Urkot, and Rekosh had followed close behind Ketahn. They stood near the edge of the pit, hides covered in water and mud, staring at him with sharp but unjudgmental eyes.

He did not doubt they had a thousand questions. Yet that raging fire burned bright and hot at Ketahn's core, threatening to consume him utterly, demanding satiation. It would not allow him to provide a thousand answers even if he'd had those answers to give.

Though a day had passed since Ahnset had brought Ella before the queen, Ketahn was no closer to being able to put what had happened—or how he felt about it—into words.

"What do we hunt and where?" Telok, who was closest to Ketahn, asked.

Time slipped away, precious moments that could never be reclaimed, lost amidst the falling rain.

"That is all we need," said Rekosh.

Ketahn's mandibles drew together, and tension rippled through his body. "Claws and Fangs," he grated. "Needle's Point."

Something flickered in his friends' eyes. Whether realization or mild confusion, understanding or sorrow, it mattered not. Only that there was no shock in their reactions, no hesitation when Telok strode forward with the other males close behind and thumped a foreleg against Ketahn's hindquarters.

Needle's Point had meant something different to them seven years ago, when they'd been young and eager to prove themselves. When they'd been too inexperienced to understand the truth of the world...the truth of the queen.

Telok stood his spear beside him and brought his lower fists together, pounding them on his chest. "You have my spear."

Another growl escaped Ketahn. Urkot and Rekosh mimicked Telok's gesture and echoed his words, their gazes unwavering.

He had no interest in leading, but the cause for the battle to come was just—and it was his own. Who better to fight alongside him than his oldest, closest friends? He clenched his fists, and the grip of his spear creaked in his upper right hand.

"We will rescue Ahnset"—Ketahn turned to face his friends fully and shifted his spear so the point was skyward as he slammed his lower fists against his chest—"and kill the rest. No mercy this day."

"We nourish the roots with blood," said Rekosh.

"May the Tangle devour their bones," rumbled Urkot.

"With me, brothers." Ketahn spun about and plunged into the jungle.

His surroundings were a blur as he ascended into the trees, tearing a path along the mighty boughs with his claws. He felt Needle's Point far ahead as clearly as he would've felt the heat of a fire. With each segment he crossed, his fury flared, growing brighter and hotter—but it was contained now, restricted to that place in his core, so close to his heartsthread, where it could be shaped into a tool like a potter's kiln or a goldworker's furnace.

Every step was another instant lost; every segment traveled was another chance for Ahnset or Ivy to come to harm. Every beat of his hearts was one closer to his ultimate death.

But he would be the bringer of death on this day. He would strike back at Zurvashi through her underlings if he could not thrust a spear into her hearts himself.

He did not look back again; he didn't need to. He knew his friends were following, just as he knew Ivy was safe in the ship no matter what dire warnings his mind produced.

Soon.

How he'd come to loath that word.

Choking back a frustrated roar, Ketahn pushed himself faster still. The storm continued to batter the Tangle, rolling thunder shook the boughs, and heavy raindrops pierced the canopy to strike Ketahn's hide unrelentingly. But he was drawing closer and closer to Needle's Point. Closer to his sister.

Closer to being able to finally—and for always—reunite with his mate.

Though the area around Needle's Point had changed much since he'd first come at the onset of the queen's war, it remained familiar to Ketahn. Rage roiled within him, eager for release, for an enemy to attack, for blood to spill; he clenched his jaw and forced that anger down. The cool rain could not ease the heat pulsing just under his hide.

Movements stiff, he signaled to his friends to slow. Together, they crept from shadow to shadow, keeping low to the branches upon which they moved. His hearts stilled for a sliver of a moment when he saw it up ahead—a ring of tall trees, their trunks stripped of branches from their roots up to nearly forty segments off the ground. Vines clung to those trunks now, their green and purple leaves lush and full but their color dulled by the weak daylight.

The area around the tree ring was overgrown with ground plants, and the only trees in that space were young, no taller than a full-grown female vrix. The Tangle was reclaiming Needle's Point, but it moved at its own pace—and it had more patience than any vrix or human ever could. What were years to towering trees whose roots had been in the ground before Queen Takari discovered the Den of Spirits?

They'd undoubtedly drunk their share of blood. Soon enough, they'd have their thirst for it quenched again.

Once, there'd been rope bridges in the trees connecting that wide central ring to the surrounding jungle, running between platforms set high in the branches from which Claws could watch for prowling thornskulls. Those pathways were all gone now, and the few remaining platforms were rotted and unreliable. So Ketahn led his friends down, keeping out of sight of Needle's Point until they were on the ground again.

Telok shifted into position beside Ketahn, and the two eased up to the edge of the thicker jungle around Needle's Point, stopping in the shadow of a twisted tree while Rekosh and Urkot guarded their flanks. The rain had less to hinder it in that swath of relatively clear land. It fell in slanted sheets, droplets rippling in the wind, creating a translucent veil through which Ketahn peered at the tree ring.

With the rain and poor lighting, he couldn't make out any of the structures that lay at the heart of the tree ring—though he guessed all but the ancient stone buildings were collapsed and overgrown by now. Only plants were visible between the mighty trunks, wild and thriving. The central area had once been cleared out, also, but this place had not been used for years.

Zurvashi had called it Spear's Point, where her warriors had gathered to prepare for their thrust into thornskull land. The tip of her mighty spear. But as Ketahn, his friends, and his brood siblings had made their first journey here, Ahnset had named it Needle's Point.

They'd chittered at the jest, both because three of their group—Ketahn, Rekosh, and Ketahn's broodbrother, Ishkal— had been weavers, and because of Ketahn's talk of slaying monsters with his needles as a broodling. But that name had held, and the group had referred to it as Needle's Point ever since.

Ketahn would have preferred to forget this place entirely.

"Poor conditions for tracking," Telok grumbled. "If only the storm had broken."

Those words—*if only*—raked along Ketahn's heartsthread like a set of wicked claws. *If only* had haunted him for a long time. Too long. And he knew it would continue to do so even when this was through, even when he was free of the queen. All the things that might have been would never stop assailing him.

His hand tightened around the shaft of his spear. When

would all this be through? When would there be an end, when would he, Ivy, and their tribe have peace?

The answer made him grit his teeth and fight back more furious heat. He'd always known the truth, had always known what it would take.

This would end when Zurvashi was dead.

Movement called his attention to the outer curve of the ring of trees. A lone figure rounded the curve, striding along the outside of Needle's Point with spear in hand. Though details were difficult to discern, he was wearing something black over his shoulder—he was a Queen's Claw.

Ketahn narrowed his eyes, straining for clarity. In addition to the black fur, the Claw was wrapped in a dark brown shroud that concealed most of his torso and head. The pale green markings on his legs could be made out only as he drew closer.

Ketahn's mandibles came together slowly, but with great force, their fangs scraping against each other. His every muscle tensed with the instinct to attack; he fought that urge and held his place.

Telok sank low, bracing himself with two hands on the tree. His attention was fixated on the Claw. "Scout or guard?"

"Watch." Ketahn kept his eyes moving to scan for other vrix.

The lone Claw halted at one of the ancient trees, swept his gaze around, and turned to walk back in the direction from which he'd come. Ketahn's thumping hearts marked the passage of time. The Claw was soon out of sight beyond the curve of the tree ring.

A few more heartbeats went by before a second Claw appeared from the opposite side of the tree formation. His blue leg markings looked closer to stony gray in the gloom.

This one moved with less urgency than the first, though his stride was longer and smoother. Ketahn and Telok watched the newcomer walk to a tree—the same tree where the other had stopped. The Claw paused there too, gave the jungle a measured look, and then went back in the direction from which he'd come.

He was soon out of sight again; the first Claw reappeared shortly after the second vanished.

"Patrolling guards," Telok said. "Not the best use of the place."

Now Ketahn made no effort to withstand his surging fury. "They do not expect a battle. They expect small, weak creatures to slaughter."

He turned his head to glance over his shoulder and let out a short, sharp hiss. When Rekosh and Urkot looked at him, he beckoned them with a wave. The pair settled into the thick undergrowth near Ketahn and Telok, their attention falling on the Claw across the clearing.

"Two outside," said Telok. "How many more inside?"

"Not enough," Ketahn growled.

"Not enough to defend it?" Urkot asked.

"Not enough to satisfy my rage."

They must have had more questions. Ketahn would have, had their roles been reversed. But they did not ask, and he appreciated them all the more for it. Now was the time for action. Talking would come later.

Despite the years that had passed since they had fought as one against the thornskulls, Ketahn knew his friends did not need to be told what had to be done. The enemy was different, but war was war. Death was death. And so long as Zurvashi lived, the cycle would remain unbroken.

The green-marked Claw began his return journey to the far side of the tree ring. Ketahn darted forward, crossing the clearing quickly and silently—not that the sound of his movement would've overcome the storm's chaotic noise, regardless. He made a few quick gestures as he reached the tree where the patrolling guards reversed their course. Wordlessly, Telok and

Rekosh broke away, heading in the direction of the green-marked Claw.

Ketahn and Urkot moved to the next tree—the last one the blue-marked Claw had to pass to complete his route. They pressed themselves against the trunk, readied their spears, and waited.

Images danced through Ketahn's mind's eye. The pair of Claws who'd been flanking the queen in The Den of Spirits, the shocked and horrified spiritspeakers, the cruelty, savagery, and unsettling satisfaction in Zurvashi's eyes.

The blood.

His mandibles spread wide, and his teeth ground against each other. Revenge... This was revenge, but it was not justice.

The blue-marked Claw stepped past the tree.

Ketahn lunged, thrusting his spear with a snarl. The blow struck the Claw in the center of his back. The shaft vibrated as the spearhead pierced thick hide, taut muscle, and hard bone.

Grunting, the Claw sagged, held upright only by the weapon run through his chest. Urkot was already before the Claw. He clamped a big hand around the Claw's throat and squeezed. Bones crunched, and, with a ragged exhalation, the Claw died.

Ketahn braced his forelegs on the Claw's back and tore his spear free. Blood spurted from the jagged wound, flowing into the muddy puddles on the ground.

Urkot caught hold of the body beneath its upper arms, and Ketahn grasped the Claw's hindquarters with his left hands. They heaved the corpse into the undergrowth between the trees and entered Needle's Point as one.

The plants were thickest around the ring of trees, and Ketahn slowed his pace so he could advance without creating too much of a disturbance. Urkot moved with equal care just behind him.

Ketahn's leg came down on something flat and solid within the undergrowth. He paused to carefully brush the leaves aside, revealing a weather worn plank of wood, its edges eaten away by insects and moisture.

There'd been a structure here, one of many that had been erected within the clearing—a simple thing used to shelter supplies from the rain. This piece of wood was but a lingering reminder of the bustling encampment that had occupied Needle's Point. A reminder of the encampment that had seemed so lively but had brought only death to the Tangle.

Ketahn continued onward, sinking lower as the vegetation thinned. The high branches around this space provided shelter from the rain, but the diminished noise of the rainfall meant he had to move with even greater care to avoid making any sounds that would alert his enemies.

As he neared the edge of his dwindling cover, voices drifted to Ketahn, made small and indiscernible by the wind. Urkot broke away just before the heart of the clearing, where the plants were only up to Ketahn's lowest leg joints, came into view.

Keeping his spear low, Ketahn crawled forward. The clearing's center lay open before him—the stone ruins choked by vines, their blocks weather stained, their carvings now faded, indecipherable impressions with meanings lost to time. The openings leading into the structures were dark, framed by shaped stones that were crumbling beneath the burdens they'd supported for hundreds of years.

Ketahn had been intrigued by the ruins when he'd first seen them, and he'd long pondered their mysteries. He'd wondered at their past, at everything those stones and the trees towering around them had witnessed, at the vrix who'd built this place.

Now he could only look at the present; even the future was too much, and his hopes for it were under constant assault.

He could make out five—no, six—figures through the gloom, gathered in a loose group before the largest ruin. Three females, three males. The females were clustered together with one of the males nearby, while the other two males were spread farther apart and turned away, watching their surroundings.

Pressing his mandible fangs together, Ketahn continued his cautious advance. The boughs overhead did more than block the worst of the rain—they deepened the shadows on the ground, allowing him to sneak closer than he otherwise might have dared. Each segment he traveled coaxed those wrathful flames within him to new strength, new heat, new ferocity.

"This is the place," someone said in a low voice that made Ketahn's hearts stutter. Ahnset. She sounded—

No. He wasn't going to waste time with that. She was alive, and he would keep it that way. Nothing else was important.

"She is lying," the male closest to the females said.

The Fang on the left shoved the female in the center—Ahnset. One of the Ahnset's forelegs buckled, and she fell onto her leg joint, splashing up mud. Ketahn caught a flash of purple eyes before her long hair, woven with beads and bits of gold, fell over her face.

His fingers curled, and his claws sunk into the soft ground. He longed for those claws to be buried in flesh rather than dirt, longed for it to be blood rather than water spattered on his hide.

"Where are the creatures?" demanded the Fang on the right.

As he drew nearer, Ketahn could make out the golden adornments on her torso, which were otherwise hidden in the shadow of the heavy shroud draped over her shoulders. His broodsister was devoid of those adornments. She'd left many of her gold pieces in Takarahl during her time with the humans, but even the little Ahnset had kept had been stripped from her. Her belt, her neckpiece, her bracelets, and the few bits of silk she normally wore, all gone.

Ahnset braced a hand on the ground, keeping her head bowed. "They are here. This is where they have made their den."

"Jardok," called the Claw nearest the females, "what say you?"

A fourth male emerged from the darkness within the central ruin a few moments later, ducking through the collapsing entryway. He tucked a shard of crystal into a pouch on his belt. "Signs of beasts denning here, but they are old. This is not the place, Hakvahl."

Hakvahl looked at the Fang on the right. "She is lying, Leteki. She has led us astray."

Ahnset lifted her head to look at Hakvahl. "What signs you have skill enough to find have been obscured by the storm."

Ketahn drew to a halt. One of the Claws standing watch was mere segments away, oblivious to his enemy's presence; his attention was turned toward the scene at the center of the clearing.

Leteki grabbed a fistful of Ahnset's hair and forced her head back. "This is what happens when we rely upon traitors."

The other Fang caught hold of three of Ahnset's arms, wrenching them back.

Leteki slid her hand up the shaft of her spear, gripping it just beneath the head, and pressed the blackrock edge to Ahnset's throat. "The truth, traitor."

CHAPTER 5

KETAHN'S HEARTS resumed the frantic rhythm they'd maintained since yesterday morning, making his entire body throb with their every beat. He glanced around, searching for signs of his friends nearby, but he saw none.

"We should bind her, hang her, and gut her like a beast," said the Fang on the left. "That would still be better than she deserves."

Hakvahl stepped closer to the females, fine hairs bristling. "The queen wants the pale creatures delivered to her. This traitor is our only means of locating them."

"I need but a few moments with her broodbrother," snapped Leteki, "and he will cooperate. We do not need *her*." She pulled harder on Ahnset's hair.

Ahnset closed her mandibles and her eyes but did not make a sound.

"Final chance," said Leteki. "Where are the creatures?"

"They are small," Ahnset rasped, slitting her eyes open to stare at her captors. "Perhaps you must look closer."

Whether his companions were ready or not, Ketahn could wait no longer.

He surged up out of the undergrowth. The nearest Claw turned his head toward Ketahn and widened his eyes just before Ketahn's spear struck him beneath his chest plates, driving upward into his chest cavity.

Nearly half a segment of the spear slid into the Claw's body. The male released a confused grunt; the light in his eyes was gone before he began to fall. With his left hands, Ketahn grasped the Claw's spear and snatched it away. The other watcher had turned as well, attention drawn by the sound of Ketahn's attack, but had failed to notice the movement behind him.

Urkot's spear burst out from the other Claw's abdomen, driven clean through from behind. The Claw cried out in pain and grasped the quivering, bloody spear shaft with his lower hands, dropping his gaze to the grievous wound. Urkot growled and swung the spear aside, dragging his impaled foe to the ground.

As Urkot dispatched his target, a thrown spear struck Jardok, who still stood just outside the entrance to the central ruin. The bit of colorful silk tied on the shaft marked it as Rekosh's weapon. Jardok staggered backward—into Telok, who'd crept up behind him. Telok caught the Claw's head with one hand, forced it back, and cut his throat with a blackrock knife.

"Traitors!" Hakvahl shouted.

Ketahn's attention darted to Hakvahl, who held his spear in an overhand grip even as he tore the axe off his belt. With a grunt, Ketahn used his spear to heave the dead Claw aside, placing the body between himself and Hakvahl just as the surviving Claw threw his spear.

The weapon hit the dead Claw's back. Ketahn had scarce registered the impact when he let the body fall away and threw the barbed spear he'd stolen from his foe.

The spear sliced through the air a handspan from Hakvahl's head to find Ketahn's true target—Leteki.

The spear hit high on her chest, close to her muscled shoulder, and only half the tip pierced her. Though the wound was far from fatal, it served its purpose—the head of spear fell away from Ahnset's throat as the impact twisted her torso to the side.

Hakvahl didn't look back at Leteki; axe in hand, he roared and charged at Ketahn.

Ketahn answered with a roar of his own and ripped his spear out of the fallen Claw. He charged to meet Hakvahl.

Ahnset swung her arm backward, hammering her free fist into the face of the Fang restraining her. The Fang's hold faltered, and Ahnset tore free, throwing herself aside and sweeping her legs into her opponent's. The Fang's balance shattered, and she fell, twisting as she crashed onto the undergrowth. She shifted her hold on her spear and thrust it at Ahnset, who caught the shaft in one hand.

Rekosh was a blur of black and red as he pounced atop the Fang, the blackrock knives in his hands gleaming with moisture. His blades rained down upon his foe faster than she could react.

Ketahn thrust his spear at Hakvahl's chest the instant the Claw was close enough. Hakvahl shifted aside, narrowly avoiding the spear head, and lashed out with his axe. Ketahn ducked the swing and reversed his thrust, dragging the spear head across Hakvahl's abdomen. The edge sliced open the Claw's hide, making him snarl.

Before Hakvahl could retaliate with a backhand blow, Ketahn used his free hands to grab his foe's forearm. His claws punched through flesh and scraped the bone beneath.

"Jungle worm!" Hakvahl raked the claws of his lower hand across Ketahn's abdomen; the heat of that pain was nothing compared to the fire of Ketahn's rage.

Ketahn dipped his head and snapped his mandibles shut on Hakvahl's extended arm. The Claw cried out, and his leg joints buckled. Dropping the butt of his spear to the ground and angling the head up at Hakvahl, Ketahn wrenched on that arm harder.

The Claw fell with the tip of Ketahn's spear poised just under his chin. His fall halted abruptly when the blackrock spearhead struck the inside of his skull. The noise he made was small, brief, and easily forgotten.

All four Claws were dead, and the fallen Fang was barely moving beneath the blood-spattered forms of Rekosh and Ahnset. Of the queen's warriors, Leteki alone remained standing. Ketahn shoved Hakvahl away and turned to face her as she tugged the spear out of her shoulder.

"I care not if she kills me for it," the Fang growled, raising her huge war spear in her right hands and the smaller barbed spear in her left, "I will deliver your treacherous heads to my queen in offering!"

She strode toward Ketahn, who spread his arms and sank low, fingers curled, and mandibles raised.

"Come then, Fang," he growled, "and have the threads of your fate severed."

Leteki let loose a roar that rivaled the thunder and increased her speed only to jolt with a grunt, stride faltering. She twisted her torso to look backward; the shaft of a spear protruded from her back, and ten segments behind her stood Telok, arm still extended from his throw.

Ketahn rushed forward.

"You jungle worms!" Leteki roared, mandibles flaring. "You worthless little—"

Her eyes rounded as she caught sight of Ketahn. She whipped back toward him, swinging her war spear in a wide, wicked arc. Ketahn dropped low, using his hands to add a final burst of speed to his charge, and drove himself upward. He struck her underside, straightening his legs to pour as much strength into the blow as he could.

Despite her superior size and weight, Leteki was already off balance due to her missed attack. The unexpected impact lifted her forelegs off the ground. Her right rear leg buckled under the immense weight suddenly placed upon it, and she tumbled aside.

The bloody barbed spear lashed out at Ketahn next. He swayed just enough for the attack to cut through the air at his side and dropped his right arms, catching the weapon's shaft with both hands. Moving with the force of Leteki's thrust, he yanked the weapon from her grasp.

She shoved her torso upright. Dirt, leaves, and blood clung to her wet hide, and fury burned in her crimson eyes. When she lifted her war spear for another blow, her dark shroud—heavy with moisture—caught on her arms. The attack came up half a segment short, the spearhead making a soft *whoosh* as it sliced the empty air.

Ketahn had already flipped his hold on the barbed spear. As he angled the weapon toward Leteki, he saw only Zurvashi's face. Saw the malice in her eyes, the cruelty, the terrible, horrifying glee. Saw the *hunger.*

She would never take anyone from him again.

If Leteki's roar had rivaled the thunder, Ketahn's surpassed it. The Tangle itself quivered around him, the sky swirled, and the ancient stones of the ruins moaned. The head of his spear hit the center of Leteki's chest. The blackrock head punched through the thick bone of her chest plate and jerked to a halt as it hit something else just as hard, but he did not relent. The shaft of the weapon bent and snapped.

Leteki hissed and spat, mandibles gnashing. Her free hands clawed at the ground for purchase, shoving her body forward despite the fatal wound she'd just suffered. Her spear swung again—but it was halted by Urkot, who grabbed the Fang's arms from behind.

Urkot let out a yell, braced his forelegs against Leteki's back, and pulled on her arms with all his might. Bone cracked.

The Fang's pained cry ended abruptly when Ketahn thrust the broken shaft of his spear into her throat. Her crimson eyes held his for several heartbeats, flickering between hatred and fear.

Ketahn tore the broken shaft free. Blood spurted from the hole in Leteki's throat and poured down her chest. Even as her muscles relaxed and her body went limp, Ketahn jabbed the splintered shaft into her throat again, and again, and again, barely hearing the guttural sounds escaping him as he did so.

All his rage could not change that face back into Zurvashi's. His fury couldn't warp reality and make it so the female before him was the queen.

"Ketahn," Ahnset gasped. He turned his head to see her shoving herself off the other Fang. Her claws were bloody, and now that he was close, he could see the dark, discolored patches on her hide; she'd suffered at the hands of her former comrades.

He finally released the broken spear shaft. Urkot lowered Leteki's carcass to the ground as Ahnset approached Ketahn. The siblings stared at one another, shoulders and chests heaving with their ragged breaths, and a thousand emotions flickered through her eyes. Her mandibles rose and fell uncertainly.

A thousand more emotions roiled in Ketahn's chest, each at war with the others. All of this...all of this because she hadn't listened. He could not fault her for trying to do right, but he'd told her. He'd *told* her.

And she had not believed him.

She had not *trusted* him.

His hand trembled as he reached up and took hold of the back of Ahnset's neck, drawing her down to touch his headcrest to hers. She closed her eyes, released a shaky breath, and placed her big hands on his shoulders. When she inhaled, her body sagged, and she fell onto the joints of her forelegs.

"I am sorry, Ketahn," she rasped. "I am—"

Ketahn pulled away from her. She dropped a hand to the

ground to prevent herself from falling, and the hurt in her eyes as she opened them nearly undid him.

"Get up, Ahnset," he growled. "We must go."

Telok, Rekosh, and Urkot were close now, gathered in a loose ring around Ketahn and his sister. All had blood mingling with the rainwater on their hides. All were tense, silent, solemn. And Ketahn... His anger had not faded, but he was tired, and his body ached. His spirit ached.

He wanted only to hold his mate and forget the rest of the world.

Ahnset's claws sank into the ground. "Please, Ketahn, I must—"

Ketahn snapped his fangs together, fine hairs bristling. "Get. Up. I do not want your words, broodsister. I want you moving."

"What is the harm in letting her speak?" asked Rekosh, voice low and uncharacteristically uncertain.

Drawing in what was meant to be a steadying breath, Ketahn turned away from his sister and plucked up Leteki's war spear. The weapon was nearly a segment longer than he was tall. He found himself fighting a sudden urge to snap the shaft in half and cast the pieces into the jungle.

His fingers tightened around the spear, the claw of his thumb digging into the wood. "There is nothing to be said." He ran his gaze over his friends one at a time. "Search for anything of use. We must return to the pit, gather our humans, and depart."

"You mean to begin our journey?" asked Telok. "You have not even told us what happened."

Ketahn looked at Ahnset, clenching his jaw against another surge of fury. His broodsister hung her head, directing her eyes toward the ground.

"Ketahn and Ahnset are here," Urkot said, his words measured and sorrowful, "but not Ella. We know what happened."

"And we will speak on it no more," Ketahn snarled. "We must go. Now."

His gaze lingered on his broodsister for a moment longer. She was speaking, her voice little more than a broken rasp, the scrape of a claw against stone, but he could just make out her words over the rain.

"I am sorry. Broodmother, forgive me. Ella…"

Ketahn walked away from her, but those words clung to his heartsthread, dragging it down, down, down into the darkness he'd only just escaped.

CHAPTER 6

Ivy stood at the edge of the break in the *Somnium's* hull, surrounded by mangled metal and severed wires. The pit was dark outside that opening, just as it always was, but the ship's lights—crimson from the interior, orange from the slowly flashing emergency light—caught the many falling droplets of water and danced on the surface of the pool.

Rain drummed on the ship's exterior. All around the edges of the crater, water streamed down into the pool from the jungle, leaving little room for other sounds.

If it kept raining like this for another day or two, that pool would reach the hole in the ship. Even if Ivy and the others hadn't already been planning to leave, they wouldn't have had much longer before the ship flooded.

A cold breeze brushed past Ivy. Goosebumps prickled on her arms beneath the sleeves of her jumpsuit, and she rubbed her hands over them. She'd changed into one to prepare for their journey; though it didn't help much against the cold, it would keep her dry.

At least the ache in her pelvis had dulled enough for her to ignore it.

Ketahn had told her to remain inside, in the safety of the sealed room, but she couldn't. She couldn't stay in there any longer, locked in a cage while he was out dealing with who knew what. While he was in danger.

She'd tried to keep herself occupied, had tended to the supplies and run through mental checklists of their preparations more times than she could count, but she'd finally accepted there was simply nothing more to do but wait. And that had left her with far too much time to worry—to reflect upon the many ways this was all going wrong.

To think about exactly what Ketahn might have meant when he'd said, *I am sorry, my nyleea.*

She closed her eyes against the renewed sting of tears and bit down on her bottom lip.

He'll be fine. He's a hunter, a warrior.

His parting words resonated through her.

I will come back to you, my heartsthread. I will always come back.

"Please come back," she whispered.

"You okay?" Cole asked from behind her.

Ivy started, opening her eyes as she turned to look at him. She hadn't even heard him approach.

He was wearing one of the jumpsuits too, the sleeves rolled up to bare his forearms, and held one of the spears they'd made in his right hand. Bathed in that red glow, he was a grim figure. His eyes met Ivy's only briefly as he walked over and stopped beside her to look out into the gloom.

"I...don't know," Ivy replied.

Cole leaned forward and swept his gaze across the darkness outside. "You shouldn't be out here alone, Ivy."

"I know. I just had to get out of there. I felt..."

"Antsy?"

"Yeah. And...trapped. Helpless."

Cole glanced at her and frowned. When he turned his face

away again, he lifted a hand and scratched at the stubble on his jaw. "Because he's out there."

Ivy sighed heavily. "Cole, I really don't want to get into it with you again."

"I'm not—" He dropped his hand. "That's not why I came out here, Ivy. Can't blame you for thinking that, but it's really not. I just…get what you're going through right now."

Her brow creased as she tilted her head. "You do?"

"I mean, I never stood around longing for a spider man or anything, but I get it." A playful smirk curled on his lips, but it died as quickly as it had appeared. "My dad was a firefighter. He wasn't home a lot, and during wildfire season…sometimes I'd go months without seeing him. When I was a kid, every day I'd get home from school and sit in the living room to do home-work, but I'd really just be watching out the window. Hoping to see his truck pull into the driveway.

"When I was lucky, I'd get to see him before bed. Those were the best nights. Sometimes I'd wake up in the morning after he hadn't come home, and I'd have this dread in my gut, you know? And then I'd see his boots next to the front door and I'd know he made it back safe. But most of the time…I just had no idea." Cole ran his fingers through his hair, sweeping the strands back as he looked up at the falling rain. "Kids at school thought it was awesome that my dad was a firefighter. Thought it was so cool, like I spent all my time with fucking Dalmatians or sitting in firetrucks with oversized helmets on.

"But I knew what he did was dangerous, and I knew every time he was gone that he might never come back again because…because when my mom died…" Cole squeezed his eyes shut and clenched his jaw, drawing in a sharp breath. "Because when she died, I heard him talking to my uncle. Saying that *he* was the one who went out and faced death every night. He was the one who was willingly facing danger to protect people. That it should have been him instead of her."

He opened his eyes and glared out of the hole in the hull. "And he never once talked to *me* about any of that. Never once told me that I didn't have to worry about him, or that it was okay to worry, or..." He shook his head and laughed without humor. "Fuck, I'm sorry, Ivy. I...didn't mean to dump my shit on you. I just know how you feel, is all I want to say. That having no idea when someone you care about is coming home sucks."

Ivy placed her hand on his arm. Cole faced her. His features held a vulnerability that he'd never displayed before.

Her heart ached for him. Even if his situation hadn't been the same as hers growing up, the result was similar—a childhood spent feeling alone. "Thank you for sharing that with me, Cole. I'm sorry about your mom and all you went through. That had to have been tough as a kid."

"Yeah. I was pretty young when she passed, so..." He looked at her hand on his arm and his frown returned, even deeper than before. "Ivy, I don't..." He released a loud sigh. "I fucked up. What I did with you, *to* you, was wrong, and all my baggage or whatever doesn't make it okay."

Ivy withdrew her hand. "It's okay. It's done now."

"No. It's not okay. What I did was not okay. And I'm...sorry."

She stared up at him, searching his face. The remorse was there, plain as day, but it was mixed with confusion and uncertainty. "I guess being threatened by a giant spider has a way of putting things into perspective, huh?"

Cole laughed and shook his head. "He's one scary son of a bitch. But actually...it was you that got me thinking. You could've let him tear me apart. Hell, you were well within your rights to have hit me a few dozen more times. You're hot and I wanted you, and I guess I was just so sure of myself, that every time you looked at me, smiled at me..."

"Yeah, that's not how things work, Cole."

"I know. I was just *that* guy in school, and I never had anyone around brave enough to tell me I was a dick."

"You're a dick."

He winced.

"But you're not a bad guy. You're learning." Ivy smiled at him. "I forgive you."

"Thanks, Ivy. That... Thanks."

They both looked out at the storm again, and the silence between them lacked the awkwardness Ivy might have otherwise expected. Unfortunately, that only gave space to her anxiety—her mate was still out there. Ivy crossed her arms and rubbed them again for warmth, wishing it was Ketahn's arms around her instead, that it was his heat and his body protecting her.

"For what it's worth, he will come back," Cole said. "He looked grim as hell when he left, but I don't think anything can stop him when he's like that."

"Thank you, Cole."

They stood there, side by side, watching the rain fall, watching the water level inch higher and higher, listening to the booming peals of thunder and feeling them reverberate through the ship.

When Ivy realized she was scratching at her forearm again— which was thankfully protected by her sleeve—she curled her fingers into a fist. The worry in her belly gnawed at her, making her feel sick, but it was nothing compared to the worry in her heart. No one in her life had ever come close to meaning a sliver of what Ketahn meant to her. And if she lost him...

She drew in a shuddering breath and bit back the tears.

No. Don't even think of it, Ivy.

Something splashed in the pool outside.

Ivy's heart froze, and her breath caught in her lungs. The sound had been barely audible over the cacophony of the storm, but it was there, she'd heard it—and based on his concerned glance at her, so had Cole.

Wordlessly, they retreated from the opening, entering the

ruined stasis room into which it led. Cole flattened himself against the wall near the break and motioned for Ivy to get down before taking his spear in both hands.

As though it hadn't been enough for her to have disobeyed Ketahn's command, she'd forgotten her own spear. He'd taught her it was her most valuable tool in the Tangle, and she'd left it back in the secure room she'd chosen to leave despite his warning.

She ducked behind a nearby cryochamber, her pounding heart setting a rhythm to rival that of the rain, and that sense of helplessness washed over her again. It wasn't very long ago that she'd hid behind one of these pods while Ketahn fought Durax.

From inside the room, the sound of rainfall was different—more distant, more surreal, and yet somehow more concentrated. It was all Ivy could hear apart from her frantic heartbeat, and she focused on it.

The sound from outside changed, becoming muffled. The change was subtle but unmistakable.

Something was partially blocking the entrance. Someone or something was entering the ship.

Ivy dropped her gaze to a long, rusted metal bar lying on the floor in front of her. Leaning forward, closed her fingers around one end and carefully lifted it, gritting her teeth as it made a slight scrape against the floor. She pulled it close to her chest.

A metallic groan emerged from the gap in the wall. Ivy released a shuddering breath and tightened her hold on her improvised weapon. It was heavy and rough, its rusted surface abrading her clammy palms, but it was better than nothing.

Something brushed over the floor of the chamber near Cole. Before Ivy could so much as wonder if it had been his boot or their unidentified visitors, there was a burst of rustling movement, a startled shout—*"Fuck!"*—and the heavy slam of something striking the wall.

All the helplessness that had consumed Ivy, all her need to help Ella and her inability to do so, coursed through her in an icy flow. But something sparked in her chest that blasted the cold back. An angry fire; a molten determination. She wasn't that naïve girl who was too timid to stand up for herself anymore. She wasn't a bystander. She was a blossoming hunter, a friend, a mate…a survivor.

And if Ketahn wasn't around to protect everyone, she would do everything she could to do it herself.

Gripping the metal rod like a baseball bat, Ivy surged to her feet and ran toward the intruder with cry.

The big vrix pinning Cole to the wall twisted, one arm darting out to catch Ivy's swinging rod in his hand. Recognition struck her the instant their gazes met.

"Ketahn," Ivy breathed, eyes widening in alarm. She released the metal rod as though it burned.

"Ivy," he growled as he tossed the rod aside. It landed with a loud clang.

"I'm sorry! I didn't know it was you. I wouldn't have—"

"I told you to stay in the chamber." His mandibles twitched and snapped together, and he released a huff. His fist tightened on the fabric of Cole's jumpsuit. "I said do not go out!"

"Well, technically, we're still inside," Cole rasped. He still held his spear in one hand, though its head was angled toward the ceiling now, while his other hand was clutching Ketahn's forearm.

"And a thread's width from having been run through." Ketahn released Cole with a snarl. Cole managed to land on his feet, but his spear fell, clattering on the floor as Ketahn turned to face Ivy fully. "Why did you disobey? Why did you place yourself in danger? If I am not here to prot—"

Ivy threw herself against Ketahn, wrapping her arms around him and burying her face against his wet, hard chest. He was here. He was *safe*. A shudder stole through her. "I was worried about you."

He tensed, and something unsettling rippled through his body. With a final grunt, he tossed down his own weapon and cocooned Ivy with all four of his arms, dipping his head to nuzzle her hair. There was desperation in the strength of his hold, but he didn't hurt her, even when his fingers curled against her back and his claws raked her jumpsuit.

Warmth flooded her chest. This was where she was meant to be, in his arms. This was where she felt right. Where she felt *loved*.

"I'm sorry I didn't listen, but I just couldn't wait in there anymore," Ivy said, turning her face to the side as tears of relief spilled down her cheeks.

"It is all right," he rumbled. "I am here, my *nyleea*."

A second vrix entered the chamber through the gap—Rekosh, carrying a bundle of spears lashed together with a silk strand. Keeping his hold on Ivy, Ketahn moved aside, allowing Rekosh past. Urkot and Telok followed, both bearing bulging bags in addition to their normal packs.

Ahnset entered last. She ducked through the opening slowly and did not lift her head even when she was through. She'd forgone most of her golden adornments while she'd lived here on the ship, but Ivy couldn't help noticing they were all gone now, even the ring Ahnset had worn on her right mandible—like she'd been stripped.

All the vrix were quiet. That wasn't necessarily unusual, but there was something decidedly morose about their silence and their postures. And Ella... Ella wasn't with them.

Ivy's mind went back to Ketahn's brief return earlier—to the way he'd acted, to what he'd said.

I am sorry, Ivy.

Cole bent down and retrieved his spear, frowning as he looked past Ahnset. "Where's Ella?"

Ketahn stiffened, and his hold on Ivy tightened. She felt his hearts thumping, hard and fast, felt the rasp in his chest as he drew in a deep breath. When he spoke, his words were low and harsh. "We must go."

He didn't answer.

Ivy's chest constricted as that feeling of dread resurfaced. She drew back and looked up at him. "Ketahn—"

"Now," Ketahn growled, withdrawing from her abruptly.

She flinched and snapped her mouth shut.

Ketahn placed his hands on Ivy's shoulders and spun her around, guiding her forward with just enough firmness to make it clear that there'd be no resisting.

"For real, Ketahn, where is she?" Cole demanded.

Telok hissed, short and sharp—a universal sound for *shut up.*

Numbing cold spread outward from the dread pooled in Ivy's belly, filling her limbs as Ketahn directed her into the corridor and toward the stasis chamber where everyone else was waiting. With each step, her legs felt heavier, her muscles less responsive, her heart a little closer to breaking.

When they reached the door, Ketahn slammed his palm against the button beside it. It opened with a rush of air. Startled faces from within the room turned their way.

Ahmya pushed herself away from the cyrochamber she was leaning against and stepped toward the doorway. A smile lit upon her face. "You're back!"

That smile died the moment her eyes met Ivy's.

Ketahn guided Ivy into the room, moving clear of the door so the others could enter behind them.

"So what happened?" Callie asked, brow pinched.

"Ella's not here." Cole planted the butt of his spear on the floor and glared at Ahnset. "Where the fuck is she? What did you do to her?"

Ahnset did not meet Cole's gaze; she kept her eyes downcast, her mandibles hanging. Urkot, Rekosh, and Telok looked to one another uncertainly before shifting their attention to Ketahn.

He didn't acknowledge their questioning glances. His fingers flexed, and his claws pricked Ivy's shoulders through the material of her jumpsuit.

"Answer me!" Cole stepped toward the female vrix. The cords on his neck were standing out, and his grip on the spear was so tight that his knuckles were white.

"Ease up, man," said Diego, hopping down from his cryochamber and putting up his hands. "She doesn't understand what you're saying."

"But Ketahn does," Lacey said, eyes leveled on Ketahn. "We have a right to know what happened to Ella."

Ivy shrugged Ketahn's hands off and turned to face him, meaning to echo what Lacey had said, but her words caught in her throat when she saw him in the bright, clear light. Vrix didn't seem to bruise easily—their hides were thick and hard, their muscles dense, and their dark skin made it difficult to spot wounds that weren't bleeding.

But Ivy saw the damage inflicted upon Ketahn now. There were numerous deep, dark splotches on his body, bruises, a few small cuts, and claw marks across his abdomen crusted with dried blood. The most startling of all was the thick bruise circling his throat that disappeared beneath his loose, wet hair on either side.

It looked as if he'd been caught in a noose.

Ivy's heart lurched, and that sickness in her belly rose again. Brow furrowing, she stepped closer to him and reached up, brushing her trembling fingertips across the dark band marring his throat. "Ketahn, what happened?"

Ketahn caught her hand, holding her fingers just out of reach of his neck. A low growl sounded in his chest, and his mandibles twitched. "I failed."

Silence seized the room, a suffocating, stifling force far

heavier than it had any right to be. It was broken by Ahmya, who softly asked, "Failed?"

"Ella is dead." Kethan's voice was low, gravelly, seething with rage.

"Fuck!" Will's face grew taut as he laced his hands behind his head and turned away from the group.

Lacey's eyes widened, and she covered her mouth. "Oh God."

"What happened?" Callie demanded, stepping forward. Her dark eyes glistened with tears, but there was fury within them. She thrust a finger at Ahnset. "We *trusted* you. All of you. Why would you do this?"

"No more talk," Ketahn snarled. "Need to go. *Now.*"

Cole spun toward Ketahn. "Fuck that shit! You expect us to go with you after this? After your own sister had Ella killed?"

Diego ran his palm over his face and swallowed hard. He glanced at Ahnset and quickly looked away, but he wasn't fast enough to hide the tears in his eyes from Ivy.

Ahnset's shoulders sank, and a shudder rippled through her. She couldn't speak English, but it was clear that she understood the humans well enough.

Ketahn's mandibles snapped together. "She did not have Ella killed."

"Bullshit!" Cole shook his head, jaw muscles ticking. "Ella would be here with us right now if your sister hadn't taken her this morning."

Ivy tugged her hand free of Ketahn's grasp and took a step back. The words were hard to force past the tightness in her throat, but she spoke them nonetheless. "What happened, Ketahn?"

Ketahn looked at her with pain and anger swirling in his violet eyes. He rasped, "We must go, my *nyleea*."

"We need to know. No one is going to follow if they can't trust you." Ivy flicked her gaze over Rekosh, Urkot, Telok, and lastly, Ahnset. "If they can't trust them."

For a long while, Ketahn stared at her, searching for something, bristling with barely contained emotion. She'd never seen him so battered, so worn, so frayed. Ivy couldn't begin to imagine what he'd been through. If it were just the two of them, she would've gladly given him the time he needed to process everything before asking him to talk...

But the others needed to know. Ivy needed to know. Though a strange numbness had settled over her, there was a spark of anger in her belly waiting to be fanned into a roaring flame—and that anger would've been so much easier to accept than grief right now.

"I did not find Ahnset," he said, keeping his gaze locked with Ivy's. "I stood before the queen when Ahnset came to Takarahl. She asked for healing. For Ella. The queen gave only death, and I...could not stop her."

Diego cursed. He ran his hands through his hair, clenched it, and stalked toward Ahnset. "Why did you take her? Why did you fucking take her?"

Ketahn let out a huff and strode to his sister. He stopped in front of her, his body forming a barrier between Ahnset and everyone else, and turned his back toward her. "To help. To get healing. To save—"

"But Ahnset knew what the queen was like," Ivy said. "She knew but took Ella anyway."

He bowed his head and curled his hands into fists, which trembled at his sides. "She knew. But did not...understand. Did not see with all her eyes."

Ahnset said something in vrix, far too low for Ivy to make out, and Ketahn's tension increased.

"Ella didn't deserve this," Diego growled. "She was already dying, but she didn't fucking deserve this." He turned and walked away, propping his elbows on a cryochamber and burying his head in his hands.

Will approached Diego and settled a hand upon his shoulder.

"She did not. But she is gone," Ketahn replied firmly, but not ungently. "You are here. *We* are here. To live, we must go."

Somehow, the dread that had lodged itself so deep within Ivy intensified. She pressed her back to the wall. "Because the queen knows about us now."

Ketahn glanced over his shoulder at his sister. "She sent Ahnset with hunters to find all humans."

"And you fucking brought her back here anyway?" Cole threw up a hand and slapped it down on his head, pulling his hair fiercely. "This is fucked. So fucked."

With a huff and a sharp shake of his head, Ketahn took a step forward. "Ahnset led them away from here."

"But then you came back," said Lacey, "which means they could've followed you."

Another frustrated sound erupted from Ketahn's chest. His fists trembled, and his leg hairs bristled. Ivy's eyes swept over Rekosh, Telok, and Urkot. They were agitated and ill at ease. And they were still holding all those extra spears, the extra bags...

"They did not," Ketahn said.

"How can you be sure?" Callie folded her arms across her chest; normally, it would've been a confident stance for her, but it conveyed only nervousness now.

"They weren't followed," said Ivy.

Will turned his head to look back at her without removing his hand from Diego's shoulder. "How could you know that?"

Cole faced Ivy. His expression was strained with anger, but fear glimmered in his eyes. "Hasn't the time for blind trust passed, Ivy?"

"It's not blind trust," she said, drawing in a steadying breath and struggling to swallow her overwhelming feelings. "Ketahn and the others left with their spears and their bags. Look what they came back with."

The other humans stared at the vrix. The air was so thick

with emotion, so electric with tension, that it was a wonder anyone could breathe. But realization gradually blossomed on the humans' faces.

"The hunters are dead, but more will come," said Ketahn. The finality in his tone left no room for argument.

And yet Ivy knew there was so much more he hadn't said—so much more he'd endured since he'd left this morning. She hurt for him, for Ella, but her anger remained. She was angry at Ahnset, angry at the queen...angry at herself, for not being able to do anything. In the quiet that settled over the group, Ivy squeezed her eyes shut. Her imagination brought up Ella's face, and—

She forced her eyes open before her thoughts could run away from her. Imaging Ella, or what she might have suffered...

It wasn't time to grieve.

They didn't *have* time to grieve.

"What are we going to do now?" Ahmya sniffled, wiping tears from her cheeks.

Callie picked up her pack and swung it onto her back. "We get the hell out of here before the queen comes looking."

CHAPTER 7

THE EXODUS from the *Somnium* was miserable. Unrelenting rain made every solid surface slippery and left the forest floor a minefield of deep puddles and mud, much of it hidden beneath layers of undergrowth and fallen leaves and branches. The jumpsuits were waterproof, and the vrix had given everyone cloak-like hides to add another layer of protection, but water was *everywhere*.

It found every tiny gap in Ivy's clothing. It found its way into her boots, dripped down her face and crept under her collar, trickling steadily lower. And it brought cold wherever it touched.

Cold and jungle still didn't compute for Ivy—jungles were hot and humid, weren't they? Rain was supposed to bring some relief from that thick, oppressive heat. But this storm had made the jungle frigid compared to what she'd become accustomed to, and it had only grown colder as the meager gray daylight faded.

They'd walked for hours, huddled close enough together that they'd often bumped into each other and tripped over one another's feet. The vrix had encircled the cluster of humans, grim protectors who'd seemed little hindered by the rain—not that Ivy had spent much time watching them. She'd kept her face down for most of the trip both to shield her eyes from the rain and to watch her footing.

Though she'd built considerable endurance traveling through the jungle with Ketahn, this journey had already sapped Ivy's energy. Between the terrible conditions, the heavy pack on her back, the flaring cramps in her pelvis, and...and Ella, Ivy was exhausted in every conceivable way. She wasn't sure how she kept her feet moving, wasn't sure how she kept herself upright.

But what she felt wasn't even a sliver of the exhaustion Ketahn must have been suffering.

Ivy tugged her cloak more snugly around herself, lifted her face, and sought her mate, blinking against the rain.

Ketahn walked at the front of their formation. The deepening gloom made him a hulking shadow. His shoulders were hunched under the weight of the bulging bag on his back, and he held bundles of supplies beneath each of his lower arms. His stride was usually confident and powerful, but now it showed only bitter determination in the face of his weariness.

Ivy's heart clenched. He was doing this for her. All of this was for her. And she couldn't help but blame herself for the weight he now carried upon his shoulders.

"I don't think I can feel my legs anymore," Ahmya remarked beside Ivy.

"Mine are on auto-pilot," Callie said from behind. "I feel like if I stop, I'm going to collapse."

Lacey chuckled, though it was airy and winded. "Remember when they used to force us to run the mile in school? Yeah, that's how I feel right now."

Callie laughed. "My friends and I were too busy talking and would always come in last."

Ivy smiled. Those days, those memories, were so far away

that she wondered if they'd even happened at all. "Same. I used to get in so much trouble for it."

Ahmya turned her head and smiled sheepishly. Her face was pale, and her cheeks were flushed. "I was usually one of the first students to finish, but I'd just keep going afterward."

"Overachiever," Lacey said with a smirk, nudging Ahmya with her elbow.

Ahmya chuckled. "Maybe a little."

"I feel like my body forgot I used to go on three mile runs every morning before work," Diego said.

Cole snickered. "Guess weightlifting didn't do me much good in the cardio department."

"Well, consider us trapped in leg day indefinitely," Will said.

They laughed, but that laughter was cut short when Callie's foot caught on a root, pitching her forward. She gasped and slammed into Ivy from behind. Ivy's eyes widened, and she released her hide cloak to throw her hands out to catch herself as she and Callie tumbled into the water and muck.

Ivy squeezed her eyes shut as water and mud splashed her face. Rocks and twigs scraped her palms and dug painfully into her legs from where Callie lay atop them. The backpack felt twice as heavy, threating to crush her.

Callie pushed herself off Ivy. "Shit! I'm so sorry."

Raising her head, Ivy wiped the dirty water from her face. "It's okay."

The rain continued falling upon her, and water spilled freely into her jumpsuit. That chill penetrated to her bones, making her shiver. But worst of all was that pressure in her pelvis. It chose that moment to reassert itself, clamping down on her insides harshly enough to make her suck in a sharp breath and sink her fingers into the soft ground.

Strong hands slid under her arms and lifted her out of the muck. She reflexively reached out, taking hold of the big, solid forearms attached to those hands as she was placed on her feet.

Through the curtain of her wet hair, she could only make out the dark shape of a vrix looming before her.

With the lightest of touches, another large hand brushed her hair aside, clearing her vision. Of course it was Ketahn standing before her, the very last traces of gray daylight reflected in tiny pinpoints in his violet eyes.

He pressed his palm to her cheek. "Are you all right, my *nyleea?*"

Ivy turned her face into it his touch. Though his hide was rough and callused, it was warm and comforting. She slid her palm along his arm to cover his hand. "I'm fine. Thank you."

Beside them, Urkot had helped Callie up, and was adjusting her backpack and cloak.

Ketahn bent forward, touching his headcrest to Ivy's forehead. He drew in a long, slow breath, and released it just as slowly. Ivy didn't miss the shakiness of that exhalation.

She frowned and cupped his jaw between her wet, chilled hands. "We need to stop, Ketahn."

It was the truth, no matter how much she dreaded it—no matter how much she feared having time for her mind to wander down paths even darker than the surrounding jungle.

"No. We must go." He straightened, pulling his face from her hands and withdrawing his touch, and began to turn. "As far as we can, we must go."

Ivy caught one of his wrists. He halted and looked back at her.

"No. We need to stop. *You* need to stop." She stepped closer to him, smoothing her hand over his arm, and searched his eyes as the storm continued around them. "You're exhausted, my *luveen.*"

Tension rippled under his hide, and his voice was a barely audible rasp when he said, "It is too soon."

"We've traveled for hours, it's almost night, and you've been through so much. So much that I don't even know about. I also haven't even seen you eat." She settled her hands on his chest; his hearts pounded beneath her palms. In vrix, she said, "Please, Ketahn. You need to rest."

Ketahn gripped her shoulders and waist. His mandibles twitched and his fingers flexed as he stared down at her, and Ivy couldn't tell whether he wanted to release her or pull her closer. His indecision, his internal struggle, wrapped around Ivy's heart like barbed wire and coiled tight. Did he really intend to push himself until there was nothing left?

"Your mate is right," Telok said as he neared them, stabbing the end of his spear into the ground in front of his foreleg. "We will gain little should we continue. Less if we must carry you, Ketahn."

"We are too close." Ketahn turned his head and looked off into the distance; Ivy knew he was looking toward Takarahl. Though he'd told her about it, the vrix city was like a place of myth to her...but perhaps *place of nightmares* was more apt a term.

Telok extended a foreleg, bumping it against Ketahn's. "The light is dying. Our little companions have had trouble enough seeing as it is, and they are weary from worry and grief. We will be safe taking shelter for the night."

Ivy reached up to touch Ketahn's cheek again, drawing his attention back to her. "We're all in this together, Ketahn. You don't have to carry it all yourself. You don't have to break yourself for our sake." Her voice softened when she said, "You're hurt."

Ketahn closed his eyes and leaned his face into her palm, brushing his hide against it. "I do not wish to see such sorrow in your eyes, my heartsthread."

"It's because I'm worried about you."

"I... We will stop."

"Thank fuck," Cole said from somewhere behind Ivy.

"There is a hollow nearby." Ketahn looked at Telok as he

covered Ivy's hand with his own. "It is large enough for all of us to shelter in."

"I know it," said Telok. "Stride with your mate. I will go with Rekosh to ensure it is not occupied."

~

*T*he hollow was at the base of an immense tree, the size of which was made only more imposing by the thick darkness settling over the jungle. A huge split in the trunk created a cave-like opening that began several feet off the jungle floor. The split was wide enough at its base to drive a car through, narrowing as it rose until the trunk came together into a solid piece again.

Apart from some debris—leaves and sticks, mostly—and the thick, soft moss clinging to the trunk and growing on the ground, the interior had been empty. It was also surprisingly spacious, at least until everyone was crammed inside.

But all that mattered was that it was dry.

All the humans had changed their jumpsuits, turning the wet ones inside out and leaving them to dry.

So much for being waterproof.

The change of clothing had only helped a little against the cold. Without a fire, the group had no choice but to huddle together for warmth as the storm raged outside. Rain poured in sheets, wind swept through the boughs, its wails echoing faintly in the hollow, and thunder rolled across heaven and earth, shaking everything with its fury.

Ivy drew her blanket snugly around herself and nestled more firmly against Ketahn. He was like a blazing furnace against her chilled body. His arms, which were banded around her, tightened.

At first, she'd argued against lying on him, not having known the extent of his injuries and fearful of hurting him further. But Ketahn had simply scooped Ivy up and put her in her usual place as he positioned himself against the inner wall of the trunk. He'd refused to let her sleep apart from him.

Despite her concerns for Ketahn, she had to admit that this position helped ease some of the discomfort in her pelvis.

Ivy swept her gaze over the others. She couldn't make out any details in the dark, but her eyes had adjusted enough for her to make out their forms. Most of the humans were asleep, having drifted off as soon as they lay down, but a few, like Ivy, were awake and restless.

Telok, Rekosh, and Urkot had positioned themselves to the sides of the opening, the latter two having eased down to sleep with spears in hand. Ahnset sat alone at the center of that opening with her back toward the group, a large, shadowed figure, silent and stationary in her vigil.

She'd separated herself from everyone since Ketahn had brought her back to the *Somnium*, and she hadn't spoken apart from a few rasped words to Ketahn on the ship. She'd just been…a presence, a mournful shade trailing behind the party as they traveled.

The person Ahnset had been two days ago was gone.

Ahnset was hurting, but Ivy could not look at her without being reminded of what the female vrix had done. Without being reminded that Ella was dead, and Ahnset was at fault. Ivy understood why Ahnset had taken the sickly human. Ahnset had been nothing but gentle and caring when it came to Ella, and never would have harmed her on purpose, but…

It was too soon for that understanding to make a difference. The loss was too raw. Having seen the strength and ferocity the vrix were capable of, Ivy could only imagine what the queen had done to Ella.

The road to hell is paved with good intentions.

Ivy's mother had been fond of that saying, yet even now, Ivy wasn't sure if she quite believed it.

Ahnset had done what she thought was right. She'd acted in an attempt to save a life. How was that any different from what Ivy had done in waking up the humans to begin with?

Ivy frowned and pressed her brow to Ketahn's chest. She just...she needed time. The anger, hurt, and sense of betrayal was still too new.

Thunder boomed outside, rattling the hollow.

Ketahn slid a hand up her back and brushed her hair from her cheek. In English, he said, "Be at ease, my *nyleea*. Rest."

"I'm sorry. There's just a lot on my mind." Ivy lifted her head to look up at him. "You should be sleeping, too."

He stroked her cheek, the tip of his claw grazing her temple. "My thoughts are troubled also. But you are safe. We are safe."

She couldn't ignore the strain in his voice, or the way his mandibles twitched downward. Laying her head back down, she slid one of her hands up his body until she reached his throat, where she gently stroked her thumb back and forth along his bruised hide. He emitted a quiet trill.

The storm filled in the ensuing quiet—and she could only find some comfort in it because Ketahn was holding her so securely, so closely.

"Which way do you mean to lead us come suncrest?" Telok asked after a while. His rough, raspy voice seemed at home amidst the rain sounds.

"The direction we have been going," Ketahn replied.

Not ungently, Telok said, "Have your wounds addled your wits, Ketahn?"

Ketahn grunted. "No."

"So you know where you are leading us?"

"I know the Tangle as well as you, Telok. I know where we are going."

"From one enemy to another," Telok growled. "What good will that do us?"

Ivy frowned. In vrix, she asked, "What does he mean, Ketahn?"

"He is leading us toward thornskull territory," Telok said.

Rekosh stirred, lifting his torso upright to look at Ketahn. "That does not seem wise."

"It is the last place the queen would expect us to go," Urkot rumbled, unmoving.

"Does that make it worth the risk?" Telok was still looking at Ketahn; Ivy could just make out the tiny reflections in his green eyes.

"After what occurred..." Ketahn drew in a ragged breath, body tensing. "Zurvashi will seek blood. The thornskulls are her enemies, and so may be a shield against her for a time."

"They are our enemies also. Have you forgotten?"

Ketahn growled. "How could I ever forget?"

"Ketahn led us into their land before," said Urkot. "I trust him now, just as I did then."

"It is not a matter of trust," Telok replied. "We did not have a pack of humans accompanying us during the war, and still the way was hard won."

A thoughtful trill sounded from Rekosh. "I would expect you of all vrix to oppose this, Urkot. You have ever scolded Ketahn for his unnecessary risks."

Urkot sat up then and folded his arms across his broad chest. "I would never have returned to Takarahl if not for Ketahn. I would have been left to rot in the mire, another fallen warrior in Zurvashi's war. I have no wish to return there, but if Ketahn believes it is the way to protect our tribe, I will follow him."

With a grunt, Telok leaned back against the wood. "Eight stride with us, for this is foolish. The thornskulls...they will not welcome us."

"Humans have an old saying," Ivy said, pausing to worry her bottom lip as she tried to piece the words together in vrix. "The enemy of my enemy is my friend. Do you...understand that?"

Ketahn's fingers pressed into her. "Yes, my heartsthread."

"Good, simple words," Urkot said. "I like them."

"I hope not too simple," said Rekosh. "Such matters are rarely so."

Telok clacked his fangs. "Words will make no difference if the thornskulls kill us the moment they see us."

"So we will do all we can to go unseen," Ketahn said. "Sleep. We have a long journey ahead."

The vrix fell silent, once more allowing the storm's sounds to devour all other noise. Sleep still felt far away despite Ivy's exhaustion. Her mind wandered—to what they might face in the coming days, to the queen, to the *what-ifs* and *could've-beens*, to whatever future lay ahead.

To Ella.

To the death she had not deserved.

Tears burned Ivy's eyes. They spilled, tickling over her skin to drip onto Ketahn's chest. What if Ivy had never awoken the others? Ella would have...

Ella would have still died.

I'm glad you woke me, Ivy, Ella had said. *I'm glad I got to see something so amazing before the end. I get...I get to be one of eight humans in the whole universe to have met the vrix.*

Ivy drew in a shuddering breath.

Ketahn's claspers curled around her hips, and he smoothed a hand down her back. Another of his hands stroked her hair. "I am here, Ivy."

Those words only made her cling to him more desperately. She wrapped her arm around the back of his neck and drew herself higher up his body to tuck her face beneath his chin, the tip of her nose brushing his neck. She closed her eyes and drew in his mahogany and spice scent.

I am here, Ivy.

Had things gone differently, he might not have been here to

say those words. He might never have escaped the queen's clutches. He might have been lost to Ivy forever.

"What are we going to do?" she whispered, her tears still falling.

He combed his claws through her hair slowly, gently, but his reply was firm. "Anything it takes to keep you safe, my heartsthread. You will never be taken from me."

"You could have died today. Or the queen, she could have... have..." Then an awful thought occurred to her. All the marks upon his hide, the bruising around his throat and wrists. Her fingers clutched at him. "Oh God. Did she force you to...?"

"*No*," he rasped, voice low and raw. "I was freed by my broodsister's mate before the queen could try to claim me." Ketahn drew his head back and brushed his rough mouth across Ivy's forehead. "No matter what might have happened, I would have found my way back to you. You are my mate, my heartsthread. I will never forsake you. I will never betray you."

CHAPTER 8

LOW GROANS and voices woke Ivy. She breathed in deep and stretched her sore, stiff limbs.

Ketahn's palm, planted firmly on her backside, pressed down to clamp her in place as his claspers stroked her outer thighs.

She blinked her eyes open as thrilling little tingles coursed over her skin. Unbidden, her sex clenched, and she rocked her pelvis against Ketahn.

"Be still, my *nyleea*," he rumbled.

Ivy froze, suddenly very much aware of the hard, prominent bulge behind his slit nestled against her core. "Oh."

All that separated them was the material of her jumpsuit. A simple flick of his claw could eliminate that barrier, and then he'd be inside her. Had they been alone, they undoubtedly would've indulged in the pleasure of each other's bodies as they'd done on so many other mornings. She craved his touch, longed to lose herself in the oblivion of ecstasy. But she and Ketahn weren't likely to have many opportunities to indulge those cravings in the coming days.

Morning light shone outside the hollow. No rain, no wind, no rolling thunder; just soft, golden sunlight.

She kissed one of the larger bruises on his chest. "The storm broke."

"Yes," Ketahn replied, his deep voice vibrating into her. "It will ease our travels today."

Ivy lifted her head off his chest and shifted to glance around the hollow. Telok wasn't here, so she could only assume he'd already gone outside. Everyone else was either awake or in the process of waking.

Cole was on his feet, one shoulder leaned against the inside of the tree trunk as he chewed on a strip of dried meat, and Will stood with his arms over his head in a stretch. Diego, sitting with a waterskin in hand, turned his sleepy eyes toward Will, running them up and down. Ahnset, who had been keeping watch before Ivy fell asleep, now sat to the left of the entrance, legs tucked against her body.

As normal as it was for people to look groggy and disoriented when they first woke up, the weariness in Ivy's companions seemed to run deeper—and she felt it, too. They hadn't even spent half the day walking yesterday and yet it had taken all Ivy's strength and then some to get through.

"I think we could all use an easier day," she replied softly.

"I know, my *nyleea*." Shifting one pair of hands to her hips and the other to her underarms, Ketahn gently lifted Ivy off him, setting her on her feet.

The instant her legs had to support her weight, that sharp, cramping pain flared in her pelvis. Ivy sucked in a breath, hunched forward, and braced her hands on her thighs, squeezing the material of her jumpsuit.

Ketahn rose behind her, sweeping her hair back from her face with one hand while grasping her shoulders with two others. "What is wrong, Ivy? What is hurt?"

"Ivy?" Ahmya asked uncertainly.

Diego pushed himself up and hurried to Ivy, crouching to look into her eyes. "What're you feeling?"

Ivy drew in a couple deep breaths and shook her head. "I'm okay. It's just a little cramping." Which was true. It'd been persistent yet tolerable all day yesterday, but the moment Ketahn had set her down, it had sharpened. She looked up Ketahn and smiled. "I'm fine. Promise. The pain is already easing."

Ketahn tilted his head and narrowed his eyes, clearly unconvinced.

"You're sure?" Diego asked.

Ivy nodded and straightened. "Yeah. Likely just...woman stuff, you know?"

"Ah. Gotcha." Diego stood with a crooked smile. "Too bad we don't have anything to help that."

"I wish."

"What is *woman stuff?*" Ketahn asked as Diego stepped away.

Her cheeks warmed as she faced Ketahn. "It's...human stuff. Normal stuff."

He grunted and caught her chin. "That explains nothing, Ivy."

She chuckled, placed her hands on his forearms, and rose on the toes of her boots to kiss his mouth. "Trust me. I'm okay."

Ketahn tipped his head forward, touching his headcrest to her forehead, and released a soft trill. "I do, my heartsthread."

"I have to pee something fierce," Callie said. She walked toward the opening in trunk, placed a hand upon the edge of the wood, and peered out before turning to look at the others. "Anyone else want to mountain woman this with me behind a bush?"

Smiling at Ketahn, Ivy pulled away from him. "I'll come."

"Me too." Lacey stood, brushed her backside off, and picked up her spear, walking toward the entrance to stand next to Callie. "How about you, Ahmya?"

Ahmya nodded, pushing herself up to her feet. "I feel like I'm going to burst."

"I will stay with you." Ketahn closed the little bit of distance Ivy had opened between them. "Bad things happen when you pee."

Ivy laughed and flattened a hand on Ketahn's chest to stop him. "Really? That was *one* time, and I wasn't even actually peeing when the velocitiger snuck up on me."

He wasn't ever going to let her live that down, especially since she had a scar on her leg as a reminder of the incident.

Ketahn cocked his head. "The *what*? I have told you, the beast was called *unac*. And you said you were going to pee. It does not matter if you did or not."

"Hold up," Callie said, arching a brow. "First, Ivy, you're going to have to explain that whole thing later, and second, Ketahn, you are not coming to watch us pee."

Ketahn let out a frustrated huff. "I will not watch you. I will watch the jungle."

Ivy stroked his chest. "We've already talked about this, Ketahn. I also won't be by myself this time."

His mandibles twitched, and he flicked his gaze toward the other humans. In his native tongue, he said, "That does not ease my worry."

"He's talking about us, isn't he?" Lacey asked, smirking. Lifting her spear, she braced her feet and took a fighting stance, jabbing the pointed end of the weapon in front of her. "He doesn't trust our mad skills?"

A large, dark figure stepped up behind Lacey, silhouetted by the morning light. Lacey started, but before she could turn, the figure had reached to either side of her, placing big hands over hers on the shaft of the spear.

Telok leaned over Lacey, his face close to her ear, and placed his lower hands on her hips. Her breath hitched. He slid her leading hand away from the spearhead and turned her other hand slightly, correcting the angle of her arm. Then, with a foreleg, he pushed her feet farther apart to widen her stance.

Lacey rolled her eyes. "Couldn't just let me have my moment, could you?"

"What did she say, Ketahn?" Telok asked.

"She thanked you for the lesson," Ketahn replied with a chitter.

"That did not seem a grateful tone." Telok turned his face toward Lacey but paused. His mandibles twitched. Hesitantly, he pressed his face into her hair and inhaled. A low trill sounded in his chest.

Ivy's eyebrows rose high.

"Um... What's he doing?" Lacey asked, standing very, very still.

"He's, uh, praising you." Ivy covered her mouth to hide her grin.

Rekosh chittered. "It seems the hunter has scented new prey."

With a grunt, Telok withdrew from Lacey. He glared at Rekosh for an instant before shaking himself and turning away. "We should leave soon, Ketahn, while the weather holds." Then he strode out of sight.

"I couldn't tell if that was hot or what," Callie said when Telok was gone. She stood with her arms crossed and her hip cocked, lips split into a wide grin. "He went *Ghost* on you."

Pink flooded Lacey's face as she lowered the spear and stood straight. "Oh, shut up. He did not."

Ivy laughed. "He really did."

"I can't believe you guys have even seen that movie," Ahmya said. "I thought I was the only one."

"It's a classic. A must see..." Callie frowned. "Well, not that we'll be seeing any movies anytime soon. Anyway, now can we go pee?"

Ivy looked at Ketahn. "We won't go far. Ahnset can come with us if that'll make you feel better."

Ahnset looked at Ivy as her name was spoken, and then flicked her gaze toward Ketahn. "Broodbrother?"

His mandibles rose and fell, and his hands curled into fists at his sides. He didn't look at his sister; his eyes remained on Ivy, and she could tell he was warring with his decision. She didn't blame him. She understood his hesitance, his distrust, his anger, and knew a lot of it stemmed from his need to keep Ivy safe.

And from his failure to do the same for Ella.

Switching to vrix, Ivy faced Ahnset. "Can you watch us outside?" She gestured to herself and the other women.

Ahnset spread her legs, rose, and bowed her head. "I will keep watch." She looked at Ketahn and placed a fist over her hearts. "I will guard your mate with my life, brother."

Finally, Ketahn looked at Ahnset. He was silent, tension pulsing from him in waves, his eyes unreadable. Then he dipped his head in a shallow nod. "I know, sister."

A shiver coursed through Ahnset's body as she closed her eyes. Bringing her other arms up, she pressed all four hands over her hearts, holding the pose for a few quiet seconds. When she opened her eyes, she retrieved her bag and spear from beside the wall, glanced at Ivy and the other women, and gestured to the outside.

"Finally!" Callie dropped her arms and stepped out of the hollow with Lacey and Ahmya close behind.

Ivy slipped her arms around Ketahn in a quick embrace. "I'll be back."

He hugged her back with his lower arms, the fingers of his upper right hand catching a loose strand of her hair. "Quickly, my heartsthread. And not far."

After a moment's hesitation, he released her.

Ahnset waited just outside the hollow, a silent sentry, until Ivy grabbed her spear and hurried after the others.

It had been dark when they'd taken shelter here, and everything looked different in the morning light. The jungle was magical when the sun hit it like this after a storm—like a fae world out of a fantasy story, too beautiful to be real. Water droplets clung to broad leaves, sparkling like crystals, the humid air caught the shafts of sunlight and broke them into bright rainbows, and the breeze smelled of earth, vegetation, and fresh rain.

The females departed, trekking down from the hollow's opening and then up an incline. They picked their path carefully, stepping on exposed roots, stones, and vegetation whenever possible. The few patches of mud they were forced to cross were fortunately shallow.

With the sunshine came heat. It bore down on Ivy's head whenever she passed through the beams of light streaming through the canopy. After yesterday's cold, she welcomed the warmth—though it would likely become its own sort of misery as the day wore on and the temperature rose.

They soon came to a place where the dense foliage on the jungle floor was broken up by several rock formations. The green and purple vines clinging to the rocks served as an appealing contrast to the pale stones, which glittered faintly where they were hit by the light. Hundreds of yellow and orange suncrest flowers were scattered amidst the vines, their petals open to drink the sunshine. The spot reminded Ivy of those old gardens she'd seen in pictures—the ones with stone walls overgrown by vines, and wildflowers growing along the rock-paved paths.

Callie stopped beside a bush and plucked several leaves from it. "Never thought this would be my life. From grad school to pissing in the woods."

"I don't think any of us imagined this," Ahmya said, tucking her long, black hair behind her ear and looking around. "Meet back here?"

"Sounds good." Lacey stepping away and disappeared between a couple trees. "I can't hold it anymore."

"Me either." With leaves in hand, Callie turned her body and maneuvered herself through the space separating some tall, viny plants.

Ahnset stopped beside Ivy and planted the butt of her spear on the ground just as Ahmya wandered off. The vrix folded her lower arms. "Tell them not far."

"Ahnset said not to go too far!" Ivy called in English.

"Got it!" Lacey yelled back.

Ivy pointed to the ground and said in vrix, "We will all meet back here."

Ahnset hesitated before she lifted a foreleg and lightly tapped it against Ivy's calf. "I will wait."

Though Ivy's anger hadn't vanished, much of it had faded overnight. She knew Ahnset was already being devoured by guilt over what had happened. Part of Ivy thought Ahnset deserved it, but another part of her, a larger part, hated seeing the once proud warrior so diminished. So...alone. Everyone made mistakes, and this...this had been a terrible one. One that had cost Ahnset nearly everything.

Reaching out, Ivy touched one of Ahnset's elbows and offered her a smile.

Ahnset tensed. She looked down at Ivy's fingers and shuddered, closing her eyes.

Ivy withdrew her hand, turned, and walked around one of the larger rocks. On its backside, it was apparent that this wasn't a simple boulder—it was a whole formation, its numerous ledges creating uneven tiers until they reached a wider, flatter portion that eventually disappeared under the dirt and vegetation. Water was pooled in depressions in many places, clear and shining, and the stone backing each of those pools showed signs of discoloration from runoff having trickled down their faces over countless years.

She stuck her spear into the ground, gathered some leaves, and piled them on a low rock ledge within reaching distance.

Once she'd dug a hole in the ground with her boot, she undid her jumpsuit, gathered the excess material in her arm, and squatted. It wasn't the easiest or most comfortable position, but Ivy managed. She nearly groaned as she relieved herself. When she was done, she used the leaves to wipe, and glanced down at them.

They were coated in blood.

Dropping the leaves into the hole, Ivy looked between her legs. More blood was smeared upon her inner thighs and stained the crotch of her jumpsuit.

"Damn it."

Of course her period had started. It made sense given the cramping, and it had only been a matter of time, right?

But this was the last thing she needed to deal with, especially now.

Rising, she covered the hole with dirt using her boot and eased closer to the rocks. She splashed herself clean, cursing as the cool water slid down her legs, then washed her thighs. Next, she sat on the stone ledge next to one of the pools and scrubbed the blood from her jumpsuit.

What the heck was she going to use to deal with this situation? It wasn't like there were any pads, tampons, or menstrual cups in the emergency supply caches.

"Twenty-second century and they still didn't consider feminine hygiene products a necessity. Go figure," she grumbled as she plunged the crotch of her jumpsuit into the water to scrub some more.

"Ivy."

Ivy snapped her head up upon hearing Ahnset's voice. The female vrix stood tall ahead of her with eyes narrowed and head cocked. Lacey, Callie, and Ahmya were behind her.

"You were taking a while, so we wanted to come check on you to make sure—" Ahmya's eyes dipped and widened. "Oh."

Heat bloomed on Ivy's face. Talk about being caught with

your pants down—literally. She was sitting in the middle of the jungle with nothing on except her boots.

"Yeah, I…kind of have an issue," Ivy said.

Callie winced. "That sucks."

Ahnset stepped closer. "You are bleeding." The little hairs on her legs bristled. "Where are you hurt?"

Ivy glanced down with a frown. She'd cleaned herself, but there was blood pooling on the edge of the stone where she sat —and a tiny, diluted stream trickling down the ledge. She squeezed her thighs together and let out a frustrated breath.

"I am not hurt," she said in vrix, looking back up at Ahnset. "It is… Um…"

Ahnset's mandibles shuddered. Fear and grief gleamed in her eyes, and her voice was unsteady. "How can you bleed with no wound?"

"Female humans bleed once every…every moon cycle. It is natural. It is a sign that we can give…that we can have a brood." Ivy placed a hand on her belly then cradled her arms, switching to English. "A baby."

Colonization had been The Homeworld Initiative's plan. It would have been Ivy's duty as a colonist to give birth to a new generation. But since waking up, the thought of having a baby hadn't crossed her mind. And it certainly wasn't going to happen now. She was a human, and Ketahn… He was vrix.

Still, she couldn't stop a sorrowful pang in her heart. She had always wanted a family, a real one, a loving one. Something unlike the cold, lonely family she'd grown up with. And Ivy knew that Ketahn would have been an amazing, protective, caring father.

Ketahn is enough. He will always *be enough.*

Ahnset's eyes flared, and the hairs on her legs settled. She stared at Ivy's belly. "You…are not harmed then?"

Ivy shook her head. "No."

"Here," Lacey said, holding out a handful of green moss. "It's obviously not a pad, but it should absorb the blood."

Ivy took the moss. It was soft and a little spongy. "Thanks."

She asked Ahnset for a piece of silk from her bag, and the other women turned their backs to allow Ivy some privacy as she fashioned something to keep the moss in place. It was ridiculous looking and uncomfortable, but it was all she could manage for the time being, and it was definitely better than nothing.

"I am really not looking forward to starting my period," Ahmya said.

Callie chuckled. "Especially when there's not a single bubble bath or piece of chocolate within a thousand lightyears."

Lacey pulled several more chunks of moss off a nearby rock. "Well, the only way to stop that would be to get knocked up. I mean, that *was* the plan, right?" She turned her head and looked at the others. "There are three guys. Any of you got your eye on one?"

"I know that one *guy* has his eyes on you."

"Oh, stop it. Telok was just correcting my form."

Callie laughed, folding her arms over her chest. "See! I didn't even say vrix, and your mind was already on him."

"He does watch you a lot," Ahmya said.

Ivy sealed her jumpsuit and looked at Ahmya, grinning. "Rekosh seems to watch you a lot too, Ahmya."

Ahmya blushed.

"So do we need to bring up the way Urkot stared at Callie's ass during her little victory dance?" asked Lacey with a smirk.

Callie gaped at her. "He did not!"

"Oh, he sooooo was. He was staring at that booty shake." Lacey turned and wiggled her backside, arms in the air as she replicated Callie's dance.

The women laughed; it felt good to do so, to have a few moments of light spirits and no worries.

Head cocked, Ahnset regarded the humans. "They are speaking of the males?"

"Yes," Ivy replied in vrix. "About how Rekosh, Urkot, and Telok have been staring at them so often."

Ahnset let out a soft chitter. "We are curious about your kind. Vrix do not hide their interest in one another." One of her hands rose to brush over her mandible; her finger lingered on the slightly paler flesh where the gold band had been, and her mandibles drooped. "Not usually, anyway."

"Do...you have a mate, Ahnset?" Ivy asked.

"Yes. But I... Her place is in Takarahl, and mine is...nowhere."

Once more, Ivy's heart hurt for Ahnset, and just like that, the anger she'd harbored was extinguished. What good could it have done? Ahnset was part of the group, part of Ivy's new family—and no one felt more grief over what had happened than her.

Ivy closed the distance between herself and Ahnset and rested her hand on the vrix's arm. "It will take time for all of us to heal, but you need to know, Ahnset... I understand. You... gave everything for a chance to help Ella, and you would not have done so if you did not think it was right. I am sorry you lost so much, sister."

Ahnset drew in a shaky breath and bowed her head. Her voice was impossibly small and broken when she said, "Ella lost more."

Ivy stood on her toes and stretched her arm up; she was just able to touch Ahnset's chin with the tips of her fingers. "Ella knew she was going to die. She said she was happy to see this jungle and to meet the vrix. To meet you. Her life was... It was *more* because you were in it. And she wanted to thank you for that."

Ahnset's huge body shuddered violently, and she closed her

eyes. That strength and determination was still in there some-where, Ivy knew it, but none of it showed anymore.

"You will always have a place with us, Ahnset," Ivy said gently.

Slowly, carefully, Ahnset bent down to lean her headcrest against Ivy's head. "Thank you, little sister."

"We should head back," Ivy said. "If we stay out here too long, the males will come looking for us."

CHAPTER 9

"*ZIRKITA*," said Will, letting some of the dirt in his hand fall through his fingers.

Ketahn clamped his mouth shut, content to let the exchange progress on its own.

"No," Rekosh replied in English. "*Zirkeeta.*"

Will's brow creased. He turned his head to look at Ahmya, who was sitting next to him on a rock beside the stream. "Isn't that what I just said?"

"*Zir...kita?*" Ahmya winced.

Ivy pressed her lips together. She was kneeling on the stream bank with a few other humans, refilling the waterskins. She glanced at Ketahn and grinned knowingly.

Ketahn smiled and somehow withheld a chitter.

But Urkot did not.

Will frowned. "He laughed again. Every time we say *zirkita*, Urkot laughs."

Rekosh let out a huff. "No *zirkita*." He cupped a hand at the side of his head. "Humans, hear. *Zirkeeta.*"

Lacey threw her hands up. "That's what we've been saying!"

The humans and vrix had been learning one another's

languages since they'd all come together, but the last two days of travel had sped the process. They'd passed much of their time swapping words as they'd trudged through the Tangle. That Rekosh seemed to be learning faster than everyone was of no surprise—he'd always had a talent for talking, even when he really should have just closed his mouth.

"*Zirkita*," said Will, Ahmya, and Lacey in unison.

Taking in a slow breath, Rekosh brought the pads of his fingers together, creating a triangle with each set of hands and making his long, sharpened claws touch at their tips. His mandibles twitched.

"Hear." He bent down and scooped up a little pile of dirt with a lower hand. "*Zirkeeta*." Then he flattened the palms of his upper hands against each other, spread them slightly, and slid a finger from his other lower hand through the gap. "*Zirkita*."

Ahmya frowned. "What does that mean?"

Cole laughed from his perch on a nearby rock. "Pretty sure he's saying dick."

"What?" Ahyma's eyes widened as she looked from Cole back to Rekosh's hands, her pale cheeks flaring red. She buried her face in her hands. "Oh, my God."

"Why the hell is he talking about his dick?" Lacey asked.

Ivy laughed.

Ahmya lifted her head and turned her betrayed gaze toward Ivy. "You knew!"

Closing the waterskin in her hand, Ivy rose and approached Ketahn. "Yeah. I went through the same thing with Ketahn, but it was funnier to watch you guys struggle."

"Ahmya's face turned nearly as red as my markings," Rekosh said in vrix. He cocked his head and turned his eyes toward Ketahn. "Did I anger her?"

Ketahn chittered. "She was embarrassed by what she was saying."

"Their kind does not prefer directness," Urkot said. "And they do not seem comfortable having their bodies exposed."

"So how do you say *zir…zirk…*that word?" Ahmya asked.

"We can't. At least, I don't think we can," Ivy replied, dropping down to sit in the shade in front of Ketahn. "Our vocal cords can't produce the right sound for it."

Sliding forward, Ketahn slipped his lower arms around Ivy and drew her back against his chest. His claspers unfurled to hook her hips. He and his mate had spent so much time at the stream near their den—whether lying in the sun, sitting in the shade, or escaping the heat in the water. They'd enjoyed many quiet days of learning, of closeness, of peace.

He missed those days. The tribe could not remain here much longer, but he would relish these moments.

"What right sound?" Will shook his head. "They're exactly the same!"

Diego flicked water off his hands and strolled over to Will from the stream, holding out a full waterskin when he neared. "Nah. There's this little clicking kind of sound in the one you're getting wrong."

Ivy relaxed against Ketahn and smoothed her chilly palms over his forearms. "Yeah. It's pretty subtle to us, but you'll start to pick up on it. The vrix are a lot more sensitive to vibrations, even really faint ones from voices."

"Guess I'll have to try to pay more attention." Will accepted Diego's waterskin with a smile and took a long drink from it.

"And we'll be sticking with dirt," Lacey said. She pointed to the ground as she met Rekosh's eyes. "*Dirt.*"

"*Zirkeeta,*" Rekosh corrected, drawing out each sound.

Lacey shook her head. "English. Dirt."

Rekosh again looked at Ketahn. "They refuse to learn now?"

Ketahn's mandibles lifted in a bit wider of a smile. "They cannot say the word, Rekosh. They cannot make the sound."

Rekosh's eyes narrowed. "You knew that from the beginning, did you not?"

"I did."

Urkot chittered, shoulders shaking with amusement. "At least you did not show them your real stem, Rekosh."

"I have no need to resort to such means." Rekosh clicked his fangs. "It simply takes some effort to communicate with these humans, and I am willing to make that effort."

A thoughtful trill sounded in Urkot's chest. "And does that willingness include your stem?"

"We need not speak of my stem any further, Urkot. If you require entertainment, there are plenty of rocks around for you to familiarize yourself with." Rekosh glanced at Ahmya, and his eyes softened. "These females are already uneasy with us. I do not wish to cause them more fear."

"Are they talking about dicks now?" Callie asked. She'd been lying on the ground a few segments away with her arm over her eyes, but now she dropped her arm and lifted her head, squinting against the sunlight. "I didn't hear any clicking that time."

Cole snickered. "Hey Ketahn, do you guys compare—"

"Dude." Diego shot Cole a glare.

"What? You don't even know what I was going to say."

Callie rolled onto her side, propping her head up in her hand. "We *all* knew what you were going to say."

The humans laughed, and—after a quick explanation from a blushing Ivy—the vrix chittered. But Ketahn's amusement didn't help him understand why humans would even think about doing such things. What did it matter how large or small a male's stem was compared to those of his friends? So long as one's mate was satisfied, it made no difference.

Did male humans need to prove themselves worthy of potential mates by proving they had the largest stems? Perhaps males with larger stems were more likely to produce strong offspring? But none of that seemed correct given the humans' preference to cover their bodies.

The conversation continued, humans and vrix teaching each other new words throughout, and Ketahn let his gaze wander. This spot along the stream was a good one. The sun was warm but not overly hot, the water was clear and cool, and the ground was blanketed with soft leaves and grass. This was the sort of place he wanted to settle with his tribe.

But he could not help feeling the absences in the group. It wasn't just Ella, though her being gone was the most impactful; Ahnset and Telok had left to keep watch, one upstream and one downstream. Ketahn wanted Telok here to share in the playful banter between friends, and he wanted his broodsister here to simply...to be part of it all. To know she was welcome.

If only he had found a way to say that to her since they'd left the *Somnium*.

His anger had been too strong, his pain and guilt too raw, and he'd only contained those emotions by pouring all his focus into the journey. What comfort could he have offered his sister when he'd found so little of it himself?

The storm had been the worst weather they'd encountered so far, but there'd been abundant rain in the two days since it had broken, slowing the vrix considerably. It was even harder on the humans. Were everyone not so burdened by their supplies and equipment, the vrix might have carried the humans and taken to the trees to speed their travels.

Every moment, Ketahn had felt an instinctual itch on his back, an anxious tightness in his gut. He'd expected to glance over his shoulder and see Queen's Claws in pursuit of the group, or Zurvashi tearing through the Tangle in a vengeful rage. He knew she would not give up.

He and Telok had worked together to hide their tracks as best as they could—at least those that would not be disrupted by the rain—but it did little to ease his worries. It was impossible to travel without leaving evidence of their passage, and they were moving slowly enough that anyone tracking them would catch up eventually, even following an obscured trail.

And all that while, Ahnset had kept herself apart. She'd spoken a little more since escorting the human females the morning after the storm, but Ketahn had spared her few words. Whatever it was he wanted to say to her, whatever it was he felt toward her, he'd simply been unable to get it out. The gap between them had opened so wide that he didn't know how to cross it.

Fingers brushed along his jaw. "You okay?"

Ivy's voice and soft touch roused Ketahn from his thoughts, and he glanced down to see her looking up at him. Her eyes were a purer blue than the sky, brimming with affection and concern, so beautiful, so deep.

And she was his.

Ketahn's claspers tightened around her hips. He craved the feel of her skin, yearned for the comfort of her body. "I will be, my heartsthread. When we are through all this, I will be."

Ivy smiled and slipped her hand behind his neck, urging him down until she could press her lips to his mouth. "I am here for you."

A low, contented trill pulsed from his core. Tangling his fingers in her hair, he touched his headcrest to her forehead and breathed in her scent, which was sweeter and headier than anything he'd ever smelled. "I know. And I will be here for you always, my *nyleea*."

Ketahn remained like that, letting his hearts thump and the stream burble, until his hide was itching with the need to move. However comfortable he'd allowed himself to become here, Takarahl was far too close—and the distance Ketahn and his tribe had traveled over the last couple days was much too short to justify any more relaxation.

There were a few half-hearted groans from the humans

when Ketahn finally pulled away from Ivy and told them it was time to leave, but they all set into motion regardless. As he helped Ivy stand and slip on her bag, Ketahn ran his gaze over the others, noting the stiffness in their movements.

He understood their weariness, understood their pain. His aches had only deepened since leaving the ship, and even he, who'd stalked the jungle ceaselessly for years, was already tired. But everyone here knew what lay behind them—at least well enough to keep their legs moving despite their exhaustion.

Once Urkot had stood and taken up his share of the supplies, he used two small pieces of blackrock to signal Telok and Ahnset. The two vrix returned from their watch positions just as the rest of the group was ready to depart.

Several humans cast longing glances over their shoulders as they left their little streamside haven behind, Ivy included. But she quickly shifted her attention to Ketahn and offered him a smile that was at once weary, bright, and hopeful.

He would find a place to make their home, and it would surpass all others in beauty and serenity. It would be what Ivy called a *paradise*. He would give these humans, his tribe, the best of this world.

He would give his mate everything.

～

The sun continued its trek across the sky. Ivy saw it directly only a few times through the dense jungle canopy as she and her companions continued their journey. Telok had taken the lead, Urkot and Rekosh the flanks, and Ketahn the rear. Ahnset, though still quiet, walked amongst the humans near the center of their loose formation. Though the group's emotions were still raw and confused, it seemed to Ivy that everyone was glad to have her close.

With a vrix like Ahnset nearby, even the biggest, meanest jungle beasts were a little less scary.

Though Ivy would've preferred to recline on the bank of the stream, basking in the midday sun and granting her exhausted body its greatest wish—stillness—she had known they were due to leave. She'd felt it deep, right down into her bones, and it had instilled her with a pervasive restlessness even as she'd nestled against Ketahn.

Her legs cursed her with every step. She couldn't blame them; she'd asked for so much from them and given so little in return.

On the plus side, my ass is going to be so toned after all this walking.

Ivy scoffed at herself. Finding the positives in a difficult situation was a great way to maintain motivation, but was that really the best she could come up with?

I'm not bleeding anymore.

Okay, so that one was better, but it wasn't quite what she'd meant. The morning after the storm, she'd been convinced her menstrual cycle had come with a vengeance. That should've meant having to deal with a heavy flow for a few days.

But there'd been no blood yesterday or today. She had, in fact, stopped bleeding before nightfall the day it had started. And though her cramping had persisted, it was thankfully mild enough to ignore as she hiked.

Though she was by no means eager to deal with her period every month, she would be glad when her body finally shook off the lingering effects of stasis and got back to normal.

She glanced over her shoulder. Ketahn walked a short distance behind her, his head turning and eyes roving; he was tall, strong, and alert despite his injuries and weariness.

When his gaze fell upon her, it was aimed low—undoubtedly focused on the ass she'd just been contemplating. Ivy grinned and put a little wiggle in her hips for a few steps. Ketahn's mandibles rose, and hunger sharpened his eyes before they lifted to meet hers.

Low as it was, she heard his lustful growl with perfect clarity. The sound went straight to her core.

The people around her, vrix and human, were all the positive she needed. Yeah, they butted heads sometimes. Tempers had flared on and off since they'd all woken, there'd been arguments, there'd been suffering and tragedy. But there was a powerful camaraderie beneath it all. This dire situation had brought all these people—who'd had so little in common— together with bonds stronger than Ivy could ever have imagined.

And Ketahn was the center of it. The core, the heart. Without him, none of this would've been possible, and all the hardships Ivy had faced were worth it just for her to see that look in his eyes when they fell upon her.

She smiled to herself. Her mate. Her lover. Her very own sexy, insatiable spider man.

That is something I never imagined myself thinking.

Ivy held onto the fullness of her feelings for him as she marched onward.

God, it felt like it had been forever since they'd last had a moment alone. Since he'd touched her intimately, since those big, calloused, clawed hands had glided over her naked body, since he'd pushed his thick cock inside her, since his alien shaft had filled and stroked her so delightfully...

Ivy caught her bottom lip with her teeth to trap the moan threatening to emerge from her throat. She yearned for that connection with him again.

Soon. Be patient.

Conversations rose and fell around her. Sometimes Ivy was involved, sometimes she wasn't, but she enjoyed all of it. Most of those conversations ended abruptly when the group encountered some obstacle—a low cliff they had to scale using exposed roots and silk strands; a wide depression that had been flooded by the rain; a patch of tangled undergrowth so riddled with fallen branches and vines that it clawed mercilessly at legs and clothing.

They overcame all those challenges, but the group's pace slowed a little more with each one. By late afternoon, those sporadic conversations had all but died, replaced primarily by exhausted huffs and puffs.

Though his face betrayed little, Ivy swore Ketahn looked more concerned every time she glanced back at him. She'd done enough traipsing around the jungle with him to know that, for all their effort, they really hadn't covered all that much ground. Ivy had never been great at judging distance, but she doubted they'd managed more than five or six miles since setting out this morning. The prior two days couldn't have been much better.

And if they'd only traveled fifteen or twenty miles since leaving the *Somnium*, that meant Takarahl was still uncomfortably close. Silly as it might have been to think in such terms, the queen was only a twenty-minute car ride away.

Ivy shuddered, dropped her gaze to the jungle floor, and pressed on a little harder. She'd already tapped into more secret energy reserves than she ever could've guessed she had; what else could she do but keep digging until there was nothing left?

Sunset was still a few hours away when the sky began to darken. Gray clouds filled in the gaps in the jungle canopy, snuffing out the pleasant rays of sunshine that had broken through the leaves for most of the day. Ivy's heart sank.

The jungle was difficult enough to navigate when it wasn't raining.

A breeze kicked up, rustling leaves overhead and sweeping between the boughs. It carried a hint of rain scent and just enough of a chill to make Ivy shiver.

Cole tipped his head back and looked up. "Going to be another fun evening."

"Could be worse," said Lacey from a little farther ahead.

Ivy nodded. "Much worse."

"How so?" Cole asked.

Ivy's mind flashed back to that tornado; no matter how many years had passed, no matter the unfathomable distance she'd crossed since, those few minutes stayed with her in stunning, terrifying detail. Oh, it could've been *so* much worse than the jungle storms they'd weathered so far.

Lacey shrugged, though her shoulders barely lifted under the weight of her bag. "Use your imagination."

Diego chuckled. "After some of the stuff we've seen here, I'm afraid to do that. Last thing I need is to imagine some terrifying monster only to find out it's real."

"There is time before the rain," Ketahn said from the rear of the group. A couple of the humans looked back at him.

"How can you tell?" asked Ahmya. Though her bag was by necessity the lightest, the woman still looked comically overburdened with it on her back. But she'd not voiced a single complaint since they'd left, and her pace had been steadier than that of many of the others.

"Feel," Ketahn replied, raising a foreleg. His fine hairs were standing on end.

"Sensitive to vibrations...and air currents," said Callie, pausing to mop sweat from her brow with the back of her hand. With her other, she hooked a finger under the collar of her jumpsuit and pulled it down, turning toward the wind. "Guess they're sensitive to humidity and air pressure too."

Will slowed down and turned to look at everyone else. "I guess it's silly to ask if we're going to stop when the rain starts, right?"

Ketahn chittered. "Yes."

"That's what I thought." Will grasped the straps of his backpack and shifted it to rest higher on his shoulders. "Can we take a few minutes to stop beforehand, then? Catch our breath and have a bite to eat while we're dry?"

A few of the others voiced their approval of his suggestion.

Tilting his head, Ketahn swept his gaze over the humans, all of whom were either slowing or had already stopped. His mandibles ticked down. In vrix, he called, "Telok, is there a place ahead to rest?"

The green-marked vrix halted. In the brief time during which the humans had faltered, his lead had increased significantly, but his raspy voice carried to them just fine. "I will scout." Then he hurried ahead, vanishing amidst the jungle growth.

Ivy envied his endurance for a moment; she was too tired to do so any longer than that.

"Walk, humans," Ketahn said, waving everyone on. "Rest when Telok finds a place."

His command was met by a chorus of exaggerated groans, but everyone trudged forward regardless. Ivy couldn't help but smile. Things were hard, but more and more, she knew they'd turn out okay. Better than okay.

A gust of wind shook the boughs above, calling Ivy's gaze upward. She'd seen photos of the redwood forest, where the trees were so tall and straight, and it had always seemed unreal to her. The trees in this forest made redwoods look like toothpicks. Sometimes just glancing skyward was almost enough to trigger vertigo—especially while those big branches were swaying.

"Oh! What are those?" Ahmya asked excitedly.

Ivy lowered her gaze to see Ahmya standing atop a fallen log, staring at something off to the side of the group's current path.

Cole stopped nearby her and stood on his toes; it nearly made him as tall as Ahmya despite the height she'd gained from the log. "Really? More flowers?"

Callie arched a brow. "Ah, so are we going to pretend you haven't stopped a few times to admire pieces of wood?"

"They had unique grains," Cole protested with little of his usual bluster.

Ahmya smiled. "Well, these have unique petals."

"We must walk," Ketahn said firmly.

Ivy turned to face Ketahn and gave him a soft smile. "A quick little detour to check out some flowers can't hurt, can it?"

Ketahn made a grumbly sound, mandibles swinging open and closed uncertainly.

Ivy held up her spear. "I'll be right beside her."

Based on the way he narrowed his eyes, Ketahn was not comforted by that.

"Ahmya wants to study the flowers?" Rekosh asked in vrix.

"Yes," Ketahn replied.

"I will watch her." Rekosh's gaze settled on Ahmya. "They are singer's hearts, Ketahn. Very rare. I would not want her to miss this chance to see them."

Ketahn waved a hand toward the flowers and released a huff. "Quickly then."

Beaming, Ahmya switched her spear into her left hand and hopped down from the log. She set forth with a vigorous spring in her step. Ivy hurried to catch up, and Ketanh strode just behind her until he reached the log Ahmya had used as her perch, which he climbed onto smoothly.

Rekosh fell into place to one side of Ahmya, Ivy to the other. Ahmya's enthusiasm was admirable—and maybe just a little contagious. Constant danger and stress made it difficult to remember that this world was full of wonder and beauty, that its alienness could inspire so much more than fear and unease.

"They're amazing," Ahmya breathed.

Even from thirty feet away, the blooms were gorgeous. Their wide, gently curling petals were each as long as Ivy's hand, their edges a vibrant pink that bled into the yellow at their centers.

The short but full clusters of stamen were turquoise, offering contrast to the pink and yellow. The blossoms were at the ends of long, thick stalks with many splitting branches that all jutted out of a large bush with star shaped, waxy looking leaves.

Ahmya turned her head toward Rekosh and pointed at the flowers. "What are they called?"

"Singer's hearts," he replied. His gaze remained on the flowers only a short while before settling upon Ahmya again. "Named for the Rootsinger, who watches over all growing things. It is said that when she willed the Tangle to sprout from barren ground, she sprinkled tiny pieces of her hearts throughout, and each of these flowers is one of those pieces. They attract many small animals because they are sweet of leaf, stalk, and petal, and so they are very difficult to find. This many blossoms in one place is rare indeed."

Though she likely understood very little of what he'd said, Ahmya had kept her big, dark eyes on Rekosh while he'd spoken. Her smile widened after Ivy translated his words.

Ivy had thought about becoming a teacher during her brief time in high school, but once she'd started dating Tanner, she'd let that little dream fall away. Never would she have guessed she'd become an interpreter.

Not like I ever would've seen myself as a survivalist roughing it in an alien jungle, either.

Glancing back, she smiled at Ketahn, who remained atop the log. He warily scanned the surrounding jungle. Everything in Ivy's life had changed because of him. She'd realized so much potential in herself that would've gone untapped, had learned so much about herself through her deepening relationship with him.

The Homeworld Initiative had promised a fresh start, but... This was so much more. Ivy felt like she'd been reborn.

She swung her attention back to her companions.

"So they are safe to eat?" Ahmya asked, bringing her fingers up to her mouth and pantomiming taking a bite. "I'd love to try one."

Rekosh nodded, trilled softly, and gestured with a long-fingered hand for Ahmya to proceed.

She stepped forward slowly, her awed eyes fixed on the flowers. Ivy followed a few feet behind her, dropping her gaze to the ground out of habit—the last few days had taught her to watch her footing, even when there were no apparent hazards.

Her brow furrowed. Like most of the jungle floor, this spot was littered with decaying leaves and debris that was broken in places by small plants struggling to survive in a world of giants, but there was something else here.

Roots. Not the big, gnarled sort so prevalent throughout the jungle, but tiny, pale things no thicker than pieces of thread. They poked up from amidst the fallen leaves, often crossing each other to create tangled little patches. Maybe they shouldn't have seemed so strange, but she had the sense that those little roots were spread out all over beneath the leaves, like a net, or a web, or...

"Rekosh," Ivy said, gesturing at the ground, "do you know what those are from?"

Ahmya made a thoughtful hum as she stopped in front of the flowering bush. "Weird. Looks like the main stems are a different color..."

Rekosh cursed just as everything burst into motion. Fallen leaves flew up into the air as things leapt off the ground, long, writhing things, all around Ahmya. Whether it was instinct or reflex, Ivy lunged forward, thrusting out her left arm. Her fingers closed on the top of Ahmya's backpack.

Feet sliding on the damp debris, Ivy reversed her momentum, tugging on Ahmya's bag. The smaller woman tipped backward.

Those things—tentacles, or tendrils, or...*vines*—swept inward with immense speed. Despite all the dirt and debris in the air,

Ivy saw those lashing vines clearly. She saw one slice through the air an inch over her companion's head. She saw one latch onto Ahmya's thigh, and a second coil around the woman's torso. She saw the thorny protrusions on another of those flailing vines just before it whipped down and snapped around Ivy's extended forearm.

Ivy heard Ahmya scream even as pain dominated her awareness—a hundred scalding needles piercing her skin, injecting her with liquid fire.

A pained cry tore from Ivy's throat, and she fell backward, dragging Ahmya down with her. The smaller woman landed heavily atop Ivy's legs. Ahmya dropped her spear and frantically clawed at the vine clutching her torso.

The world around Ivy was utter chaos. Thrashing vines, swirling leaves, shouts and cries and too much motion to track. She thought she heard Ketahn call her name, but his voice was swept up in the cacophony. Everything was happening so fast.

Ivy let go of her own spear as fire blazed up her caught arm. The pain was too intense to think around; it was relentless, pervasive, by far the worst she'd ever experienced. So she acted without thought, without hesitation.

Her free hand fumbled along her leg until it encountered her survival knife. She curled her fingers around the weapon and tugged it free just as a huge, dark form appeared over her and Ahmya.

Rekosh.

He was speaking in vrix, but his words were too harsh and fast for Ivy to understand amidst all the noise. Only one thing mattered—his claws were already tearing at the vines binding Ahmya. At least two of his arms were blurs of motion, fighting back the vines that were flailing all around.

God, this was like those movies where the tentacles of some horrifying leviathan rose from the deep to grab a ship and its sailors.

Gritting her teeth against the pain, Ivy set her blade to the vine coiled around Ahmya's midsection. A warm, viscous yellow substance leaked from the vine as the knife bit deep, oozing over Ivy's fingers.

The pain on her arm began to fade, leaving only a dull echo in the wake of that molten agony. She was distantly aware of her hold on Ahmya's bag slipping, but her fingers refused to tighten. Her arm was going numb.

Probably not a good thing.

Definitely *not a good thing.*

She sawed at the vine all the quicker.

A shadow loomed over Ivy. Something big clamped around her left arm just below her elbow, while something else caught hold of her backpack. More of the yellow ichor spattered her as the vine around her forearm was torn apart by a clawed hand. She was tugged out from beneath Ahmya unceremoniously; the last drag of her knife against the vine constricting the smaller woman's torso nearly severed it completely.

"No! Ahmya!" Ivy's feet touched the ground, and her knees buckled, but she was held upright by her backpack.

"I have you," Ketahn growled.

She looked at him then. He was holding her numb arm up with one hand and had another clamped on her backpack. The vines were gone from around her arm, and the sleeve of her jumpsuit was shredded, spattered with yellow ichor, bits of dirt and debris, and...and crimson. Blood. She could see a few small puncture wounds through the tears, but she couldn't feel any of it.

Ketahn bent down and twisted toward her, hooking an arm around the backs of her thighs. He lifted her off the ground, taking her weight on his shoulder, and sped away from the violently thrashing vine monster. She tried to brace herself by planting her hands on his back. Only her right hand obeyed.

The numbness crept up to her shoulder and pushed onward, preceded by a hint of fire.

Ivy desperately sought Ahmya within the chaos. Rekosh emerged from the storm of kicked up leaves and whipping vines with the woman clutched against his chest. His hide glistened with droplets of blood in at least a dozen places and splatters of yellow ichor in many more, and there were thorny tendrils clinging to his arms and legs, but he was upright.

Ahmya, however, was much too still.

"Take her," Ketahn said.

Something gripped her backpack again, and it was slipped off her back with little resistance from her arms. Then Ketahn pitched her forward.

Ivy's stomach, which was already twisted into knots, lurched, but her fall was brief; a set of large, powerful, but gentle arms caught her. Ahnset.

Ivy saw the other humans in her peripheral vision, but she kept her eyes on Ketahn. He touched her cheek with the pad of a finger—she barely felt it—and then turned to rush back to Rekosh.

She wanted to call to him, to tell him to come back, to be careful, but no words would emerge.

An unhappy sound resonated in Ahnset's chest, resonating into Ivy. But all Ivy could do was watch.

Ketahn called something out. Urkot charged up beside him and collected Ahmya from Rekosh's arms, immediately retreating from the vine monster. As soon as he was clear, Ketahn and Rekosh plunged back into the battle.

Ivy's heart skipped a beat. It might also have leapt into her throat, but she couldn't feel her throat quite well enough to tell for sure.

"Let me take a quick look at her arm," Diego said from nearby.

Ahnset shifted her hold on Ivy, presumably to enable his

examination. Ivy found just enough strength to turn her head and keep the battle in view. Diego was probably touching her arm, turning it to inspect the wounds, but she didn't care.

Her mate was over there. And Ivy was stuck here, useless.

At the edge of Ivy's vision, Urkot arrived with Ahmya, and Diego went to them.

Ketahn shouted something to Rekosh—something like heart root or heart branch—as he hacked at the lashing vines with his claws and a gleaming blackrock knife.

Rekosh's reply was swallowed in the cacophony. He turned toward the singer's hearts bush, mandibles twitching, and lunged at it after an instant's hesitation.

All those vines that had been flailing about, seeking flesh, drew inward toward Rekosh. Ivy realized then that they were all coming from the same source—the base of the singer's hearts bush. A wide swing of Ketahn's spear intercepted a great many of them, but several made it through.

Rekosh crashed into the bush and grabbed at something inside with all four hands. A low, bestial growl, as pained as it was furious, escaped him as the vines lashed against his back and curled around his limbs, but he was not deterred; he threw his weight backward.

The plant tore out of the ground, shedding those waxy leaves and pink and yellow petals everywhere. But it wasn't just the singer's hearts bush that he'd uprooted—it was something else, something that had been hidden inside. Captured in his arms was a thick, bulbous central cluster the size of an exercise ball. It was a dull blue green, and all those vines ran from its top; the whole mass pulsed and shuddered as the vines moved.

From the bottom dangled large, dirt caked roots that split and narrowed into a weblike network of thread-thin tendrils leading under the carpet of fallen leaves.

Another vrix darted past Ahnset and Ivy—Telok, holding a

pair of axes with black stone heads. He tossed one of the axes to Ketahn as he neared.

Ketahn caught the weapon by its haft just as Rekosh slammed the plant down on the ground. In a flurry of motion, the three vrix hacked the plant apart with axes and claws. The viscous fluid running through the vines splattered the jungle floor, and ruined pieces of vegetation rained all around.

"Shit," Diego spat from somewhere to the side. "We need to get her to clear ground and get this jumpsuit off."

"Fuck. *Fuck.*" That was Cole. "When they were talking about carnivorous plants or whatever, I thought they meant something like those fucking fly traps!"

"Yeah, well I guess we're the fucking flies," Lacey said.

Ivy glanced at them. Her head moved sluggishly, as though burdened by an immense weight. Urkot held Ahmya in his arms, and Diego was before her, checking the many tiny holes in her clothing. His face was grim—just like it had been when he'd told Ivy and Ketahn about Ella.

Drawing in a heavy breath, Ivy struggled to reach up and touch Ahnset, to signal her, to tell her that she needed to help Ahmya. It didn't work.

Diego snapped his fingers in front of Urkot's face; the vrix had been focused on his fellows, and only then looked down at the man before him.

"We need to move her"—he pointed to somewhere out of Ivy's vision, somewhere closer to the log Ahmya had climbed onto only minutes ago—"over there."

Urkot's gaze dipped to the tiny, unmoving woman in his arms and returned to Diego. With a grunt, the broad vrix turned and carried Ahmya in the direction Diego had indicated.

"My heartsthread."

Ketahn's agonized voice reached into Ivy's soul and squeezed. With no small amount of effort, she turned her eyes toward him.

Her mate was covered in the sticky goop from the plant that had tried to kill them, and she counted at least half a dozen cuts on his hide from its thorns.

No. No, if they were all hit by those thorns...they'll...they'll be paralyzed too. They'll...

Ivy's breaths quickened and grew more ragged, and her heart raced.

Ketahn crooned and leaned over Ivy to cup a hand on her cheek.

She knew he was smoothing his fingers over her skin and hair, but she wasn't sure if she actually felt it or only imagined the sensation.

"I see the fear in your eyes," he whispered, "but you need not hold it, Ivy. The poison has stilled your body, but it will pass. I promise you, it will pass. You will be well very soon."

Her throat worked as she struggled to get out a word, a name, managing only a strained whimper.

"Ahmya will be well, too." Ketahn moved his face even closer, filling up her whole world with his presence. "I weave my word into a bond. She will be well."

Ivy let out a shuddering breath and let her eyelids fall shut.

CHAPTER 10

KETAHN'S HEARTS thumped with all the gentleness of a charging yatin. His hide tingled in the few places it had been broken by the thorns of the firevine plant, but he'd taken little of its poison, and the pain was already fading.

Ivy had not been so fortunate.

Anger and fear warred inside Ketahn, and once again, they were useless to him—as useless as they were persistent. He drew in a breath that was filled with familiar scents; the jungle, Ahnset, Ivy, human blood.

Had Ketahn reached his mate sooner, he might've freed her arm before she'd been filled with enough poison to bring on this death-like slumber. Had he remained close to her, he might have recognized the danger before anyone was hurt.

Had he denied the request to examine the singer's hearts, Ivy would not have suffered any of this.

His hands clenched—the upper pair around the hafts of axe and spear, the lower upon themselves.

"We are exposed here," Telok said. "Ketahn, we must go."

The firm voice of his friend roused Ketahn from those

consuming thoughts, though it could do nothing to banish them.

My mate is wounded.

My mate is still. Far too still.

Mandibles jittering downward, Ketahn lifted his head and turned it toward Telok.

Telok answered Ketahn's unspoken question without hesitation. "There is shelter nearby."

"Guide us." Ketahn looked at Ivy again and brushed his thumb under her jaw. Her heartbeat pulsed there, slow but steady. He forced himself to withdraw from her, pausing only to secure the axe to his leg with a leather cord before extending his arms.

"Come, humans!" Telok called.

Ahnset bent toward Ketahn and carefully laid Ivy in his waiting arms. He cradled his mate against his chest. The limpness of Ivy's body was an immense weight on his heartsthread.

"Search for anything that fell," Ketahn said to Ahnset, "but do not linger."

"As you say, broodbrother," Ahnset replied, tapping a knuckle to her headcrest. She stepped around him and strode toward the firevine.

"What's going on?" Callie asked. "Where are we going?"

"Walk, humans. Follow Telok." Ketahn lifted Ivy's injured arm and tore off the end of her sleeve. He broke the ring formed by the cloth and wrapped it around her arm again, covering her wounds.

"I need to treat their injuries," Diego said.

The human healer was leaning over Ahmya, who remained in Urkot's arms. The other humans had clustered behind him to stare at the wounded female's motionless form. Rekosh was beyond them. His eyes were intense, crackling with anger and worry, his leg hairs were standing on end, and his fingers were curling and stretching repeatedly. As he paced back and forth over the same few segments of ground, his body displayed none of its usual grace.

"When we stop," Ketahn said, moving toward Telok, who'd already begun walking.

Diego stepped in front of Ketahn. While the other humans wore uncertainty and shock on their faces, Diego's eyes were focused and steady. "Ketahn, they need *mehdikal* attention."

"Blood smell is in air," Ketahn growled. One of his legs dug into the ground, forcing aside the dirt and vegetation. That was all he could do to keep from pushing Diego away and continuing after Telok. "We must shelter."

Ivy felt heavier with each thump of Ketahn's hearts. Firevine poison was not deadly to vrix, and he prayed it was not deadly to humans... But he could not forget the sweetfang root. He could not forget those torturous days of wondering whether his mate would survive. And the effects of this poison had already proven far stronger for Ivy and Ahmya than Ketahn had ever seen in any vrix.

Diego clenched his jaw and cast a glance around. What was there to be seen but unforgiving jungle? Here, spears would be the only defense against any predators lured by the scent of blood.

Instinct told Ketahn to leave, to bring his mate high into the trees where she would be safe, and to treat her wounds with his silk. To care for his mate as he was meant to. Everyone else was preventing him from properly tending to his female. They were endangering her further.

But he understood that such instincts would not always help his mate. Denying her the care of a healer familiar with her kind, who possessed tools beyond the comprehension of the vrix, would only increase Ivy's risk of lasting harm.

Just as Ketahn was about to tell Rekosh or Urkot to pick Diego up and carry him, the human dipped his chin in a shallow nod and stepped aside.

The humans kept close together, walking to Urkot's right. Rekosh strode to Urkot's left, hardly looking away from Ahmya. Ketahn kept a few segments behind them. His fingers brushed over Ivy's jumpsuit or along the loose strands of her hair ceaselessly, and he hummed, soft and low, just as he'd sometimes done during the rainstorms that frightened her so much.

He did not know whether he meant to soothe Ivy or himself.

Diego glanced over his shoulder at Ketahn. "I need to know what we're dealing with here. That thing have some kind of *tahkzin?*"

Ketahn grunted. "*Tahkzin* is like poison?"

"*Teknik lee,* poison is a type of toxin that's *in jestid*," said Callie. Her voice was thinner and more strained than usual. She cleared her throat and shook her head. "That would make this a *venum*, which... Well, I guess this isn't the time."

Cole laughed humorlessly. "Yeah. Not the time."

"Yes, like poison." Diego waved a hand impatiently. "What are its effects?"

"Pain. And it makes prey...sleep." Ketahn's hold on Ivy tightened, and he found himself struggling to restrain his own strength.

"Does it wear off?"

"If firevine's hold is breaked."

"They're going to wake up, right?" Will asked, his wide eyes directed at Ahmya.

Ketahn nodded, staring down at his Ivy. "They will."

All Ketahn's ferocity, fury, guilt, and willpower bent toward that idea—Ivy would wake up. Once the poison's effects faded, she would be fine, and all she'd have to show for her ordeal would be a few tiny scars.

Ketahn *needed* that to be true.

He would accept no other outcome.

Telok led the tribe to a rocky outcropping on a low hill. The stone formed a wide but shallow cave with a low ceiling that angled downward sharply at the back. Apart from a few patches of moss and piles of fallen leaves and debris, the ground within and around the cave was smooth, bare stone.

The entire tribe would not be able to fit inside, but it would be enough to shelter the humans and most of the supplies should the gathering clouds bring rain.

At Diego's direction, Callie and Will kicked aside the debris and spread blankets inside the cave, while Cole and Lacey gathered several clean pieces of cloth and a couple waterskins. Diego dropped his bag on the ground, tugged it open, and removed the box he called a medkit from within.

Rekosh paced outside as the humans made their preparations. His gaze wandered erratically, often unfocused, but it always returned to the small, motionless figure in Urkot's arms. Blood had trickled from some of Rekosh's wounds, leaving trails on his dark hide, and he was still opening and closing his hands repeatedly.

Though Ketahn presented calm outwardly, he saw all his emotions reflected in Rekosh's behavior. He told himself everything would be all right, that Ivy and Ahmya would recover before the night was through, that they'd be ready to travel with the climbing sun.

He didn't allow himself to argue against any of that.

"Bring them both here!" Diego called.

Ketahn gestured to Urkot, and the two strode forward. They ducked to enter the cave; Ketahn was forced to drop so low that his underside nearly scraped the rock beneath him, and even then, still had to angle his head sharply aside to avoid bumping his headcrest on the ceiling. As gently as he could, he laid Ivy on the blankets beside Diego.

Urkot placed Ahmya down on Diego's other side. He withdrew his hands from her slowly, his movements measured and made with immense care.

A low, unhappy sound rumbled from Rekosh—not quite a growl, but not far removed from one.

Ketahn released Ivy with great reluctance, moving even slower than Urkot had despite knowing that every moment was of the greatest importance.

He trusted Diego. The male was a healer, trained in the human ways; no one else in the Tangle was more knowledgeable or capable when it came to treating these humans. But Ketahn could find no comfort in that.

"Return to me, my *nyleea*," Ketahn said, his voice far lower and more ragged than he'd expected. All that rage, all that fire, and yet he could offer his mate little more than those pleading, broken words.

Diego had arranged several of the items from the medkit on a scrap of clean white cloth atop the blanket, as familiar and comfortable with his tools as Urkot with hammer and chisel or Rekosh with needles and thread. Then he looked into Ketahn's eyes. "I will do everything I can to make sure she's okay."

A growl threatened to escape Ketahn. He wanted assurance —he wanted a promise, spoken with confidence and finality. Tension rippled through him as he fought the urge to force such words out of Diego's mouth. But Ketahn held it all inside. Words would do neither Ivy nor Ahmya any good now.

Ketahn tapped Urkot's leg with his own and backed out of the cave, straightening as soon as his head was clear. Urkot did the same, briefly bracing a hand on the ceiling to steady himself.

"Callie, Lacey, come help me out," Diego said as he leaned over Ahmya and carefully caught the bloody fabric of her jumpsuit between finger and thumb.

The small human did not react when Diego lifted the sticky material from the skin around one of her many wounds.

Keeping her arms crossed over her chest, Lacey nodded and stepped toward Diego and the injured females. She looked a little paler than usual, but her gaze seemed to be clearing.

Callie placed a hand on her chest and stared at Diego with wide eyes. "Me? But... But I was a chemist. I... I don't—"

"Well, now you're an honorary nurse," Diego replied with an impressive blend of gentleness and firmness. "You got this."

"Okay. Okay." She entered the cave and knelt beside Ahmya, across from Diego, flicking her thick, dark hair over her shoulder. "What do you need us to do?"

"We need to get her jumpsuit off." Diego reached to the holder on the leg of his own jumpsuit and drew his metal knife.

Rekosh's pacing halted suddenly, and he turned his whole body toward Diego. "What need has he for a knife?"

"Trust him to his work, Rekosh," said Ketahn, fixing his gaze on his friend.

One of Rekosh's lower arms was dangling at his side, and the continued movement of his fingers was slower and stiffer than before.

"I should tend her," Rekosh said. "It is my duty."

Ketahn's mandibles twitched, and he only barely stopped himself from looking at Ivy again. "Diego will tend her."

Rekosh growled. He folded both sets of arms across his chest and stared down at Ahmya, who looked somehow even smaller lying on that blanket with Callie, Lacey, and Diego around her. Callie had unfastened the seam of Ahmya's jumpsuit, and now she pulled it open to reveal the shirt beneath.

Blood had blossomed around each of the small tears in the white fabric, leaving a crimson path across her abdomen.

"I found all I could," said Ahnset from behind Ketahn.

Ketahn turned to see his broodsister approaching. She carried a pair of small, barbed spears in addition to her war spear, and Ivy's and Ahmya's bags dangled from one of her lower hands. He strode to meet her, feeling his heartsthread grow tauter with each step he took away from his mate.

Ahnset set down the bags and spears with some of the other supplies that had been cast off upon the tribe's arrival. Then she raised her other lower hand, holding it to Ketahn with her flattened palm up.

Ivy's knife lay on Ahnset's hand, its grip pointed toward Ketahn. The tool looked so tiny there, so insignificant—like it was no more deadly than the needles with which a young Ketahn had imagined himself slaying monsters.

He reached for the knife, but before he could grab it, a harsh growl called his attention back to the cave.

Rekosh lunged into the cave, his long, clawed fingers reaching for Diego. Callie and Lacey scrambled away from the vrix with a cry, but Diego remained in place despite the gleam of fear in his eyes.

One of Rekosh's hands caught the chest of Diego's jumpsuit just as Urkot inserted himself in front of the spindly vrix, halting Rekosh's lunge by wrapping two thick arms around the weaver's middle.

Several of the humans gasped or cursed; despite only five of them being awake, Ketahn could not tell who had made which sounds, only that they were shocked and scared.

Ketahn raced to them, fine hairs bristling. Only as he neared did he see that Ahmya's shirt had been cut open, baring her chest. That crimson trail ran across her abdomen and beneath her small breasts—more than a dozen tiny wounds visible, and undoubtedly more hidden by the position of her body. Several of those wounds had thorns protruding from them.

Diego's nose holes flared with his heavy breaths, but his eyes were steady, locked with Rekosh's.

"Release him, Rekosh," Ketahn growled. His muscles were abuzz with tension, and a dense, heavy lump hung in his gut. He had no desire to hurt his friend, but he would not allow harm to befall Diego either.

"I will not watch another male lay his hands upon her like this," Rekosh said with a snarl. He strained forward.

Urkot grunted and spread his legs wider, denying Rekosh even a few more thread widths of reach.

"You have no claim upon her." Ketahn placed a hand on Rekosh's extended arm, keeping his touch as firm but unthreatening as possible. "And he is not making one."

Rekosh turned his face toward Ketahn, his crimson eyes swirling with pain and guilt. "It is for me to tend her. To make up for my failure."

The energy crackling in the air was volatile enough to make Ketahn's hide tingle with uneasy heat. His heartsthread thrummed, and he could sense Ivy's presence just behind him, could sense his own failures pressing in from all around.

"Tell him it's just to get to her wounds," Diego said evenly. "I'm just trying to help her."

Ketahn conveyed Diego's message, though he guessed Rekosh had already had a good notion of what the human said.

"It should be my silk to bind her wounds," Rekosh rasped. The stiffness of his body wavered.

When Ketahn told Diego what Rekosh had said, the human shook his head. "Nothing from his ass is getting anywhere near these cuts."

Ketahn dipped his chin, indicating one of the blankets beneath Ahmya. It was silk. "Where do you think that is from?"

To Ketahn's surprise, Diego chuckled. "Shit. Got me there."

Rekosh huffed and regarded Diego with narrowed eyes. Slowly—very slowly—he released his hold on the human's clothing. Not ungently, Urkot pushed Rekosh back, and the weaver stood upright once he was clear of the low ceiling.

Will and Cole were standing nearby, eyes wide and postures uncertain, while Callie and Lacey stared up at the vrix from their places on the cave floor, no less uneasy than their male counterparts. Ahnset and Telok were nearby also, their eyes wary.

Ketahn kept his loose hold on Rekosh's arm until they were both outside and Urkot had released the weaver.

Diego called Callie and Lacey back and resumed his work like nothing had happened.

Rekosh's hands curled into fists. He stood with his head bowed, caught in uncharacteristic silence, his overwhelming emotion flowing from him more readily than the blood from his wounds.

"Sit," Ketahn said, thumping a foreleg against one of Rekosh's. "I will see to your wounds."

In silent reluctance, Rekosh walked closer to the discarded supplies and lowered himself onto the ground.

"Ahnset, Telok" —Ketahn looked at them—"we must remain here tonight, but the blood scent is strong. See to our defenses."

With quiet words of acknowledgement, the two went to work, using branches and brambles to block the approaches to the cave.

"Lacey, go ahead and remove Ivy's bandage," Diego said. "Get her wounds cleaned up."

Ketahn drew in a deep, burning breath and held himself utterly still. These humans would not harm his mate. They were helping.

They were *helping*.

No good would come of him storming into the cave and forcing Lacey aside. No good would come of his insistence to aid his Ivy by himself.

The two male humans standing outside the cave were staring at the injured females. Will appeared to be in a state of startlement, but Cole's expression was harder—grim and determined if a bit pale. His was the face of someone who'd endured hardship, who'd pushed himself through suffering and pain, but who had not grown used to seeing the innocent ravaged by life's cruelties.

"Cole, Will," Ketahn said, drawing their attention to him.

"Make fire. Little flames." He walked along the cave mouth for a few segments before tapping a spot on the stone floor with a foreleg. "Here."

Will blinked and swallowed. "Fire? Yeah. All right." He nodded to himself. "Fire. We can do that."

Cole frowned at Will for a few moments before his gaze briefly shifted to Ahmya. "Yeah. No problem. Let's, uh...see if there's anything dry enough."

As the two males began their search, Ketahn felt that pull, familiar and urgent, to go to Ivy. Another pull, deeper and more savage, urged him to purge the surrounding jungle of threats, to feed the roots with the blood of anything that was even slightly dangerous to his mate. His fury had not died since his confrontation with Zurvashi days ago. The battle with the Claws and Fangs at Needle's Point had not satisfied his rage; it demanded further release.

In this, at least, vrix and humans seemed little different—they endured hardships and worry best when they could keep themselves occupied.

You will wake soon, my nyleea, *and I shall hold you in my arms until the sun's fire has burned out.*

Not even two full eightdays ago, Ketahn would never have entrusted the safety of his mate to anyone but himself. He found it difficult to do so even now, after having lived with these humans for days, after working, hunting, and surviving along-side them. But he could not ignore the lessons he'd learned.

He could not do this alone. None of them could do this alone. Yet when it came to mates, whether claimed or not...the vrix would ever be at war with their own instincts. Just as Ketahn had been with his since the moment he'd awoken Ivy and taken her as his own.

Did the humans ever face similar struggles?

Ketahn grunted, shook his arm to relieve the lingering tingles caused by the poison, and strode to Rekosh.

Rekosh did not look up as Ketahn sank down beside him. One of his lower arms lay across his bent forelegs, while the elbows of his upper arms rested on his uppermost leg joints. His hunched, tense posture made his long-limbed body look bent out of its natural shape.

"You need not aid me," Rekosh rasped. "I will tend myself soon."

With a soft chitter, Ketahn removed his bag and swung it to his front, setting it on the ground between his forelegs. He opened it and rummaged within for his waterskin and some cloth.

Turning his head slightly, Rekosh watched Ketahn's hands. "You should be with her. You should be tending her."

"I want nothing more than that." Ketahn folded a piece of silk and poured some water on it. "But I also want blood. I want vengeance."

Wake soon, my heartsthread. Only you can soothe my fury.

Rekosh faced forward again. "The firevine is no more. We have won our vengeance."

Ketahn used the cloth to wipe the blood away from Rekosh's upper arm. Rekosh's hide pulled taut, but he made no other sign of pain or discomfort.

"You know as well as I that it is not enough. It cannot sate the beasts that have been roused at our cores," Ketahn said.

Rekosh's mandibles fell, and he lowered his head along with them. "Threads and words. Such has been my world, Ketahn. But for that accursed war, what do I know of beasts and blood thirst?"

"Enough to know I speak true. My world was once the same as yours."

Silence gripped Rekosh. He remained unmoving as Ketahn cleaned his wounds save for a few erratic twitches of his mandibles. When he finally spoke again, his voice was low and raw. "You placed your trust in me, Ketahn, and your mate came to harm under my protection."

Anger roiled in Ketahn's chest, bitter and thick as sludge. "No matter how hard we fight, Rekosh, no matter how steadfastly we watch, we cannot shield anyone from all harm. Firevines are no easy thing to spot, even for me and Telok. You acted swiftly enough to save them. That is all that matters."

"Were it not for your Ivy, we would have been weaving a death shroud even now. One of those vines would have caught Ahmya by the throat, but Ivy dragged her down just before it could strike." Rekosh shivered, and an uneven buzz rattled in his chest.

The swelling of pride in Ketahn's hearts clashed with his rage and worry. He was proud of his female's quick reaction, of her selflessness in trying to save Ahmya despite the danger to her own life, but he would rather she had never been in such a situation.

"I am sorry, Ketahn," Rekosh said.

Tilting his head, Ketahn regarded his friend anew. The way Rekosh had spoken, the way he had acted, since the encounter with the firevine was unlike him. Rekosh had always possessed fire at his core, but he'd controlled it—he'd wielded it as delicately and precisely as he would a needle. To see him come undone like his was startling.

There was more than simple guilt behind his behavior. And Rekosh's protectiveness toward Ahmya... That was no simple thing, either.

But this was no time to reflect upon such things. Dark times would only be worsened by dark thoughts.

Ketahn chittered again as he gathered sticky silk from his spinnerets. "If you mean to make apologies, Rekosh, there are several others far more deserving than I."

Rekosh grunted; the sound extended into a long, unhappy trill.

"See the good in it, my friend," Ketahn said. "It will give you a reason to do your favorite thing—talk."

Rekosh chittered, and his mandibles twitched up a bit. "And it shall be made all the sweeter because you will be forced to repeat every word I speak in the human tongue."

Ketahn huffed and pressed a wad of silk into one of Rekosh's wounds a little harder than necessary, coaxing a low hiss from the weaver.

CHAPTER 11

IVY'S EYELIDS opened after what must've been a thousand years, and the darkness that had surrounded her for all that time was finally banished. Brow furrowing, she stared up at flickering orange light dancing across a stone surface. She felt...heavy. It reminded her of what she'd experienced as they'd initiated her stasis on the *Somnium*, or that sensation of being weighed down when she climbed out of the pool after a long swim, like her body had just remembered gravity was a thing and was over-compensating for it.

Conversation swirled in the air nearby, the voices low and restrained whether belonging to vrix or human. It was backed by the crackling of a fire and the sighing of wind through leaves. All those sounds were so comforting, so familiar, that they might've been enough to soothe Ivy to sleep had she not just awoken from oblivion.

Had she been sleeping?

What had that plant done to her? She recalled the pain, the numbness, the fear, and Ketahn's reassuring voice...

Then nothing.

Ketahn.

There was a warmth along the right side of her body. She forced her gaze away from the ceiling to look beside her. Ketahn was there, legs folded snugly against his hindquarters with his underside on the floor. His pelvis was pressed against Ivy, and his claspers were draped over her middle, gentle but possessive. He was looking toward the fire, somewhere to Ivy's left—or rather he was looking toward the people talking over there.

Ketahn's arms were bent back slightly, hands resting on the upper joints of his legs. One of his fingers tapped his hide erratically.

The last time she'd seen him, he'd been splattered with the vine monster's yellow ichor. Now he was clean, silky hair hanging freely about his shoulders, its purple and white strands catching the firelight.

She lifted her hand from the ground and pressed her palm against his abdomen.

Ketahn's claspers tensed, and his attention snapped down to her, violet eyes wide and gleaming. He said her name—it was a sigh, a rasp, and a growl all at once—and leaned over her. One of his hands covered hers on his abdomen, while another cupped her face, thumb brushing her cheek.

"Are you in pain, my *nyleea?*"

Ivy shifted her body. It wasn't until she moved her left arm that she felt the soreness. The sting was reminiscent of those goat head stickers she'd once stepped on as a kid, where the pain would linger for days, or the aftermath of a shot. She flexed her arm back and forth; there was some tightness where her skin pulled.

"Just a little, but I'm okay," she said.

That quickly, his arms slipped around her, and he lifted her off the ground, hugging her to his chest. Ivy's breath hitched. He released a trill that resonated into her and then drew in a deep breath, undoubtedly taking in her scent. One of his hands cupped the back of her head, engulfing it as he held her close, his claspers stroking her hips and the outsides of her thighs. Ivy brushed her nose along his neck and breathed him in too.

"Thank God," Diego said, his voice filled with relief.

"How are you feeling, Ivy?" Callie asked.

Ivy turned her head to look at the others; that was all the movement Ketahn allowed her. His fingers curled, and his embrace strengthened. She understood his reluctance to let her go. Had their circumstances been swapped, Ivy would have felt the same and would've been clinging to him just as urgently. Nothing would have been able to pry her away.

Lacey, Callie, and Will were around the small fire, the latter of whom was lying down with his head propped on his backpack. Diego sat near them with his back against the cave wall, knees drawn up and hands dangling off them. His head was tipped back, his eyes were closed, and his face was a bit strained.

It was dark outside—middle of the night dark—but the fire's glow reached far enough for Ivy to see Rekosh and Telok out there, hunched over as they worked on something with their hands. Ahnset and Urkot were nowhere to be seen, and neither was Cole. Was he out on watch with the missing vrix?

And then there was Ahmya, who lay motionless upon a silk blanket just a few feet away from Ivy and Ketahn.

"I'm fine," Ivy said with a frown. "And...Ahmya?"

"Sleeping." Diego lifted his head and opened his eyes. "She took a lot more of that venom into her system than you did, so she might be out for a while still." He pushed himself to his feet and walked, slightly hunched, toward Ivy. "How's your arm?"

"Sore, but it's not numb anymore."

Diego glanced at Ketahn before returning his attention to Ivy. He held out his hand. "Can I check it out?"

A low growl rattled in Ketahn's chest, and his body tensed.

She chuckled. "It's okay, Ketahn. I'm not going to disappear."

Ketahn exhaled, heavy and slow, and his tension gradually eased. Though he didn't release her, he allowed Ivy enough freedom to turn toward Diego and extend her injured arm.

It was the first time Ivy had looked at her wounds directly. Her jumpsuit sleeve had been torn away, leaving her arm bare, and sure enough, there was a band of purple bruising around faint, pink scars left by the thorns.

"Man, you bastards are scary possessive," Diego muttered as he took hold of Ivy's wrist. With his other hand, he massaged up her arm. "Feel all that?"

"Yeah."

He gently probed near one of the sealed wounds.

Ivy jerked, hissing through her teeth. She doubted anyone heard it over Ketahn's snarl.

"Sorry," Diego said, releasing her. "But good news is there doesn't appear to be any lasting damage. The tenderness should pass in a couple days."

Ivy settled her hand on Ketahn's shoulder. "Thanks, Diego."

"Just glad you're still with us, Ivy." Smiling, Diego dropped his gaze to the sleeping woman. "Ahmya too."

Ivy followed his gaze with her own. They'd covered Ahmya with a dark silk blanket that made her face look so pale, but the blanket was rising and falling steadily with her slow breaths. "She's going to be okay, right?"

"Yeah. It's just a waiting game on when she'll wake, but her vitals are all good."

Will raised his hand in a wave and grinned. "Nice to have you back in the world of the living, Ivy."

As Diego stepped away and sat on the ground next to Will, Lacey dragged her bag closer, thrust her hand inside, and pulled out one of the ration bars from the *Somnium's* emergency stash.

Picking up a waterskin, she stood and held both the water and the ration out to Ivy. "Hungry?"

"Starving actually," Ivy replied.

That produced another grumble from Ketahn, but he said nothing, lowering her so she sat on the blanket in front of him.

Ivy's eyes lingered on him before she leaned forward to accept the food and drink from Lacey. "Thanks."

Lacey smiled. "No problem."

As Lacey returned to her spot by the fire, Ivy sat back, opened the ration bar's wrapper, and lifted her gaze to study Ketahn's face.

For someone who couldn't really change his expression, there was a lot of emotion in it. His mandibles seemed uncertain as to whether they wanted to be raised or lowered, drawn close together or spread wide apart, and his eyes gleamed with far more light than they should've reflected from the fire.

Ketahn canted his head. "What is it, Ivy?"

"You just seem...agitated."

"Ah, my heartsthread..." He leaned down and nuzzled her hair with his mouth. "This day has been difficult. Your hunger only reminds me that I have failed as your mate. I have failed to provide and protect."

Ivy raised a hand and cradled his jaw just beneath his mandible, holding him in place. "You haven't failed anything, Ketahn. Not me, not our tribe. You've done everything you can for us and more. You've pushed yourself, you've been beaten and battered, you...you could have *died*." She stroked her thumb across the hide of his face. "We are here, we are safe, we have food. That is all that matters."

"You are right." He trailed his knuckles along her cheek, his touch delicate and soothing. "All that matters is right here."

Ivy smiled and leaned into his touch.

Callie cleared her throat. "Not to, uh, break up this lovely moment, but...where are we going? Are we just going to keep on running? How far do we need to go?"

Ketahn grunted, but his mandibles rose in a slight smile. "Never one question from a human. Why always many?"

"And that, ladies and gentlemen, is called *deflecting*," said Lacey with a chuckle.

His mandibles twitched. "I do not know your words."

Diego laughed. "Does that work with Ivy?"

Ivy snorted and settled back down on the ground. "Only when he's purposely being stubborn." She took a bite out of the ration bar. It was dry, bland, and hard, but it was food.

"I should try that one sometime," Will said with a grin.

Callie smirked at Will. "Yeah, I don't think that'd work out so well for you considering you're not an alien and all that. But really, Ketahn...what's the plan? Where are we going?"

Ketahn shifted atop the blanket, turning so he faced the others. "Far."

Callie arched a brow. "Far?"

He nodded. "We go as far as we must. Away from Takarahl. Away from the queen. More far than she will follow."

A flash of rage swept through Ivy. She swallowed the lump of chewed up, grainy food and took a long drink from the waterskin to help it go down easier. In her mind, she cursed the queen with every swear word she knew. All this was because of Zurvashi. All this was because she couldn't just let Ketahn go. She was covetous, obsessed, and she'd been spurned by the object of her desire.

Hell hath no fury like a woman scorned.

At least when that woman had been cruel and vindictive to begin with.

"Will she stop following?" Will asked.

"I...do not know. Now we go into danger, into the land of her enemies, so we can be safe. She will not think to look there."

"We're dead," Lacey said, adding a stick to the fire.

"No." Ketahn's voice was firm; the doubts and guilt he'd expressed only minutes ago seemed to have vanished. He ran his palm down the back of Ivy's hair.

She looked up.

His eyes blazed into hers, their violet aglow with the flickering firelight. "We will live."

CHAPTER 12

WHEN KETAHN OPENED HIS EYES, the firelight on the cave ceiling was the muted red of dying embers. The quiet conversations of earlier in the night had been replaced by the pattering of rain on the surrounding jungle. Cool air touched his hide—at least where it wasn't covered by blankets or his mate.

Beyond the cave, all was dark, but he could now make out the shadowy forms of nearby plants thanks to the diminished glow of the fire.

Tightening his hold on Ivy, he shifted to sit with his back against the wall. The others were asleep. Callie, Lacey, Diego, and Will were packed around the fire, their bodies indistinct beneath a tangle of blankets. Ahmya lay closer to Ketahn and Ivy, still bundled in blankets of her own. One of her little feet was poking out from beneath those blankets.

Rekosh's hand rested but a finger's length away from Ahmya's exposed foot. Rekosh himself was sprawled out with only his torso inside the shelter, looking as though he'd meant to tuck Ahmya's foot back under the blanket when he'd fallen asleep.

Telok was also outside the cave, his shoulder leaned against the rock face. A large-leafed plant over his head shielded him from the rain.

Ketahn breathed in deep, relishing his mate's sweet scent. He focused on her—on her weight, her warmth, her softness, on the way her body sculpted to his whenever she lay atop him this way.

He'd almost lost her again. The Tangle had almost claimed another person Ketahn cared about.

A person Ketahn *loved*.

The fire's glow was reminiscent of the crimson stains on spearblossom petals, and thinking on that would've made it easy for Ketahn's mind to linger on the past. So many had fallen. The threads of his fate were surely dripping with blood, like a web upon which raindrops had gathered.

We are here, we are safe...

That is all that matters.

Ivy's words were as true now as they'd been when she'd spoken them earlier. Death had not claimed any other members of their tribe, and no one had suffered serious injury. They'd survived another day.

With a soft trill, Ketahn trailed his fingers up and down Ivy's back. She hummed and snuggled against him. Her hair was draped over one side of his chest, and her warm breath fanned across the other, both tickling his hide.

He should have added wood to the fire to chase away the chill, but he could not bring himself to move. To waste even a single moment of this peaceful time with his mate was unthinkable. They rarely enjoyed such quiet lately; for this little while, he wanted only to hold his Ivy and pretend there was no one else in all the world.

Ketahn had not been awake long when Urkot and Cole returned to camp. Both were wearing shrouds made of cured hide over their necks and shoulders to protect them from the rain, yet both were soaked regardless.

Cole shed his, letting it drop to the ground, stood his spear against the outer wall, and ducked into the cave. "I'm fucking beat." He swayed on his feet as he passed the fire, stopped, and knelt before it. Adding more wood and leaves, he blew on the coals to coax them back to life. Then he lay down beside the other humans and threw his arms over his eyes.

Ketahn carefully slid Ivy off him. When she stirred, he hushed her, smoothed her hair back, and told her to sleep. She curled up beneath her blanket, and Ketahn tucked it snugly around her.

Urkot halted near Telok. "All was quiet."

"That is good," Ketahn replied as he stood—at least as much as the low ceiling allowed. Hunched forward with head and back brushing the stone, he stepped out of the cave. The instant he was able, he straightened fully and stretched his stiff limbs and back.

Telok grunted and ran his gaze from Urkot to the slumbering humans and back again. Bracing his hands against the stone behind him, he pushed himself up.

"You should have come sooner," Ketahn said, leaning into the cave to pluck up his spear.

Urkot's mandibles were low, and his eyes were on Rekosh. "The two of you needed rest."

"He does, yes. But I am not so worn as to not contribute."

"You are a fool, Ketahn, if you think you have not contributed," Telok said. He gathered his spear from its place against the stone wall and strode forward. "I will share this watch with you."

Ketahn lifted his mandibles in a smile. "I am glad for it."

"I held vigil with Cole on that side of camp," Urkot said, gesturing toward suncrest. "Ahnset still watches from the other side."

"Is she not returning to sleep?"

An uncertain buzz rattled in Urkot's chest. "She refused.

Said the rest of us need it more, and she is happy to watch for danger while we do."

Ketahn huffed, turning his gaze in the direction Urkot had indicated.

"I will take the suncrest side," Telok said, tapping Ketahn's leg with one of his own. "You see to your broodsister."

Even as he nodded, Ketahn glanced over his shoulder at his mate. Only her tousled golden hair and her face from her nose up were visible; she'd drawn the blanket up far enough to cover all the rest. But her brow was smooth, unblemished by worry, and her breaths were soft and even. Sight of her drew hard on his heartsthread, beckoning him closer to her. How could he leave her alone after what had happened? How could he even think to let her out of his sight?

To watch over her, I must step away. To guard her—to guard them all—I must sit apart a while.

And who else in all the Tangle would watch over Ivy and the others as fiercely as Urkot and Rekosh while Ketahn was away?

"I will," Ketahn said. "Urkot, see if you can help Rekosh into the cave. He need not lie in the rain after what he has suffered today."

Urkot thumped a leg on the ground and tapped a knuckle against his headcrest. Telok strode toward his chosen place to watch, and Ketahn strode toward his.

He found Ahnset just outside the ring of brambles and branches she'd helped build around the camp, leaning against a tree. She'd donned a silk shroud, the wet fabric glistening in the rain, but did not have the hood up. Her hair was bound in a single thick bundle that hung over her shoulder.

"You must rest too, sister," Ketahn said as he approached her.

She didn't respond, didn't even move save the slightest lowering of her chin.

A very different sort of pull on Ketahn's heartsthread brought him to a halt just behind her. Again, he was aware of the distance between them, a chasm wider and more frightening than the maw of any beast of legend. And he rejected it. He would not suffer such a thing, not after all that had happened.

What time he was to have with those he cared about was too precious to waste like this.

"I will not deny my anger, Ahnset," he said. "I will not deny that some part of me hated you for what you did."

Ahnset released a shuddering breath, and her head fell farther.

"But I know you, broodsister," he continued. "However else we have changed, I know the truth of you, because that has remained constant. I know you wanted only to help Ella. I know you acted in desperation because it seemed the rest of us did not.

"And...we did not. We did little for her because there was nothing to be done. The Ahnset I have always known would not accept that. You are one of the fiercest warriors Takarahl has ever seen, Ahnset, and you are thus because you always fight for those who cannot. You will always fight, whether it is for an innocent weaver trying to pay tribute or a sickly creature you barely know. And I would not have you feel guilt for that."

"By my actions, Ketahn, eight was sundered. Eight was made seven." She turned her head to look at him over her shoulder. "Eight humans. That was a sign, Ketahn. That was sacred. And I broke it."

Ketahn strode around to Ahnset's front. When she did not look at him again, he reached up and took her face between his hands, forcing her to meet his gaze. "Zurvashi broke it, Ahnset. If the Eight are real, it is she who has disrespected them, she who has reviled them."

"She could not have harmed Ella were it not for me."

"And she would have harmed me further were it not for you."

"The harm she has done to you spans years, Ketahn, yet I

urged you to go to her. I did not listen. I did not... I did not *see*. And now...now I have brought a curse upon us by making seven of eight. By sundering that sacred number. By—"

"Hear me, Ahnset. Hear my words." He straightened his legs, rising higher until his face was immediately before hers and their mandibles brushed against each other. "Our tribe is not eight. It never was. It began as two—as Ivy and Ketahn. Then it was nine when we awoke the other humans. When you came with Telok, Rekosh, and Urkot, we were thirteen. Now it is twelve.

"And it would always have been. For you would have left had things gone differently."

"I would have taken her place. I should have. I should have challenged Zurvashi there. Should have made her suffer for all she has done, for all that I was too blind to see."

Ketahn shook his head. There was fire in his chest, fire and tension, roiling maddeningly. "No, Ahnset. No. You do not inflict suffering. You are a protector. You are the shield. But shields cannot stop every blow. That does not make a shield useless. The other humans need you. I need you, sister, and I am sorry I made you think otherwise."

She closed her eyes as her head fell forward, headcrest coming to rest against Ketahn's. Her forelegs pressed against the outsides of his, her broad shoulders shook with a shuddering breath, and the mournful rain continued to fall.

"You are ours, Ahnset," Ketahn rasped, "and I am sorry you gave up so much to be ours. I never wanted you to lose anything."

One of her hands cupped the back of his head. "I have not lost my broodbrother. I have not lost my new sister. I have not lost our friends. That is enough, Ketahn."

But Ahnset had lost her mate. Her heartsthread.

They stood like that for a long while. The rain trickled over

Ketahn's hide, washing away much of the burden that had weighed upon his spirit.

"I see things as they are now," Ahnset said. "I see them as they are…"

He pulled away from her again and looked up into her eyes when she opened them. "Never forget, broodsister…never forget how they could be. How they should be."

"I will not."

"Now go and sleep. You are the strongest of us, and I would not have you falter as we travel tomorrow."

She chittered, the sound at once sorrowful and amused. "It would take more than a single sleepless night to hinder me."

Ketahn's mandibles rose. "I do not doubt it, Ahnset. But rest all the same."

Ahnset touched her headcrest to his again before withdrawing. He watched her turn and walk back to camp, watched until she was out of sight, and then assumed her place against the tree, planting the butt of his spear in the mud.

As Urkot had said, the jungle was quiet, and Ketahn could not stop his mind from wandering back to the cave—back to Ivy. He was different than he'd been when he'd first found her. He was…more. More in so many ways, in too many ways to define. In ways he could not even recognize.

And he knew now, he understood, that it was largely due to her spirit. Ivy was so small, so delicate, so unthreatening. Outwardly, she and her kind truly seemed like creatures the vrix would have treated as prey. But she'd lent him such strength in the time he'd known her.

All he'd wanted over the last seven years was peace and solitude. To forget Zurvashi and what she'd done, to forget the suffering and loss caused by her rule. To turn away from everything and everyone he'd known and see only to himself.

Thanks to Ivy, he understood how wrong that had been. How selfish. He understood that it was, in its own way, cruel. A

different sort of cruelty than the queen's, but cruelty nonetheless. To have forsaken everything and everyone to spare
himself the fates they were enduring…

Ivy had given him hope and love and joy, but she'd given him
that strength too, and it had allowed him to embrace everything
else. It had allowed him to stride forward and risk himself to
better the lives of those he cared about.

She had shown him that trust was not a thing to hide away
and never use. She had shown him that relying upon others was
not a weakness. And she did not see him as weak for his failings,
did not see him as lesser when he exposed his vulnerabilities.
She only saw *him*. Her mate, her love. Her heartsthread.

They had survived this day together. Ketahn and Ivy, all their
tribe. They would survive the next, and the next, and on and on
until their times had come, and they would look back on their
lives and feel pride for overcoming hardships, for claiming
peace—for claiming the lives they wanted.

They would weave their own fates forever onward, the will
of the Eight be damned.

CHAPTER 13

"How are you feeling?" Ivy asked as she handed Ahmya a waterskin.

Ahmya accepted it with a strained smile. They'd been traveling for more than half the day, having set out before the sun had fully risen, and if Ivy's arm was hurting after the thorny vine monstrosity's attack, Ahmya had to be in much greater pain. Thankfully, they were finally crossing some easier terrain. Their journey over the last few days had been fraught with endless mud, twisted roots, and uneven ground that had caused many slips and falls.

Today had been almost leisurely in comparison, especially now that the clouds had parted to let the sun shine bright and clear through the canopy.

"I feel like I've been hit by a car. Everything hurts." Ahmya rubbed at the fabric of her jumpsuit just below her sternum; though Diego had sealed all the little puncture wounds beneath, Ahmya's abdomen was just as bruised as Ivy's arm. "I've been pricked by rose thorns more times than I can count, but this…"

"Bet you'll never want to touch a flower again," said Cole.

Ahmya arched a brow. "Why would I not want to touch a

flower again?" Opening the waterskin, she brought it to her mouth to drink.

"Really? After that?"

"It wasn't the flower. It was the thing hiding *inside* the flower. The firevine. I...just need to be careful next time. Be more aware of my surroundings."

"We didn't even know what to look for, so we couldn't have known." Ivy ran her hand through her hair, sweeping it back. "We do now."

"Ketahn never told you about those things?" Lacey asked from behind, quickening her steps to catch up to Ivy.

"He's told me about a lot of hidden dangers in the jungle, but we've never come across anything like that until yesterday."

"Would hate to see what else is hiding out here."

Callie, who was walking farther ahead with Will and Diego, glanced over her shoulder. She grinned. "Come on you slackers. You're falling behind."

Cole scoffed. "Who the hell are you calling a slacker?"

"Right?" Lacey said. "You're the one who refused to wake up this morning until Urkot poured water on your head, Callie."

With that reminder, Callie sent a dark glare in Urkot's direction.

The humans laughed.

Even with everyone awake and moving—packing supplies, eating breakfast, stretching after another night of sleeping on the ground—Callie had remained snuggled under her blanket. Nearby conversations hadn't roused her, and when Lacey had nudged Callie with her toe, the woman had only offered a groan, pulled her blanket over her head, and fallen back asleep.

Despite the language barrier, it had been clear to the humans that the vrix were anxious to move on. Urkot had attempted to wake Callie gently, rubbing her shoulder with a big hand. Ivy swore she'd heard a muttered *go away* from somewhere under the blanket.

So Urkot had drastically altered his methods. He'd plucked up a nearby waterskin, tore Callie's blanket away, and upturned the waterskin over her head.

Watching Callie sputter and shriek had been the comedic relief they all needed after yesterday's events.

Callie had been sour toward Urkot ever since.

Something tapped Ivy's backside. She turned her head to look up at Ahnset, who was now keeping pace beside her. Even the giant female had been in better spirits this morning.

Ahnset narrowed her eyes and said in vrix, "You are falling behind."

Ivy grinned. "So are you."

"I cannot watch you humans from in front."

"That is what we are doing. Watching. From the back."

Ahnset chittered. "So my sister is sharing in my duties?"

Ivy squared her shoulders. "Yes. It is a…chain."

"A *chayn*?"

"Ketahn watches you, you watch us, we watch them. So we are all watching, right?"

Ahnset glanced over her shoulder. "Then who watches Ketahn?"

"Well…I do. Every moment I can." It wasn't a lie. Ivy often sought her mate, needing to reassure herself that he was near.

"I do not think he would refuse were you to do so now." Ahnset looked down at Ivy again. "From closer."

Ivy gasped, hand flying to her chest in mock astonishment. "*Ahnset*, are you trying to push us to mate? When we should be traveling?"

Ahnset chittered again, mandibles twitching upward. "No. But I see you both longing. You have been often apart since we left, and it is a burden upon both of you."

Ivy looked back at Ketahn, and her heart ached at the sight of him. It was as Ahnset said—since leaving the *Somnium*, they'd had little time together, and they weren't likely to have much more in the near future. Not until they found a safe place to call home. Ivy had woken alone this morning and hated it.

Smiling, Ivy reached out and brushed her hand over the female vrix's foreleg. "Thank you, Ahnset."

Ahnset settled a big hand over Ivy's shoulder, stopping her as the others continued ahead. Her legs spread out wider, and she lowered herself, bending her head forward. "It is you who I must thank, Ivy. You have given my broodbrother joy he has not known in a long while. You have given him purpose he has not known in just as long. And...you have given me understanding when I did not think I deserved it."

Ivy stepped forward and slipped her arms around Ahnset the best she could, hugging her tight. Though she fought to keep her tears at bay, they won the battle, filling her eyes and trickling down her cheeks.

She'd grown up in a family that had never felt like family, and now, with Ketahn, Ahnset, and the others, she had one. A real one. That had sparked a sense of belonging, of being needed and loved, that Ivy had never had. "Your thread is woven with ours, Ahnset."

Ahnset shuddered. Her fingers flexed on Ivy's shoulder, but Ivy could feel the vrix's restraint; even with the involuntary motion, Ahnset was acting with great care. Finally, Ahnset took hold of Ivy's arms and withdrew.

"Now"—Ahnset turned Ivy toward Ketahn, placed a hand on her back, and gave her a push—"go to your mate."

Ketahn's roving, vigilant gaze settled on Ivy, and his head tilted. He slowed his pace as another little nudge from Ahnset set Ivy's feet in motion. Grinning like a fool, Ivy walked toward him; his mandibles rose in response to her smile.

"What did you speak of, my heartsthread?" he asked.

"Well..." She tucked loose strands of her hair behind her ear as she fell into step beside him. "Ahnset said we should sneak off and have kinky, dirty, hot sex." She wiggled her eyebrows.

"Did she? That is strange of her…" His eyes flicked toward Ahnset briefly, and he released a thoughtful trill before bending and scooping Ivy up into his arms. "But it has been a long while."

Ivy laughed, throwing her arm around his neck as he cradled her against chest. She twirled her fingers in his silky hair. "It has been."

"My broodsister did not really say that, did she?"

Her grin widened. "Does it matter?"

He chittered, and the sound rolled into a deep, hungry growl. "No."

The vibration of that growl stimulated her nipples, sending a bolt of arousal straight to her core. She had to bite her lip to hold in the moan that threatened to escape. Somehow, that sensation had been stronger than any she'd felt there before.

Sighing heavily, Ivy rested her head beneath his chin, resigning herself to taking pleasure simply from being in his arms. "Alas, there shall be no quickie for us, as we have to stay with the group."

Ketahn huffed and held her a little tighter. "They will not miss us if we are only gone for a few…what is the human word?"

"Minutes?"

"No. The longer one. Hours?"

"They'll definitely miss us if we disappear for hours."

"That is how long it will take for me to see to my mate's needs."

Ivy laughed, then turned her face against his neck and groaned. "You're not supposed to be making me horny right now, Ketahn. We have ground to cover, remember?"

"Ah, my *nyleea*, those sounds you make…" He drew in a deep breath, and something shifted just beneath Ivy's backside—his claspers, drawing closer against his pelvis. "But you are right.

We must put the needs of our tribe before our desires. At least until those desires become needs."

Ivy's pussy nearly wept at his words.

Down girl, down.

What she felt now sure seemed like a need.

She wanted more than anything for him to carry her off into the trees so she could again feel him inside her, thrusting deep, their tribe be damned. She *craved* him.

Except they really did need to keep going. Ivy and Ketahn's time would come.

Resting her cheek on his chest, she lowered a hand and traced the hard planes of his chest with her fingertips, trying to ignore the needy ache between her thighs.

"I spoke with Ahnset last night," Ketahn said.

Ivy snapped her head up and met his gaze. "You did?"

"Yes." A low buzz ran through his chest, more subtle than his other sounds but impossible to miss. "I apologized to her."

Once more, tears welled in Ivy's eyes. She hurriedly wiped them away. It seemed like any little thing could make her an emotional wreck these days. "I'm glad. I didn't like seeing you two so distant."

Ketahn lowered his head, touching his headcrest to her forehead. "I do not wish to waste time in anger."

Ivy rested her head on his shoulder and flattened her hand over his hearts. They beat strong and steady beneath her palm.

Ketahn continued onward in silence, and Ivy took comfort in his closeness, in the gentle swaying of his stride, in his familiar scent. She glanced up. The bruising around his neck had already faded, but it remained fresh in her memory.

"Are you happy, Ketahn?" Ivy asked after a time. "Despite... the queen and everything that's happened. Are you happy with...the choice I made?"

"Ah, my heartsthread." Ketahn combed his claws through her hair. "We cannot know what will come. But that does not mean we should falter in doing what is right for fear of where those strands will lead us." He brushed his hard mouth over her forehead, his version of a kiss. "I am happy. I am full of pride. I am full of love. For Ivy Foster is my mate, and no one on any world can claim such fortune."

Warmth blossomed within her. Her guilt wasn't for waking the others from stasis, but for the suffering Ketahn had endured. She wished she could erase that suffering, that he could live in the peace he so longed for.

Soon. We will get there soon.

Ivy kissed his chest. "I love you."

"Hey, that's no fair!" Lacey said, drawing Ivy's attention to her. The woman stood with her arms crossed over her chest and a playful smirk on her lips. "Here we are walking like chumps, and you get the royal treatment."

Ivy laughed. "I'm sure if you asked, Telok would be happy to carry you."

Lacey snorted, her already flushed cheeks darkening. "Ahem. *Anyway*, uh, the others are stopped up ahead. I think Telok wanted me to hurry you over. He kinda waved in this direction and barked *Ketahn come.*"

"Is something wrong?" Ivy asked, brow furrowing.

"No, I don't think so. I got the sense he's just tired of you two being so slow."

Ketahn chittered. "We are not slow. We are watching the rear."

Lacey rolled her eyes. "You've been watching *a* rear, that's for sure."

His mandibles drooped. "What do you mean, Lacey?"

"My ass," Ivy said with a chuckle. "You've been watching my ass. And she's not wrong, so don't deny it."

"I would be watching it now were it in sight." He squeezed one of Ivy's ass cheeks.

Lacey arched a brow. "Wow. These vrix really aren't that different from human guys. Bunch of lust-crazed animals."

Ivy laughed. "You have *no* idea."

"After hearing you on the *Somnium*, I kind of do have an idea…"

Ketahn straightened, drawing his shoulders back and angling his chin up. "I said I would make my claim on my mate known to all the jungle."

This time, it was Ivy's turn to blush, but she wasn't really embarrassed. She liked that the others knew she was Ketahn's. She certainly never gave a damn while they were in the moment either.

"Bunch of freaky sex fiends." Lacey cleared her throat and tucked her hair behind her ear. "So, yeah, we should catch up with the others."

Ketahn followed Lacey, keeping Ivy securely in his arms—and one of his lower hands firmly on her backside. That only reminded Ivy again of how long it had been since they'd made love, and it took quite a bit of willpower to prevent herself from getting all hot and bothered again, especially when she imagined that hand sliding a little higher between her thighs.

The others had gathered beside a wide stream. Sunlight sparkled upon the water's surface, inviting and warm, dancing with the shadows cast by the broken canopy overhead. Large, moss-covered boulders stood along the stream's edges and jutted out of the water. Clusters of flowers lined the banks, some with long stems bent down, their bright blossoms reflected in smears of color on the rippling surface.

Ketahn lowered Ivy, releasing her legs and keeping his strong hands upon her until she found her footing.

"This is beautiful," Ahmya said.

Cole, who stood at the edge of the water with an uncharacteristically contemplative smile on his lips, nodded. "Yeah, it's pretty alright, isn't it?"

Callie stepped forward and toed the water with her boot. "What I wouldn't give for a bath right now."

Ivy, recalling those lazy hours spent lounging by the stream with Ketahn, also looked upon the water longingly. "Me too."

"So let's stay." Will turned toward the others. "We've been pushing for days. We're all exhausted." He waved at Ahmya. "I know she's hurting after what happened yesterday, even if she hasn't said anything."

Ahmya ducked her head, her hair falling to cover her eyes. "I don't want to slow everyone down."

"You do not slow us," Ketahn said gently, "but we did not go far yesterday. We must go now."

The small woman's lower lip trembled, and she crossed her arms over her chest. "I'm sorry. I know that was my fault."

"What did you say to upset her, Ketahn?" Rekosh demanded, striding toward Ahmya. Carefully, he hooked her hair with his claws and tucked it behind her ears.

Ahmya peeked up at Rekosh. Her dark eyes were glossy with unshed tears.

Ketahn huffed. "Not your fault, Ahmya. It is okay. But we must walk now."

Ivy pressed her hand against his abdomen. "Let's stay."

He covered Ivy's hand with one of his own and looked down at her.

She didn't hear his grumbling, but she felt it under her palm. "We're all tired and worn, Ketahn. I think it would do everyone's spirits good if we had an evening to relax."

"We had that yesterday," he replied.

Ivy scrunched her face at him. "I wouldn't call getting stabbed by thorns and falling into a poison-induced sleep relaxing, Ketahn. You know no one was relaxing yesterday." She reached up and grabbed hold of his mandibles, pulling him down. "*You* need this too."

"They want to stop, do they not?" asked Telok from his place atop one of the boulders that was surrounded by water.

"Yes," Ketahn said, not looking away from Ivy. "I told them we must—"

"This is a pleasant place to rest," Telok said. "I am for enjoying what sun we may have before the next rain."

"As am I," Rekosh added.

"I was going to say we should stop to eat anyway," Urkot called. "These humans have eaten little but sticks of dust. They need meat."

"By which you mean *you* need meat," said Ahnset with a chitter.

"They're agreeing with us, aren't they?" asked Diego.

Ivy arched a brow at Ketahn.

He narrowed his eyes and dipped his head farther, cupping the back of her head with a hand. In a low, deep voice, he said, "I will submit, my *nyleea*."

She smiled, closed the distance between them, and pressed her lips to the seam of his mouth. "Thank you."

"Fuck yeah!" Cole tugged off his boots, tossed them aside, then grasped the collar of his jumpsuit. He opened it and shoved it down, baring his ass.

"Really, Cole?" Callie demanded, dropping her head back to look at the sky.

"I don't know what you're waiting for."

"We've lived together for like two weeks. We're not ready to see your dick swinging around."

Cole jumped into the water. "Your loss!"

Ivy shook her head with a laugh and drew away from Ketahn. "Maybe Ahnset can take us females a little farther upstream?"

"Definitely," said Lacey, holding a hand up to block Cole out of her vision as she hurried toward Ahnset.

Ketahn's eyes widened. "No. No, you will stay with me, Ivy."

Ivy tilted her head and raised her brows. "You want the other males to see me naked?"

His mandibles fell and drew together. With a growl, he placed his hands on her shoulders, spun her toward Ahnset, and pushed her forward. "Keep them safe, broodsister."

CHAPTER 14

"OH MY GOD," Callie moaned as she lowered her body into the water. "I could close my eyes and almost imagine we're in some five-star spa resort."

"I can't say I've ever been to a spa"—Ivy set her folded jumpsuit on top of large rock—"but this is as close to nature as you can get."

She could occasionally hear Cole's shouts from downstream, followed by some deeper voices, all made faint by distance and the sound of flowing water, but it comforted her to know they were all near in case something happened. Ahnset hadn't led them too far from the males; they'd gone around a bend just upstream, out of sight but not out of earshot. There was more open water here, and the warm, abundant sunlight bathed Ivy's skin.

Like many places in the jungle, it was a little piece of paradise.

Even Ahnset was enjoying a moment of peace. She lay on a large rock near the shore, basking in the sun, with one of her forelegs dangling in the water.

Grabbing a few leaves of *nath'jagol*—cleanleaf—from the pile beside her bag, Ivy stepped into the stream; the water came up to her knees. Her skin immediately prickled with the chill. The stream bed beneath her feet was covered in smooth stones that were thankfully not slick with algae, allowing her to easily wade deeper. She spread her arms over the surface as the water rose to her chest. Her nipples tightened to hard points from the cold.

"I've never gone skinny dipping before," Ahmya said from the bank.

Ivy turned and looked at her.

Ahmya had undressed, but she stood with her jumpsuit clutched against her chest to shield her small breasts, belly, and pelvis. Her toes wiggled restlessly in the grass, and she chewed on her bottom lip. Her body was a mess of black and blue bruises where the firevine had grasped her, making the rest of her skin starkly pale in contrast.

Callie righted herself and chuckled. "Get that little booty in here!"

Ivy offered Ahmya an encouraging smile. "I know it's intimidating. It took me a little while to put aside those inhibitions, but you get used to it. It's just us and nature."

Lacey, who was still clothed and looked just as nervous, stopped beside Ahmya. "I've never gone skinny dipping either, but hey, you're one step ahead of me."

Ahmya shifted her weight from foot to foot. "I just feel so...exposed."

"We'll go in together. Sound good?"

"Sure."

Lacey opened her jumpsuit, withdrew her arms from the sleeves, and pushed it down, leaving her in her white shirt and shorts. Taking hold of the hem of the shirt, she clenched it, and hesitated with her lips pressed together. Finally, she pulled the shirt up and over her head and tossed it aside. Her shorts quickly followed.

Ivy's eyes rounded when Lacey straightened.

A long, crooked, slightly puckered scar ran across Lacey's belly from hip to hip amidst silvery stretch marks. A similar scar marred each of her arms, spanning from the insides of her elbows up to her armpits, and there was another pair on her inner thighs. They all had a jagged, uneven look, like they'd been crudely stitched and poorly healed.

Water splashed as Callie stepped up beside Ivy. "Shit, Lacey! What happened?"

Lacey's red hair fell forward as she looked down. She lifted her hands to her middle, covering the long scar on her belly. "Let's just say the Homeworld Initiative had certain...requirements for enrollment that I didn't meet, and I did something stupid to reach them." She forced her hands down and her face up. "It's... It's a thing of the past. I am no longer that person."

Ahmya touched Lacey's arm. "You don't have to talk about it. We understand."

"She is ashamed of her scars?" Ahnset asked.

Ivy looked at the female vrix. Ahnset had raised her torso and was staring at Lacey with her head cocked. With all that had happened lately, Ivy had never really taken the time to study Ahnset very closely. Of course a vrix who'd spent her life as a warrior had scars.

In the sunshine, those scars were clearer than ever. Some were paler that her black hide, some darker. They reminded Ivy of Ketahn's scars—cuts and stab wounds, gashes, even one on Ahnset's upper left shoulder that looked like a it had been a burn.

"Scars mean different things to humans," Ivy said in vrix. "For many of us, they are...pain instead of pride."

Ahnset dipped her chin, staring down as she lifted her arms and studied the scars upon them. "Can you speak my words to her? To Lacey?"

Ivy nodded, and all four women watched as Ahnset leaned forward and spoke.

"Say that scars *were* pain. She should not look upon them with shame. She does not have to feel pride, but when she sees them, she should take pride in herself. Because she survived whatever left them. Because she, like each of you, is strong."

Biting the inside of her cheek, Ivy fought back a fresh swell of emotions as she translated what Ahnset had said. Though Ivy's physical scars were nothing compared Ahnset's, Lacey's, or Ahmya's, she carried scars deep below the surface that had been left by the trials she'd endured in her short life. She knew Ahnset had spoken to comfort Lacey, but her words meant so much to Ivy too.

Tears shone in Lacey's eyes, and she smiled. "Thank you." She cleared her throat and grabbed some leaves from Ivy's pile of cleanleaf, offering some to Ahmya. "Come on. Let's get in instead of standing here with our tits hanging out."

Taking a deep breath, Ahmya drew away her jumpsuit, dropped it next to Lacey's clothes, and accepted the offered leaves. The two women stepped into the stream together.

Lacey hissed. "Jesus, that's cold." She ducked down until the water was up to her chin.

Ivy chuckled and handed Callie some cleanleaf before crushing a few for herself. "You get used to it."

Ahmya hummed as she swam farther in. "But it feels so good."

The strong fragrance of gardenia and lemon flooded Ivy's senses as she scrubbed the crushed leaves over her chest. They fizzled the moment they met her wet skin. This wasn't the hot and steamy bubble bath everyone must've dreamed about, but it was something, and Ivy had come to enjoy bathing in nature. There was something relaxing yet thrilling about it.

And she especially loved it when she was with Ketahn.

The corners of her lips curled up at the thought of him.

She loved how his violet eyes would focus on her body, loved how they'd darken with desire, how they'd burn for her, and she loved how, in the end, he'd always lose his tenuous self-control and it would lead to frenzied, passionate lovemaking.

Warmth gathered in her core, and her sex clenched, aching with sudden need.

God, it's been way too long.

"I cannot tell you how glad I am that I opted for body hair removal when THI offered it," Callie said, snapping Ivy out of her lustful thoughts. "Otherwise, I'd be putting this jungle to shame right about now."

Ivy laughed, dipping beneath the water to wash away the *soap*—and to cool her now heated skin. "Same for me."

"I, uh…didn't get the full treatment," Lacey said. She stood in the deeper water near Ivy, scrubbing *nath'jagol* into her wet hair. Most of her body was submerged. "For obvious reasons."

"Me either," Ahyma said as she treaded water nearby. "I was…too embarrassed. I'd never had a wax done before in my life, especially you know…down *there*, so all that laser stuff…" She shivered.

"There's nothing wrong with not doing something you aren't comfortable with," Ivy said.

Callie chuckled. "I've had a few Brazilian waxes done, so I guess I was used to stuff like that going on down there. But oof. I had this one girl once that was new, didn't really know what she was doing, and let me tell you, that shit *hurt*. I never screamed so loud in my life. I swear she must've ripped off several layers of skin while missing the hair entirely. What THI did with their laser treatment was like a soothing massage compared to that."

The women laughed.

Ahmya looked down at the water. "I wish I could be that

TIFFANY ROBERTS

brave and confident. Getting a Pap smear is one thing, but the Initiative technicians were so cold and clinical, and I just couldn't bring myself to lie on the table and spread my legs in front of a room full of people when the time came."

Ivy cringed. "That part *was* really uncomfortable."

"I already felt like cattle being poked and prodded. That was just a step more than I could take."

"And that's okay, Ahmya," Callie said. "You are plenty brave. Look at where you are now. Who cares if you didn't get your pubes removed before you flew across the universe?"

Lifting her gaze, Ahmya smiled. "Yeah, who cares? I did the part that mattered, right?"

"You did," said Lacey. "Jumping into a new life... That takes more courage than most people understand. And what we've done here, well..."

Callie grinned. "Guess we're taking new life to an extreme."

Lacey waggled her eyebrows. "Ivy still has us beat with her eight-legged lover."

Tightness flitted through Ivy's chest. She knew it for what it was—a reflex that had been shaped by years of being judged. But it was fleeting, gone as soon as it had come, because there was no judgment here.

Ivy smiled. "Six-legged. He's a vrix, not a spider."

Lacey waved a hand nonchalantly. "Details, details. He still shoots webs out of his ass and is scary as fuck."

"The vrix look scary," Ahmya said as she washed herself, "but most of the time, they're actually...pretty sweet."

"Are you thinking of Rekosh, Ahmya?" Callie asked, grinning wide.

Ahmya ducked her head, but not before Ivy saw the blush staining her cheeks. "He's just kind to me. I'm not...I'm not thinking of him in *that* way."

"Mhmm."

Ahmya snapped her gaze back up. "I'm not!"

168

"Keep telling yourself that. I bet you're wondering if his cock is as red as his—"

Ahmya lunged for Callie, dunking her head under water.

Callie came back up, arms thrashing, sputtering and laughing. "So there is fire in you."

"He's...a *spider*." Ahmya whispered, body shuddering as her face scrunched.

Callie snickered. "Vrix."

"We're not really going down that road, right?" Lacey asked. "We're not really going to talk about their dicks while we're all buck-ass naked a few hundred feet away from them?"

"It's probably what the guys are talking about," Callie said with a shrug. "Besides, I'm curious. I'm also freaked out and definitely don't want to fuck one of them, but I am curious."

Lacey jabbed her thumb in Ivy's direction. "You could always ask the expert over here."

All eyes turned toward Ivy. Her eyebrows rose. She couldn't fault the others for their curiosity—Ivy had been just as curious in the beginning with Ketahn. Still, that didn't stop her cheeks from warming.

"Um, well..." Ivy cleared her throat and glanced down at the water. "I can only say with Ketahn that his, uh... Its color matches his markings."

Callie pumped her arm. "I knew it!"

Lacey covered her face with her hands. "That's all I'm going to be picturing now."

"A rainbow of cocks?"

Well, that was definitely what Ivy was picturing now. She chuckled.

Lacey laughed, drawing her hands away. "You're horrible."

Callie snickered. "Well, you have your answer now, Ahmya. A red rocket."

"Oh, my God." It was the last thing Ahmya said before slowly submerging herself, leaving only the long, dark wisps of her hair floating near the surface.

That's one way to avoid a conversation, I guess.

Ivy chuckled.

After they were done washing, the females spent a little time swimming in the slow running stream. Though no one said it, Ivy didn't doubt they all had the same thought—there was no telling when they'd have time to relax like this again. Nothing was certain out here, nothing was guaranteed. And that only made these moments more precious.

When they finally pulled themselves out of the water, the women laid out a blanket and joined Ahnset on the rock, letting the sunshine dry their skin.

Lacey, sitting with her knees hugged to her chest, tipped her face up to the sky. Her long, damp hair hung down her back. "It's times like this when you can almost...forget."

"Forget what?" Ahmya asked.

"The crash and...Ella."

Ahnset stiffened behind Ivy's back and turned her head toward Lacey. Ivy settled her palm on Ahnset's hindquarters in silent comfort.

"Is it... Is it wrong that when I think of everyone who died in the crash, I feel sad but no real connection, but Ella being gone is like this big hole?" Lacey asked, her voice low. "I only knew her for what? A week?"

"It doesn't matter how long it was," said Callie, dropping her gaze to the water. "She was our friend."

"She was our family," Ivy said. "Our tribe."

Ahmya looked around, her black hair shimmering in the sunlight. "She would have loved this."

Lacey opened her eyes and smiled. "Yeah, she would have."

"What do they say?" Ahnset asked.

Ivy looked at her, switching to vrix. "They said Ella would have liked it here."

Ahnset turned her face toward the sun and closed her eyes. With the light directly on her, the hide of her neck and upper chest looked just a little paler than the rest of it—the place where she'd worn that thick, gold-adorned neck piece. Every time Ivy had seen Ahnset, the vrix had been wearing all those decorative pieces that largely hid the body beneath. Devested of all that, Ahnset looked plain, but she also seemed more...herself.

"There is a place in Takarahl called the Den of Spirits," Ahnset said softly. "They say the spirits of all vrix who came before dwell there, watching over us, guiding us. That is where Ella died. But...I do not think her spirit would have remained in that place. She would have returned to the Tangle. Returned to you."

Opening her eyes, Ahnset lifted her mandibles just a little in what Ivy could only see as a smile. "I believe she is here now, with us. Seeing all the things she longed to see. Free of pain, free of suffering... And I hope she will forgive me one day. But more, I hope she is at peace."

Tears stung Ivy's eyes. She rose on her knees and slipped her arm around Ahnset's hindquarters, resting her head there. "She is, Ahnset. And she has."

Ahnset rested a hand upon Ivy's back, dipping her chin and closing her eyes.

"What did she say?" Ahmya asked.

Giving Ahnset a gentle squeeze, Ivy drew away and looked at the others, repeating as well as she could all the female vrix had said.

"We should make something here," Lacey said. "A memorial. We could...say our goodbyes in this place."

Ivy repeated Lacey's words in vrix. Ahnset made a low, thoughtful sound, and for a few moments, stared down at her upturned hands. When she finally spoke, tears spilled from Ivy's eyes.

The other humans looked to Ivy for an explanation.

171

Ivy cleared her throat. "She, uh, said that she would rather carry Ella with us. Until we find a new place to make our home. And that we should remember Ella in that place, and make sure she is welcome, because...because there are no goodbyes. Because Ella will always be with us, and even if it hurts sometimes, it is a beautiful thing."

CHAPTER 15

"I DO NOT UNDERSTAND. Why do they insist upon covering themselves in cloth no matter the weather?" Urkot asked.

Ketahn glanced in the direction the females had gone and pressed the tips of his legs into the dirt to fight his persistent urge to go to Ivy. Though he wasn't happy about being separated from his mate, he trusted Ivy and Ahnset, and he knew the females' reason for wanting to bathe apart from the males was important to them.

But he could not claim to truly understand the reason itself.

He released a huff. "Because humans are bound by *mah dess tee.*"

Telok attempted—unsuccessfully—to repeat the word. "Is it some sort of sacred law?"

"I do not recall the spiritspeakers giving any such law," said Urkot.

Rekosh chittered. "The humans do not worship the Eight, Urkot."

"What? How could they not? What else is there?"

"More than any vrix has ever imagined," Ketahn replied, returning his attention to his friends.

Urkot's mandibles twitched, and a contemplative trill rose from within him. "You still have not explained *mah dess tee*, Ketahn."

Out in the stream, Cole spun around, throwing his arms wide. He'd waded far enough for the water to reach only to his mid-thighs, leaving his soft, wrinkly, dangling stem visible. "What the hell are you guys waiting for? The water's great."

Perhaps *mah dess tee* wasn't something all humans were bound by. Ivy had shed hers during her time with Ketahn, but she'd regained it around the other humans. Cole, however, had shown no hesitation in baring his torso from the beginning—which none of the females had done.

"Damn, man." Will turned away from the stream, scrubbing a hand over his mouth and chin and tucking his other arm across his belly.

"I do not fully understand it," Ketahn said to Urkot. "Ivy said most humans are uncomfortable with others seeing their uncovered bodies."

"Seems foolish," said Telok.

Urkot watched Cole, head tilted. "Vrix females cover themselves."

"No," said Rekosh, "they adorn themselves. Not to hide but to draw attention. And the whispers I have heard say it was not the same before Zurvashi. The elders have said she was jealous of the male's markings, so chose to cover herself in gold that she would outshine every male. With her as queen, it became fashion."

"The queen *jealous* of males?" Urkot snorted. "Whose head is full of rocks, Rekosh?"

"What are you talking about?" Cole asked.

"Human *mah dess tee*," Ketahn replied in English.

"What?"

"*Mah dess tee*," Diego said.

"Tch. Who needs it?" Cole braced his fists on his hips and

widened his stance; his arms served as arrows pointing straight at his stem. "New world, new century. We can make whatever rules we want."

Diego chuckled. He stood near the water's edge with his arms folded across his chest, having moved neither nearer to nor farther from Cole. "I think that kind of thing is best discussed by everyone before we make any decisions."

"That's fair. But you"—he pointed at the other males, vrix and human both—"need to get your asses in here now. You won't regret it."

Diego's mouth slanted into a smirk. "You asking me to get naked with you, Cole?"

"Fully clothed or dick swinging in the wind, man," Cole said with a laugh, "doesn't matter to me." He put his arms out to the sides again and walked backward. The water gradually rose to his waist; a shiver coursed through him as his stem went under.

"Cold, huh?" Diego unfastened his jumpsuit and pulled it open. He looked at Ketahn. "*Mah dess tee* is all about comfort and *aygen see*. It's different for everyone, you know?"

He pulled his arms free of the jumpsuit's sleeves and shoved it down. He was also wearing the white undergarments beneath. As he stepped out of the jumpsuit, he continued, "And that's always been the problem back on Earth. Too many people *projekting* their *moralitee* onto others, trying to make them feel ashamed for who they are. For their bodies, for their confidence, for who they love." His eyes flicked toward Will, who was still turned away, for an instant.

"And it's all a bunch of bullshit." Cole sank down until the water reached his chin. "Just a bunch of different ways to divide us up."

Diego kicked his jumpsuit aside and pulled his shirt off over his head. "Yeah, pretty much. Our species sure has a talent for bullshit."

Ketahn translated for his friends as well as he could, but he didn't understand everything himself. This was a glimpse into human ways like he'd never quite had—and he knew so much was missing from that glimpse. But it was something. It was a tiny bit more insight into his mate and the world in which she'd lived.

"They have strange ways," Urkot said.

Telok lowered himself atop the boulder, dipping his legs into the water. "Our ways must be just as strange to them."

Diego shoved down the white undergarments, exposing his stem. Like Cole's, it hung in the open air between his legs, though his emerged from a patch of dark hair.

Rekosh trilled and narrowed his eyes. "While we are speaking of strange..."

Urkot grunted, staring along with Rekosh.

"Come on, Will." Diego beckoned with one hand and walked into the stream. "Don't be shy."

Will glanced at Diego over his shoulder. His eyes rounded, and his tongue emerged to sweep across his lips. "I, uh... I'm good, guys. Really."

"There's that knack for bullshit Diego was talking about!" Cole called. He'd moved to the middle of the stream, where he was swimming against the lazy current.

"You don't have anything we haven't seen before," Diego said with a grin.

Clearly those words did not apply to the vrix.

"Come on!" Cole ducked his head under water. When he emerged, his pale hair hung in his face. He whipped it away, spraying water into the air.

Nose holes flaring with a heavy exhalation, Will looked at Ketahn for support. There was something in his expression that ran deeper than human *mah dess tee*. Perhaps Ivy would have been able to identify it, but Ketahn could not.

Ketahn strode forward, removed his bags, and set them on

the ground with the other supplies. He said in English, "I cannot choose for you, Will."

Urkot thumped a leg on the ground. "Are we joining them?"

Ketahn chittered. "I cannot choose for you either, Urkot."

"Get in! The more the merrier," Cole said, lifting a hand out of the water to wave. "Plenty of room for all you big bastards."

Diego reached the deeper water and sank into it with a sigh. "That's quite a change of tune, Cole."

Will turned back toward the stream and folded his arms over his chest. "Yeah. Haven't you been all *humans gotta stick together, we don't need no aliens* this whole time?"

"Sorry, Will, can't hear you from all the way out here," Cole replied. "You'll have to get in the water!"

Pressing his lips together, Will huffed. His already rigid posture stiffened further, and his fingers pressed into his arms, depressing the jumpsuit's fabric. He tapped his foot on the ground in a gesture reminiscent of vrix thumping their legs.

Ketahn stepped into the stream. The recent rains had left the water cooler than usual, making it a welcome relief from the heat of the unimpeded sunshine.

Diego let out a contented sigh and tipped his head back. "At this rate, the stream will dry up before you ever get in."

"Fine." Will swallowed and set his hands to opening the jumpsuit, fingers shaking slightly. "You guys win. You happy?"

"Yup. You will be too once you get in the water," said Cole.

Will kicked off his boots and turned away from Diego and Cole to remove his clothing, grumbling to himself. Rekosh added his supplies to the pile and entered the water near Ketahn, glancing back at Will several times as he moved.

"Staring will not help him, Rekosh," Ketahn said as he lowered himself into the stream. He could feel the gently flowing water lifting the dirt of the day's travel off his hide and carrying it away.

Though it felt good, he much preferred when it was his mate's hands cleaning him.

"I cannot deny my curiosity," Rekosh replied.

"They look small and soft," Telok said.

Urkot trudged into the water. Despite days of rain and having been away from Takarahl's tunnels for so long, his hands and lower legs retained that faded look. Stone dust must have become part of his hide during his time as a delver.

On the bank, Will removed his underclothing, gathered it up along with his jumpsuit, and set them atop his bag. His shoulders rose with a deep breath. After slowly exhaling, he turned around. Unlike Diego's, Will's body had no hair.

Urkot tilted his head. "Do their stems always hang like that?"

A crease formed between Will's eyebrows, and he frowned. "You guys are really weirding me out."

Cole stood up and took a few steps toward the bank. "Just get in the water already, William!"

"I cannot imagine my stem always being out," said Telok. "Too vulnerable."

Lifting a hand, Will gestured toward Ketahn and the other vrix. "They're saying *zirkita*. They're talking about my—" His eyes widened, and he dropped them to his now exposed stem. He covered his pelvis with a muttered curse and twisted away.

Ketahn chittered, and Cole and Diego laughed.

"Finally, you say the right word," Ketahn said.

Diego grinned, but his eyes softened the expression. "Just think about all the times we've stared at the vrix, Will. We need to remember that we look as alien to them as they do to us." He waded to the bank, water streaming down his light brown skin as he emerged from it. He made no effort to cover himself. "They've been walking around naked this whole time."

His stem looked different. A little smaller than it had been, perhaps, and the strange, fleshy pouch under it was more compact now.

"That doesn't—" Will looked at Diego, gaze dipping briefly. Again his tongue slipped out to slide across his lips. "Doesn't, um...help."

"Would it help if I said you don't have anything to be embarrassed about?"

Will didn't look away from Diego, and there was a hint of something in his gaze again, something familiar but which Ketahn couldn't quite identify. After some more gentle coaxing, Will followed Diego into the stream.

"About fucking time," Cole said, lying back to float on the surface.

"I'm in now." Will splashed water in Cole's direction. "So you going to answer my question? I'm not going to complain about this change in your attitude, but even you have to admit it's pretty jarring."

Cole blew out through his lips, spraying mist into the air. "What, about the vrix?"

"Yeah."

"It's just... After all the shit that's happened, I guess I just figure they're all we got, right? Mad as I am about Ella, I know deep down, like in the bottom of my heart, they don't mean to hurt us. And I don't want to see anyone else get hurt, so...peace and love or whatever. They're pretty cool in their own ways."

"I'm shocked, Cole," Diego said with a grin. "I never would've guessed you have a heart."

Will chuckled. "You think he had one of those *grinch* moments, then?"

"I wouldn't go so far as to say his heart grew three sizes... Maybe by an extra half."

"Ah, fuck you guys." Cole splashed water at the other humans.

"Perhaps their stems are always out as a way to attract mates," Rekosh said, clearly unaware of the nature of the humans' conversation.

Urkot submerged himself to his shoulders and reached down to scrub at his legs. "Then why do they cover themselves?"

Telok grunted and laid his spear over his upper leg segments. "A mate cannot be attracted by a hidden stem. And I do not see how something so small and grub-like could attract *any* females."

"But their females are also small," Rekosh replied. "And they all seem to be soft things. Perhaps that makes them desire other soft things?"

"I cannot imagine my stem swinging freely all the time," said Urkot. "That does not seem safe or comfortable. Does it not hit their legs as they walk?"

Rekosh folded his arms across his chest and drummed his claws in a slow, thoughtful rhythm. "That could be why they cover their stems. To prevent the swinging."

Will let out a shaky breath as he sank down to get his torso into the water. "They're still talking about our dicks."

Laughing, Diego turned toward Ketahn. "What do you guys want to know?"

Ketahn didn't hesitate to relay what his friends had been discussing. Again, Cole and Diego laughed. Even Will chuckled a little, though he still seemed uncomfortable.

Diego explained with good natured patience, introducing new human words—penis, testicles, flaccid, erect, and shrinkage. He explained that their stems swelled with blood when they were aroused.

"Or sometimes when you first wake up," Cole added, dubbing the occurrence *morning wood*.

Ketahn and the vrix did not understand what that had to do with trees. The humans only laughed, long and loud, at the question.

Their humor faltered when Ketahn asked about their stem tendrils and was forced to explain—with a series of hand gestures to demonstrate his words—what he'd meant.

Cole's face scrunched up. "That's fucked up."

Diego made a deep, contemplative hum. "Does that do something for your females?"

Ketahn again used some hand gestures to supplement his human words. "Mating is sometimes a battle, and females may fight. A female can force the male and his seed out of her if she chooses, if she thinks he is not strong or not worthy. The tendrils...caress her inside, to make her open within so his seed may reach her eggs."

"Damn," said Cole. "That sounds, uh...rough."

For the first time, Ketahn found himself wondering what his tendrils did for Ivy. Each time they'd emerged within her, they'd brought her immense pleasure, and he'd not once felt the sort of resistance in his mate that was said to be common in female vrix—and he'd never heard of a male's tendrils bringing a female enjoyment enough to make her scream.

But those thoughts only made him long for his mate even more.

The males continued to wash and swim in the water, using cleanleaf from Telok's bag to scrub themselves. Though the conversation did not die out, it was broken by long periods of silence—but there was an ease in that silence, a comfort and familiarity, that Ketahn wouldn't have imagined possible between vrix and humans an eightday prior.

Even Cole was relaxed and less confrontational than normal, just as Will and Diego had said. Ketahn could not guess what had brought about the change in Cole, but he was glad for it. There were enough threats for the tribe to face without warring amongst themselves, and Cole had fed much of the unease between vrix and human. Over the last few days, however, he had been more...thoughtful. More restrained. Quieter, and slower to anger.

The quiet and serenity was shattered when Rekosh asked, "What is it like to mate with a human female, Ketahn?"

Ketahn had not been prepared for that question, and he found himself unable to respond immediately. In his silence, a thousand words spun through his mind like the interconnected strands of a web. A thousand words to describe the joy, the pleasure, the sense of rightness when he joined with his mate.

He thought of her warmth and softness. He thought of the way her skin sometimes rose in tiny bumps under the lightest of touches, of how her body responded to his fingers and tongue, and how his words alone could make her slit drip. In his mind's eye, he saw that gleam in her eyes, equally hungry and loving, saw the color on her cheeks as she gave in to her desires.

He could almost feel her body pressed against his, could almost feel her hot, slick walls bearing down on his stem, drawing him deeper, clutching for more, could almost feel the maddening scrape of her nails across his hide.

His desire roared into a blaze at his core. His stem pressed against the inside of his slit, and his blood ran hot despite the cool water surrounding him. By the Eight, how he hungered for Ivy.

And she was his. All those sensations, all those experiences, had been her gifts to Ketahn, shared with him and him alone. They were for no one else.

Ketahn's mandibles rose. "Unlike anything."

However simple, however vague, however inadequate, those words were undeniably true. And they were what finally pushed his yearning beyond his control. For too long, he'd denied himself his mate. Fear, loss, rage, and desperation had pushed him onward, and they had obscured his reason for doing all this—Ivy.

Even as the other vrix asked him to tell more, Ketahn stood and strode to the bank. He barely noticed the cool breeze flowing over his wet hide, barely felt his fine hairs standing, barely felt the rivulets trickling down his body. His hearts thumped heavily despite his lack of exertion, and his stem pulsed, held in only by his claspers—which itched to hook around Ivy's hips and tug her close.

But as he walked in the direction the females had gone, he did hear Telok chitter and say, "That must mean it is good. Very, very good."

CHAPTER 16

Ivy cast a longing glance back at the stream as she and the other women dressed. They'd sat on that boulder for as long as they could, soaking up the sunshine, talking, laughing, and attempting to learn more vrix words while teaching Ahnset English. It'd been fun. It'd been rejuvenating.

It'd been what they'd all needed.

Ivy's skin was sun-warmed, her hair loose and dry, and her limbs relaxed. She was thankful they'd had this time, for tomorrow they would again be running for their lives.

The hair on the back of her neck rose.

Ivy stilled as she was bending to retrieve her jumpsuit, turning her eyes toward the jungle ahead. She hadn't heard anything out of the ordinary, but she sensed something there, watching, waiting. She couldn't explain it. Her brow creased, and her skin prickled in awareness.

There's nothing there, Ivy. You're thinking of the queen and getting paranoid. They couldn't have caught up to us already.

Could they?

It was likely just some curious beastie checking out the humans.

"Hey Ivy, can I ask you something?" Lacey said.

The question snapped Ivy out of her thoughts and made her start. Reflexively plucking up her jumpsuit and bringing it up to her chest, she looked at Lacey. "Yeah, sure."

Lacey, already dressed, adjusted the strap of her bag on her shoulder. Indecision warred upon her face. She opened her mouth, closed it with a frown, then ran a hand through her long, damp hair before finally speaking. "If you had known what was going to happen before you boarded the *Somnium*, would you still have done it?"

Would I have?

The answer came to Ivy without hesitation. "Yes."

"Wow. Didn't even need to think about it, huh?" Callie asked.

"My life on Earth wasn't a happy one. I had nothing there, had no one. But here, I found happiness. It's not easy, but I have…"

"Ketahn."

Ivy smiled, and her voice softened when she said, "Yeah. I have Ketahn."

Ahnset, who was standing a little apart from the others with spear in hand, turned her face toward the jungle and scanned the foliage. Her mandibles twitched restlessly.

Callie chuckled as she sealed her jumpsuit. "Never in my life did I think I'd ever hear a woman say they were happy having sex with a spider."

Ivy laughed, shaking her head. "Vrix, not spider."

Callie waved her hand nonchalantly, "Yeah, yeah." She looked around. "I'm glad you found something here. I don't know if I could answer that question in the same way. This… isn't exactly what I dreamed of doing."

"Same," Ahmya said, slipping her feet into her boots.

"What about you, Lacey?"

Lacey stared down at the ground, browed deeply furrowed.

"I don't know. I...think I would have." She shifted her gaze up to meet Ivy's. "Earth was shit for me too. But this place... I don't know."

Ivy offered her an encouraging smile. "We'll make a place for us here. We'll make a home."

Lacey's lips curled into a small smile, and she nodded.

"Not like we have a choice," Callie said, "but we might as well make the best of it. It could have been worse."

Ahmya cocked her head. "How so?"

"We could have landed on some ice planet. Least the weather is nice enough here for skinny dipping."

The women laughed, and Ivy smiled. It felt wonderful to talk and joke so easily with them.

Family. This was her new family, her real family, brought together not by blood but by circumstance, bonded by tragedy and shared struggle. And she felt closer to them than she ever had to anyone in her life—anyone apart from Ketahn. She was more grateful for them than she could ever express.

Callie grinned. "Should we prank the guys and steal their clothes?"

Lacey snorted. "Something tells me Cole wouldn't care. He'd strut around with his dick hanging—"

Leaves shook nearby.

Faster than Ivy could perceive, Ahnset darted forward, placing herself between the women and the source of the sound with her spear at the ready. Her body was rigid, and the hairs on her legs stood on end. But she lowered her spear as a dark figure emerged from the greenery before her.

"Why did you not announce yourself, broodbrother?" Ahnset demanded, tension lingering in her posture.

Ketahn's eyes, shining violet in the bright sunlight, were fixed upon Ivy. He stalked toward her without slowing, not even casting a glance at his sister as she stepped aside and growled.

Ivy's brow creased, and she clutched her jumpsuit to her chest. "Ketahn? Is something wr—ah!"

He dropped his upper hands to her hips and plucked her off the ground like she weighed nothing. Ivy's world tilted as he slung her over his shoulder. She flung her arms out to flatten her palms on his back and brace herself, dropping her jumpsuit in the process. Her hair fell all around her face, obscuring her view with a curtain of golden locks.

Ivy turned her head, blowing hair from her face as she tried to push herself up. "Ketahn, what are you doing?"

A large, rough hand smoothed up her thigh to grip her bare ass, holding her in place. "I have need of you, female."

Those words sent a blast of heat straight to her core and stole the air from her lungs. Her sex clenched. All those earlier sensations, those cravings she'd had while in his arms, came rushing back tenfold.

"Wow. I...can't say I'm not jealous of that," Lacey said.

"No kidding," Callie replied. "He's like...Tarzan but with extra legs and stuff."

Ketahn pressed the tips of his claws against Ivy's skin, producing thrilling pricks. "Bring her things to camp, Ahnset. We will return before suncrest."

Then he was in motion, carrying her away from the stream in that smooth, quick stride. Ivy managed to lift a hand and sweep her hair aside.

The other women were watching her—Ahmya with red-stained cheeks and rounded eyes, Lacey and Callie with knowing grins. But they soon disappeared from view.

Ivy returned her hand to Ketahn's back and twisted to look toward him. His hold on her only strengthened as he added another hand, curling his fingers around her inner thigh, one of which grazed her pussy and made her breath hitch. He rumbled and lifted that digit again, deliberately stroking her sensitive flesh with his knuckle.

"It was you watching me, wasn't it?" she asked.

He turned his face toward her and breathed in deep. "Yes."

"I felt something out there. But I didn't..." Her eyes narrowed as she recalled that she hadn't been alone beside the stream. She wriggled on his shoulder in an attempt to get down. "You creep! You were watching us!"

He smacked her ass, making Ivy hiss. Though the sting was brief, it left a heat that seeped into her and turned to liquid between her thighs. Ketahn soothed the hurt he'd caused with a calloused palm.

"I beheld only you, my Ivy, my heartsthread, my brightest light." He grasped her hips, his hands nearly encircling her fully, and lifted her off his shoulder.

He slid her down the front of his body, her softness against his hardness, and the rasp of her nipples over his hide made her shiver. Once her feet were on the ground, Ketahn's claspers hooked around her hips, and he produced a low trill as he again inhaled deeply. Ivy tipped her head back.

Ravenous eyes boring into hers, Ketahn brushed a foreleg along her inner calf.

Ivy reached up with both hands and slipped her fingers into his hair. She stood on her toes as she pulled his head down, bringing their mouths together. Desperate to taste more of him, she parted her lips, and he obliged by slipping his long tongue into her mouth.

Her eyelids fell shut, and she pulled herself into his embrace, letting his strong hands hold her upright when her knees felt weak. But all too soon he withdrew his tongue, all too soon he pulled his mouth away. She whimpered in need and moved her head to follow.

One of his hands caught her hair and tugged her head back, exposing her neck. With a low, hungry growl, he ravaged her throat and the underside of her jaw with his hard mouth and clever tongue. His slit parted against her belly, and the firm, slick head of his cock pressed against her skin, radiating heat and thrumming with the beating of his hearts.

Ketahn's mouth trekked downward, and soon his tongue was upon her breasts. Ivy moaned as she gripped his hair. He twirled that tongue around her aching nipples, and her back arched reflexively as sparks of pleasure raced through her, each stronger than the last. That delightful, torturous sensation was already building at her core, the one that made her belly flutter and her toes curl, the one she desired so much—but only with him, only from him.

But Ivy wanted—*craved*—more. She was so wet that her arousal dripped down her inner thighs.

Ketahn slipped one of his lower hands around her backside and up, again brushing her sex. But he did not relent this time. That finger stroked her slowly, teasingly, gathering and spreading her essence. It trembled with the same consuming need that drove her. Another of his lower hands slid up her torso to cup her other breast. He used the pad of his calloused thumb to knead her nipple, lavishing the sensitive bud.

Ivy closed her eyes and gave in to the pleasure he bestowed upon her. It'd been so long, too long, since she'd felt his intimate touch. She caught her bottom lip between her teeth, muffling her moans as her body rocked in time with the strokes of his fingers, and pulled his head closer as he took her nipple into his mouth. The sensations were stronger than ever before, sending bolts of desire straight to her core. Her breath hitched and her hips bucked when his sharp teeth bit down on the tender flesh of her breast, but he soothed the pain with a curl of his sinful tongue.

"Ketahn." Ivy opened her heavy-lidded eyes. "I need you. Now."

Ketahn's hold on her tightened. He pressed his headcrest to her chest, and his breath was hot on her skin when he growled, "I yearn for you."

Sliding his hands from her hips to her ass, he straightened, drew his forelegs closer, and was about to lift her when she dropped a hand to his arm, stopping him. His eyes met hers.

Ivy twirled a strand of his hair around her finger before running her fingertip along his jaw. "Lie on your back for me."

He tilted his head. "I do not understand."

She smiled, released his hair, and traced the hard seam of his mouth. "I want to claim you."

His claspers drew her closer still, and more of his cock emerged from his slit. It was throbbing, slickened steel, and its heat pulsed into her, only enhancing the needy ache at her core. His low chitter was absolutely devilish. "My little mate means to claim me?"

The seductive purr in his voice nearly undid Ivy then and there. She battled the urge to lift her hips and slam herself down on his shaft, to take him without care for how, but her desire to put her claim upon him this way won out.

Ivy leaned toward him until her lips were a hair's breadth away from his. "Yes."

A shuddering breath escaped him. He opened his mouth, giving her a glimpse of those wicked fangs and his long, purple tongue.

"I cannot overpower you," she whispered, "but I will conquer you all the same."

"Ah, my *nyleea*..." His tongue slipped out to tease the corner of her mouth. "You already have."

Keeping her eyes locked with his, she smoothed a hand down his chest and abdomen until she reached his slit. She traced its outer ridges with her fingers before dipping her hand farther to wrap around the base of his shaft. "Then surrender to me, Kethan, my *luveen*." She stroked him once, twice, thrice, taking pleasure as he shuddered anew and released a harsh hiss in response to her touch. "Let me claim you."

He squeezed her ass, pulling her more firmly against him as

he pumped his hips. She felt desire emanating from him, felt him struggling against his need, against the instinctual frenzy that often overtook him. Part of her hungered for that.

But just as it seemed he was about to succumb, he let her go and withdrew, claws grazing her skin in a final, fleeting attempt to maintain contact. His blazing eyes locked with hers as he lowered himself onto the ground and lay back, propping himself on his lower arms, and bent his spindly legs to either side. His extruded shaft twitched in the air, glistening with oils.

She'd never imagined seeing Ketahn like this, sprawled out before her, surrendering himself to her—ceding control. And God, he was beautiful. All those things she'd once thought monstrous had become things she loved, and she cherished every bit of his body. There was such grace in his form, such strength. But it was always the fire in his eyes that drew her back again and again. That fire, that passion, possessiveness, kindness, and desire, would draw her in forever.

Ivy stepped over Ketahn, positioning herself above his belly. His claspers were already reaching toward her. As she lowered herself, Ketahn drew his torso upright to meet her. She placed her hands on his shoulders and pushed him back until he was fully lying on the ground again. Thighs to either side of his waist, she settled atop his abdomen.

His body was hard and hot, everything she wanted, and her sex thrummed against him. Ketahn's cock, hotter still, was nestled along her ass, and his claspers were struggling to grasp her—but they couldn't reach.

Ketahn moved his upper hands to her hips. Ivy grabbed his wrists and pulled his arms away, leaning forward to guide them over his head and onto the ground. Denying his touch like this was difficult, so damned difficult, but she knew it would pay off. She knew it would heighten every sensation to come.

That didn't make it any easier to endure the void inside her, which only he could fill.

Ivy curled his fingers around some roots jutting from the dirt. "Hold these."

Ketahn grasped the roots, his mandibles spreading to brush the sides of her breasts. He ran his tongue up the valley between them. "And my lower hands?"

Those lower hands touched her knees and trailed along the outsides of her calves, teasing her with their claws, leaving thrilling tingles in their wake.

She sat back, lifted one knee off the ground, and settled it atop his lower forearm, pinning it in place, and then repeated the movement for the other. "You are bound, my *luveen*. You are conquered."

"I am yours, my *nyleea*," Ketahn rasped. Faint tremors ran through his body, each of which roused a new spark of pleasure in her pussy.

Barely holding in a moan, Ivy placed a hand on Ketahn's chest. She raked his hide with her nails, teasing him just as he'd teased her, and leaned her weight on that arm. As she lifted her hips, she reached down with her other hand, trailing it across the hard ridges of his abdomen until it reached the apex of his slit. Her fingers dipped within and skimmed the bulging base of his shaft before she grasped it. Ketahn grunted. She angled the tip of his cock to her entrance. She was already dripping wet, needing him, aching for him.

Ivy stared into his passion-filled eyes. "You are mine, Ketahn. You will always be mine."

And then she pressed her pussy down, taking his cock into her body. A sound spilled past her lips, a blend of pleasure and pain, and she bit her bottom lip as she forced herself to take more of him. Despite her arousal, despite the natural oils coating his shaft, his sheer girth always stretched her upon entry.

Ketahn closed his eyes, tipped his chin up, and growled as a shiver coursed through him. His body tensed and strained beneath her as though he were holding himself back from taking control. "Ivy…"

Flattening her palms on his chest, Ivy slammed her hips down, seating herself completely. She gasped. Ketahn filled that emptiness inside her; he filled her to bursting, heart, body, and soul, and she still wanted more, still needed more of him. She could feel the rapid, pulsing beats of his hearts in her core.

He pulled his lower arms out from beneath her knees effortlessly. That little drop to the ground only sent him deeper, wringing another gasp from Ivy, and she curled her fingers against his chest.

Ketahn's hands settled on her thighs and smoothed up toward her hips. He lifted his head, briefly meeting her gaze before his attention dipped to the place where their bodies were connected. The spark in his eyes swirled into an inferno. His claspers hooked around her ass and pulled her even more firmly against him, and his hips twitched up. Every movement, however slight, teased her with fresh pleasure that threatened to steal her breath and shatter her mind.

Ivy lifted herself, relishing the slow drag of his cock along her inner walls and the greater width toward the top of his shaft, before dropping back down again. She moaned. In this position, he felt bigger, and he stroked her in ways that wildly amplified her burning need. She set to riding him slowly, wanting to feel every inch of him as he slid in and out, wanting to take him deeper and deeper yet never able to take him deep enough.

A thrill flitted through her core and spread outward, encompassing her until every bit of her skin tingled with awareness—she felt the tiny droplets of sweat trickling over her flesh, felt the kiss of the humid air, felt the heat and power radiating from her mate, felt their love crackling in the air like lightning.

The roots cracked in Ketahn's grip. He growled, rough and

long, and dropped his head back, squeezing his eyes shut. The vibration of that growl thrummed between Ivy's legs, stimulating her clit. To either side, his legs scraped the ground. His fingers flexed on her hips, his claws biting and cutting, but Ivy didn't care. The pain only added to the ecstasy coursing through her veins like liquid fire.

She quickened her pace, unable to deny her desire. Unable to deny her consuming need for her mate—for all of him. Her breath came in short, ragged pants, her heart raced, and the tingling on her skin intensified as she came down upon him again and again, as she marked him with her fingernails and her scent, as she rode faster and faster and her desperation increased.

"Ketahn," she rasped. Her thighs quivered, and her sex tightened around his cock. She was there, *right there*, but her release was trapped behind this utter, merciless ecstasy.

Ketahn snarled, and the tension within him increased tenfold. She heard the roots snap, saw dirt and dead leaves fly into the air, and she welcomed him as he sat up. His upper hands hooked under her thighs while the other pair dropped from her hips to her ass, kneading and caressing as he pushed her on harder still. His every breath came with a guttural, ravenous grunt.

And despite his frenzy, despite his lust, he tipped his headcrest against her forehead with tenderness and stared into her eyes. Stared into her soul.

This new position brought their chests together. The friction of his hide against Ivy's nipples added a maddening layer to her pleasure that made her body feel like it was melting into his. Her every muscle trembled, and her breaths were too shallow to fill her lungs, but there was no room for air when she was so full of him. Her Ketahn, her mate, her *luveen*, her love.

Her heartsthread.

Heat erupted between her legs and consumed her wholly. She cried out, clutching at him, as those flames licked every nerve, stoking her pleasure higher and higher, and she lost herself to rapture.

As she lost herself to the feel of him.

Ketahn's world was his mate. Her warmth, softness, passion, and scent. Her breath was his air, her sounds his music, her body...*his*.

Ivy shuddered in his arms, her sex fluttering and constricting around his stem. Her essence flowed freely, coating his hide, marking him with her scent, driving him beyond pleasure, beyond thought, beyond everything. And all the while his peak eluded him, taunted him, mocked him with its long absence.

He needed more. Needed to seize control, to take what she so wanted to give him.

With a snarl, Ketahn rolled aside, reversing his position with his mate. His forelegs lashed out and slammed down on the ground to either side of her. One of his upper hands caught her wrists and pinned them over her head. He angled her hips up and drove into her, claspers latching onto her thighs to deny her escape as she cried out in a second climax.

Ivy's pale skin was tinted pink, her kiss-swollen lips were parted, and her half-lidded eyes shone with lustful light as they stared up at him. Her sex squeezed his stem, her thighs squeezed his hips, and she arched her back, lifting her breasts toward him.

"Ketahn," she breathed.

The pleasure gathering at his core was too much; it threatened to destroy him, to tear apart his spirit and mind, and he welcomed it. He craved it. He needed it. He thrust into her faster, harder, his grip on her tightening with each pump of his hips, the tips of his legs sinking a little deeper into the ground.

The mating frenzy had seized him, and he could not stop. He didn't want to. Ivy's strained cries in response to his pounding thrusts told Ketahn she didn't want him to stop either.

Ketahn hammered into her deeper than ever, forcing her to take all of him, and snarled, "Mine!"

His body convulsed. Ecstasy forced him to bend forward, torso curling over his mate, as his rear legs dug in for purchase. He slammed into her one final time. Scalding seed swelled his stem just as his mouth brushed over Ivy's shoulder. His seed erupted inside her, and he bit down.

A gasp burst from Ivy, followed by a scream. Ketahn's tendrils vibrating and caressed deep inside her sex. Quivering, she wrapped her legs around his sides and dug her heels into his back. She ground her sex against his slit as her cries filled the jungle.

He shuddered again and growled against Ivy's shoulder, his claspers locking her in place as her movements coaxed out more of his seed.

He held her like that until the haze of the mating frenzy left him and the last of his tremors faded. He loosened his jaw, releasing her shoulder from his mouth but not lifting his head away. There was a strange taste on his tongue—it seemed familiar, but he could not name it.

Ivy's body relaxed beneath him, and her legs fell away to either side, dangling limply over his. She hummed contently. Her fingertips brushed his hand, which still held her wrists.

"Mmm, I love it when you miss me," she purred as she turned her face to kiss his headcrest.

Ketahn breathed in her scent, and the air caught in his chest.

He smelled blood.

He *tasted* blood.

With a hiss, he let go of her wrists and shoved himself

upright, eyes falling immediately upon her shoulder. Blood welled from the distinct marks left by his sharp teeth.

"What have I done?" Raising his hindquarters off the ground, he hastily drew silk from his spinnerets and gathered it into a sticky wad with his back legs before passing it to his hand. "I am sorry, my heartsthread. I did not mean to harm you."

Ivy's brow furrowed as she watched him apply the silk to the bite mark. "You bit me? I...don't even remember you doing it." She chuckled and looked up at him. "I guess I was distracted."

Once the last of the tiny wounds was sealed, Ketahn gently covered her shoulder with his palm. Her skin was warm and sweat dampened, and her heartbeat was steady and calm despite what he'd done.

"I gave you my word, Ivy. That I would never harm you."

She settled a hand over his. "Ketahn, it's fine. *I'm* fine. I don't even really feel it. I mean, I'm sure it'll sting later, but...I kind of like it. It's not like I haven't bitten you while lost in the moment." She frowned. "Is it...wrong of me to like it? To want your mark on me for others to see?"

His mandibles fell, and his heartsthread pulled taut in his chest. He cupped her cheek with another hand and stroked his thumb over her soft skin. "No, my *nyleea*. It is not wrong."

Lifting her other arm, she skimmed his mandible with her fingers before stroking along his jaw. Once more, her lips curled into a smile. "Then don't feel guilty for it. I'm stronger than I look, Ketahn. I'm not going to break with a little rough sex. And this love bite was *so* worth it."

Ketahn trilled and rubbed the seam of his mouth across her lips. Her words had eased the pressure in his chest, leaving only the elation of what they'd just shared.

She kissed him and grinned. "Also, it's not like you were going to eat me, right?"

"Ah, but I told you I would not eat you before I had a real taste, human..." He slipped his tongue out; she parted her lips and accepted it into her mouth, meeting it with her own tongue in a slow, sensual dance.

He broke the kiss reluctantly, lifting his face away from hers. Even more reluctantly, his claspers released her, and he withdrew his stem from her hot sex. He regretted both actions immediately. He missed her taste, her heat, the snug embrace of her body, missed it all enough to growl at the loss. Worse, his seed spilled from her slit and dripped onto the ground.

Instinct demanded that his seed remain inside her. It needed to take root, to sprout—and his instincts did not care that she was human and he was vrix.

He cupped her sex, using a finger to push his seed back inside. Ivy's breath hitched, and she arched into his touch. Before she could react further, Ketahn rolled onto his back, dragging her with him to lay her face up atop him with his hand still between her thighs. His claspers secured themselves around her hips.

Ivy sighed and relaxed atop him. She slipped a hand up and tangled her fingers in his hair while smoothing her other palm along his arm until it rested on the hand between her legs. "I missed this. I missed us."

Wrapping an arm around her middle to clamp her in place, Ketahn let his two free hands roam over her body in light, leisurely touches, relishing the times when her flesh raised in tiny bumps or she shivered in delight. "As did I. To have you so close and yet always out of reach..."

This was what he'd needed, this connection.

He'd needed her.

Though it had only been days since he'd escaped Takarahl, it felt like he'd spent years apart from Ivy, and each day had weighed upon him eightfold more than the last. All he'd wanted to do since returning to Ivy was hold her, be with her...lose himself in her. But the tribe's survival had taken priority. Because the tribe's safety was Ivy's safety, their security was her security. And he needed her as far away from Takarahl and the queen as she could get.

To finally have these precious moments alone with her... This meant everything. Their connection was only stronger for the time apart, was only more solid for the trials they'd faced. They were not nearly far enough away for his comfort, and they still had so much distance to travel, but another day without *this* would have pushed Ketahn to madness.

One of his hands slid up her belly and covered her breast, squeezing the yielding flesh appreciatively. His stem stirred behind his slit, and his claspers twitched. He did not understand how he could be so satisfied and yet so hungry at the same time —but such was his relationship with Ivy. He could never be more content than when he was with her, and he would never have enough. He would ever thirst for more.

Ivy moaned, arching to press her breast into his palm, and rocked her pelvis against his fingers. She chuckled. "So much for bathing."

"The stream has not run dry," Ketahn purred, curling his finger into her folds. He found that little nub that brought her such pleasure and slowly circled it. "And I am not ready to return to the others. This time belongs to us."

Her breath quickened as her knees fell wide open. "Won't they wonder where we're at?"

"They know. They all know." He turned his head and nuzzled her hair, drawing in her scent. It had changed over the last several days, becoming stronger, sweeter, fuller. It was even more enticing than he'd ever dreamed possible. His stem pushed out, sliding between her inner thighs and along her slit. The heat from her core pulsed into it, producing a low growl in his chest. He didn't try to fight it. "And if they did not know...I will make sure your cries carry to them."

Ivy tilted her head back and closed her eyes, clutching his

hand. Her hips undulated against his finger as her essence flowed. "Ketahn...I need you."

"Yes," he hissed. Grasping his stem, Ketahn guided it to Ivy's sex and pushed in deep, thrilling in her tight, wet heat and the moan that escaped her lips. "Claim your mate once more, my heartsthread."

CHAPTER 17

A STABBING PAIN in Ivy's pelvis jolted her awake. She whimpered, dug her fingers into Ketahn's chest, and drew her knees up as the pain intensified. Brow creasing, she opened her eyes. Everything was dark. Rain drummed atop the shelter they'd constructed of leaves, branches, and silk, falling just as heavily as it had been when Ivy lay down with Ketahn to sleep yesterday evening.

She sucked in one deep breath after another, releasing each slowly, shakily, hoping they would dull the cramping. They didn't. Nausea twisted in her belly.

Ivy squeezed her eyes shut. The pain flared, becoming so strong that she couldn't hold back a cry as she shifted onto her side, curled up, and banded an arm around her middle.

Ketahn stirred beneath Ivy, his arms tightening around her. He raised his head. "Ivy?" His voice was thick and gravelly with sleep, but there was already concern within it.

"It hurts," she rasped against his hide, pressing her forehead to his chest.

His chest rumbled uncertainly, and he eased his embrace, stroking his claws through her hair. "What hurts, my *nyleea?*"

TIFFANY ROBERTS

Bile rose in her throat. She clenched her teeth and shoved at Ketahn's arms, breaking his hold and scrambling off him to hurry blindly toward the shelter's opening.

Rain poured down on her, trickling into the open collar of her jumpsuit to run over her skin, as she crawled out of the shelter and forced herself upright. She had only taken a few steps before she doubled over, hugging her belly, and vomited. Acid burned her throat, a harsh contrast to the freezing raindrops pelting her.

One of Ketahn's hands settled on her back, while two others gathered her loose, soaked hair and pulled it out of her face. He said something in a very low voice that was swallowed by the sound of the rain—her name, perhaps, or *my mate*.

Spitting the foulness from her mouth, Ivy cried.

Ketahn looped an arm around her and pulled her against his side, accepting most of her weight against his body. "Please, Ivy. Not this. Not again."

"I-I don't know w-what's wrong. It feels like s-something is tearing me apart inside."

His fingers flexed on her back, claws pricking her skin, as he snarled something in vrix she couldn't make out. He twisted away from her to look back.

"Diego," Ketahn barked before leaning his body over Ivy's. "Come out of the rain, my heartsthread."

Ivy took a few breaths, waiting for the nausea to resurge; thankfully it didn't. "Okay."

Ketahn scooped Ivy into his arms, clutched her against his chest, and turned to the shelter. One of the solar lanterns was on within, bathing the space in a cool white glow that made the water outside sparkle with reflected light.

Ducking down to fit under the roof, Ketahn carried Ivy inside. Diego was already awake, spreading a blanket on the ground beside the lantern. He glanced at Ivy as Ketahn brought her closer.

"Need to get those wet clothes off her," Diego said, holding up second blanket. When Ketahn growled in response, Diego continued, "She's freezing and soaked, man. Whatever's going on, that's not going to help. You can cover her with this."

Ketahn held Ivy just a little closer, but ultimately, he loosened his grip to help remove her jumpsuit. She was trembling with her teeth chattering when she reached for the blanket Diego offered. Once it was wrapped around her, Ketahn laid her down atop the other blanket Diego had prepared. She was only vaguely aware of the others being awake and watching her with worried expressions.

Diego settled a dry, cool hand over her forehead, then her cheek. "You're a little warm." Eyebrows lowering, he tilted his head, frowned, and touched his fingertips to Ivy's shoulder beside the web-sealed bite mark. "What's this?"

"My mark," Ketahn growled.

Diego's eyebrows rose. "Oh. I, uh…all right then. Doesn't look infected at least." He cleared his throat and took hold of her wrist instead, checking her pulse. "So what's going on, Ivy?"

"Pain." She pressed a hand over her pelvis. "Here."

"What kind of pain?"

"Sharp. I…I've felt it before, but not l-like this."

Diego frowned and hovered his hands over her lower body. "May I?"

Ivy nodded, letting her arm fall to the side.

He lowered his hands and pressed his fingers on her lower abdomen. Ivy grunted, gritted her teeth, and took in a deep, shaky breath. He worked his fingers lower.

Ketahn caught Diego's wrist with a snarl. The hairs upon his legs rose, and he vibrated with menace. "What are you doing, human?"

Diego stilled and looked up at Ketahn. "I'm not going to hurt her, but I need to examine her."

Ivy curled her fingers around Ketahn's arm. Her skin looked so pale against his dark hide. "It's okay, my *luveen*."

Ketahn's eyes met hers. The white light made their violet so much brighter, which only enhanced the helplessness glimmering in their depths. This was the same way he'd looked when she was sick after eating sweetfang root weeks before. He would stand against any beast in the jungle for her, no matter how dangerous, and she had no doubt that he would find a way to triumph...but he couldn't do anything here, and that was crushing to him.

He released Diego's arm with a frustrated huff. Ivy slid her hand into Ketahn's and laced her fingers with his. He tightened his grip—not enough to hurt, but enough to tell Ivy that he was willing his strength into her as he settled down beside her.

Diego resumed his exam, pressing against her belly and pelvis firmly. "There's some swelling here. When was your last menstrual cycle?"

"I...I had some bleeding a few days ago. I th-thought it was my period, but i-it only lasted a day."

"When was your last one before that?"

Ivy might've laughed if not for the agony gripping her. "A hundred and sixty-eight years ago."

He sat back on his heels. "You haven't had one yet?"

"No, I thought it was the s-stasis."

"It could be that..." Uncertainty crossed his features, and he flicked a glance at Ketahn. "What else are you feeling?"

"I'm a little nauseous still."

"And you haven't had anything strange to eat or drink?"

"No."

Ketahn's mandibles clacked together. "Heal her, Diego."

Diego sighed. "It's not that simple, man."

Ketahn leaned toward the human, producing a threatening rumble in his chest. "Make it simple. Heal her."

"Hey, Ketahn..." Will settled a hand on Ketahn's shoulder.

Snarling, Ketahn spun toward Will with fingers splayed, claws at the ready, and forelegs rising.

Ivy's heart stuttered. She pushed herself into a sitting position despite the fresh pain it caused and threw a hand out, grabbing one of Ketahn's wrists. "Stop!"

Ketahn stiffened. His body was hard as stone and just as unmoving for several of Ivy's thumping heartbeats, and with his limbs and mandibles spread, he was a predator out of nightmare, something no human could hope to overcome. Will had stumbled backward and fallen onto his ass, and was now staring up at Ketahn with wide, terrified eyes—but there was determination in his gaze too.

Will swallowed thickly, wet his lips with his tongue, and said, "He'll do his best, Ketahn. I know he will, and so do you. But you have to let him work."

"Just be here w-with me, Ketahn," Ivy said softly, trying to control her shivering. Another twinge in her pelvis had her sucking in a sharp breath. "I know you feel like it's not enough, but it means everything right now."

He remained statue still as moments passed, not breathing, not making a sound. His mandibles moved first—they twitched inward and fell. As soon as they were down, the tension bled from his body. He released a heavy, shuddering breath, brought his forearms together, and bowed his head.

"I am sorry, Will. Sorry to you all."

"I get it," Will replied, sitting forward. "I know what it feels like. But it's like you and Ivy say, right? We're all in this together."

"Yes." Ketahn rose from his apologetic pose and slowly extended a hand to Will. "We are. I did not wish to scare you."

Will nodded again, drew in a deep breath, and accepted Ketahn's hand. Ketahn helped him back onto his feet in a smooth motion that suggested Will's weight was as negligible to him as Ivy's. Then Ketahn turned back to Ivy and Diego, easing down so his underside was on the ground. He took Ivy's hand in his own again and held it with a gentle possessiveness that warmed her heart despite everything.

Clutching the blanket to her chest, Ivy lay back down.

"Do your breasts feel tender?" Diego asked.

Though Ivy was freezing, her cheeks warmed. Ketahn stiffened once more, mandibles flaring, but Ivy squeezed his hand, calming him.

"Yeah," Ivy said. "They've been pretty sensitive lately."

"And you woke from stasis over two months ago?"

"Yes." She pressed her lips together against another flare of pain in her pelvis.

"And given that the days are longer here, it's been more than that. None of these symptoms during that time?"

"No."

Diego glanced at Ketahn. "How long have you and Ketahn been...having sex?"

"W-why? I don't understand why that would make me feel like this. This only began a few days ago."

"Look... THI didn't train any non-crew medical personnel on stasis sickness. This could be part of that. I don't think they fully understood all the potential side effects or how long they might last without the proper attention, and I definitely don't have the equipment to tell for sure. But the symptoms you're describing do match something I *am* trained on."

"What is it?"

"Don't you dare fucking say what I think you're going to say," Callie said from behind Diego, eyes wide.

"I *really* need to stress that I can't tell you this for certain, okay? I need you to understand that it's really impossible to tell at this point without the right equipment." Diego ran a hand through his hair and drew his lips back. "The nausea, the spotting, the pelvic pain, the swelling in your belly, and tender breasts are...are signs of pregnancy, Ivy."

All the air rushed out of Ivy's lungs with a single word. "*What?*"

"Like I said, I can only speculate."

"Jesus," Cole said.

"That is one crazy ass speculation, Diego," Lacey said.

Ivy stared at Diego in shock. She pulled her hand from Ketahn's as she sat up and cradled her belly. Pregnant? "That's..." She shook her head. "No. No. I'm *human*, and Ketahn's a...a..."

Ketahn made an uncertain trill and settled a hand on Ivy's arm. "I do not understand his words, my *nyleea*. What did he say?"

She looked up at Ketahn, searching his inhuman, mask-like face. "He thinks... He thinks I'm pregnant. That you and I..." She angled her head down, scrubbed her palms over her face, and stabbed her fingers through her wet, tangled hair, pulling it back. "A broodling, Ketahn. That you and I made a broodling."

Ketahn stared down at her in utter silence—perhaps the heaviest, most heart-wrenching silence she'd ever endured. Shock and confusion were clear in his eyes, which sought *something* in her gaze, but she couldn't guess what was happening behind them. His mandibles twitched up and sank down, repeating the motions erratically.

She couldn't deny that his silence hurt, even if she completely understood it. Even if it really couldn't have lasted more than a few seconds.

"How?" he rasped. "How... I...do not understand, Ivy." His eyes dipped to her belly, and he tilted his head to the side. "I do not understand. Our... We are different."

"Ketahn?" Rekosh eased closer. "What is wrong with Ivy? We do not know what is being said."

"Diego said Ivy's body has...accepted my seed," Ketahn replied in vrix.

Rekosh's red eyes widened.

Ahnset buzzed, her legs moving restlessly as she looked between Ketahn and Ivy. "But she is human!"

"By their eightfold eyes…" Urkot uttered.

"Don't vrix…lay eggs?" Ahmya asked.

"Oh, my God. No, no, no…" Ivy turned terrified eyes toward Diego as she clutched at her stomach. "Am I? Am I going t-to—" Her breath grew ragged, and her skin tingled as panic seized her.

Eggs? Am I going to lay eggs?

Diego leaned forward and settled his hands on Ivy's shoulders. "Breathe, Ivy. Breathe."

With no small amount of effort, she did as he'd instructed. The air felt thick, and it was a struggle to get it into and out of her lungs, but she did it.

"I want nothing more than to be able to put your worries to rest," Diego said, "but I'm not going to lie to you, okay? I don't know. I don't know what's going to happen, don't know *how* this happened, don't even know if I'm right. All I can promise you is that I will do everything I can—*everything*—to help you through this."

Tears blurred her vision. She was scared; scared of the unknown, scared of what was going to happen, scared…for the thing possibly growing inside her. If Diego was right, if she was truly pregnant, then whatever was in her womb… She didn't know if it was human, or vrix, or something else entirely. All she knew was that it wasn't supposed to exist.

"How is this even possible, Diego?" Ivy asked.

His hands squeezed her shoulders, and he shook his head. "Best guess I have is all the stuff they injected us with. They said it was supposed to hypercharge our immune systems and help us adapt to the environment on Xolea, so maybe…"

"Maybe it was way more effective than they thought?" Callie asked.

"Or we've just pushed it beyond its intent."

"If those compounds did affect us like that, if it can send the human body into a state of adaptation so strong that her body actually changed to accommodate his sperm and procreate..." Callie let out a humorless laugh. "That's so far beyond what they told us it would do that it's criminal."

"I'm not gonna start sprouting extra legs or some shit like that, am I?" Cole demanded.

"Don't be ridiculous, Cole," Lacey said.

"It's a legit question!"

"Could be that adaptive stuff combined with the fertility drugs they pumped us full of," Diego said. "Maybe there was some reaction between the two?"

Callie frowned. "Well, it's not like we were intended to have sex with any aliens. They wanted us to procreate, and well"— she waved at Ivy—"it worked. I mean, *if* she is in fact pregnant."

A shiver stole through Ivy, and she clenched her belly, unable to hold back a whimper as another cramp twisted her insides.

Diego looked back at Ivy. "If that is the case, then you're at the beginning stages of your pregnancy, Ivy, and your body is working to grow new life." He withdrew his hands and sat back with a deep frown. "Or...it's your body trying to reject it. All we can do is wait."

Or...it's your body trying to reject it.

Ivy sucked in a sharp breath as she stared at Diego, tears falling down her cheeks. How could those words strike her so deeply when she feared the very thing she could lose?

Because whatever it was that she might've been carrying within her had been created with Ketahn. Because whatever it was, be it vrix, human or...or both...

It was *her baby.*

It was something made from love.

Tentatively, Ketahn reached toward her, settling a big hand over hers, which were still on her stomach. He'd been so

211

confused, so quiet during the conversation, but as he looked into her eyes now, she saw that familiar passion, that determination, burning in his gaze. He stroked the back of her hand with his thumb. "Our broodling is growing inside you. My heartsthread…"

He bent forward and gathered her in his arms, blanket and all, and drew her snugly against his chest. Dipping his head, he brushed his mouth across her forehead in something between a tender kiss and a nuzzle. "I weave my word into a bond, my *nyleea*. Nothing in this world shall harm you or our broodling. You are the heart that beats outside my chest."

CHAPTER 18

KETAHN BLINKED RAINWATER from his eyes and tugged down the hood of his shroud. The covering had offered little protection over the last few days; it had been long since soaked through. By now he doubted whether it or any of his other belongings would ever be dry again.

The seven days that had passed since Diego voiced his suspicion that Ivy was carrying Ketahn's broodling—that she was *pregnant*—should have been filled with joy and eagerness. Instead, they'd been fraught with uncertainty, struggle, fear, and rain. So much rain. The jungle floor had become one immense, muddy puddle with all manner of debris floating on its murky surface and all sorts of hazards hidden just beneath.

In most places, the water was no deeper than a human's ankle, but that was enough to obscure a root waiting to snag a foot or a depression ready to catch a boot that had been set down with too much weight.

The few respites from the rain had been brief—hardly long enough to wrestle a fire into existence and steal some warmth from the meager flames. The humans had all lost some of the color in their skin, and it was not uncommon to see them shivering or hear the faint clacking of their teeth. Even Ketahn felt the cold by now; it had seeped into every part of him, down into his bones. Only his heartsthread held any heat, and that would never be snuffed out so long as he drew breath.

He longed to have more quiet time with his mate, longed to speak with her of the future, of all the hopes and fears that had arisen with word of a possible broodling. He wanted to talk to Diego to learn what could go wrong. To learn what to expect from all this.

He wanted his tribe's suffering to end.

Ketahn's eyes shifted to Ivy, who walked a couple segments ahead of him. Her gaze was downcast, and she moved with care, testing the ground in front of her with each step. Despite that care, she looked off balance.

She looked exhausted.

And why wouldn't she? There was more than the exertion of travel behind her weariness. Her pain had thankfully subsided the same day it had begun, though it had done so gradually over the course of the morning, but her illness had persisted. Diego and the other humans called it *morning sickness*. The name made little sense to Ketahn; Ivy could be gripped by it at any time of day or night, and nothing could stop her from emptying her stomach once it began.

It was not nearly as bad as her illness after eating sweetfang root, but Ketahn felt echoes of the same helplessness each time she was ill. Especially concerning was how little she'd been eating. She had argued that it was pointless when she felt this way, as the food would end up wasted, but it conflicted with Ketahn's deep instinct to provide for her.

Whether human, vrix, or wild beast, no creature could survive without enough food.

Ivy, like all the other humans, seemed to be driven by willpower alone. The rigors of this journey had drained most of their strength, and the rain had sapped away whatever remained. Now there was just what they called *tenacity*. Now there was just a deep-rooted determination to survive.

He was awed by the humans' willpower even as he wished they had never needed to use it like this.

Ketahn's mandibles fell. He'd helped as much as he could, had taken bags and supplies to lighten the burdens of his companions, had even carried Ivy a few times, but none of it was enough, and some part of him regretted leaving the crashed human ship. At least there, Ivy had had shelter. At least there she'd had warmth.

And by now, she and the other humans would have been trapped in that ship, completely cut off from the Tangle—from fresh food and water. From sunlight, from the wind, from the scents of blossoming flowers and growing plants.

In his hearts, he understood that would have been too much to sacrifice for safety, especially when that safety came with dangers of its own.

He knew little of human offspring, knew little of the way their broodlings—their *babies*—grew, but he knew about vrix eggs. Those eggs needed to be tended. They needed to be kept warm, safe, and still. Many female vrix swathed their eggs in fluffed silk and kept carefully fed spinewood sap fires nearby. Some refused to leave their hatching dens as those eggs developed, eating only when brought food by friends and family.

Having Ivy out here...it was the same as her egg being out here too, exposed to the wind, the rain, the cold, to the mud and filth, to the teeth of every hungry predator in the Tangle. But having her near Takarahl would have been worse.

Having her near the queen would have been far, far worse.

Ahmya cried out up ahead. Ketahn looked toward the sound to see her falling. She landed face down with a splash, sending up muck and water all around her. Her legs bent as she struck the ground, lifting her feet into the air; one was clad in a boot, the other bare.

The humans nearby her moved to help, but Rekosh was faster despite having been farther away. He was at her side before her feet even came down again, sinking low and reaching out with two hands to pull her from the muck.

She came up sputtering. Rekosh held her upright as she coughed out water and mud, her little body shaking.

Hers had not been the first fall, though it looked to have been the worst. Between the many obstacles, the uncertain footing, and the trudging gaits of the increasingly weary humans, Ketahn was only surprised that no one had yet been injured.

Cole crouched near Ahmya and picked up her fallen spear, shedding mud from it with a sharp flick of his wrist. Behind her, Diego bent down to retrieve her boot, which was still standing in the last place she'd set it down. It came free only with some difficulty. When he upturned it, water poured out.

Ketahn turned so he could divide his attention between his companions ahead and the jungle behind. His grip on his spear tightened as he fought back a swell of impatience. The best thing for everyone would have been to stop and rest, but he could not bring himself to call for it. More than ever, he was aware of Takarahl behind them, still far too close.

This rain had slowed Ketahn's tribe significantly, and it would have slowed any Claws hunting them. But even delayed by rain, the Queen's Claws could move faster than Ketahn and the humans had during dry weather.

As though sensing his troubled thoughts, Ivy looked at Ketahn and offered him a soft smile. She was as beautiful as ever —perhaps even more so now that he knew of the life growing inside her—but he did not care for the paleness of her face, or the way her lips had lost so much of their pink.

"We're okay," she said. "Don't worry."

He tilted his head and released a short chitter.

Ivy's smile stretched wider. "Yeah, I know. Impossible. But we'll be fine because we're together."

Ketahn closed the short distance between them, wrapped an arm around her, and touched his headcrest to her forehead. "We will be, my heartsthread."

She embraced him for several heartbeats before they withdrew from one another. Despite everything he was carrying, his arms felt empty.

"Do you pain?" Rekosh asked, drawing Ketahn's attention back to him.

Ahmya spat to the side a couple times and shook her head. "The mud broke my fall."

Rekosh tentatively released his hold on Ahmya, reached back into his bag, and tugged out a piece of cloth, handing it to her. She used it to wipe the mud from her face and hair before returning it with a quiet thanks. Diego handed her the boot, and she bent forward to put it on.

She wobbled almost immediately, throwing an arm out and waving it to reclaim her balance, but it was too late. She pitched forward.

Rekosh swept her into his arms before she could fall, clutching her against his chest. "I have you, vi'keishi."

Little flower.

Ahmya stared up at him with wide eyes, her dark hair clinging to her cheeks. Rekosh placed a hand on her head, gently guiding her to lean it on his chest, and she curled up in his arms, nestling against him.

"Don't see why you'd want to go for a swim when we've been wet nonstop all week," Cole said. There was a little humor in his voice, a little teasing, but mostly Ketahn heard only weariness.

"Walk, human, or you will swim next," said Ketahn. He placed a hand on Ivy's shoulder and guided her forward, causing a pang of guilt in his chest as he did so.

Cole chuckled, tucked his and Ahmya's spears under his arm, and continued in the direction they'd been going. "Bossy ass spider."

Ketahn watched Ivy walk. For nearly an eightday, he'd studied her movements, seeking even the faintest signs of pain. He saw none now, but she lifted her legs like they weighed as much as boulders. He moved closer to her, supporting her with an extended hand or foreleg whenever it looked like she was about to stumble or fall.

His protective instinct warred with itself. They needed to continue onward, needed to travel far enough to be safe. But now more than ever, this journey was not safe for Ivy or any of the tribe. To protect her, he needed to stop...yet stopping would only mean different danger.

"Telok, watch for a place to shelter," Ketahn called in vrix. "I do not think we can travel much farther this day."

Telok signaled his understanding from the head of the group and increased his lead, climbing a root to get above the jungle floor. He led them along the same path they'd followed since the day Ivy had awoken in pain—keeping the stream several dozen segments to their left but matching its course. It would lead them to the mire that had become the edges of thornskull territory after the war, an area that had once been deep within the enemy's land.

Had they been able to travel in the trees, they'd have reached the mire days before.

Ketahn could not say how much farther they had walked— no more than two hundred segments, at best—when all five vrix halted at once. The humans stopped a moment later, turning their confused and tired gazes toward the vrix.

Callie slipped her bag off her back, settled it atop a log to keep it off the muddy ground, and rolled her shoulders. "What's wrong?"

"Vibrations," Ketahn said. "Shaking in the ground."

The calls of all manner of beasts echoed between the trees in a chaotic, panicked jumble. All around, creatures of various sizes scrambled up trunks and across branches, while others took flight with fluttering wings.

"This bodes ill, Ketahn," Ahnset said, gaze darting from creature to creature. The fine hairs on her legs were raised, as were those of the other vrix, Ketahn included.

Will held a hand over his eyes to shield them from the rain as he looked around. "Is something coming? It's not one of those yatin things, is it?"

"I don't feel anything," said Lacey.

A hissing sound rose over the rain—not the hissing of an agitated beast, but of rushing water. The water around Ketahn's legs rippled.

Cole glanced down at the water moving over his feet and then in the direction of the stream. "What the—"

"Into the trees!" Telok called, hurrying toward the rest of the group along the branch he'd climbed onto.

By the time anyone could so much as utter a curse, the water on the jungle floor had risen nearly a hand's length. Leaves and twigs floated on the surface, flowing around the plants and stones jutting out of the water. Ketahn rushed forward and grabbed Ivy. She twisted to throw an arm around his neck, not making a sound as he carried her toward Telok. He felt the fast, hard beat of her heart, felt her breath on his hide.

The other vrix and humans were in motion, scrambling to Telok, who cast down a thick strand of silk he'd tied to the branch. Clutching Ivy close to his chest, Ketahn leapt onto a nearby tree trunk and climbed. Bits of wet bark broke off beneath his claws, but those claws sank deep into the wood beneath, their grip strengthened by his desperation to get his mate to safety.

Once he was high enough, he jumped onto Telok's branch. The impact of his landing sent a rumbling through the wood that was answered by another vibration—a fresh surge of flood water.

He looked down to see the water higher still—nearly to Lacey's waist.

Ahnset, though burdened with the largest share of supplies, snatched Will and Lacey out of the water and charged up a broad root. Rekosh was already climbing with Ahmya. Callie stumbled, falling to her knees as she reached for something under the water.

Urkot caught her by the back of her jumpsuit, halting her before her face could go under.

"My bag!" she cried.

He lifted her fully out of the water and threw her over his shoulder. Her hands were empty. She shouted something in protest, but Urkot did not release her. He strode toward Diego and Cole, who had waded to Telok's hanging strand. Telok was already securing a second strand near the first.

Ketahn set Ivy on her feet, briefly taking her by the upper arms. "Stay here. Be careful. The wood is slick."

Her cheeks had pink splotches, her breath was ragged, and her heart still raced, but her eyes were steady. She nodded and brushed her fingertips along his jaw. "Go help."

He didn't allow himself another touch, didn't allow himself even a lingering gaze; he turned away from his mate, telling himself she was safe, promising himself she would be okay, reminding himself that the rest of the tribe needed him.

Rekosh grabbed hold of the branch and held Ahmya up. Ketahn took her from his friend and helped the little human find her footing before continuing to his broodsister.

Ahnset climbed with naught but her overwhelming might, her claws shredding the tree trunk. But her progress was slow—the weight of her body, the bulging bags on her back, and the humans tucked under her lower arms was nearly too much for her strength alone to overcome. Her claws were tearing free on their own far too frequently; she was fighting a doomed battle against slipping.

Ketahn drew a thick strand of silk from his spinnerets, passing it to his hands, which quickly wound it into a loose coil. He called his sister's name and tossed the strand to her.

Ahnset glanced his way and pulled a hand free to reach for the rope, but she immediately began to slide down. She slapped her hand against the trunk again, sinking her claws deep, and repositioned her legs.

One of Will's arms darted out, catching the rope just before it would've been out of reach. His movement put more strain on Ahnset. Ketahn's hearts squeezed as her big body shuddered, her muscles bulged, and she scrabbled to resecure her hold. The strap on one of her bags snapped, and the bag tumbled down into the now churning water below.

Lacey was repeating a human curse over and over, clinging to Ahnset in desperation. Will, though wide-eyed with fear, began looping the strand around Ahnset's middle.

Ketahn cut the strand on his end and dropped his underside onto the branch. Using arms and legs, he wound the silk around the bough. His altered position brought everyone still below into view—Urkot was hauling himself up one of Telok's strands with Callie over his shoulder, while Cole and Diego, now standing in water past their waists, had taken hold of the other strand.

The flow of water had grown stronger. The two humans swayed against the current as they struggled to wrap the strand around their hands for secure grips, shouting at one another over the roar of the flood.

Bracing his legs on the branch, Ketahn caught his silk line in all four hands.

Ahnset met his gaze. No words were needed. She leapt away from the tree, pushing with arms and legs. Lacey and Will screamed. Ketahn gritted his teeth, snapped his mandibles together, and hauled back on the strand. Ahnset and her humans swung through the air, the tip of one of her legs skimming the water's surface.

They flew under the branch and around to the other side. Ketahn twisted his head to watch as Ahnset appeared behind him and threw her upper hands out to latch onto the wood. Then her momentum faltered. Her claws tore great gouges in the bark as she slipped.

Ripping his hands free of the strand, Ketahn dove toward his sister, catching her forearm in his hand. Rekosh was at his side an instant later, taking hold of Ahnset's other arm. All three vrix growled and pulled with all their might. The branch shook and groaned, humans cried out, their voices blending into one indecipherable noise, and every muscle in Ketahn's body burned.

But Ahnset rose.

He didn't realize Ivy and Ahmya were there until he saw their arms reach out between him and Rekosh. The two females grasped Will and Lacey's hands and helped them out of Ahnset's hold and onto the branch.

Finally, Ahnset planted her legs atop the bough.

Rekosh darted off to help Urkot finish his climb while Ahnset bent forward, panting, and the humans steadied each other. Ketahn ignored the wailing aches in his body; not everyone in his tribe was safe yet.

He looked at Telok, who was hauling up the remaining strand. Diego was out of the water but for his boots, teeth bared and expression tight as he held on. But Cole had taken a lower grip on the strand and was still waist deep—though his feet were now undoubtedly off the ground, and he was at the mercy of the current, which fought to pull him away.

Ketahn's eyes widened. A branch longer than he was tall was riding the flood water toward Cole, surrounded by debris. Ketahn eased past Ivy and the others to help.

Telok's gaze landed on the approaching branch. He wrapped

the rope around his hand once more and pulled harder, lifting Cole's thighs above the surface.

The bark beneath Telok's rear leg claws gave way. He slipped, and the rope sagged.

Cole fell back into the water just as the floating branch reached him. The gnarled bough struck his stomach and carried him backward, pulling Diego into the water too—and snagging the strand.

One of Cole's hands lost its grip on the rope, and his body stretched out as though he were performing that strange human belly swim. His now free hand pushed at the branch and the surrounding debris, but he couldn't get loose.

Telok hooked his legs around the bough beneath him and pulled with a snarl.

Diego rose again, still holding tight. Cole began to emerge also, his fearful eyes fixed on the length of silk between him and Diego.

The length of frayed silk.

The big branch came up with Cole, along with many smaller, thorny branches caught upon it. Water poured from the mess, nearly drowning out Cole's shout.

"Fuck!"

The strand snapped. Diego jolted upward with the sudden release of tension, legs swinging wildly. He cried out when his weight came down again, jerking the strand taut around his hands.

Cole plunged into the flood along with the debris that had snagged on him.

"Pull Diego up!" Ketahn called as he reversed his direction on the branch to follow the water's flow. He gathered a new strand from his spinnerets while he moved and tied a loop at its end; he could only hope he would have enough in time.

Cole battled to keep his head above the water as the current swept him along and spun him about.

Ketahn pushed himself faster to get ahead of Cole, legs threatening to slip on the slick bark with each step. He jumped across a several segment wide gap to position himself on a branch directly above Cole's path.

Readying his strand, Ketahn hooked all six legs around the branch, swung himself to hang upside down from its underside, and lowered the silk.

The strand's end fell toward the water, dangling just above the surface, but the wind blew it aside as Cole neared. Hearts thumping and hairs bristling, Ketahn flicked his wrist. The small movement coursed along the length of the silk, reaching the bottom just as Cole's head dipped under water.

The loop of silk slipped over Cole's raised arm. Ketahn tugged, drawing the loop tight around Cole's arm, and then added just enough slack to the strand to whip it around in circular motions, winding it around the human's limb.

Cole's searching fingers found the silk and closed around it. Ketahn pulled up.

The human's head and shoulders surfaced. He coughed and lifted his free hand to wipe his wet hair out of his face. As Ketahn drew him a little higher, the resistance on the strand intensified far more than it should have, even with the extra weight of the branches and twigs Cole had become tangled with.

With another curse, Cole sucked in a breath, closed his mouth, and turned his face away. The churning water broke against the debris before him and splashed his head. That water was still getting deeper before Ketahn's eyes.

"My bag is caught!" Cole yelled between sputtering breaths.

Ketahn tightened his hold on the branch and the strand, keeping the line taut. "Your knife!"

Cole dunked his free hand into the murky water. He leaned down, shoulders dipping under the surface, then his neck, his chin. His nose holes flared, spraying water with each heavy breath. He turned his chin up when the water touched his lower lip. Tremors coursed through the strand, created by the water current that wanted only to carry this human away.

Ketahn glanced toward his companions. They all stood on that wide branch nearby, watching Ketahn and Cole with hope and fear warring on their faces.

Cole brought his hand up again, shoving at the branches with renewed vigor. The gleaming blade of his knife jutted from his fist. Water splashed as he hurriedly worked the knife under the strap of his bag. The struggle was brief; tough as the yatin leather was, it could not hold against the sharpness of the metal blade.

Ketahn pulled again.

Cole rose quickly, bag lost beneath the flood water. He batted off the thorny branches that had snagged on his jumpsuit, snapping some and tearing others away. The burden on the strand grew immediately lighter.

When he'd finally pulled Cole all the way up, Ketahn climbed atop the branch again and lay on his belly. His limbs were heavy—this ordeal had sapped all his strength, and his exhaustion was made only worse by the dull aches permeating him.

Cole sprawled out beside Ketahn, staring skyward, chest heaving with his ragged breaths. "Shit."

"I did not truly mean for you to swim, human," Ketahn rasped.

The human laughed, though it was weak. "A week ago... I swore you wanted to...kill me."

"We are tribe. Touch my Ivy, I kill."

Cole coughed, the rough sound coming from deep in his chest. "Got it. Thanks, Ketahn. Probably doesn't mean much after everything, but thanks."

"No thanks." Ketahn flattened his hands on the branch and shoved himself up. Below, the flood water continued flowing, the surface deceptively calm despite the powerful currents running beneath. "Must climb."

The laughter that emerged from Cole was surprisingly warm and genuine. "I've done enough climbing for one lifetime, but I guess you're the boss."

"Not boss," Ketahn replied, lifting his mandibles in a smile, "vrix."

CHAPTER 19

THERE DIDN'T SEEM to be any part of Ivy that wasn't cold. Ketahn drew her closer against the living furnace that was his body as she shivered, and she huddled into his heat gratefully.

As much as everyone had wanted to lie down right on that branch and sleep for a week after narrowly escaping the flood, Ketahn had urged them onward. Their slow, painstaking journey across the branches had finally led them to a rocky cliffside where they'd discovered this cave about forty feet above the floodwater.

Though it wasn't necessarily warm inside, it was dry, and Ivy was glad to be out of the rain and resting.

There was a small fire crackling, made from the debris they'd found in the cave—dried twigs and what must have been some sort of long-abandoned nest. But even that couldn't vanquish the cold that had seeped into Ivy's bones. All the humans had gathered around the fire with nothing more than damp blankets wrapped around them, their clothes having been cast off to dry—if anything could ever dry in this weather. The vrix sat close behind the humans, doing everything they could to generate warmth in the small space.

Despite the material of their jumpsuits being waterproof, days of travel with constant rainfall had given all that water ample opportunity to find every opening in those suits. A waterproof exterior didn't make much difference once water got underneath.

Outside the cave, the light was dying, and the rain continued. When the vrix called it the flood season, they'd meant it—literally. Had the crater where the *Somnium* crashed flooded also? Ivy couldn't imagine still being on that ship, trapped behind those doors, knowing it could be weeks or months before she'd see daylight again.

She dropped a hand to her belly. She hadn't done so intentionally, but her thoughts had frequently been seized by a... protectiveness over what was possibly growing inside her.

No, not *possibly*. She knew. She knew Diego was right, knew there was a new life taking shape within her, and her desire to safeguard that little life grew with each passing moment.

Will rubbed a hand over his face. Out of the three men, he alone wasn't growing a beard. "How much did we lose?"

"I lost my bag," Callie said.

Cole tossed another twig into the fire. "Mine too. Had to cut it loose."

"One fell from Ahnset," said Ketahn, his voice rumbling into Ivy from behind. "Lost spears also."

"We still have plenty of ration bars and hydration packets." Lacey ran a hand through her hair, pulling it back from her face and fluffing it. "The rest of the stuff wasn't necessities, and we would've lost most of it overtime anyway. It was just extra weight. We can make more clothes, blankets, and spears."

"Yes. And we will hunt for food."

Diego smirked. "Don't think we're lacking water either."

"I am *so* done with water right now," Callie muttered.

Ahmya drew her blanket tighter around her body. The fire's

orange light flickered over her features, making her cheeks look hollower. "How long will the flood last?"

Ketahn turned his head toward the mouth of the cave. A steady stream of water fell just beyond—runoff from above that formed a small waterfall through which the group had passed when they'd entered. "As long as it will."

Ivy heard the weariness in his voice, and it made her heart ache. He'd shown such strength and resolve during this journey —just as he always did—but she could only imagine how his body felt. He'd had no time to recover from the beatings he'd suffered in Takarahl before plunging into the jungle with the group, and he had pushed himself hard ever since.

She smoothed a hand up his chest until her palm was over his hearts. Their rhythmic pounding flowed into her, harmonizing with that of her own. Ketahn trilled softly and combed his claws through her hair, taking extra care with her tangles, as he coaxed her to rest her head against him.

Cole laughed to himself and shook his head. "You know, I've been on worse camping trips."

"Really?" asked Will.

Cole grinned. "Nah. We always had beer at least. That'll help you ignore a lot of shit."

Lacey pursed her lips to the side and stared into the fire. "All things considered, this isn't really *bad*, is it?"

Ahmya arched a brow. "You don't think being chased by a queen hell bent on killing us bad?"

Lacey chuckled. "Well, aside from that. That's not fun. My whole body hurts, I'm tired, and we've come close to death a couple times, but I also... I feel alive. Maybe for the first time in my life, I feel really alive."

"Real danger has a way of putting everything in perspective," said Diego.

Callie frowned. "Never realized how much I was living on auto-pilot on Earth until I woke up here. Everything was routine. And there were just...so many expectations. I doubt much of that would have changed if we had made it to Xolea."

"Would have just been a whole new routine," Will said.

"While popping out babies."

"We dodged that one," Lacey muttered.

Ahmya snickered.

"Would've been no shortage of work, I guess," said Callie.

Diego leaned back against Ahnset's hindquarters. "I can't decide whether or not that's a good thing. I was a workaholic."

"I can imagine, with you being a nurse. You must be really passionate about it."

"Yeah, I guess I am."

"How'd you go from workaholic nurse to colonist on a crashed ship?" Will asked.

"My mom was a nurse, and she worked so hard. But she always had a smile for everyone...always put a smile on people's faces, you know? I wanted to do that, too. Wanted to be just like her. So I dove right into nursing school after high school. I met a woman named Angela in college, and we hit it off. She was aiming for law school. Smartest person I ever knew. We wound up moving in together, and after a year, we got engaged.

"But I was driven. Wanted nothing more than I wanted that degree, than I wanted to help people. I started volunteering as a paramedic, throwing any hours I didn't spend studying into that. And I just...really didn't have any time for her. Didn't *make* any time for her. She wasn't really doing the same for me either, though. We were just so focused on school, on our careers, and we just...weren't ready to settle down, I guess. We made the mutual choice to separate. Cleanest breakup I'd ever had, but... still hurt."

He looked down at his hands in his lap, turning his palms up. "I don't regret the choice I made. I graduated and got right to work, and it felt good to help people. Felt good to have my mom give me that special smile, the one she saved just for me, and tell me she so was so proud. And then, uh…not long after…"

Diego bowed his head and shook it. "She passed away. My dad didn't take it well and crawled into a bottle. He didn't make it but a few months before he was gone too. And I just threw myself into work. I took every damn shift they had, and when there weren't any, I asked for stuff to do. I lived at the hospital. And I thought I was handling it.

"I was good at my job. I made people feel good, I helped them, took care of them, just like my mom. That kept me going. That was how I was honoring her. But I never…never let myself grieve. I came home one day after a double, could barely stand upright, and I put my keys on the stand by the door and looked down. I had this picture of my mom and dad there, smiling and happy…and I lost it."

He lifted a hand, raking it through his hair. "Curled up on the floor and cried for hours. And when I didn't have any more tears, I lifted my head and looked around and realized…I was alone. I didn't have anyone. And I had spent the last few years of my parents' lives busting my ass to make them proud instead of spending time with them. So…the choice to get on that ship was easy. I promised myself it would be different this time. I promised myself I would be happy.

"Maybe nothing would've changed on Xolea, but…man, I really, really needed things to be different. And it is now, and a lot of this sucks, but"—he lifted his gaze and swept it around, smiling as it stopped on Will—"I'm glad to have people I care about again. I'm fucking glad I'm not alone anymore."

Will's dark eyes flared, and he ducked his head. "Yeah."

"So, what about you, Will?"

"W-what about me?"

Diego's smile widened. "I think most of us got on that ship to get away from something. Share that burden with us." He brushed his knuckles against the side of Will's thigh. "If you're ready, I mean."

Will stared down at where Diego had touched him. "If I'm ready…" He gave himself a visible shake and released a heavy sigh. "Don't think I'll ever be ready, but might as well do it anyway, right?"

He leaned forward, propping his elbows on his knees, and ran his tongue across his teeth. "I was always into computers. Ever since I was a kid and my dad helped me build one for gaming. Used to play with him and his buddies all the time so, uh… Well, I learned some colorful language at a young age, and they made me swear I'd never let my mother hear any of it. I also learned some coding, too, messing with mods and stuff like that.

"So as I got older I figured that I wanted to work with computers. That was easy, didn't even really need to think about it. The IT stuff came naturally to me. And I was so happy that *something* about me was easy to figure out, because there was so much about myself that confused me. Stuff that even now I'm not sure I've come to terms with."

His eyes flicked up to Diego briefly before he continued. "I pretended to be into girls even when I got to high school because I thought that was expected of me, but it was never… right. And since I was always playing these military shooters with my dad and his friends, and the jokes they'd make, I didn't…I didn't want them to think there was something wrong with me. So I struggled for a long time. I hated myself and I went through all that stuff that I guess a lot of people go through, but you always feel impossibly alone when you're experiencing it.

"And it was just tearing me apart because I loved my dad, and we had such a strong relationship, but I convinced myself he'd hate me if I told him. My mom knew, though. She never said anything, but she knew. She used to say *In your time, Willie.*

We'll always be here when you're ready. And I knew she would be, but him?"

Will reached down and picked up a waterskin from the cave floor, unsealing it and pouring water into his mouth. He drew in a steadying breath when he was done. "I went to an IT college, finished top of my class and all that, and my dad was so damned proud of me, and God did I want to tell him. I wanted nothing more, but I couldn't. I just...any time I tried I'd freeze up.

"I worked a couple jobs at some big corporations. The money was really good, but it just wasn't clicking for me. I was restless. I wanted to just...go away. Anywhere that I didn't have to be me. Then I saw this recruitment ad for the Homeworld Initiative, and I figured why not? I probably wouldn't get hired, but it couldn't hurt to apply, right? It felt good to at least try for something so different. And they hired me. So I accepted and went to the crew training, and it all set in. I was going to leave Earth. I was leaving it all behind. Couldn't get much more extreme than that."

Will laughed to himself, but that laughter was belied by the glimmer of tears in his eyes. "And my parents were so proud. My dad would brag that I was doing something real, something that would make a difference for all mankind. And I felt the clock ticking, watched the days change on the calendar, counted them down to takeoff. And I still couldn't tell him.

"The day before the launch, THI had a family event for all the crew members. A big party to send us off and let us get our goodbyes in. My mom and dad came, and I finally mustered the courage to take him off to the side. And I was stuttering and stumbling over my words, trying to say what I'd wanted to say for so long, and he looked me in the eye and told me it was okay. Told me that he knew, and he wished I'd told him sooner. That he wished he'd known how much I had struggled with it.

That he was sorry to have made me feel like I couldn't talk to him about it.

"And he said that no matter what, I was his son and he loved me, and he would tell people until the day"—Will's voice shook, and those tears welling in his eyes spilled—"until the day he died that his son was on the *Somnium*, that his son was a hero, and that there'd never been a father as proud of his child as he was of me."

Bringing a hand up, Will wiped the tears from his cheeks. "And the next day I boarded the ship. I was still reeling from the whole thing, you know? Finally have that moment with my dad and it's so much more than I could've ever hoped, and then I had to leave forever. We were doing our final system prep before takeoff when a friend of mine, Ian Johnson, mentioned he was jealous because I had a shift with a woman he really liked who he'd met in training.

"The crew was great, don't get me wrong, but there was a kind of weird vibe among us, you know? Ian hadn't really approached her because, well...I guess it just felt like anything we did before takeoff didn't matter anymore. It was all going to be in the past." Will chuckled bitterly and shook his head. "I had spent years denying who I was and what I wanted. I mean, it probably got me onto the crew because there was this unspoken bias against being queer, but I wanted to be done with pretending."

"Breeders," Cole said. "That's what they wanted from passengers and crew both, man. Fucking breeders."

Callie scoffed. "Cole, you were the one talking about how we need to repopulate the human race ourselves not all that long ago."

"Yeah, well, I haven't had sex in a hundred and seventy years or whatever. Can you blame me?"

"It's not like you were *awake* for all those years."

"And it's been just as long for all the rest of us," Diego said, grinning. "Well, almost all." He tilted his head toward Ivy.

Ivy laughed as her cheeks warmed.

I'm apparently fulfilling that role as a breeder anyway.

"We all knew what we were signing up for when we joined the Initiative," Lacey said.

"We did." Diego gestured to Will. "Go ahead."

Will took another drink from the waterskin. "Yeah. Anyway, I wanted to put that pretending behind me. And I didn't want to see a friend go through the same thing. So I offered to swap shifts with him. He was reluctant, but I told him he'd never have a better chance to get to know her. Even if nothing came of it, right? So he agreed, we put it in, and it got approved.

"We were working one year on, five in stasis, teams of four in each section. There'd always be a med tech and a computer tech awake to handle any issues. My cycle was off because I swapped with Johnson. I worked three shifts. Three years. And then...Ivy woke me up."

He released a shaky breath. "And the shift that was active when, uh...when the...the crash happened. It was the one I traded. Johnson was working in my place. He should've been asleep in the cryochamber, not me. But I...I pushed him to..."

"You didn't know what was going to happen, Will," Ivy said, drawing away from Ketahn slightly as she turned toward the man. "You never could have known."

"It's *my* fault, Ivy. He's dead because I convinced him to change shifts. Dead because of me. Because—"

"Will," Diego said firmly, calling other man's attention. "Don't do this to yourself, man. It's not your fault. None of it was. None of this is. Choices have consequences, and most of the time, they're completely out of our control. But that doesn't mean you did anything wrong. That doesn't mean you don't deserve to be here."

Diego leaned closer to Will and placed a hand on Will's

thigh. "Whether it was meant to be this way, whether you believe in fate or not, you're here. And I am happy that you are."

Will stared down at that hand, surprise etched upon his features. He raised his own hand, hesitating for but a moment, before covering Diego's. "Didn't you, uh...didn't you say you had a...a girlfriend?"

"Yeah. Had a couple boyfriends before her, though."

Will's head snapped up, and his eyes widened when they met Diego's. "Y-You did?"

Diego chuckled and turned his hand, lacing their fingers together. "I did."

"It's about time," Callie said, crossing her arms over her chest. "Been watching you two eye fuck each other for days."

As the humans laughed, Ketahn offered some translation to the vrix; there was a lot that had been said that even he wouldn't have understood, but he got the important points across.

When he was done, Ahnset was stared down at Diego and Will—stared at their linked hands. "They...are mates now?"

"Only they can answer that," Ivy said in vrix. "But I think it is a start."

"They are males."

Ivy nodded.

"Yet they show this without shame? Before all of us?"

"Humans have different ways," Ketahn said, placing one hand on Ivy's shoulder and cupping the underside of her jaw with another. His thumb stroked her chin slowly.

"There are humans who still look down on it on Earth. But here..." Ivy looked up at Ketahn and leaned into his touch, trailing her fingertips along his arm. Warmth blossomed on her chest at the fierce gleam in his gaze. "We are free to love who we will here."

CHAPTER 20

KETAHN STOOD at the edge of the murky water and looked across it. Thick green growth floated atop it in places. Other spots were choked with vine-like plants that had broad, flat leaves drifting upon the surface, or stalks of tall grass with edges sharp enough to draw blood from human flesh if not navigated carefully. Rotting logs and branches jutted from the water, some overgrown with hanging moss. Trees grew from the few visible patches of land in clusters, while many more rose directly from the water, their mighty trunks stained by the fluctuating water levels. Twisted roots of all shapes and sizes ran above and below the surface—a network of potential pathways even more tangled and hazardous than the jungle boughs.

He'd never wanted to see this place again. He'd never wanted to return to this mire, where so much had been lost to put an end to the queen's war. And after spending two days in that cliffside cave, waiting for the rain to ease and the floodwaters to recede, some part of him must have believed he wouldn't actually get here. That he wasn't foolish enough to come.

But they'd left that cave yesterday and trudged through the ravaged jungle. More and more, Ketahn had felt as though he were striding away from a spear poised at his back—striding straight toward another aimed at his chest. After reaching higher ground, they'd found the place where landslides had allowed part of the rain-swollen mireland to pour into the area around the stream. They'd reflected upon it with awe and had expressed thanks for their fortune in escaping unscathed. Then they'd moved on.

Now they were here, and they could not turn back.

"I can't decide if this is better or worse than the flood," Cole said.

"I think worse," said Lacey. "Maybe much worse."

Cole laughed. "Well, I haven't almost drowned here yet, so I guess I'll hold off on making up my mind."

Will arched a brow and stared at Cole. "How are *you* staying so positive?"

"It's that shit Diego said the other day. You know. About almost dying really making you think."

"Ah, so I did see smoke coming out of your ears the other day," Diego said with a grin.

The humans laughed, even Cole.

But Ketahn could find no amusement in their words. He had been restless during their time in the cave; his worry had deepened, and the dread that had come to den in his gut had grown heavier. Surviving the flood had not dislodged his feeling that they were fast approaching some disaster.

Whenever he looked at the other vrix, he saw the concern in their eyes too—Telok and Ahnset especially.

"Hear me, humans," Ketahn said, turning to face his tribe. "Thornskull grounds begin here."

"Not much ground," Callie said, staring out over the water.

"They once claimed much of the jungle we have crossed," Ketahn replied. "We fought them. Took the ground from them. But the queen has no want of this place and left it to them."

"Why did she fight for land she didn't want?" Ivy asked. She sat astride his hindquarters, her hands upon his lower shoulders and her inner thighs pressed to either side of his torso. Her closeness and heat comforted him, at least in part because he could more readily protect her like this.

But that comfort couldn't stop his insides from twisting, couldn't banish his looming sense of foreboding. "She must crush her enemies. That is her way."

Lacey crouched near the water's edge and dipped the end of her spear in, parting the thick surface growth. She wrinkled her nose. "Are we walking in this?"

Telok stepped to Lacey, placed a hand over one of hers, and guided her spear out of the water. She started, looking up at him with confused eyes. He shook his head.

"I guess that's a no," Will said.

Ketahn studied the others. Despite resting for two days in the cave, they were worn down, and he feared they would soon sink into despair—all as they reached what was likely to be the most trying part of their journey.

He filled his lungs with warm, wet air, nearly shuddering at the pungent odors of rot and foul water. "We will use ground, root, and branch to cross. This water hides hungry mud and beasts. Do not drink, do not go in. You humans know my words?"

A few humans nodded. The rest voiced their understanding.

Ivy braced a hand upon one of his upper shoulders and swung her leg to the opposite side of his hindquarters. "At least it's not pouring. That's a positive, right?"

Ketahn brought a leg up to steady Ivy as she slid off him. With her down, his unease increased; she was far too close to the water for his liking. He barely resisted his instinctual urge to snatch her off the ground and carry her far away from this place.

"We should not do this, Ketahn," said Telok. He'd released

Lacey's hand, but remained near her, fine hairs standing. "We will find no peace here."

"Then where, Telok?" Ketahn demanded, mandibles spreading.

"Anywhere," Rekosh said. "Anywhere but this place. Thornskulls will not remain idle if they find us on their ground."

Urkot folded his upper arms across his chest. "Then they must not find us."

"You believe we can hide from them in their lands?" Telok asked. One of his forelegs scraped the ground. "You are no fool, Urkot, but yours are foolish words."

Ketahn clenched his fists, fighting back a surge of memories that threatened to overwhelm him. "We came here before, and they did not know until we attacked."

Telok growled. "Have I remembered wrong, Ketahn? For I do not recall having a pack of humans with us when we made war on Kaldarak. I have said such to you already."

"Will the...thornskulls try to kill us when they see us?" Ivy asked in vrix.

"Yes," Telok snapped.

"No," Ketahn replied at the same time. He huffed. "They will watch. They will not attack until they know why we have come."

Ivy frowned. "Will they let you talk and make...peace?"

"I do not know, my heartsthread." He turned to face Ivy and took her cheeks between two of his hands, stroking them with his thumbs. "But we will not meet our ends by their spears. I promise."

She covered his hands with her own. "I know."

"They are not likely to attack until we have crossed the mire," said Ahnset.

Ketahn and the others looked at her. For the first time since before she'd brought Ella to Takarahl, Ahnset stood tall, firm, confident—not a Fang any longer, but a warrior. A protector.

"How could you know that?" Telok asked.

"They fear Zurvashi. The death she...*we* brought upon the thornskulls was great, and they are much fewer than they were. They will be loath to risk starting a new war with her."

"And when they realize we are not allied with her? That we are not her Claws?" Telok asked. "By the Eight, we cannot fight all of them, even if they are fewer."

Ketahn looked at his mate. "Ivy, what is it you said before?"

She met his gaze. "You mean when I said the enemy of my enemy is my friend? But as Rekosh said, it is not that simple."

"But it *is* more of a chance than we would have with the queen," Rekosh said with a chitter. "Call me a fool, Telok, for I see no way but forward."

Urkot thumped a leg on the ground and touched the scar of his missing arm. "We have come too far to turn back now."

"Protector, shield me," Telok hissed. He glared at the ground for a moment before releasing a long, low growl. "Ketahn, I have followed you through this mire once before. You know I will follow you again. But I do not wish to lose any more of our tribe."

"You think I wish to lose more?" Ketahn asked, his voice thick. He lowered his hands from Ivy's face and turned toward Telok. "Everything I have is here, Telok. *Here.* You, my brothers. My broodsister. My tribe. My mate. Everything." He advanced a step. "I would not risk any of you if I thought there was a better way. I have begged the Eight to grant us an easy path. I have cursed them, cursed myself, for my failures. How many times have I been close enough to kill Zurvashi? How many times have I failed? Failed to protect everyone, everything? To protect Ella?"

Telok held his place, posture rigid. "We all have failures to torment us, Ketahn. We all have given up everything but what is right here. If you say we must leap into flames to save those we long to protect, I will do so—but I will always speak my concerns to you."

Ketahn's rage cooled as quickly as it had sparked. "You are not the reason for my anger, Telok. I am sorry."

"I know. But this path...it is dangerous, Ketahn, and it will be painful." Telok gestured toward the deeper mire. "Some of the things we left in this place are better forgotten."

Ketahn clenched his jaw, and his mandibles twitched downward. How could he ever forget?

"If we go back, we go to the Claws," Ivy said. "And all the ground we have crossed, all the...the time, would be for nothing."

"I, um...I don't understand everything they're saying," Ahmya said, stepping closer to Ivy, "but I think I get what's going on. Can you tell them that we're in this together? That we understand the dangers, and we're willing to face them to make new lives for ourselves?"

Lacey stood. "It's not like we have much choice. Fight on or die, right?"

"We can do without the dying part," Callie said.

Diego chuckled. "I agree."

Ivy shifted her attention to Cole and Will.

Will flicked a glance at Diego and smiled. "Yeah."

Cole shrugged and smirked. "I'm in. Got that deck to build, remember?"

Callie laughed. "You know, after all this hype, that had better be the best deck in the whole damned world, Cole."

"Oh, it sure as shit will be."

"Yeah," said Diego, "because it'll be the only deck in the world."

Cole shook his head, though his lips stretched into a grin. "You guys are dicks."

"Takes one to know one."

"Guess you got me there."

"I..." Telok tilted his head, staring between the humans. "They are talking of stems again, are they not?"

Ketahn chittered. "I do not think so. They are calling each other stems."

"Well, they are as soft as their stems," Urkot said.

"They call their stems *decks*?" asked Ahnset.

"I think that is something different. Their word is *dick*," said Rekosh.

"*Deck*," Ahnset repeated.

"*Dick*," Rekosh corrected.

"Ah, fuck," Cole said, throwing his hands up. "This is that whole *zirkita* thing again, isn't it?"

"You guys started it." Lacey rolled her eyes. "Always talking about your dicks."

"For the record, I had very little involvement in those conversations," said Will.

"Anyway," Ivy said with a grin, looking up at Ketahn, "what we were trying to get at before was, we understand what we are up against, and we are ready to face it."

CHAPTER 21

"I THINK I just saw another one of those...*things*," said Ahmya.

Ketahn glanced in the direction she was looking. The green growth on the mire's surface had been broken several segments away, revealing dark water beneath that betrayed only the faintest of ripples.

He'd seen several of the eshkens himself as they'd traveled, often on the edges of his vision. The creatures were slick, black forms that would break the surface for an instant before dipping under again, sometimes making a tiny splash, sometimes making no sound at all. In places where the water wasn't overgrown with the greenish slime, he'd spied the eshkens' long, dark shapes swimming in the murk.

He agreed with Telok's assessment; the eshkens were likely following the vibrations created in the water every time the tribe crossed a root. It was why Ketahn's companions had called the creatures muckstalkers during the war—the beasts always lurked nearby.

Callie wiped sweat from her brow with the back of her sleeve. She'd pulled her thick, curly hair back and tied it into a loose braid, keeping most of the strands out of her face. "I just might start freaking out if I see another of them."

"You're not already?" Cole asked.

"This is me calm. You haven't seen me freak out yet."

"What about the time we got attacked by those boar-elephant things and—"

"Cole." Callie stared at him with her lips pressed together.

"We were all scared, but—"

Somehow, Callie stared *harder*.

Cole waved a hand and shook his head. "All right, all right."

"I think we all held it together pretty well considering," Lacey said.

Ketahn grunted. "You fought well. But now you must walk instead of talk."

"Always a *partee* pooper, huh?"

"I do not know *partee*, but I have not made poop on it."

A laugh burst from Ivy. She slapped a hand over her mouth to muffle the sound, but it escaped again when Diego said, "If you don't know what it is, how do you know you haven't pooped on it?"

The other humans joined in her laughter, and Ketahn raised his mandibles in a smile. Their amusement seemed genuine; that meant a lot after the day they'd had so far.

Progress through the mire had been slow, though not as slow as Ketahn had expected. They'd crossed solid ground where they could but had largely used branches and roots for passage—possible here because so many of them were lower to the ground than elsewhere in the jungle. Once the group had determined the best way to get both the humans and the supplies up to and down from those elevated pathways, travel had been smoother.

Many of the trees here had vast webs of twisting, tangled roots branching outward from their bases, running both above and below the water. Such roots formed natural bridges in many locations, but the crossings had not been easy. There'd been many slips and near falls, and everyone in the tribe had experienced a jolt of fear at least once when the wood beneath them groaned and wobbled.

As though the new beasts, plants, and pathways were not enough to occupy Ketahn's attention, there were the thornskulls to watch for. The tribe would undoubtedly be spotted by thornskull scouts before reaching the far side of the mire—it could not be avoided—but Ketahn wanted to know when that moment came. The thornskulls had enough advantages here already; Ketahn would not allow them the advantage of surprise, also.

A high-pitched shriek caused Ketahn to halt. He spun around with spear raised and mandibles spread wide to find Callie bent over and frantically swatting at her long hair, which had come undone from its braid. Her words were too quick and jumbled for him to understand.

Urkot strode up behind her. He placed one hand across her shoulders, thumb curling around the side of her neck, to still her, and then with another plucked something out of her hair.

Cole recoiled. "Oh fuck, what the hell is that?"

"*What is it?*" Callie demanded.

Ketahn glimpsed spindly, wriggling legs and a flutter of tiny wings from the thing in Urkot's grasp. Urkot squeezed his finger and thumb together. There was a crunch, and a thick, yellow-green ichor oozed out of the creature and onto Urkot's hand. He flicked the thing away.

"You safe, female," Urkot said in heavily accented English, sliding his hand up to the back of Callie's neck to guide her upright again. "It gone."

Callie shuddered, her face twisted in disgust behind her tousled hair. "Ugh. I hate bugs." She flicked her gaze toward Urkot. "Not you. I mean, spiders aren't even really bugs anyway."

Urkot canted his head, mandibles twitching uncertainly. "Not spider. Urkot."

Callie chuckled. "Yeah, we've already had that drilled into us. Not spider."

He lifted his hand from her neck and smoothed it down her hair. With a thoughtful trill, he took a curly lock between his forefinger and thumb, raised it from the rest, and rubbed it gently. In vrix he said, "So soft. It is like fluffed silk."

Arching a brow, Callie reached up and delicately plucked her hair out of Urkot's grasp. "Not sure what you just said but, um, thanks big guy."

Urkot thumped a fist against his chest. "Urkot."

"Yeah, I know." She tapped her own chest. "Callie. Thought we were way past introductions."

With a huff, he shook his head. He cupped her jaw, squeezing her cheeks just a little to make her lips part, as he drew her closer. "Say. Urkot."

Callie's brow creased, and her hands came up to grasp his arm. She looked into his eyes. "Urkot?"

He purred and said in vrix, "My name sounds right in your voice, female."

Ivy, who stood near them, glanced up at Ketahn with a small smile.

"What's going on?" Cole asked.

"Um, not sure," Callie said.

Rekosh chittered. "You look at her with the same gleam in your eyes as when you look upon freshly shaped stone."

Urkot withdrew his hand from Callie's face and turned his head to glare at Rekosh. "And you look upon your little flower with the same gleam in your eyes as when you look upon freshly woven silk."

"Ah, but she is so much more than that."

"And Callie is much more than a piece of stone."

"There is much I would say," Telok said from the rear of the group, "but I have no desire to become the next target."

"Come," Ketahn said with a chitter. "We must go." He beckoned his companions and led them onward, climbing onto another weblike cluster of roots. He selected his path with care, testing for rotting wood, spots that would dip too close to the water, and patches slippery with slime or moss.

And memories attacked him as he went. Those memories had been surfacing all day, emerging from the depths of his mind like muckstalkers from the dark water. He'd led his group of Claws this way seven years ago. He'd crossed these roots, these branches, had braved this mire while it had been entirely unknown to him, and he'd battled his enemies from one end to the other.

Ketahn stepped off the web of roots, legs briefly coming down on a small patch of soft ground before he followed a long root up. Its narrowness would force the tribe to walk along it one at a time, but it was the only bridge across the next stretch of water.

Ketahn and his companions had made the path Zurvashi's forces had followed through the mire. He and his companions had bled for it. His friends had given their lives to win her war. His broodbrother had died for it.

Ketahn could almost feel Ishkal's weight in his arms, growing heavier as the vrix's strength drained, could almost feel the warm blood flowing over his hide. And in his mind, Ketahn saw Ishkal's purple eyes staring up at him, their light fading, fading, fading...

Ishkal's bones were out here along with those of many other fallen vrix, swallowed by mud and murky water, their broken bodies long since having been torn apart by beasts.

Ketahn's hearts clenched as the guilt he'd long carried flared. If only he had marked the places his companions had fallen. If only he had been able to bring them back to Takarahl, where they could have been laid with their kin.

If only he'd been able to bring them all back alive.

Wood cracked behind Ketahn, shattering the mire's unsettling quiet, and the root trembled, sinking by at least a hand's span. Several humans made sounds in response—gasps, cries, words uttered in horror and surprise. Dread seized Ketahn's insides as he spun around, a hundred potential disasters flashing through his mind.

Before he fully understood what he saw, he threw himself forward with arms outstretched.

Diego and Lacey were falling, but Ketahn was too slow, too late.

Lacey's red hair was wild around her head, a harsh contrast to the muted greens and browns of the mire. Both she and Diego met Ketahn's gaze; the startled looks on their faces were terribly clear in that moment.

Ketahn landed on his belly hard, making the root shudder. The two humans hit the water with a great splash, bits of splintered wood raining around them. Ketahn saw the shaft of Diego's spear in the water for a moment before the stone head dragged it down and it vanished into the gloom.

The section of root now directly in front of Ketahn's face was barely half the width it had been before—a large, rotted chunk had broken away.

Ivy called his name, and he looked up to see her peering around Cole, who'd been next in line after Lacey. She and Cole stepped toward Ketahn.

With a sharp hiss, Ketahn raised a hand, palm toward them.

Cole froze, his leading foot not yet fully down. Ketahn felt wood groaning beneath him, felt tremors coursing through the root. He felt it sink again by a thread's width. His hearts pounded hard enough that he feared they'd shake the rest of the root apart.

Movement below called his attention downward. Diego and Lacey struggled to get their heads above the surface, coughing and sucking in great lungfuls of air once they were up. The layer of green growth atop the water had been disturbed, leaving a rippling circle of black water a few segments wide around the two; they looked like they were suspended in nothingness, about to be swallowed by it.

"Shit." Diego wiped water and muck from his face as he stood, raising his chest out of the water.

Lacey rose beside him, sweeping her soaked hair back with her free hand. Her other still clutched her spear. She took in another breath, this one slower and deeper, seeming to calm herself—until she glanced around.

She shook her head, shedding excess water. "Oh, no. No, no, no. Not fucking happening."

"Are you hurt?" Ivy asked. Her eyes were wide with concern.

Something made a soft splash in the water not far away.

"Not yet," Diego replied with surprising calm.

"Ketahn," Telok called, "muckstalkers!"

Ketahn glanced toward him. Telok was with everyone else on the ground at the far end of the root, having not yet climbed up. Dark shapes were visible in the murky water nearby. The eshkens had been gathering there, where the root touched the water—where they would've felt the vibrations as the tribe traversed it.

Now those dark shapes were swimming toward Diego and Lacey.

Wrapping his legs around the root, Ketahn rolled himself to its underside. The root bounced and wobbled, but it held. Ketahn could only hope the rot had not spread entirely across the damaged section. Hanging as low as he could, he extended an arm to the humans below.

Diego reached up. His fingertips brushed Ketahn's, and they both strained, stretching their bodies farther. Then Diego sank by a claw's length—more than enough to leave him out of Ketahn's reach.

"It's the mud," Diego said.

Grasping her spear in both hands, Lacey raised it to Ketahn. He took hold of the shaft and pulled up.

Knuckles paling with the strength of her grip, Lacey held fast, rising from the mud with no small amount of resistance. But as her torso emerged from the water, the strain on her arms increased.

"No, no, no," she cried again as her hands began slipping.

Ketahn's thoughts echoed her words.

A long, dark shadow flitted through the water near her. Ketahn loosened his grip on her spear, letting her sink back into the water, and thrust his own spear down hard. It hit something solid. The shaft trembled with the creature's thrashing, and black blood clouded the already dark water.

"Be still," Ketahn snarled.

More of the eshkens rushed in to take the place of the first. Lacey and Diego cried out in alarm, the former losing her hold on her weapon entirely. Ketahn quickly reversed his grip on it and set it to work even as he shook the first creature free of his spear.

"Yeah, okay. Still and calm. No problem," Lacey said, her voice thick with what Ivy called *sar kazum*.

The root shuddered, creaked, and groaned as Ketahn thrust the spears into the water as fast as he could. He attacked anything that moved around the two humans. If the root gave out, it would be Ivy in this water. It would be Ivy swarmed by these creatures.

Ketahn could not accept that.

By your eightfold eyes, see that the root holds, or it shall be my wrath to shake the Tangle.

.   .   .

$\mathcal{T}$he hot, humid air could not keep the chill out of Ivy's blood as she stared down at the churning water. Ketahn's spears lashed out again and again, but there seemed no end to the dark shapes swirling around Diego and Lacey.

The two humans had leaned closer together, back-to-back—bag-to-bag—Diego having fished out his knife. Even with Ketahn's speed, the frenzy in the water only seemed to worsen. How long before someone was bitten? Before someone...

A roar from the other end of the root demanded Ivy's attention. Her eyes widened as Telok leapt into the water near the shoreline, sinking up to his second leg joints. Raising his spear overhead in one hand, he lowered himself and splashed wildly with his lower arms and his forelegs.

One of the eel things surfaced before him. Ivy glimpsed a gaping maw filled with jagged, gleaming teeth before Telok's spear came down on the creature, slamming it back under.

And still Telok continued his splashing, taking another step away from the shore.

Ivy looked down. Several dark shapes flitted away from the pack around Diego and Lacey, called by the new disturbance. Telok was trying to give Ketahn some space to get the humans out of the water, but there were still too many of the muckstalkers.

"Cole," Ivy said suddenly.

"Huh?" He started turning toward her but stopped when she placed her hands on his shoulders. "What is it, Ivy?"

She hurriedly untied the drawstring of his pack and then tore the bag open, plunging both hands inside to rummage through the contents. Cole swayed with the force of her movements; the root shook with the force of Ketahn's movements. Finally, she uncovered a bundle of silk rope at the bottom of his bag.

Cole glanced over his shoulder as she pulled the rope free.

Understanding sparked in his gaze, and he didn't speak as Ivy turned around so her bag was toward him. She uncoiled the rope.

Ivy felt him open her bag, felt him search it, felt him pull something free. When she faced him again, he was already uncoiling the rope he'd taken from her pack. Shoving aside all the thoughts that threatened to overwhelm her—*my friends are down there about to be eaten; my mate is dangling upside down over a killer-eel-infested swamp; this root is damaged and could break at any moment*—she tied one end of the rope into a large loop, just like Ketahn had taught her. He'd said it would draw tight around whatever was inside when the rope was pulled.

She prayed she had done it correctly.

Beside her, Cole was trying to follow her example, but he let out a frustrated growl. "I'm not getting this right."

Ivy glanced at the shore. Telok was the embodiment of speed and ferocity in the water, which seemed alive all around him. The muckstalkers were leaping at him, latching onto his legs, thrashing and wriggling as he battled them with spear and claws and filled the water with their blood. Urkot and Rekosh had joined him, though neither had gone quite as deep. All three continued splashing to draw as much attention as possible.

Ahnset stood on land with the other humans, her spear at the ready and her gaze wary. She undoubtedly knew that if anything else decided to come investigate the commotion, she was the final line of defense.

Handing Cole the first rope, Ivy grabbed the other from his hands. She quickly undid his work and made a new loop, somehow managing to do so without a mistake despite her fingers trembling.

She and Cole tossed the ropes down to Diego and Lacey simultaneously.

Cole's line landed just beside Diego, who had sunk up to his collarbone. He was breathing quickly, face streaked with dirt and muck. Ivy's loop fell over Lacey's raised arm. Both humans hurriedly grasped the ropes and drew them over their heads and shoulders until they were under their arms.

"To land," Ketahn growled as he skewered another muck-stalker. He lifted the spear out of the water and swung it hard, dislodging the writhing creature.

"We need to pull them up," Cole replied, bracing his feet on the root.

"The root might break." Ivy wrapped her end of the rope around her fists. "If we pull them straight up, it could put too much pressure on the wood."

"Fuck." Cole glanced toward land, nostrils flaring with a heavy exhalation. "You better not fall, Ivy."

"I don't plan on it." Ivy turned toward land and started walking. All she needed to do was keep a hold of the rope and get to the others on the shore.

She shut out the chaos around her, all the splashing and shouting, the growls and grunts, the strengthened stench that had arisen from the disturbed water, and focused on the root in front of her. Focused on setting her feet down one after the other, quick and careful.

The rope began to run out of slack as Ivy neared the end of the root. If she pulled hard enough to free Lacey from the mud, she'd be pulling the woman away from Ketahn—away from her only protection.

Like tearing off a bandage. Just have to do it quick.

"Help me!" Ivy called just before she jumped down.

She landed in the water, boots sinking immediately into the mud, but the water here was only shin deep. Tightening her hold on the rope, she slung it over her shoulder, leaned forward, and put all her strength and body weight into charging ahead.

Will, Ahmya, and Callie rushed to Ivy, arriving just as Cole hopped down beside her. The other humans grasped the ropes, their voices frantic. Ivy couldn't make out what they were saying over all the other noise. But it didn't matter. All that mattered was getting her friends out of this situation.

Her muscles, tired from so many days of hard travel and uncomfortable sleep, screamed in agony. Ivy gritted her teeth and pushed on, trudging toward land. The silk rope trembled and pulled taut, straining against the resistance on the other end, but it was moving, it had to be moving.

Something huge loomed in front of Ivy. She lifted her gaze from the muddy ground to find Ahnset standing tall before her.

The female vrix stabbed the butt of her spear into the ground and reached out with her left hands to grasp Ivy's rope. With her right hands, she took hold of Cole's. Mandibles spread, legs braced wide, and violet eyes fierce, Ahnset pulled.

The ropes jerked forward. Ivy and the other humans stumbled and fell with the sudden momentum, but Ahnset didn't slow. Hand over hand, she dragged the ropes to shore with increasing speed.

Ivy turned to see the male vrix still battling the creatures near the shoreline, all of them covered in muck, blood, and at least a few bite wounds. Just beyond them were Diego and Lacey, racing on the water toward land at the ends of the taut ropes.

With another roar, Telok dipped into deeper water and swept his arms and forelegs up and out. Several of the black muckstalkers flew into the air, jaws snapping and bodies flailing, riding a spray of filthy water. His arms came back down just as Lacey neared. He scooped her out of the water, sweeping her high and cradling her just beneath his chin. Forelegs kicking and stomping, he began a slow retreat.

Ivy could almost feel the mud trying to catch his legs with each step, but Telok's strength—or perhaps his fury—was too great to be restrained.

Rekosh seized Diego as the man's bag hit the bottom in the shallow water, hauling him up to his feet and half-carrying him back to land. Urkot thrust his spear into the water one more time. When he pulled it out, a pair of the killer eels were impaled on its end, their sleek, slimy bodies writhing. Then he too retreated.

Ivy pushed herself up and helped her friends get to their feet. Her breath was sawing in and out of her lungs, her hands hurt where the rope had been coiled around them, and she was certain she was shaking, but all her concern in that moment was turned toward Ketahn.

Still dangling from the underside of the root, he lifted his gaze to her. He'd been splashed with all manner of filth, and even from that distance, she could see his chest heaving with his great breaths, but he raised his mandibles in a smile.

Well, from her perspective, he'd lowered them—but an upside-down smile was a smile all the same.

She didn't look away from him until he'd hauled himself back atop the root and had begun a cautious return.

Telok and Rekosh carried Lacey and Diego to the only truly solid ground—a low boulder that was half overgrown with moss. The vrix set down the humans gently; only Rekosh backed away. Ivy and the others hurried over to them.

"You are pain?" Telok asked in halting English, hands on Lacey's shoulders as he raked his gaze over her.

Lacey curled her arms around her belly and leaned forward. Her lips parted with a slow, shaky exhalation, and water dripped from her long hair, which was dark with muck. Her face looked far paler than normal, which made Ivy's heart stutter.

Diego didn't look to be in much better shape. With Will's help, he lay back on the rock with knees bent, face turned toward the sky, and eyes closed. His chest rose and fell with deep breaths just as uneven and erratic as Lacey's.

"Fuck," Diego rasped.

Kneeling beside Diego, Will looked at the man uncertainly.

"Lacey," Telok said firmly. "You are pain? You are"—he looked to Ivy with a pleading light in his green eyes unlike anything she'd ever seen in them.

"Hurt," Ivy said softly. "Lacey, Diego, are you guys hurt?"

Lacey shook her head, but the movement was so slight that even her dangling hair barely moved. Telok, seemingly unconvinced by this, ran his hands over her body, checking every one of the several new tears in her jumpsuit, some of which revealed bloody skin beneath.

Diego lifted his head from the rock and looked down at his body. His jumpsuit was similarly torn in a few places. Letting out a heavy sigh, he lowered his head again. "Bastards caught me a few times, but nothing serious. Also, I'm pretty sure I shit myself, but I don't think that counts as hurt."

Callie laughed, the sound short and far more relieved than amused. "Correct. Bruised pride does not count as a wound."

Lips curling into a smile, Diego chuckled. "Shouldn't I be the one to decide that? I'm the only medical professional here, after all, whether there's shit in my pants or not."

"Keep joking like that, and I'll make sure you have a real injury to nurse," Will said, giving Diego a light punch on the shoulder.

Diego turned his head to look up at Will, his smile widening.

Telok captured Lacey's chin and forced it up. She met his gaze, eyes unfocused, and blinked a few times before clarity returned. Whatever Telok communicated to her, he did so without words.

"I'm okay," she said softly. "A few bites, but I'm okay. Because of all you guys."

"And we are going to disinfect the hell out of all those bites," said Diego, "as soon as my legs don't feel like jelly anymore."

A tremor ran through Telok, and he bowed his head, lightly touching his headcrest to Lacey's forehead. She closed her eyes and remained that way.

"They are well?" Ketahn asked in English from behind Ivy.

She turned to smile at him, nodding. "Yeah. They're okay."

Ketahn dipped low as he reached her, snatching Ivy into his arms and lifting her in a tight embrace. The thunder of his hearts beating was a welcome comfort to her. She finally let go, finally let herself relax, and just melted against him.

"You did well, my heartsthread," he rumbled.

"Urkot, *what* are you doing?" Rekosh asked in vrix.

Ivy turned her head to look at Urkot. He was holding a dead muckstalker in his lower right hand, bending his wrist up and down to make the carcass flop.

"Thinking," Urkot said without looking up.

"About?" asked Ahnset, head tilted.

Everyone was looking at Urkot now. Mandibles twitching, he turned to face the rest of the group.

Callie's brow furrowed. "Uh, Urkot..."

"You say..." Urkot grunted after speaking those simple words in English, staring down as though he'd find more words scattered on the ground. "You say good?"

"What do you mean say good? What's good?"

Urkot raised his upper left arm, exposing the scar on his side below it. Then he pressed the dead muckstalker's head against the rough scar tissue and waggled his wrist again, making the eel's body flap up and down.

"*Heh-lo,*" he said, waving the eel-arm a little faster. "Say arm good?"

Ivy was pretty sure there wasn't anyone there who wasn't laughing or chittering at that, but she couldn't tell for sure over her own laughter—which welled up from her belly, rich and full and terribly cathartic, bringing tears to her eyes that might not have been caused solely by her amusement. And as she laughed, she clung to Ketahn all the tighter.

He squeezed her against him, drawing in her scent through is nostrils as he nuzzled her hair.

In that moment, Ivy felt more like she was part of a family than ever before, and she knew it was not only her bond with Ketahn that would last forever. This was her tribe, these were her people.

And she would fight for them.

CHAPTER 22

THE SWAMP WAS FAR NOISIER by night. Animals made their calls in the anonymity of darkness, some creating a gentle ambiance not unlike the night songs of frogs and crickets, others much harsher but thankfully more infrequent. There was more activity in the water, too—more splashes and ripples, as though all sorts of creatures were emerging from it now that the daylight was gone.

Ivy barely suppressed a shudder as she recalled the creatures Diego and Lacey had escaped from earlier in the day—bloodthirsty crosses between eels and leeches that the vrix called eshkens.

She'd be happy to never see one of them again, but she knew that wouldn't happen. The tribe wasn't out of the swamp yet.

And yet oddly enough, Ivy found these night sounds soothing. They should've unsettled her, as they meant so many more creatures—unknown things she couldn't even imagine—were creeping through the dark, but...they made the swamp feel more alive.

During the day, everything had been so quiet. Every little sound had been amplified by that relative silence—every tiny splash became something big and terrible, every creaking piece of wood became the groan of some unseen monster. And with those muckstalkers following the group all day…

Those slimy creatures had made Ivy think of vultures. They'd made her feel like she was a dying animal walking through a desert with those massive birds circling overhead, just waiting for a chance to get a bite of her.

She still hadn't shaken that feeling, even though she knew it was silly. This place was about as far from a desert as she could get without being in the middle of the ocean.

Ivy nestled back into Ketahn's embrace and sighed. He'd carried her up onto a high branch and leaned against the tree trunk, drawing her atop him like he always used to do in the den they'd shared. It was his warmth, his solidness, his strength, that truly comforted her. It was Ketahn who'd seen her through all these trials.

He dipped his chin and brushed his mouth over the top of her hair, mandibles teasing her ears and jaw with touches that were impossibly gentle considering the long, sharp fangs at their tips. A low, contented rumble sounded in his chest.

Stars twinkled through a break in the clouds overhead—a patch of the deepest blue and purple spattered with countless glittering lights cut out of the expansive black and gray. Even in this place, with all its muck, hidden terrors, foul odors, and slime, there was beauty to be found.

Ketahn shifted one of his lower hands, settling it on Ivy's belly, which she couldn't deny was just a bit rounder than it had been before; she could've told as much by the slight curl of his fingers and palm. And that was a little frightening. With a normal human pregnancy, she wouldn't have been showing at all this soon, so unless she'd somehow gained weight in the last month…

This was all too new, too uncertain. She didn't know what to expect of this pregnancy, what it would do to her, or how long she would carry the baby.

She didn't know if the hybrid baby would even survive.

Ivy swiftly shoved that thought away, feeling sick to her stomach. She didn't want to think about that for even an instant.

"Ah, my heartsthread," he purred, rubbing her stomach slowly, reverently. His touch eased her, helping to sweep aside her troubled thoughts and bring her back to this moment.

Ivy smiled and placed her hand over his, tipping her head back against his chest. She could sit like this forever, forgetting about the world, forgetting about everything but her mate.

Her mate...and her child.

The voices of her tribemates, who had made camp on a large tree nearby, drifted to Ivy. Telok had discovered a place where a massive trunk split into dozens of branches that spread outward in all directions, creating something as close to a platform as they would find in nature. With the strategic placement of a few blankets and some silk, they'd managed to make a fairly comfortable spot that almost felt like a house.

Camp hadn't been set even a few minutes when Ketahn had picked Ivy up and carried her away. His only response to their companions' questions had been that he needed time alone with his mate.

Ivy knew exactly what they'd all been thinking. She'd been thinking the same thing. But when they'd come up here, he'd just moved her into this position and sat in content silence. And that was okay—they were both dirty and exhausted, splattered with who-knew-what kind of sludge from the swamp, and the comfort of their closeness was enough. Just being held by Ketahn was enough.

"We should go back soon," she said, nestling more snugly against him.

"Soon," he replied, holding her a little tighter.

Smile widening, she closed her eyes. She loved being around the others and had come to care for all of them. They really were her family. But she would never tire of these moments with Ketahn. These moments alone, these moments of peace, when silence didn't need to be filled in with conversation, when there were absolutely no expectations but to simply exist with one another.

Someone laughed back at camp—Diego by the sound of it. It was followed by more laughter from the others, made spritely by distance and the swamp's other sounds.

"I'm glad everyone is all right," Ivy said.

Ketahn hummed his agreement. His claspers squeezed her hips, and his big hand continued its lazy motion up and down her belly. They weren't going to sleep here on their own, Ivy knew that would be foolish, but it would have been so easy to give in to her weariness, turn her face against his chest, and drift off.

Ivy lifted her other hand to Ketahn's cheek, stroking her palm down to his jaw and trailing her thumb along his neck before sliding her hand up again. He leaned into her touch.

The swamp continued its alien music, and the dark clouds continued their trek across the night sky. This place, this planet, this universe, cared nothing for beings so small and insignificant as Ivy and Ketahn. They were no more consequential than two specks of dust. She could understand how such a thought might frighten some people, could understand the dread that some people found in it.

But Ivy was at peace with that knowledge. What did the universe matter when she had her mate? What did any of it matter when she had *love*? This was everything. Whatever path her thoughts took, they always came back to that, time and again. This was everything, and for her, it was forever.

"Ketahn?"

"Yes?"

"How do you feel about…this?" She squeezed his hand upon her belly. "It has to be strange, right?"

With a thoughtful grunt, he stilled his hand. He kept it there on her stomach, fingers spread, strong and secure, as possessive as it was protective. "Yes. Like finding small, frail, two-legged creatures that fell from the sky, or realizing that one of those creatures is my heartsthread. Strange…but right."

Ivy's heart clenched with his words. She turned her face up to look at him. He was already looking down at her, his eyes faintly glowing violet in the starlight. Eight eyes that had been unsettling to her all those weeks ago, but had become so endearing, so comforting, so familiar.

"How long does it take a vrix egg to hatch?" she asked.

"Four moon cycles."

Ivy tensed, and the air locked in her throat.

Four months? *Four months?*

That…that didn't mean she would give birth so soon, did it? She was still human. That had to make some difference, didn't it? But why else would she be showing so early if the baby wasn't growing faster than normal? Why else would she already be having these symptoms?

Because this baby isn't human…and isn't vrix.

And if what Diego had said was true, if her body really had changed to accept Ketahn's seed, did that mean Ivy wasn't exactly human anymore? Or was it just her eggs adapting to accept his sperm?

The most frustrating part—the scariest part—was that she would never know the answers. However much she thought about it, she'd only ever come up with simple guesses about a process that was undoubtedly complex, a process that even the scientists who'd created the injections for the Homeworld Initiative hadn't fully understood.

And it wasn't those scientists who had to deal with this. It wasn't THI facing the consequences. All those people were long,

long gone. Ivy, Ketahn, and their baby would have to figure it all out, and the best they could do for now was hope everything would be okay.

There was no *What to Expect When You're Expecting Vrix Babies* for Ivy to read. She didn't have friends or family who'd already gone through this because she was the first. She was making history here.

But when people talked about those great historical moments, about those groundbreaking firsts, they rarely mentioned just how terrifying those occurrences had been for those involved.

And as much as I want this with Ketahn, I am terrified.

Ketahn cupped the underside of her jaw, his long fingers curling to stroke her cheek. "What troubles you, Ivy?"

"I'm worried. About everything, of course, but mostly... about this." She pressed his hand more firmly on her belly. "I've never done this. In a lot of ways, no one has ever done this."

His hold tightened, but there was nothing painful or uncomfortable about it—there was just adoration, security, *love*. "I have never seen an egg hatch. My brood was my mother's last. But we will see our broodling birthed together, my *nyleea*. You will hold our broodling in your arms, and you will smile, and it will be brighter than the stars, moons, and sun combined."

Ivy smiled up at him. "I didn't know vrix could be such poets."

"*Poh ehtz?*"

"Someone who makes pretty words."

Ketahn trilled and guided her to tilt her head aside, lowering his face to the spot where her neck and shoulder met. One of his hands unfastened the top of her jumpsuit before hooking the collar with a finger and pulling it aside. He skimmed his rough mouth over her skin. The flow of his warm breath made her shiver with anticipation, and her nipples hardened into achy points.

"My words will never be worthy of you, my heartsthread," he said, proceeding to peel open her jumpsuit and drag it down her arms, baring her breasts to the air. "So I will do. All I can, I will do, and always for you. Ever for you."

He covered her breast with one of his large hands, and Ivy's breath hitched when he caught her nipple between finger and thumb and pinched it. Desire sparked in her as he rolled that sensitive bud and kneaded the surrounding flesh. She arched back against him, craving more of his touch, and heat bloomed in her core.

"Your scent drives me to a hunger like I have never known, Ivy." Ketahn's tongue slipped out, sliding over the scars left by his bite and continuing up her neck. His slit bulged against her backside, his hardening cock trapped within.

Ivy closed her eyes, reached up to hook a hand behind his head, and buried her fingers in his hair. "Ketahn, I'm dirty."

"You are delicious, female," he growled before licking her again—slowly, deliberately, wickedly. The hand on her belly shifted, forcing the jumpsuit open the rest of the way, and then dipped into it. Those long, strong, callused fingers slid down, down, down to exactly where she wanted them. They delved between the folds of her pussy. "And you are in need."

Ketahn stroked her, spreading her essence, taking extra care with his claws as he brought those fingers back up to circle her clit. Ivy gasped, her hips bucking. His claspers tightened around her hips and stilled her as a rumble vibrated in his chest. He covered her other breast with another hand.

Those dexterous fingers continued their steady, languid rhythm, applying exactly the right pressure to coax a response from her body. She squeezed his wrist just to have something to hold onto. The heat that had sparked low in her belly built higher and higher, unfurling ecstasy in her veins. Her pelvis undulated in time with his strokes, her breath grew heavy, and she arched her back more, tightening her grip on his hair as she turned her face toward his.

"Ketahn," she moaned, spreading her thighs wide and draping them over his legs.

"I love the songs you make for me"—he shifted the hand on her chin to brush a finger over her bottom lip—"but you must be quiet, my *nyleea*. This is for us alone."

Both his breath and his hair that had fallen over her shoulder tickled her skin. Even their soft, barely-there caresses were amplified by her awareness of Ketahn and his touch. Ivy fought the sounds threatening to escape her. And still, Ketahn kept tracing those maddening circles around her clit.

The pleasure coiling within her sharpened, and she tried to chase it, but his claspers locked her in place. Her blood sizzled, and her hot, liquid essence dripped down her ass as she writhed against him. Ivy whimpered.

"Shh." His hiss sent a fresh thrill through her. "Silent, Ivy. But look at me that I may see you crying out inside." He pinched her nipples.

Ivy gasped and opened her heavy-lidded eyes, meeting his gaze.

"You need more?" His voice was a barely audible rasp, but it blazed through Ivy, shaking her to her core.

"Please, Ketahn," she whispered, desperately rocking against his finger. "I need you inside me."

His low, ragged growl almost made her come right then. He peeled her jumpsuit farther down, and those claspers eased their hold so he could lift her backside off him. She felt his cock spring free of his slit immediately, brushing between her inner thighs. Even without his guidance, she was already angling her hips to meet him. He spread her open with two fingers and drove his shaft deep into her.

Ivy bit down on her lips to silence her cry. She didn't know if her teeth had drawn blood and didn't care. All that mattered was this. Was *him*.

He pushed ever deeper into her, stretching her, forcing her body to accept his girth, and withdrew only the barest amount to thrust in again. And she accepted him greedily, her sex tightening and slickening with her impending climax. She panted, her toes curling. His fingers curved, pricking her flesh with his claws, and another vibration coursed through her with his growl.

And then he was hammering into her, his movements fast, hard, fierce, contrasted by the reverent caresses of two of his hands as they teased her breasts and explored her skin.

Every stroke of his shaft pushed her closer to that edge. She panted, suppressing her moans, and though her eyelids threatened to fall shut, she kept them open to stare into his eyes, which were like gleaming gems in the night.

"My mate, my *nyleea*. Ah, my heartsthread." Once more Ketahn found her clit and stroked it in time with his thrusts.

The pressure within her grew into something unfathomable, impossible, something that would surely be her end because it was too great, too intense, too much. The vibrant violet of Ketahn's eyes flared, and glaring white filled Ivy's vision, blasting apart the darkness and plunging her into a torrent of ecstasy.

Ivy's lips parted with a soundless cry. That white-hot pleasure permeated her being; it had consumed her, had become her, and there was nothing in the universe but those sensations and her mate. Her sex clamped tight around his cock as heat flooded her core.

Sound welled up from her chest, but Ketahn covered her mouth with his hand, muffling the cries she was helpless to prevent.

Ketahn's big body shuddered, those powerful muscles tensing beneath and around Ivy as his thrusts grew deeper, more forceful, and more erratic. His chest reverberated with a sound that would've undoubtedly built to a roar, but he silenced himself by clamping his mouth on her shoulder—in the same spot he'd marked already.

He released a savage growl the same instant his molten seed erupted within her. His claws pressed into her flesh, forcing her down onto him until she couldn't possibly take any more of his shaft. And then she felt *them*—those alien tendrils that unfurled from his cock and delivered unspeakable pleasure. She squeezed her eyes shut and cried out against his palm, abandoning herself to the whirlwind of sensation.

She felt his hot seed spill inside her again and again as her sex contracted around him, milking Ketahn for everything he had to give and more. She trembled, thighs quivering, as she rode the waves of rapture.

When Ivy floated back down and opened her eyes, that brilliant patch of star-filled sky was the first thing she saw. Her skin was flushed and coated with perspiration, and her pussy pulsed with the aftermath of what they'd shared. She felt the prick of his claws, the solid grip of his claspers, and the dull pain on her shoulder where his fangs had broken her skin. But for the first time in days, Ivy felt light. She released the tension in her limbs and settled against him.

Everything felt…right.

His hand slid down from her mouth to curl around her chin as he relaxed his jaw and withdrew his teeth. Those tendrils were still fluttering within her, but their motions were leisurely now, like they'd expended all their energy but were loath to depart. Ivy certainly wasn't going to complain.

But her lingering pleasure couldn't distract her from the concerned tone in his voice when he quietly asked, "Did I hurt the broodling?"

Ivy blinked. "What?"

"The baby." He covered her lower belly with a hand, his

touch so gentle but uncertain. "If it is inside you, and I am inside you…"

The laugh spilled out of her before she could stop it, and she swiftly covered her mouth. Did he really think he was poking the baby with his cock?

Well, he is an alien, and his kind lay eggs. He doesn't know about any of this, so of course he's going to worry…

Shaking her head, Ivy turned her face toward him and lowered her hand once she'd regained her composure.

Ketahn's mandibles twitched, but his gaze was unwavering. "Why do you laugh?"

"I'm sorry. It was just something so…*human* to say. There are men back on Earth who think the same thing, men who don't understand how women's bodies work." She caressed his jaw and the base of his mandible. "No, Ketahn. You did not hurt it. My body is strong and is protecting the baby, and it was made for, well…*this.*" She grinned and wiggled upon his cock. "It can take a little pounding."

He trilled, and his claspers tightened, pinning her in place. He rasped, "Be still, my heartsthread. Should I fall to frenzy now, all the mire will know we are here."

Ivy hummed. "I love it when you lose control."

Another deep sound vibrated within him, and his cock twitched. "Now is not the time, Ivy."

She sighed dramatically and combed her fingers through his hair. "I know, I know. You just feel too good."

He responded only by grunting and wrapping his arms around her securely, neither allowing her further movement nor withdrawing from her sex. His hand remained protectively upon her belly, occasionally caressing her bare skin, and a few times, he carefully brushed the seam of his mouth over the place he'd bitten. Ivy soon felt her weariness settling in again. Only Ketahn could make a place like this feel safe. Only he could make it comfortable.

Ivy wasn't sure how much time had passed when he finally stirred, and she didn't really care. She knew it was time to go even if she didn't want to. Wordlessly, Ketahn withdrew from her, and she briefly clamped her thighs together to fight back the immediate sense of emptiness left in his wake. It still didn't make any sense that he could always leave her feeling at once sated and ravenous.

Ketahn shifted into a more upright position, and Ivy sat up. Together, they righted her jumpsuit, drawing the sleeves back up, straightening the fabric that had bunched around her knees, and sealing the front.

With Ketahn's arm holding her steady, she lifted her hands to gather her hair, meaning to tie it back. But as she was doing so, she happened to turn her head and glance down.

Her breath hitched, and her heart jumped.

Amidst the shadows below, a large, indistinct form crept across the ground in the direction of the tree where everyone was camped, silent and barely discernable from the surrounding darkness. Without prying her eyes away from the slowly moving shadow, she pressed a hand to Ketahn's chest, curled her fingers, and raked her nails across his hide.

He turned his head to follow her gaze with his own, and his limbs tensed.

Within that shadowy form, there was a faint flash of blue— eight tiny points of it, there and gone.

Like a vrix's eyes briefly catching the starlight.

CHAPTER 23

KETAHN KNEW EXACTLY what that approaching shadow was. He ignored the disbelieving, arrogant voice in his mind insisting that he'd done everything right, that his eyes were mistaken, that this was not possible, and trusted his instinct instead.

The Queen's Claw had arrived.

Wrapping his arms around Ivy, Ketahn drew her to his chest and twisted away from the Claw, shielding her body with his and hiding as much of himself behind the tree trunk as possible without falling off the branch.

His hearts pounded, their thunderous beats resonating throughout his body. The fine hairs on his legs stood on end, and his mandibles swung closed; only by tensing his jaw to the point of pain was he able to keep his fangs from striking each other. And that dread in his gut grew even heavier—enough so that its weight seemed likely to drag down this whole tree.

Ivy trembled in his arms, her little fingers pressing hard against his hide like she couldn't possibly hold him tight enough. Her breaths came quick, short, and hot against his chest, but they were quiet.

The Claw had raised his gaze, but he wasn't looking at Ivy

and Ketahn—his eyes were directed toward the tree where the tribe had made camp for the night. The tree from which voices even now emanated, so distinct from the mire's other sounds that they were unmistakable despite being so muted.

At the base of Ketahn and Ivy's tree, the Claw halted. Ketahn found himself staring almost straight down at the other male. Faint starlight fell upon the Claw, granting the fur slung over his shoulder dull, silvery highlights, but it was too weak to overcome the shadows gathered between the folds of the Claw's black shroud.

Lifting a hand, the Claw beckoned.

Movement from farther out caught Ketahn's attention. Four more figures slunk out of the dark mire growth, keeping so low that they were nearly crawling. All were clad in black shrouds and carried spears.

Holding his breath, Ketahn reached for his bag, which he'd hung on a nearby branch before settling down with Ivy earlier, and the spear fastened to it. She tensed, pressing herself more firmly against him. He stretched his arm; his muscles ached with the strain, but the bag was dangling at the far side of the branch.

"That one," said one of the Claws below, pointing toward the large tree that sheltered the rest of the tribe.

Ketahn clenched his jaw and shifted his body, leaning toward the bag. His upper arm extended past the branch into the open air; his shoulder and head followed.

"The queen will be pleased," another of the Claws said.

"Only when she has what she wants in her hands will she be pleased," a third growled.

"You have seen her, Zirket," said the second Claw. "She wants nothing as much as Ketahn and those creatures."

Zirket? Ketahn knew that name. Zurvashi had greatly increased the numbers of the Queen's Claw for her war, and there'd been many more than Ketahn could ever have remembered, but Zirket was familiar. He'd followed Durax; their group had earned some renown for their prowess, though Ketahn had always thought their success had been won despite their leader's lacking capability.

Ketahn's claw brushed the strap of his bag, but he could not work it beneath well enough to lift the bag free. He swallowed his frustration and cast aside the discomfort in his shoulder. Ivy continued to cling to him, her heartbeat so strong that he could feel it through his chest.

"You know Teznak speaks true," the first Claw said. "We will be rewarded."

Zirket growled. "You know nothing of the queen, Arjat. The Prime Claw spent years trying to please her, but it was never enough. Our only reward will be living another day."

"You are a fool, Zirket."

Ketahn glanced down. Two of the Claws were glaring at a third—likely Arjat and Teznak glaring at Zirket, whose head was turning slowly as he studied his surroundings. The other two who'd not yet spoken were watching the group's rear.

"I am leader." Zirket snapped his fangs with a sharp hiss. "And though I did not ask to be sent on this hunt with a pack of broodlings, I have come to serve my queen's will."

Releasing a slow breath, Ketahn bent at his waist, granting himself the last bit of reach he needed. His finger finally hooked securely beneath the bag's strap.

Teznak snarled. "The queen's will is that we find the traitors and drag them back to her, bound but alive."

"The queen commanded I find them and lead her to wherever they are hiding," Zirket replied.

Ketahn carefully lifted the bag off the short but thick branch from which he'd hung it. Every muscle in his body flexed to keep his arm steady, to prevent the bag from shaking even slightly—to prevent even the gentlest bump against the wood.

Arjat gestured harshly toward the other tree, though he did

not look away from Zirket. "To ignore this opportunity would be folly. Imagine the glory were we to be the ones to catch them all. Imagine the rewards."

"Imagine a pack of broodlings believing they could capture five warriors who were amongst Takarahl's fiercest during the war against Kaldarak." Zirket ended his words with a low buzz.

"We do not know if there are five," said Teznak.

Ketahn straightened, finally withdrawing from that exposed position, and drew his bag close. He glanced down at Ivy. She had her face buried against his chest, and wisps of her hair dangled over her cheeks.

"Yet you mean to attack?" asked Zirket with venom in his voice.

Ketahn caught Ivy's chin with one hand, forcing her to tilt her head back and look up at him. Her eyes were rounded, gleaming with fear and uncertainty in the dim light, a far cry from the passion that had been alight in them only moments ago.

And still, even here, even now, with danger only segments away, he could not help but be stricken by her otherworldly beauty.

Nothing would take her from him. Whatever odds he faced, he would always find a way to protect her. Always.

He'd never had a quarrel with Zirket—nor with any other Claws save Durax, the envious former Prime Claw—but Ketahn's hearts smoldered with hatred now. He could not help but hate anyone or anything that put such fear into his mate's eyes.

Ketahn did the only thing he could in that moment—he looked into Ivy's eyes and let all that he felt for her rise to the surface. The love, the desire, the fierce protectiveness, the instincts that said she was his and his alone, that would drive him to shatter this entire world if that was what it took to protect her. The vow that he would let nothing hurt her, would let nothing take her.

And her fear faded. Not entirely, but enough for him to know that she understood. That she trusted him. Raising a hand, she curled her fingers around his wrist and nodded.

"You said yourself, Zirket, the journey to this mire took five and a half days from Takarahl during the war," said Arjat. "How mighty can these traitors be if they have taken threefold as long?"

"The queen is two days behind," Teznak said. "By the time we return with a message and lead her here, the traitors and their creatures will have moved on."

Zirket released another growl, this one long, low, and furious. "Eight shield me from your foolishness. That is why we will send a message and continue to follow."

"We can take them *now*," said Arjat.

"We will confirm they are there and send a message," Zirket replied firmly. "Laresh, climb high enough to see their camp. We must know their group exactly to satisfy the queen."

One of the two that had been silent grunted in agreement. Ketahn's hearts sped. The threat to Ivy, the danger, was about to draw even closer, and his instincts were torn.

Fight and destroy the threat—but risk the safety of himself and his mate.

Run and hide—but risk the safety of his tribe.

He spent no time debating the options; the threat to his mate was far more immediate, and he would not willingly endanger Ivy or their broodling.

Guiding Ivy back a step, Ketahn broke their embrace. Hands moving faster than his thoughts, he swept the bag over her shoulders, cinched the strap so it was snug, and freed his spear from its tie. Ivy pressed her lips into a tight line, and her nose holes flared with her exhalation.

Vrix claws scraped bark below.

TIFFANY ROBERTS

Ketahn pushed Ivy back a little more and twisted so his hindquarters were toward her. She knew what he intended without needing to be told. Ivy climbed onto him, wrapping her arms around his abdomen and hooking her legs around his waist. His claspers clamped down on her shins.

Reaching back with a lower arm, he held her as tight as he could, but the awkward angle did not allow him much strength. It was the best he could do with the time they had.

Mandible fangs drawn together, and jaw clenched, Ketahn climbed. His racing heartbeat urged him faster and faster, and his muscles stiffened as he fought that urge. Giving over to speed would create too much noise.

Ivy pressed her cheek against his back. Her breath fanned across his hide, matching the frantic pace of his hearts, and her shuddering limbs clutched him.

Ketahn rounded the trunk, moving to the side opposite the Claws. The higher he climbed, the tauter his heartsthread became. He'd not had time to secure Ivy to him with silk as he usually did. The angle of his hindquarters provided her some support, but not nearly enough, and her body was worn after two eightdays of grueling travel.

She was not likely to survive a fall from this height.

That thought roused Ketahn's anger. Rage stirred at the heart of the dread he'd been carrying for so long, impotent and restrained until it found its claws and began to tear its way out. How many times would he have to put his mate through dangerous situations like this simply to escape the looming danger posed by Zurvashi? How long would Ivy have to suffer because the queen refused to be denied what she desired?

"Scents here," called Laresh from somewhere below. "Vrix and something else. Mating scent."

Ivy sucked in a sharp, quiet breath, and her fingers bit into Ketahn's hide.

"They must have stopped here before making their camp," said Teznak.

"Are they actually mating those creatures?" asked Arjat.

Zirket silenced them with a hiss.

"Fresh," said Laresh. "It is still wet."

"Sakahn, go up with Laresh. Search this tree to the top. You two, watch our surroundings. Our prey is near."

More claws bit into bark near the base of the trunk, producing barely a whisper. Panic blossomed in Ketahn's chest, threatening to spread through him, to take control.

These Claws, these cowards, these beasts that served the queen, were going to find his mate. They were going to find his Ivy. And Ketahn had nowhere to go.

The fires of his fury roared and swelled, consuming that panic and leaving naught but ash behind. His only true fear would forever be of something happening to his mate, to their broodling, but that fear would not hinder him.

No, that fear would become the terror of his enemies.

He hauled himself up onto one of the thicker branches and halted his ascent. He could climb and climb until he reached branches too small to support his weight, and then what? Would he climb right into the sky, climb to the stars and swim through the empty black between them?

With something solid beneath Ketahn and his body upright again, Ivy's hold on him relaxed, though only barely. He brushed his knuckles across her lower back before withdrawing the arm he'd bent backward to hold her.

She understood the vrix tongue. She knew what was happening. Her chest pressed rhythmically against his back as she struggled to slow her breathing, as she struggled for calm.

Ketahn drew a hasty strand of silk from his spinnerets, keeping his movements small and silent. He passed Ivy the end of the strand. Their hands worked together to swiftly wrap the silk around their middles, and Ivy pulled it tight and tied it securely as soon as they were done.

He leaned to one side to glance down, then to the other. Though he'd seen only glimpses of Laresh and Sakahn, there was no questioning the situation. The two Claws were climbing on opposite sides of the trunk, barbed spears at the ready, eyes glinting with reflected starlight. Their progress was slow and deliberate; they were scanning every branch they passed, searching, hunting.

But Ketahn was not prey.

Taking hold of one of Ivy's wrists, Ketahn pulled her arm away from him and pressed the shaft of his spear into her palm. She curled her fingers around it. He felt her weight shift on his hindquarters as she withdrew her other hand. A moment later, that hand returned to Ketahn's front, holding the grip of her metal knife to him.

He accepted the small weapon; its grip didn't even span his palm, and its blade was barely as long as his finger. But he'd seen the humans make use of the weapons, and he knew the blade would penetrate vrix hide and bone as readily as any blackrock shard.

More heartening was her understanding despite no words having been exchanged between them. They would have to fight, and the spear was all that could give her a chance of competing with a vrix's longer reach.

She moved the spear behind Ketahn and adjusted her position, scooting her backside forward and squeezing her thighs more firmly around his waist.

He glanced at her over his shoulder. Fear lingered in her eyes, but it was no brighter than a single tiny star against the vastness of the sky. Much stronger was that determination he'd come to admire so much. Ketahn tipped his head to the right. Ivy nodded and took a two-handed hold of the spear, pointing the tip toward the right side of the trunk.

Ketahn turned his attention to the left. Rage burned hotter and hotter in his chest, and its heat spread to his limbs, flooding them with vengeful strength.

Not his Ivy. Never his Ivy.

Each moment was marked by the pounding of his hearts, which had finally slowed to something steady—something dangerous. He could smell his foes now despite the pungent mire odors on the air. Male vrix, oiled wood, and damp fur. The stench of the Queen's Claw.

The scrape of claws on bark meant the climbers were just below Ketahn. In his mind's eye, he saw Laresh and Sakahn climbing, saw their muscles straining, their shrouds and furs dangling, saw the polished blackrock of their spearheads gleam with reflected starlight. That vision quickly turned red—he would see their blood spill before this was done.

A black, long fingered hand rose into view near the base of the branch and sank its claws into the wood. The fingers flexed, and the vrix attached to that hand drew himself higher.

Ketahn's muscles bunched, restless with that furious energy. The human knife felt good in his hand; though small, it had excellent balance and comfortable weight.

The Claw he was watching—the first climber, Laresh—pulled himself up in a burst of speed. Ketahn solidified his stance atop the branch and lunged at the attacker, upper arms darting out to grab hold of the Claw. His fingers caught on the fabric of a heavy shroud, his claws biting through to sink into the hide beneath.

Ivy jolted atop Ketahn, her weight shifting to the right hard and fast enough to make Ketahn sway. Ketahn heard a startled growl, heard the distinct sound of blackrock punching through flesh, heard Ivy's soft but savage grunt.

Ketahn sank his leg claws into the bark as Ivy's weight shifted again, left then right, once more producing the sound of a spear striking its target.

With a choked cry, the Claw she'd hit fell. Branches snapped below Ketahn, but there was no heavy thump to announce a body hitting the ground.

Laresh snarled as Ketahn heaved him up off the branch. Bark cracked and crumbled under Ketahn's legs as he took on his foe's weight. The Claw slid his hand closer to the head of his spear and thrust it at Ketahn.

With his lower hand, Ketahn caught the spear shaft just behind the head and forced the thrust wide. Laresh's scrambling legs found the branch, gaining some purchase and relieving some of Ketahn's burden. The ensuing struggle was chaotic—limbs swinging, mandibles gnashing, each vrix's legs seeking any means to disrupt his enemy's balance.

Ketahn pulled hard on the spear. The Claw lurched toward him, and Ketahn met his foe with Ivy's knife, plunging the blade into Laresh's abdomen. Ripping the blade free, he stabbed again and again. Bone crunched and flesh squelched, defenseless against the rapid attacks.

Ivy's thighs squeezed Ketahn's waist, and she hooked an arm around his middle to hold on through the savagery of his attacks.

Males shouted below. Sakahn rasped a response from much closer—only a few segments under Ketahn, at most.

Laresh grabbed at Ketahn, but his struggles were weakening. Ketahn wrenched the spear out of the Claw's grip and shoved Laresh hard against the tree trunk, clearing his view to the ground.

The dark form of a Claw stared up at him, blue eyes glowing in the starlight.

Ketahn tugged the coil of rope attached to Laresh's spear free, keeping the end in one hand, reversed his hold on the weapon, and threw it. The rope uncoiled as the spear darted toward its mark. Those blue eyes far below widened.

The spear struck the blue-eyed Claw in the belly, plunging

deep. By the sound of his startled, pained curse as he staggered backward, he was Arjat.

Laresh snarled and pushed away from the trunk, tearing the axe from his belt. Blood poured from the wounds on his abdomen and spattered the branch. He swung his axe at Ketahn.

Growling, Ketahn shifted aside to dodge the axe's wild arc. He shoved his enemy again, adding to the Claw's momentum, but Laresh recovered his balance quickly and spun toward Ketahn. When Laresh lashed out once more, Ketahn whipped the spear rope up, looping it around the Claw's extended arm.

Another fierce struggle ensued. Ketahn's claws sliced Laresh's hide, shedding fresh blood, and the metal knife landed several more times. Ketahn's blood-slickened hands moved without conscious thought, manipulating the silk rope to weave it around Laresh's flailing arms and, finally, around his neck.

The Claw's only free arm darted forward, straight for Ketahn's face. As Ketahn swayed back to avoid the blow, he felt Ivy shift; her legs tightened, her backside rose, and her chest pulled away from his back.

The head of a spear darted past Ketahn's cheek from behind, close enough for him to feel the air disturbed by its passage. Laresh scraped his forelegs on the branch and tipped his torso backward. The spearhead punctured the tender hide at the base of his throat, sinking just deep enough for the barbs to catch.

Ketahn clutched the spear with one hand and surged forward, slamming his forelegs into Laresh's chest. The Claw, already off balance, fell off the branch with a startled grunt, and the spear tore free with a spray of crimson.

The strand tangled around Laresh—which was tied to the spear in Arjat's gut below—fell over the top of the branch with him, pulling taut within a moment.

Arjat cried out in pain as the rope jolted him off the ground and several segments into the air before the spear tore free from his gut. His entrails spilled out with it. Laresh slammed into several branches on his way down, breaking smaller ones and bouncing off the larger ones until he finally crashed to the ground with a heavy thud.

A few branches down from Ketahn, Sakahn was dragging himself up, having managed to catch himself during his fall.

Ivy let out a shaky breath that Ketahn felt against his hair and eased back, relinquishing her hold on the spear to wrap her arms around his abdomen. "Are you hurt?"

"No," he replied. He barely felt anything through the thrumming battle haze that had swallowed him. "Signal the others. *Wiss ull.*"

Her hair brushed up and down against his back; he saw her nodding in his mind's eye. After a couple failed attempts, she made that shrill, piercing sound that humans could produce by shaping their lips a certain way and blowing. Though she could not do it as loud as Cole and Callie had once demonstrated, it was loud enough to carry back to camp—and any unknown vrix lurking nearby would have no idea what manner of creature had made such a noise.

If the battle sounds had not already alerted Ketahn's tribe, the *wiss ull* would.

"We must go," Zirket growled at the base of the tree. "We must carry the message!"

Ketahn clenched his teeth and spread his mandibles. The queen was likely to catch up to his tribe whether she received word from these scouts or not, but it would happen much sooner if that message was delivered.

"Hold firm," Ketahn said.

Somehow, Ivy squeezed him even tighter. Ketahn leapt down from branch to branch until he reached Sakahn. Grasping the vrix's hair, Ketahn tugged Sakahn's head back and stabbed him in the throat with Ivy's knife. He twisted the blade and flicked it outward as he pulled it free.

The sound of blood spilling onto the bark was like pouring

rain—a crimson storm that would not end until Zurvashi was no more.

Ketahn kicked the dying male off the branch and raced away in pursuit of the other Claws, who were two dark, indistinct shapes flitting across the scant ground, fleeing in the direction from which they'd come. No more than a few dozen segments ahead of them was an area where the trees gave way to still, murky water and densely grown tall grass.

Ivy squeaked when Ketahn jumped, crossing a wide, open-air gap to the next tree. The bough bounced beneath him, its leaves shaking and rustling. Using both his legs and his arms, he tore from one side of the tree to the other, swinging, leaping, and climbing without pause. Without the obstacles that made the mire ground difficult to traverse, he was rapidly closing the lead his enemies had gained—but his advantage was reaching its end as he entered the tree's farthest branches.

He charged forward. The narrowing branch dipped under his weight just as the front Claw—Teznak—neared the edge of the tall grass. When the branch came up again, Ketahn used it to launch himself into the air.

Ivy gasped, her body tensing and her hold on Ketahn strengthening. Her nails bit into the hide of his chest.

Zirket shouted to his companion, urging him onward, and skidded to a halt, turning around as he did so.

Ketahn's leap passed the peak of its arc. He angled his spear down as his descent began.

Mandibles spreading wide, Zirket lifted his head to look up at Ketahn. His eyes rounded, and starlight highlighted the fine hairs on his legs as they stood. He began raising his spear.

Before Zirket could defend himself, Ketahn's spear struck him in the center of his chest. With all Ketahn's weight and momentum behind it, the weapon smashed through the Claw's chest plate and into one of his hearts. Zirket fell, and Ketahn came down atop him with jarring impact, driving the spear deeper still. Ketahn felt the crunch as the spearhead pierced Zirket's back and sank into the ground.

For all the force behind the blow, the sound Zirket released was decidedly small and weak. A low grunt, more startled than pained, that crumbled into a broken, drawn-out wheeze.

Agony radiated through Ketahn's leg joints, which had absorbed some of the impact when they'd hit the ground, and pulsed along his legs. His palms burned from the scrape of the spear shaft.

One of Zirket's hands rose and fell, clutching at the uppermost segment of Ketahn's foreleg. He raked Ketahn's hide with his claws, but there was not enough strength behind them to inflict any damage. Zirket's mandibles twitched weakly. He stared up at Ketahn with a wild but far-off light in his eyes.

He opened his mouth to speak. Only a choked sound and frothy blood came out.

Zirket's body went limp beneath Ketahn, and a final, rasping breath escaped him.

"Oh, my God," Ivy whispered, face pressed against Ketahn's back.

Pushing himself up, Ketahn lifted his gaze and growled a curse; the only sign of Teznak was in the broken stalks where the Claw had plunged into the grass. Ketahn had no doubt he could follow Teznak's trail easily enough, but to continue this chase now would be foolish, especially while Ivy was with him.

His friends must have heard everything. They would arrive soon, and they would hunt the surviving Claw and ensure the message never reached Zurvashi.

From somewhere amidst the tall grass, Teznak's voice carried into the night air. His words were harsh, distressed, and too low for Ketahn to understand. But he understood the sounds that followed—the grass thrashing, the grunts and growls of a struggle, the pained cry cut short.

Ketahn exhaled, allowing his muscles to finally relax. His

friends had already intercepted the survivor, had already ended the bloody, unexpected conflict. Now he and Ivy could return to camp and—

"Did something...get him?" Ivy asked, her voice barely audible over the mire's sounds.

Ketahn's mandibles snapped together as realization struck him. His friends would have come from the opposite direction —from behind Ketahn and Ivy. There was no way any of them, even Telok, could have known to circle around like that, no way any of them could have done it so quickly without Ketahn noticing during the chase.

But the sounds of that unseen struggle had not been created by a vrix battling a beast.

His already thundering hearts beat faster and louder, hammering his chestplate. He released his weapon and sank down to pry the spear from Zirket's grasp and tug the axe off the dead Claw's belt.

Weapons at the ready, he retreated, keeping low and not turning away from the tall grass.

"Ketahn, what's wrong?" Ivy whispered.

He silenced her with a short hiss. It was too late, he knew that, but his every instinct was to protect his mate, to keep her safe, to keep her hidden. To cling to the desperate, impossible hope that there was still a clean escape—not just from Zurvashi, but from this situation.

"Ketahn," Rekosh rasped from somewhere behind, "are there more?"

Ketahn swiped a hand down through the air, signaling for Rekosh to be quiet, and continued his careful retreat. He allowed himself only the briefest glance over his shoulder.

Rekosh and Urkot had arrived with their barbed spears, each wearing a heavy silk shroud that covered most of their colorful markings. Both sank into stances similar to Ketahn's, taking positions on either side of him as he neared.

The grass swayed in the wind. Mire creatures made their calls, and somewhere close, something splashed into water. Ketahn's hearts continued their frantic beating.

Some instinctual part of him insisted he flee, that he take Ivy far away, that he use his speed and prowess to outrun any enemy that meant her harm—and leave behind all their friends. That urge, though quickly crushed, made his insides twist and coil.

Something shook the tall grass. The motion was followed by a moment of stillness just long enough to make Ketahn wonder if he'd imagined the shaking, and then it resumed.

Ketahn, Rekosh, and Urkot leveled their spears, pointing them toward the grass. Toward the approaching foes.

The long, tightly packed stalks parted, and a large figure emerged. Built as broadly as Urkot but nearly as tall as Ketahn, the male thornskull met Ketahn's gaze with dark eyes and continued striding forward, stopping only when he was several segments clear of the grass.

Hard, spiky growths on his headcrest and shoulders granted him a menacing appearance. His hide was dull and rough looking, slathered with dried mud, and broken blades of grass, fallen leaves, and specks of dirt clung to his thick legs. In one hand, he held a barbed spear, which he stood on the ground. Over his opposite shoulder was a large, dark form.

Again, Ketahn's instincts roared. Protect; attack; destroy. Close the distance between himself and his foe and end this *now*. But he held himself in place.

Like the Queen's Claws, thornskull hunters never traveled alone.

"Shadowstalkers," the thornskull said in a deep, gravelly voice. He heaved the burden off his shoulder, dropping it on the ground before him.

Teznak landed in a heap, limbs bent at unnatural angles and hide glistening with blood, and did not move again.

Ketahn was more aware than ever of Ivy on his hindquarters, clinging to him. Ivy, so vulnerable. So precious.

The grass shook more, in several places this time. Rekosh and Urkot angled their weapons outward as seven more thornskulls strode into the open. All of them stared at Ketahn's group with dark, unreadable eyes. All of them bore their spears with casual familiarity.

Ketahn would make them regret their arrogance. He growled, spreading his mandibles wide.

The first thornskull chittered. "We must share words."

CHAPTER 24

KETAHN HELD his gaze on the first thornskull, though his focus was split between all eight. He, Rekosh, and Urkot could win this battle, but they would not do so unscathed. *Ivy* would not emerge unscathed.

"Then speak," he said.

The thornskull tipped his head toward the tree, where the rest of Ketahn's tribe awaited. "We will share words in your wild den."

"Speak here," Ketahn replied. "I will not welcome foes into my camp."

With another chitter, the thornskull took a step forward. Ketahn held his place, spear steady, though everything within him cried out again to get Ivy away from here.

Ivy's muscles flexed, and she spoke his name in a quiet, a shaky breath.

The thornskull gestured at Teznak with one lower hand, then at Zirket with the other. "Your foes."

"So we are friends?" Ketahn asked.

"No. We two are abound by bloody threads. You have killed

mine. Many. It is in your eyes, true under moons and stars. But you have killed yours also."

Ketahn's chest burned, and his hands itched with yearning to release his weapons and seek his mate, to comfort her and draw comfort from her through touch. "My belly is filled with blood. I hunger for it no longer. I seek only to lead my tribe across the mire in peace."

"Then we must know. We must receive your words and find your *khahal*. We must know your hearts. Your spirit."

"I understand receiving our words," said Urkot, thumping his leg on the ground, "but the rest sounds like it can only be done after we have been torn open."

The thornskull jabbed his spear into the ground and advanced another step, turning all four of his palms to the sky, lifting his arms, and bowing his head. "You are warriors. Your *shar'thai* burns bright. If we give you death, it will be as warriors, not as beasts."

"Little comfort," said Rekosh.

"The mire is not a place for comfort." The thornskull lowered his arms and raised his eyes to meet Ketahn's gaze again. "You hold no trust, and I know. I feel. We hold no trust for you and yours. But I give these words now, and you may know their truth.

"Mine have followed since morning. We strode in your trail. We watched. You do not wear her marks, you are not blackfurs or goldhides, so we did not give war. And your little creatures..." He flicked his gaze past Ketahn, clearly looking toward Ivy even though she was mostly hidden by Ketahn's body.

Ketahn dropped his free hand, settling it over Ivy's knee and squeezing possessively. It had been difficult enough to accept his friends looking upon her. To learn that the thornskulls had done so without his knowledge for an entire day...

"They make our minds into storms," the thornskull continued. "What are they? Why do you bring them here, and why are yours here? Our questions are many, more than the stars, but we only watched.

"You did not know, purple one. Many times, you almost looked. Almost saw. But mine learned from yours. From your warriors, your hunters. From you. Any time, we could have given war. You would not have seen until too late. Do you know my *khahal*, shadowstalker?"

Ketahn released a long, heavy breath. He'd been careless lately. Unobservant. Distracted. And it had endangered the people he cared about. Years ago, he would never have missed a thornskull hunting pack following him—though the thornskulls he'd faced years ago hadn't possessed the skill to do so.

But as frustrating and frightening as it was to know his tribe had been watched during their time in the swamp, the knowledge brought some hope. The restraint shown by his old enemies meant there was a chance they could be friends—or at the very least that they didn't have to fight.

Moving slowly, Ketahn pointed his spear skyward, standing its butt on the ground beside him. "I understand, thornskull. You could have attacked any time you chose."

"And I am glad we did not. We have witnessed you, purple one. Your *shar'thai* is brightest of all, and we are stronger for seeing. Mine will remain behind, and I will go with you as one." Again, the thornskull gestured toward the camp. "We will share words in your wild den. Amongst your *vekir*, your tribe. If I must, I will leave my weapons."

Those words roused memories in Ketahn—memories of Zurvashi, so arrogant and yet fearful enough to deny weapons of any sort to all but her own guards within her presence. Though Ketahn had never wanted to be a leader, such was his role, and he refused to be a leader like the queen. He refused to taint every interaction with distrust and overwhelming pride.

He could not so quickly shed his misgivings, but Ivy had taught Ketahn that he could look past them at least briefly—that there was always a chance he was wrong, but it took a little blind trust to find out.

"We are warriors," Ketahn said, thumping his chest with the hand holding Ivy's knife and bowing his head toward the thornskull. "That does not change when we lay down our weapons. You say you wish to share words in our camp. I say be welcome so long as you come in peace."

"I give no vow of what will come after," the thornskull said, "as I cannot guess your *khahal*. But as guest in your wild den, I will come and go giving peace."

Urkot grunted. "I find little comfort in his words. Now or later, what difference does it make if they mean to kill us?"

"All the moments between still have meaning," said Rekosh. Following Ketahn's example, he stood his spear with its point skyward. "And what is more meaningful than moments spent trying to end what Zurvashi began those years ago?"

Buzzing thoughtfully, Urkot also stood his spear. "I wonder if it would have made a difference then."

"We may share words of the past," said the thornskull. "We may share words of battles and courage, blood and death. We may share words of what is to come. But in your wild den. It makes ill fortune to give such words where the dead rest."

"I am called Ketahn tes Ishuun'ani Ir'okari," Ketahn said. "What are you called?"

The thornskull slapped his chest with his upper hands. "Garahk ki'Tuun, Slayer of the Golden Walker."

Rekosh tilted his head. "The Golden Walker?"

"One of yours." Garahk grasped the shaft of his spear and tugged it out of the ground. "She stood beside your Blood-drinker Queen in the last battle. I could not give death to your queen, but the Golden Walker had a fierce *shar'thai*. She was the greatest foe I have slain, and I do her honor by carrying her name."

To have slain a Queen's Fang, this Garahk had to be a

formidable warrior—but Ketahn had never been intimidated by such, and certainly would not be now, especially while he had Ivy and their broodling to protect.

"Come, Garahk ki'Tuun, Slayer of the Golden Walker," Ketahn said. "Let us go and share words."

Garahk turned to face the other thornskulls. "Watch, my brothers. More blackfurs may be crawling in our mire."

"You trust these shadowstalkers after all theirs have done, Garahk?" asked one of the thornskulls, dark eyes hard set upon Ketahn.

"I give my trust. They give their trust. Such is the way to learn a vrix's *khahal*." Garahk waved his companions back. "Go watch. I will find you in small time."

Though none of them displayed any pleasure at that order, the thornskulls withdrew, carrying their spears back into the tall grass and vanishing from sight one by one. Garahk watched them off; Ketahn, Rekosh, and Urkot did as well, all three wary.

Then Garahk faced Ketahn again, and the group walked back toward the camp. Ketahn waved for Rekosh to take the lead and fell back to the rear again, bidding Ivy watch behind them. He would have led the thornskull himself, but the thought of Ivy being fully exposed to Garahk's gaze was too unsettling for Ketahn to accept.

That did not stop Garahk from looking at Ketahn over his shoulder. "You are protective of your little creature."

Ketahn angled his body to better shield her from the thornskull's gaze and snarled, "She is mine."

"This I know. You shared bodies, shared pleasure. I witnessed with eight eyes. She is your heartsflame?"

Ivy's body—especially her cheek—warmed against Ketahn's back. "D-did he just say what I think he said?" she whispered in English. "It's hard for me to make it all out. It's like...like he's speaking with a very thick accent."

"Yes," Ketahn replied, fury burning low in his gut. Their

295

mating had been meant for only the two of them, and to know that their bond, their passion, had been watched by someone else, someone unknown…

Garahk trilled softly. "We have heard these creatures make words. But those words are more strange from close than from far."

"So they were…watching?" Ivy asked. "Watching us?"

Ketahn nodded.

Ivy pressed her forehead between his upper shoulders. "Ugh! That's…that's not right. I understand them watching because we're in their territory, but to watch *that…*"

"You know its words?" asked Garahk.

"I do," Ketahn growled in vrix.

As they neared the tree, Urkot signaled with two pieces of blackrock, producing a sharp, quick imitation of Telok's typical rhythm.

Telok leaned out of cover high above. Even from that distance, Ketahn didn't miss the twitch of Telok's mandibles, or the way he angled his spear down just a little more sharply.

Ketahn and his companions made their climb in silence, Ivy holding on tight as ever. Ketahn's weariness made itself known throughout. His muscles ached, and each beat of his hearts spread a dull, throbbing discomfort through him that sank deep into his bones. But it went beyond flesh and bone; he was tired in his spirit too. He'd long since wearied of running, of spending each day unable to escape the threat of Zurvashi's retaliation, unable to see the sun through the long, dark shadow she cast.

When they reached the camp, the rest of the tribe was understandably wary. Telok and Ahnset had placed themselves in front of the humans, who'd clustered together in a tight ring with their weapons directed outward.

Ahnset leveled her spear at Garahk's throat, mandibles spread.

Ketahn hurriedly unfastened the rope around his middle, helped Ivy down, and strode forward, grabbing the shaft of his sister's spear and pushing it aside.

"What is this?" Ahnset demanded, her intense gaze fixed on the thornskull.

Telok squeezed his spear hard enough to make the wood creak. "I would also know why you have brought a thornskull amongst us."

The humans, now joined by Ivy, stood firm despite their ragged appearances, drawing upon that hidden strength Ketahn couldn't begin to measure.

"He is Garahk ki'Tuun," Ketahn replied.

"Slayer of the Golden Walker," Garahk added.

A deep growl rolled from Ahnset's chest.

Ketahn reached up and caught her mandible, guiding her face toward his. "Broodsister, I need your trust. And I need you to grant a little of it to him."

"I need to know why," she said. "Need to know what happened."

"The Queen's Claw found us. They followed our trail and stopped at the very tree Ivy and me were in. We slew them. The thornskulls killed the last before he could escape."

"And that makes us friends now? Do you— No, you remember. Of course you do. And so you know why this...this is *foolish.*"

"It is more than we might have hoped for, broodsister. Trust. For a little while, at least." Ketahn released his hold on Ahnset and met Ivy's gaze. "Tell the other humans what is said, my heartsthread, as well as you are able. We are a tribe, and we all must know what is being discussed."

She nodded. "I will."

Pushing Ahnset's spear down and away, Ketahn let go of it. "Garahk has come to our camp in peace to speak with us. While he is here, there is no war between us."

"As you say, broodbrother," Ahnset uttered.

"Garahk. Sit." Ketahn pointed to the center of the tree, where blankets and fluffed silk had been used to soften the uneven convergence of branches. Then he looked to the rest of the tribe, meeting their gazes one by one in quick succession. "We must keep watch, but I want all to listen. What is said here may well alter our coming days."

Garahk lowered himself in the place Ketahn had indicated, settling his underside atop one of the blankets. He folded his four rear legs and tucked them against his hindquarters, but his forelegs he positioned in front of himself. He laid his spear across them and removed his hands from the shaft to hold his palms skyward. "I come to your wild den and offer peace, Ketahn tes Ishuun'ani Ir'okari."

Ketahn eased himself down before the thornskull, laying his own spear across his forelegs. He'd never engaged with a thornskull in this manner—had never learned much of their ways. All his interactions with Garahk's kind had begun and ended in violence. "I accept your offering, Garahk ki'Tuun, Slayer of the Golden Walker, and I offer peace in return. Let me be only Ketahn while you are my guest."

The thornskull chittered and lowered his hands. "Then it is only Garahk, as well."

"I know what I see, but it cannot be real," Telok rasped.

"We shattered the barrier between what is real and impossible a long while ago," Rekosh said, offering a gentle chitter of his own. "I think we will see much more that cannot be before we are through."

Ketahn glanced at his friends. They'd spread out around the edges of the camp, forming a loose ring to stand guard. The humans had separated from their earlier grouping to join their vrix companions. For Ketahn, it was a confirmation of what he'd already known—though they were outmatched in most ways, these humans would fight alongside the vrix to defend their tribe.

"Perhaps we were fools to believe anything impossible," said Ketahn, returning his attention to Garahk. "I would hear your words and share my own."

Garahk's gaze flicked around, undoubtedly studying the nearby humans. "Yes. Many words, many questions. I must know, Ketahn. Why have you come?"

"My tribe seeks a place to make our home."

"Not so simple as your words sound." Garahk tilted his head. "Why near to Kaldarak and not your Takarahl? Yours have taken enough ground from mine."

Ketahn shook his head and curled his hands into loose fists, resting them on his foreleg joints. "We do not wish to take your ground. Only to find a place to live in peace."

"Mine know little peace when yours stride amongst us."

"And that may be true of us, Garahk, but not because we bring war to you."

Garahk slapped his palms on his uppermost foreleg segments, producing a jarring sound. "Always shadowstalkers give war. For long and long, through the lives of many broodmothers. And sometimes mine give war too. Mine are warriors. Mine have much *shar'thai*. We know it is for warriors to make battle and to die, and we are not sad. They are honored in death. Mine see yours fight and see strength. We respect, we learn, we honor yours.

"But your Blooddrinker Queen gave different war." Garahk's fists curled so tight they trembled, but he made no move to grasp his weapon. "Her *shar'thai* is strongest, but it is not bright. It is dark. She gives war to weavers, menders, and shapers, to spiritspeakers and growers. To broodlings. We give war to your warriors. Do you see, Ketahn? Do you know?"

Rage, bitterness, and guilt whirled in Ketahn's gut, a sickening storm that made him want to roar into the night sky and rake his claws across his own hide. "I know."

"From every foe, mine learn. From your blackfurs, we learn to stalk. To hide. To hunt. We learn from *you*."

That was the second time Garahk had said as much, and Ketahn could not ignore it now.

"You know me, Garahk?"

"I know you. I witnessed you. Many of mine longed to be the one to slay you, Ketahn. Much honor would have come. Only your queen would have given more. To mine you were Spear in Shadows. You were death, unseen, unheard."

Ketahn stared into the thornskull's eyes. "Each vrix here fought your kind during the war. Many of your kind are dead by our spears."

Garahk leaned back, propping his lower hands on the branches beneath him. He swept his gaze around again, mandibles twitching. "I know. And you and yours carry scars with pride, as do me and mine. I am honored to be amongst you. This wild den is bright with *shar'thai*."

"I do not see anything glowing," said Urkot, "especially not this...*shar'thai*."

Chittering, Garahk brought a hand to his chest, placing it over his hearts. "*Shar'thai* is like the fire in a warrior's hearts. It gives courage, gives strength. The brighter it is, the greater the warrior."

"It sounds like you speak of spirit. Everyone has a spirit, warrior or not."

"No, not spirit. Like spirit, but not the same. It is for warriors only. If shadowstalkers saw with all eyes, you would know it. You would see now. There is much honor for me here, to be amongst such *shar'thai*."

"Even after that war, you are honored to be amongst us?" asked Ahnset, voice low and hard. "After watching us kill your friends, your family?"

"My words were true, female," Garahk said. He thumped a fist against his chest. "I am warrior. You are warrior. I know you, even without your gold shell. You strode with her, and you slew many of mine. But they were warriors also. They met their fate. No warrior can say when their flame will go out, or who will smother it."

"The queen thinks differently," growled Telok.

"Your Blooddrinker Queen..." Garahk hissed and clacked his fangs. "From her, mine learned only one thing."

"What thing?" asked Ketahn.

"Hatred."

That quickly, Ketahn's rage surged ahead of his other emotions, solidifying and becoming something deeper, something stronger, something driving—because it had grown so much from his own hatred.

"Mine honor our foes," Garahk continued. "We tell stories of our enemies. I know many stories from the war, some witnessed by my eight eyes. We do not give hate, we give thanks. Thanks for combat, for learning, for the chance to grow and become stronger. Only your queen has earned our hate."

"She has earned the hate of many of ours also," Ahnset said, mandibles falling.

Rekosh made a troubled buzz. "But hate alone is not enough to topple the queen."

"That is why you killed the blackfurs?" Garahk asked. "You give hate to your Blooddrinker Queen, and give war to her warriors?"

"That is a simple way to say it, but yes," Ketahn replied. "Only Zurvashi has earned my hate."

Garahk studied Ketahn. "And you hers, or her blackfurs would not hunt you."

"It takes little to earn her hatred," Rekosh said. "It is much harder to avoid it."

"It is not hate that makes her hearts beat," said Ketahn.

A thoughtful grunt rumbled in Garahk's chest. "Few shadowstalkers come to the mire. What ground mine held was taken by the Blooddrinker, and this place gives nothing for yours. But when they come, they are blackfurs, and they watch. Sometimes they take from mine—our food, our supplies, our lives. All so we remember her. So we do not forget that we live only because she does not yet choose to kill us all.

He leaned forward, closer to Ketahn, and lowered his voice. "All this because she wanted our mender roots. Our *daiya* gave her an offer. Our root for her crystals. Long have yours and mine given war to each other, and always have we seen your crystals with wonder. They are as *shar'thai* trapped in stone. Your queen took our root and gave death. So I say give me your words, Ketahn. Give me your *khahal*. Why does she hunt you?"

Give me your khahal—*give me your truth.*

"Zurvashi wants me as her mate," Ketahn said. Even after all this time, saying the words aloud made his chest tight and his insides feel knotted even as the fires of his fury flared. "I refused her many times. Defied her many times."

Garahk dipped his chin toward Ivy. "For your creature."

"For my heartsthread." Ketahn looked at his mate, and so much of the discomfort brought on by talk of Zurvashi faded at the sight of her. All these risks, all this hardship, it was all for her. For her and their broodling. "Zurvashi means to kill them also."

"No such creatures dwell on our grounds. What are they?"

"We are human," Ivy said in vrix as she strode to Ketahn and stood beside him, shoulders squared and back straight. "And we come from very, very far away."

"It can make vrix words." Garahk trilled. "Though it makes them more poorly than you shadowstalkers."

"You are the ones who speak poorly," Urkot muttered.

"I must wrestle meaning from your words, Three-Arm."

Urkot seemed about to charge forward, but Rekosh halted him with a sharp hiss.

"I do not give war," Garahk said, lifting his palms to the sky again. "I give only jest."

Ivy placed a hand on the side of Ketahn's face and turned it toward her. Her features were hard set and solemn, but a glimmer of fear lingered in her eyes. In English, she whispered, "We don't have time to waste, Ketahn. We need to ask him for help."

Ketahn covered her hand with one of his own. "Help? They did not attack. To ask for more…"

"We have to tell him what we heard. What the Claws said." She cradled his face with her other hand and leaned close, blocking out the rest of the world. "We have to warn them and offer *our* help in exchange."

"Ivy, this is—"

"Listen, please. Because…because you know this, but I don't think you'll really acknowledge it until it's said out loud." Ivy drew in a deep breath, seeming to search his gaze, and pressed her lips together for a few moments. "We can't keep running, Ketahn. She's not going to stop, and we're not going to outrun her. If we keep going like this, she will find us, and we're definitely not going to be in a state to do anything about it."

He opened his mouth to reply, to tell her she was wrong, to tell her that they couldn't stop, but no words came out. Because she was right. He did know it, and he'd known it for a long while—since well before the Claws had arrived. He'd felt it at his core.

Tonight had only given him proof that he could not argue.

If he'd known fear before, the feeling that swept through him in that moment was something else entirely—something impossibly larger and darker. Something that felt so unavoidable, so consuming.

Ketahn gently guided Ivy's hands down and turned his head

back toward the thornskull. Garahk's gaze was intent upon him, communicating his unspoken question.

"My mate said I should ask your aid, Garahk," Ketahn said.

"Ah. I do not wish to give you war, Ketahn," Garahk said. "Peace you may have, but aid…that is much to ask."

"I know, but I do not ask it without offering aid in return."

Garahk chittered, mandibles twitching. "What have you to offer? You are few, and you carry little."

"The Blooddrinker Queen."

Garahk's mandibles fell, and his hands curled into fists again.

"She is following," Ketahn continued. "Her Claws said she was two days behind. We killed those, but she has many more, and she will have Fangs as well."

"Fangs…they are the ones that wear golden shells?"

"Yes," said Ahnset, stepping forward. "And she has trained many of the younger ones to mimic her cruelty."

"What does this mean to mine?" Garahk asked, looking from Ahnset to Ketahn. "Her blackfurs are already swallowed by the mire. She hunts you. We have given her no war."

Ketahn released a huff; what he was about to say was the truth, and speaking it made him feel ill. "There will always be war from her. She will always take, always kill. If not this day, the next, or the one after that."

Garahk grunted. He opened his mouth and snapped it shut, making his teeth click together. "If mine gift her you and yours, we would have no fear of her fury."

"Whether you have seven or seven hundred more of your kind waiting around this tree, Garahk, you will not take us," Ketahn said, unable to keep a guttural note from his voice. "I weave my words into a bond. You will not take us."

Chittering, Garahk lifted his hands and turned his palms up. "Now I have witnessed your *khahal*, Ketahn. Mine thought you the chosen of the Hunter. But the blessing of the Protector is upon you also. We will give the Blooddrinker nothing. Nothing more than what she has taken already. But I do not know what more I may give you."

"And if I say I will give you Zurvashi's death?"

"By the Eight, Ketahn, what are you offering?" Telok demanded.

"Do you seek to start a new war?" Rekosh asked.

Garahk chittered again, but the sound was cut short by a disbelieving snort as he stared into Ketahn's unwavering eyes. "You are more bold than I knew, Spear in Shadows. Or more foolish."

"Both," Ketahn said.

"Broodbrother, do you understand what you are doing?" asked Ahnset.

The humans exchanged uncertain glances and words when Ivy explained what Ketahn had said.

"We've just spent weeks running from her. Now we're going to turn around and fight?" Will asked.

"Ivy, I'm sorry, but I think he's gone insane," said Lacey. "This damned swamp is driving us all crazy, but he's the first one to truly lose it."

Diego, who was standing beside Ahnset with his arms folded across his chest and his spear tucked through them, smirked. "He knows what he's doing."

"He does," Ivy agreed, placing her hand on Ketahn's upper arm. "He knows exactly what he's doing, and it's the only way. Even with the storms and flooding, they already caught up with us. We *can't* run anymore."

"How, Ketahn? How will you give us your Blooddrinker Queen's death?" asked Garahk.

"She will come for us," Ketahn replied.

"If she strides, she does so with her blackfurs and goldshells. Mine cannot stand against her army. We are too few."

"That is why we will make ready to receive her." Ketahn

covered Ivy's hand with his own, squeezing it gently. "And ensure she never crosses the mire again."

"Spear in Shadows," Garahk said with a chitter, slapping his palms on his legs, "you are bold indeed. I will take you to my home, and you will share words with my *daiya*. She will find much honor in meeting you."

"Your home?" Ahnset asked warily.

"Yes, my home. Kaldarak."

Even without looking at them, Ketahn knew the exhalations of the other vrix had not been made in relief.

CHAPTER 25

Everyone had remained wary, but the tribe chose to place their trust in Garahk and accompany him to Kaldarak the next morning. The terrain was difficult, and the group had to stop on occasion when Ivy was sick, but they made good time.

Of course, that progress was only possible because the thornskulls carried most of the supplies, allowing the humans to ride on Ketahn and the other vrix.

Half a day's travel brought them out of the swamp. The jungle on this side had all the trees and plants Ivy had grown accustomed to, but it was hillier and contained far more bare rock. That seemed fitting—the jagged outcroppings and cliffs matched the thornskulls well.

They shared a camp with the thornskulls that night, exchanging food and stories, with the humans answering what felt like thousands of questions from their curious guides. Ivy's understanding of the thornskull dialect had improved greatly during the trip. She still had to listen intently to understand, and there were a few words she didn't know, but the thornskulls' vocabulary was largely the same as Ketahn's. They simply spoke with slightly different pronunciations, inflections, and phrasing.

The unexpected camaraderie gave Ivy hope that this would work out—but part of her didn't trust that hope. A few thornskulls appeared uneasy in the company of Ketahn and his friends, and several more often looked between Ivy and Ketahn before exchanging hushed words, though they never openly offered insult or provocation.

Garahk was key in maintaining peace. He was the leader of their group, but the way the other thornskulls respected him and obeyed his wishes gave Ivy the sense that he was more important than that.

The next morning, Garahk sent two of his companions ahead to bring word to their *daiya* that he was returning with guests. Then he led the rest of the group onward under a warm, brightly shining sun.

Another half a day's travel brought them to a rocky ridgeline. Garahk bounded to the crest, turned to face them, and eagerly waved them up. Pride gleamed in his eyes. Ivy had to remind herself that as childlike as that light seemed, it was coming from a seven-and-a-half-foot tall spider with spikes on his head and shoulders.

Ketahn climbed up to stand beside Garahk, carrying Ivy on his back. Her breath had hitched when she looked down from that ridge.

Ivy had never seen Takarahl. With only Ketahn's descriptions to go by, it had become a place of myth in her imagination —shadows and eerily glowing crystals, monsters prowling in dark tunnels, spider webs hanging along ceilings and walls. She knew it was wrong, that there were many vrix who called the place home and had found comfort and happiness there, but she couldn't shake her mental image. Zurvashi had turned Takarahl into a foreboding place—into a monster's den, or a tomb holding unspeakable horrors.

The contrast between her imagined Takarahl and Kaldarak was so strong that the latter seemed even more unreal, though it stood right before her eyes.

Her first glimpse of Kaldarak would be forever emblazoned in her memory.

The ridge overlooked a wide valley backed by tall, rocky hills. The valley itself was filled with greenery from which several immense trees rose. And structures filled those trees—buildings and platforms made of wood, leaves, thatch, and undoubtedly silk. They ringed the trunks and sat on branches. Rope bridges and nets spanned gaps, connecting the structures to each other. In a few places, grayish smoke billowed into the air, though most of it was diffused by the leaves above.

Thornskulls, made tiny by the distance, moved on the platforms and bridges. It was impossible for Ivy to tell how many of them were there, but she was both heartened and frightened by the numbers.

This was a village. A city.

And yet the most wondrous thing of all was on the hill beyond those trees, where a huge stone building, perhaps a temple, stood overlooking the village. Its base was wide and solid, with each ascending tier narrower than the first; nothing was quite even enough for her to really consider it a pyramid, but that was the closest thing she could compare it to. Vines and plants clung to the stone in many places, but they made it no less impressive. If anything, the vegetation only made the structure appear more ancient and otherworldly, an aesthetic enhanced by the waterfall flowing from its front that filled the air around the base with mist.

Tall stone figures jutted from the top, clearly in the shape of vrix—and Ivy couldn't guess how big those statues were.

Kaldarak was wondrous, even more so because no one in the tribe could ever have imagined they would come here. Who could've guessed that their best hope for survival, for salvation, would be amongst Ketahn's old enemies?

The awe from his guests seemed to please Garahk. They followed him down into the valley, where he greeted several sentries, before finally coming to a place to ascend. It was like a large spiral staircase winding round and round one of the huge trunks, leading ever higher.

Ivy's heart fluttered with excitement and worry as Ketahn carried her up.

A treehouse village was something out of a fairy tale. She couldn't keep her gaze from wandering while they followed Garahk along bridges and platforms. There were dozens of thornskulls here working—weaving, carving wood, crafting spears and tools, preparing food. And so many were startlingly colorful.

The male thornskulls were the inverse of Ketahn's kind. Their hides were bright reds, yellows, oranges, and greens, even a few in pristine white, all with black spots on their hindquarters, backs, and shoulders. Even the females had some color—though most were some shade of brown, many had hindquarters in earthy reds and oranges.

The males were summer; the females autumn.

Their coloration was almost as much of a surprise to Ivy as this city. Garahk and his companions had kept themselves covered in mud during their travels, hiding the skin beneath, and Ivy understood why. They'd have stood out immediately in the drab swamp otherwise.

But for all there was to see, Ivy couldn't ignore the stares. Cold, scrutinous, sometimes distrustful. Every thornskull who noticed Garahk's guests stopped whatever they were doing to stare in silence. The air was soon filled with palpable tension wholly at odds with Ivy's wonder and curiosity.

"I'm getting the feeling we're not very welcome here," Lacey said from her perch on Telok's back, who was positioned at the rear of the group.

"No shit," Cole replied. "I mean, it's not easy to decipher their expressions to begin with, but they seem to have the glare down."

"Are we...safe here?" Ahmya asked.

"Yes, *vi'keishi*," Rekosh said, voice smooth and soothing. "I keep you safe."

"So they're *not* going to tie us up and roast us over a spit?" Will asked.

"No," replied Ketahn with a chitter. "They eat raw."

"Damn man, that's some dark humor." Will frowned and cocked his head, staring at Ketahn. "It *is* a joke, right?"

Diego chuckled. "If so, it was pretty well done. Unlike us, if they're going to eat us raw."

Lacey snickered, while Callie chuckled.

Garahk looked back at them and cocked his head. "What do your creatures say?"

"Humans. We are humans," Ivy said in vrix. "And they are worried you will eat them."

The thornskull chittered and snapped his mandibles. "No, no eat. *Hyu-nanz* would not give enough meat."

"What did he say?" asked Callie.

Ivy pressed her lips together to hold in a laugh, knowing she shouldn't have found Garahk's reply funny, especially considering she as worried too. She wasn't sure if everyone else would have been amused. "Just that he's not going to eat us."

"Suuuure he did."

"He did," said Ketahn. "We must trust. Vrix no eat humans."

"Yet," Callie added.

"Oh, stop," Lacey said with a chuckle. "You just might tempt them."

Garahk stopped and looked at Lacey. "What is that sound they make?"

Lacey arched a brow. "Uh…why is he staring at me now?"

Callie snickered. "You must have tempted him."

Telok shifted his torso to shield more of Lacey from the thornskull's view. "It is how they chitter."

"Ah. It is"—Garahk glanced skyward, mandibles twitching— "a pleasing sound."

"Well, it's nice to know we at least sound nice," Ivy said quietly as Garahk turned and continued onward.

"They are so young," Telok said a short while later.

Ivy looked around again, and only then did she realize it. So many of the thornskulls were smaller and slighter than Garahk and his warriors—adolescents compared to adults. Yet they were all working, all doing a part.

"War claimed many," Garahk said. "My brothers and sisters. Many brothers and sisters, many mothers and sires. Half of Kaldarak or more."

"I am sorry for what we did," Ahnset rumbled.

Garahk snapped his mandibles and waved a hand dismissively. "No sorry. War claimed many of yours also."

"Yes. In…many ways."

"Because of your Blooddrinker Queen. She is why. We fight, warriors die, we go on." He gestured toward some of his people who were staring. "She did not let Kaldarak go on."

"She wanted you broken," Rekosh said.

"Yes. But we heal. We mend. We find our strength. And if you, Spear in Shadows, make real your words, Kaldarak will live again."

Ketahn placed a hand on Ivy's thigh and gave it a squeeze. His voice was harsh and firm when he said, "For my mate and my tribe, I will make real my words. For yours and mine."

Garahk chittered and thumped the butt of his spear on the wood planks beneath him, gesturing at the onlookers as he said in a raised voice, "Share my words. These ones are friends, and all will give them peace. Go."

The onlookers dispersed, hurrying along the walkways in different directions. As Garahk led on, he relayed the same message to any other thornskulls who stopped to watch—which was essentially all of them.

"Some are following," Urkot said.

Ivy glanced back to see at least fifteen thornskulls trailing behind their group on various levels of the village, keeping their distance but not bothering to disguise their curiosity. Some of them were broodlings. Small with large eyes, long, gangly legs, and teeny tiny spikes on their headcrests and shoulders, they were…adorable. Ivy thought of the life growing inside her.

What will our baby look like?

"They want to know why you come. What your *hyu-nanz* are," said Garahk.

He led them across one more bridge, which brought them to a broad platform with a wide, thatch-roofed building set atop it. The angles of the structure gave it a natural feel—more like a large nest than a home—that reminded Ivy of the den she and Ketahn had left behind. A lot of these places were reminiscent of their den…

It gave Ivy a little much needed comfort, but it was bitter-sweet. She missed their time in the den, the place she had considered home more than anywhere she'd ever lived.

We will make a new one.

But it wasn't the building. It was Ketahn. So long as Ivy was with him, she was home.

Garahk strode to the entrance, which was a tall, arched opening formed of intertwined branches and vines from which hung thick strips of brightly colored silk. He looked at Ketahn over his shoulder. "We have come to my *daiya's* den."

Ketahn tilted his head, and both Rekosh and Telok made soft, skeptical sounds.

"This is your *daiya's* den?" Ahnset asked incredulously. "No guards? No defenses? No…"

313

"Splendor?" Rekosh offered.

"Yes. Zurvashi would sooner burn a den like this to ash than dwell within it."

Garahk snorted and stomped a leg on the platform. "Your Blooddrinker Queen knows only to give war. Only to destroy and burn. My *daiya* is not as her. My *daiya* is warrior, mother, sister, weaver, and grower. All mine need, she is. Do you know my words?"

This den, coupled with Garahk's description of his *daiya*, further eased Ivy's nerves. She'd first thought the thornskulls' *daiya* was the same as a queen, but Garahk always used *jikarai*, the vrix word for queen, when referring to Zurvashi. *Daiya*, it seemed, was something humbler, something more selfless. A leader worthy of respect and adoration as opposed to one who *demanded* such.

Ivy smiled. "She gives herself to yours. Not takes."

"Yes, *hyu-nanz* Ivy. My *daiya* gives herself."

"You share words like I am not here, *luveen*," someone said from inside the den. The voice was deep and powerful, but there was a softness and warmth to it not unlike that in Ahnset's voice.

"Ah, but you are always with me, *nyleea*"—Garahk tapped his chest—"wherever I go. I carry you. Your *shar'thai* is my strength, for you are my heartsflame."

"You were strong before I was yours, Garahk," the *daiya* replied. The silk hanging over the entryway lifted and swung aside, and a female moved into the opening. "To you I give wisdom, not strength. Would that you use it a—"

The *daiya's* words died as her eight black eyes looked past Ketahn and fell upon Ivy—and Ivy stared right back.

The *daiya* was big. Tall, yes, though Ivy guessed Ahnset was at least a head taller, but mostly just *big*. Like the male thornskulls, she was built broad and solid, with spiky protrusions on her headcrest and shoulders. Her hide was reddish brown, which brightened to a purer red on her hindquarters, and her hair was a rich mahogany. She wore no adornments that Ivy could see, just a vibrant green silk cloth hanging around her waist with several pockets sewn onto it that contained tools—crude spools of thread, needles of various sizes, and a small knife.

In many ways, she was even more intimidating than the females of Ketahn's kind. She bore several scars of her own, undoubtedly earned in battle, and Garahk had just said she was a warrior, but... But there was something calming about her presence.

The *daiya's* eyes flicked past Ivy to look at the others. "Shadowstalkers and...creatures. The words you sent little prepared me for this sight, Garahk. I cannot know which is stranger to see in Kaldarak."

"I did not have words to make you know," Garahk said, turning his palms up and bowing his head.

Again, the *daiya* raked her gaze over Ivy and the others, mandibles twitching. "No words could have been enough. Only by my eight eyes could I know. Yet my questions are many and more."

"We can answer them for you," Ivy said in vrix.

The *daiya* flinched, her eyes flaring. She opened her mouth and snapped it shut. "It makes words."

"We speak. We are like you inside. Just...different outside."

"Its words sound more strange than the shadowstalkers'," the *daiya* said with a low buzz. She looked past Ivy and the other humans and cocked her head as though seeing the crowd of thornskulls beyond for the first time. She shifted aside, holding the cloth up and out of the way. "Enter. We will share words."

Ketahn stepped forward, only to be stopped by Garahk, who extended a foreleg.

"I give trust, Ketahn tes Ishuun'ani Ir'okari," Garahk said. "Do not harm my *nyleea*."

315

"I weave my words into a bond, Garahk ki'Tuun, Slayer of the Golden Walker. I will not harm your *nyleea*. And I trust you will not harm mine."

"I give my vow." Garahk bowed his head and withdrew his leg.

Ivy smoothed her palms down the outsides of Ketahn's upper arms. "We'll be okay."

Ketahn dropped a hand to her knee, grasping it with a blend of possessiveness and tenderness. "We will."

He entered the den. It took Ivy's eyes a moment to adjust to the dim light, but the space soon came into focus. The den was large and oval shaped, with several wide, low windows. The air was filled with fragrance—flowers, both exotic and familiar, hung in clusters from the ceiling, some fresh and some dried. There were swaths of cloth and furs hanging in other places and laid on the floor, and to one side was what appeared to be a large loom and countless tools, threads, and pieces of silk for weaving and sewing.

Just like in Ketahn's den, there were clay pots and baskets woven directly into the wall that likely contained foodstuffs and other supplies. A few spears of varying sizes stood near the entrance along with some knives and hatchets, all with black-rock heads.

Garahk entered and strode across the den. Ivy followed him with her gaze.

The thornskull stopped in the far corner, where crude boxes built from slabs of stone stood on either side of a large pile of fluffed silk and cloth. The openings of those boxes faced away from the pile, revealing bowls inside each that held low, blue-green flames. They radiated heat that Ivy could feel even from her place near the entryway.

It took her a few moments to realize what rested within the soft pile.

Eggs.

There were five of them, similar in size to watermelons—or to newborn human babies. Their textured bronze shells gleamed when the light touched them. If Ivy were to have imagined dragon eggs from a fantasy world, they would've looked something like these.

Awe filled her. She lowered a hand to her belly, cradling its gentle curve, cradling the tiny life inside.

For Garahk to allow Ketahn and the others—who had once been his enemies—into his home with his mate was one thing, but to allow them in here with something as precious and fragile as these, his soon-to-be broodlings, proved that he and the *daiya* truly sought peace with Ketahn's people.

Ivy untied the silk rope around her waist, letting it fall away. She drew her leg over Ketahn's hindquarters and turned, sliding off his back. He shifted and barred her from leaving his side with his left arms. She looked up at him, but he wasn't looking at her. Ketahn's eyes were also focused on the eggs, and Ivy knew he'd reached the same conclusion she had—but he didn't seem to know what to think about it.

She took hold of his arms and guided them down as their companions entered the den. Once Ahnset, the last of their group, had stepped inside, the *daiya* dropped the silk curtain.

"I welcome you to my den, shadowstalkers and..." The *daiya* glanced at Garahk.

"*Hyu-nanz,*" he said.

"*Hyu-nanz,*" the *daiya* echoed, buzzing softly. But her attention swiftly returned to her mate, and she snapped her mandible fangs and thumped her leg on the floor. "Do not think our guests have made me forget that you have entered our den covered in mud, Garahk."

He chittered and looked down at his mud-slathered chest. "One more heartbeat without you in my eyes would bring my death, my heartsflame."

"We will share words later."

"We will share much more," he purred.

Ahmya gasped softly. "Are those...eggs?"

"Yes," Ketahn replied in English. "They show much trust to bring us here."

"Wow," Will said, his attention also on the nest.

He and Ahmya weren't the only ones; as the humans dismounted the vrix, all their gazes fell on the nest.

Garahk's mandibles spread, and the fine hairs on his legs rose as he realized the focus of his guests.

"We mean no threat," Ivy said as quickly and as clearly as she could in vrix. "We have never seen vrix eggs before. We find them...beautiful."

Garahk huffed and cocked his head, his posture taking on an uncertainty Ivy hadn't expected from him. "Your eggs are different?"

"Humans do not lay eggs." Ivy placed a hand on her belly once more. "We carry our broodlings inside."

"Very small broodlings to have fit inside you," Garahk said as he leaned down to adjust the silk around one of the eggs.

"We have much to learn of each other," the *daiya* said. She looked upon the nest, and her eyes both brightened with pride and softened with affection. "This brood is our first. I often find myself staring. To see them as eggs... I cannot imagine what they will be like when they hatch. I know only that I will give all of myself to them and hope that it will be enough."

"Enough?" Garahk chittered and strode to her, reaching up to draw her head down and touch headcrests. "My *nyleea* is more than enough. She is more than any deserve."

The *daiya* trilled contently.

Ivy smiled as she watched the pair. It warmed her to see this kind of affection between vrix. She'd seen brotherly affection between Ketahn and his friends, had seen him and his sister display their love for each other, but this...

The *daiya* withdrew from her mate and brushed her hands

over her face. "I will not be happy if you left your mark on me in mud, Garahk."

"I will give my mud-mark somewhere, *nyleea*, be it on you or the floor," he replied. "It is true under sun and sky."

She gave him a shove—a surprisingly gentle, playful shove, especially considering her size and build—and turned toward Ketahn and Ivy. "It has been long since a shadowstalker last strode in Kaldarak. Not since my mother lead as *daiya* have we had one of yours as a guest."

Ketahn tilted his head. "One of ours was a guest in Kaldarak?"

The *daiya* spread her arms, palms up. "Long ago, as I said. She came years before the war, while I was a broodling still. A Fang who said she would not serve your queen. My mother gave her a place here, and she was my friend until her death."

"You are speaking differently," Rekosh said carefully.

She chittered. "Yes, and my *luveen* does not care for it. From that old friend I learned to speak in your way. All these years later, it still comes easily to me."

"It is not your voice, my *nyleea*," Garahk said.

"It is no matter whether I am of two voices or one. Garahk has brought you here, granting you far more trust than I might have offered. But he has my hearts in his keeping and holds all my trust. So I will not worry, and instead follow my curiosity. These *hyu-nanz* are unlike anything I have seen. But a group of shadowstalkers pursued by their own hunters? I know not which questions to ask first."

"If you wish to hear it, I will tell you all, *daiya*," said Ketahn.

"Let it be only Nalaki," she replied.

Garahk grunted, mandibles spreading. "Nalaki ka'Naghi, Slayer of—"

"Please, my *luveen*," Nalaki said with a gentle chitter, "there is no need. We may have respect without titles, yes?"

"By your words, heartsflame, I will act."

"My thanks. Now, shadowstalker"—Nalaki returned her attention to Ketahn, though her focus seemed to flick between him and Ivy—"I would hear all." She motioned to the floor with a hand. "Find comfort and rest. All of you."

Nalaki lowered herself onto the floor, folding her thick legs and tucking their tips beneath herself. Garahk joined her after returning to the nest and adding a viscous substance from a clay jar into one of the fire bowls, making it flare. Ivy and the others followed their example, sitting in a loose half-circle on the rugs and furs that covered the floor. Ivy herself sat in front of Ketahn, smiling when he wrapped his arms around her and hooked his claspers over her hips.

"This *hyu-nanz*," Nalaki said, dipping her chin toward Ivy, "you are protective of it."

"Yes," Ketahn rumbled, holding Ivy a little tighter. "She is my mate."

The thornskull recoiled and snapped her mandibles together. "Your mate? These creatures are not vrix. To mate one…it is like mating a beast. Perhaps to keep one as a pet—"

Ketahn growled, forelegs rising to either side of Ivy, and Garahk placed a hand on Nalaki's forearm.

"They are mates," Garahk said, "as sure as you and I. True under sun and sky, under moons and stars, by my eight eyes and the eightfold eyes."

Nalaki's eyes widened as she held her mate's gaze. She let out a soft breath, and she visibly eased before turning back to Ketahn and Ivy, drawing her forearms together in an apologetic gesture. "I am sorry, shadowstalker. There are no creatures like these in all the Tangle, and none other than vrix that can speak. I do not mean to give insult."

Ivy placed a hand upon one of Ketahn's forelegs, and he lowered them, his fine hairs settling.

"I understand," Ketahn replied. He drew in a deep breath,

undoubtedly taking in Ivy's scent. "But she is bound to me, and I to her. She is my heartsthread."

A low, uncertain buzz sounded from Nalaki's chest. "They are so small. So delicate. So…strange looking. How have you mated this creature without breaking it?"

Ivy had answered similar questions often enough that the response came out in vrix without her even consciously meaning to speak, even as a blush burned on her cheeks. "We are not as delicate as we look."

"My *nyleea* is strong," Ketahn replied. "Small as these humans are, their *shar'thai* is bright."

She smiled and tucked loose strands of her hair behind her ear. "We are not so different from your kind, Nalaki. We are like you."

Nalaki's mandibles twitched close together. "The way you shape sounds is strange. And why do you bare your teeth?"

"It is a smile," Ivy replied. "For my kind, it shows kindness and friendship."

"A…*snyull*? For most creatures, baring teeth is a threat."

"Humans are not like most creatures," Ketahn said.

"I do not doubt your words. I would know more of these *hyu-nanz*. But first let us share names that we may be friends, and then you may share your story."

Beginning with Ketahn and Ivy, the tribe introduced themselves. Nalaki repeated each name as it was spoken, struggling with the human names a little—particularly Will and Ahmya's, which relied upon having lips to pronounce properly.

Then Ketahn told the story, with Ivy and the other vrix adding bits and pieces. Ivy had lived through much of it herself, but hearing the parts she hadn't experienced personally, hearing in even greater detail than ever about Ketahn's confrontations with Zurvashi before that final day in Takarahl, dredged up all her heartache and anger. All the helplessness and pain she'd endured while she could do nothing but watch him suffer rose to the surface.

And to know that all of it had occurred over a few short months... She felt every single day that had passed since she'd awoken in this alien world, felt them like a weight that had settled on her shoulders, not nearly heavy enough to drag her down but not so light as to be ignored. In some ways, each of those days had been a lifetime. All the same, looking back now...that time had passed in the blink of an eye.

She'd gone from hopeful colonist to stranded survivor, from stranded survivor to a vrix's mate, from mate to makeshift leader of a small-scale exodus to save what remained of her people, all in a matter of weeks.

Though there were undoubtedly parts of the story Nalaki either didn't understand or wasn't likely to believe, she absorbed it with little comment, listening with respect and attentiveness. When Ketahn was finally done, the *daiya* folded her arms across her chest and bowed her head. For what felt like forever, she remained that way, silent.

Ivy pressed her lips together, willing her heart to stop pounding, willing their host to say something, anything, so they could know what fate awaited them. She didn't think the thorn-skulls would turn them out—or worse, turn on them—but she couldn't know for sure.

Finally, Nalaki spoke. "Much of what you say cannot be true. Creatures from a place amidst the stars...such cannot be without the many hands of the Eight taking part, and why would the Eight form things such as these *hyu-nanz*? Yet I sense your *khahal*, Ketahn. I know you do not lie, for these *hyu-nanz* sit before my eight eyes. And if Zurvashi is coming to our lands..."

Ketahn let out a low, gravelly, unhappy sound. "She is coming. Because she is hunting us."

Nalaki lifted her upper arms, gathering her long, silken hair in her hands and drawing it over her shoulder. With startling dexterity for fingers so large and thick, she began weaving her hair into a loose braid. "My mother was *daiya* before me. She was wise and just, as I have tried to be. When Zurvashi demanded mender root from our growing patches, my mother offered trade. But Zurvashi did not want trade. She wanted only to take. When we refused, she gave war.

"My mother led Kaldarak in battle. She began her fight on the farthest reaches of our lands, those places beyond the mire, and slowly she was pushed back, and back, and back. Zurvashi was more than a warrior. She was as a beast, uncaring of who she destroyed. Thirsty only for blood.

"I fought alongside my mother. I was with her when she fell to the spears of your Fangs, and I avenged her with my own. I had ever been content to weave, to carve, to grow. To do all but make war. Yet I had no choice, because Zurvashi craved nothing other than war."

Her fingers stilled, and she stared down at that long, shimmering hair as though it were foreign to her. "I became *daiya* then, painted by our spiritspeakers in my mother's still warm blood, and I fought to preserve what remained ours. Kaldarak was the heart of our land. Kaldarak could not fall. I commanded ours to return home and defend it to the last. We prepared our defenses, ready to finally exact revenge on the Blooddrinker Queen. I was ready to die here, spear in hand, happy so long as that spear was buried in her chest.

"But she did not come. She found the mire distasteful and retreated after she drove us across it. She thought us broken, and perhaps she was right. Our numbers are half what they were before her war. And I have done all I can to heal my kind. To build our strength. To keep our *shar'thai* strong—but to keep us alive more so." Nalaki turned her head to look at the nest in the corner, to look at those precious eggs bundled there, soaking in the warmth.

"You have led the beast that would be the end of my kind straight to us, Ketahn." Nalaki returned her gaze to Ketahn. Her eyes were unreadable, her posture solid and unyielding. "If your words are true, and I know they are, she will come for you. And she will come *here*, to Kaldarak. My people hold hate only for her, but they would be glad to never see her again. We have avoided war with her all these years, do you understand? We knew we did not have the strength to stand against Takarahl."

"I understand, Nalaki," Ketahn said, "and I am sorry. This fight does not belong to you or your kind. It is mine. But I would ask you to stand with us regardless."

"You ask much, shadowstalker."

Ivy nodded, pushing aside the sorrow Nalaki's tale had instilled in her. "We do, but...this is for our future. For our broodlings. Our friends. Our tribe. And for yours also. So long as Zurvashi lives, her shadow will hang over Kaldarak. There will always be that hatred. There will always be that fear that one day she will thirst for blood again. Garahk told us her Claws still come and take from you, that sometimes they kill. Is that not as much as war? We ask you to help us end all that."

"We do not have the numbers to withstand her army," said Nalaki.

"I do not believe she strides with the full strength of Takarahl," Ketahn replied. "To be so close behind, she could not have roused all her warriors. She hunts only us, and she thinks the humans too weak to be a threat. She believes the same of Kaldarak."

"And she has grown increasingly fearful of betrayal," said Ahnset. "She would not leave Takarahl unguarded while she was away."

Nalaki huffed, settling her lower hands on her leg joints. "And against even half the strength of Takarahl we would be outmatched."

"Do not share such words," Garahk growled. "One of ours is as three of theirs."

"Ah, my *luveen*." Nalaki shifted to face her mate and leaned down, pressing her headcrest to his. "My pride in Kaldarak is as great as yours, but I will not lie to them or to you. We would flood the ground beneath us with the blood of our foes and still not win."

"We may end this without the need for such a battle," said Ketahn.

Nalaki lifted her head and looked at Ketahn. "How, shadow-stalker?"

"We will meet her, ready for battle, but she will face me alone. And I will slay her."

Ivy inhaled sharply and snapped her eyes up to her mate. "Ketahn, no."

"Broodbrother, do not be a fool," Ahnset snapped.

Telok, Rekosh, and Urkot all said similar things at the same instant, though none matched Ahnset's volume.

Ketahn settled a hand upon Ivy's shoulder, right over his bite mark, giving it a gentle squeeze. "It is as it must be. As you said, my *nyleea*, we cannot run. If we must fight, it will be me who fights. This was ever about me. I will gladly face her alone to spare the rest of you from her wrath."

Ivy searched his face, her heart pounding rapidly, ice flowing through her veins. She shook her head. "She'll kill you," she said in English. "And when she kills you, she will turn on us. All of us. You can't stop her alone, Ketahn."

"Wait, what?" Cole said. "He's planning to face the queen by himself?"

"She will not kill me," Ketahn growled, drawing Ivy tight against him with one hand over her belly. "But if we war with her, many of us will come to harm. Many of us will die, even if we win."

325

"Why would she fight you alone?" asked Nalaki. "If she is so sure of Takarahl's strength, she will simply take you."

"Because she seethes with rage, and she will not be able to resist a chance to conquer me before all."

"Zurvashi has long wanted Ketahn as her mate," Rekosh said. "But he made a fool of her before all and chose a human in her stead. Now she wants him as a conquest and breeder only."

Telok rested his lower elbows on his leg joints and leaned forward. "And she will not rest until she has him. She does not suffer attacks to her pride, and Ketahn has wounded it far more than any before him."

"The question must be asked, Ketahn," Nalaki said, drawing in a long, slow breath as she met and held Ketahn's gaze. "Can you defeat her?"

"I have fought her more than once, and I have done her harm," Ketahn replied.

"That is not the same."

"It is not, but Spear in Shadows has slain our female warriors," Garahk said. "I have witnessed him. If any male could slay the Blooddrinker Queen, it is he."

"If nothing more, I will wound her," Ketahn said, voice low and rough. His gaze flicked to Ahnset. "And it will be enough for another to end her in my stead."

Ahnset tensed. "Broodbrother..."

"I will not go to my death," He lowered his chin to rest atop Ivy's head, and his hand flexed on her belly.

Ivy covered his hand with her own and squeezed it tight as tears stung her eyes. She'd known the danger they were in, had known what was after them, but she'd never allowed herself to imagine life without Ketahn. Their future was meant to be lived together.

Anger burned in Ivy's gut, mingling with her terror at the possibility of losing her mate. Her throat constricted. She would *not* let Zurvashi take him from her. She would not.

"You are not allowed to die," she rasped.

He wrapped her in all four arms and curled his forelegs around her, cocooning her in his warmth and strength. "Even if I fail, I will not die. I weave my words into a bond, my heartsthread. Zurvashi will meet her end, and we will have our peace."

Ivy turned and huddled against him, clutching at his chest and pressing her lips together as she fought to keep her overwhelming emotions at bay. For a time, there was only silence and Ketahn; Ivy felt his heat, his heartbeat, his rough but welcoming skin. But still, he did not bring the comfort she longed for in that moment. Her sense of foreboding was too great, and the unknown stretching before them was too vast.

It was Nalaki who broke the silence and pulled Ivy back to reality, her voice warm and gentle. "We need not speak more of such matters now. You have all journeyed far and hard, and you have earned nothing if not rest."

She looked to Garahk and chittered. "My mate will take you to the temple, where you may bathe. He is certainly in need of cleaning himself. We will have food and a place for you to rest when you have finished."

"Did she say food?" Cole asked. "Because I swear I recognized that word."

Diego shook his head with a smirk. "Of course you would catch *that* out of everything else that was said."

Cole pressed his hands to his stomach. "Dude, I'm starving!"

"The last time we had a fresh meal, you ate as much as Urkot," said Callie, rolling her eyes.

Urkot sat up straighter, turned toward Callie, and tilted his head. "Urkot no eat."

Despite everything, Ivy smiled. These little moments really were everything—they made all the struggle, all the risks, worthwhile. She could not shake her dread, but she wouldn't

327

succumb to it. She would be strong for Ketahn, just as he'd been strong for her.

She met Nalaki's gaze and smiled. "Thank you. For everything. Even this small kindness is more than we could have hoped."

CHAPTER 26

ONCE AGAIN, Garahk led Ivy's little tribe through Kaldarak. Once again, thornskulls gathered on the surrounding platforms and walkways to stare, now in even greater numbers.

After their conversation with Nalaki, Ivy wasn't nearly as unsettled by those stares as she had been upon arriving in the village. Garahk put her even more at ease by speaking to many of those onlookers as he walked. His words varied, but his message did not—the *daiya* had accepted these outsiders into Kaldarak. Ivy, Ketahn, and the others were to be treated not merely as honored guests, but as though they'd hatched in these very dens.

Ivy leaned against Ketahn's back, hugging him tight as he followed Garahk. The mud-covered thornskull had done so much for them already. Here amongst his own people, he was a beacon of warmth and positivity, and Ivy saw the change in the other thornskulls when he spoke to them. She saw the suspicions in their eyes soften and fade, saw their tense postures relax.

Soon, Ivy's tribe was receiving words of welcome instead of wary stares.

The uncertainty of the future loomed over Ivy, immense, dark, and ominous, but for now she refused to acknowledge it. For now, she just let herself feel content. She just let herself feel at home.

Kaldarak really was a place out of a fairy tale. Its many bridges, buildings, and platforms looked cozy in the sun dappled shade. The air was warm and humid, but just enough of a breeze flowed through the boughs to provide some relief. The usual jungle sounds were still present—the rustling leaves and distant animal calls that had become so familiar—but this place had something else, something Ivy hadn't realized she'd been missing for all this time.

It had that gentle buzz that rose and fell like lazy ocean waves, that hum of chatter and activity. That sound that only happened when people were together, working and talking. When people were living.

Garahk led them higher and higher, until finally they reached what must've been the uppermost level of Kaldarak. As Ketahn climbed onto a platform behind the thornskull, Ivy found herself looking up at the sky, which seemed so much larger than it had anywhere else in the jungle. Swathes of blue, a little deeper and purer than that of the Earth sky, peeked through breaks in the clouds. While most of those clouds were fluffy and white overhead, they darkened to the gray of coming rain toward the horizon.

Then Ketahn was up fully, and Ivy's breath caught. From their current vantage, she could see *everything*.

Her eyes fell first on a distant cliff. Its rocky face plunged into the thick jungle below, the pale stone fraught with clusters of plants and hanging vines. She smiled when she realized that it was the place from which she'd first spied Kaldarak, a high point overlooking the valley. Alien birds sped over the canopy near the cliff, tiny specks of bright blue and red against all the green and purple.

Then Ketahn turned and trilled, calling Ivy's attention forward. She sat up higher and looked over his shoulder.

The temple stood straight ahead, more massive than she could have imagined. Though it was still a few hundred feet away, she could see some of the detail in the stonework from here, the carvings that had faded over untold years, the subtle patterns and designs that made the whole structure look far more sophisticated than it had at first glance. There was no mistaking the statues atop the temple now—they were vrix, four male and four female.

The Eight.

She really didn't know much about vrix religion, but she knew those statues depicted their gods.

The waterfall pouring from the temple's front glittered in the sunlight, and the mist it produced shattered that same light into a faded but beautiful rainbow.

And leading to that temple was a bridge. A very, very long bridge that sagged in the middle because it was so long, a bridge that was swaying in the breeze even without anyone walking on it. Yes, there were ropes running like handrails on either side; yes, the wooden planks connected by the silk *looked* solid enough. None of that changed the fact that Ivy and her companions were about to cross a few hundred feet of open air on a sagging, unsteady bridge.

Ivy swallowed hard and scanned the hillside. There were three other bridges stretching toward the temple, all lower than this one—and only one other of which anchored at the temple itself.

Before she could open her mouth to ask why they hadn't used one of the lower bridges—like maybe the lowest one that was far enough down to look tiny from here—Garahk stepped onto the bridge, and Ketahn followed close behind.

She sucked in a breath, dropped back down onto Ketahn's

hindquarters, and clutched him as tight as possible with arms and legs alike.

Though she wasn't walking on the bridge herself, she felt it bounce and sway beneath him. She squeezed her eyes shut and pressed her face against his back. He'd carried her through the trees more times than she could count. They'd climbed high, high up, much higher than she would ever have gone on her own, and she'd grown accustomed to that. Even if she'd never fully shed her fear, she trusted Ketahn. She knew he wouldn't let her fall. No matter how high he climbed, he had her.

But she did *not* trust this bridge.

Especially not when the others stepped on behind Ketahn and the thing started to shake and sway even more.

Ketahn chittered softly and laid one of his lower arms over hers, covering her hand with his.

"Please use that to hold the rope," she rasped. "All four hands."

He chittered again, much deeper and fuller this time; the sound might've made her heart flutter if her stomach wasn't already flipping because of the bridge's movements.

"I am steady enough with six legs alone, my *nyleea*," he replied.

Ivy felt his other arms shift. Her heart leapt into her throat, and she clung to him impossibly tighter. "Don't you dare!"

With an amused trill, he returned his arms to their previous positions.

That did little to ease Ivy; though her heart sank back down, her stomach sank along with it. "I think I might puke."

Ketahn tensed. "Do not do so upon me, human."

Despite how unsettled her belly was—and despite that consuming fear—she chuckled. "I can't promise anything."

He huffed and growled, "You are fortunate we are going to bathe."

Somehow, after what felt like the longest, most harrowing

journey of Ivy's life, Ketahn stepped off the bridge. As soon as the swaying stopped and Ivy knew he was on solid ground, her whole body went limp. Her legs dangled to either side of him, her arms fell, and her cheek smushed against his back as she blew out a long, shaky breath.

When she finally opened her eyes, she glanced back toward the bridge, trying not to let herself acknowledge the fact that they'd have to cross it again to get back.

A few of the others were still crossing—including Cole, who was on foot, grinning from ear to ear with his hair fluttering in the breeze.

"I can feel you guys hoping I fall," he said, grin unwavering.

"Why would we? It's nice to have someone around that makes the rest of us look good," said Lacey.

Diego smirked. "I wouldn't hope for it. I'd just push you and be done with it."

Cole laughed and shook his head. "Yeah, well, I bet one of the vrix would lasso me with some butt rope and I'd be okay. Would probably even be fun, like bungee jumping or whatever."

Lacey pinched the bridge of her nose and sighed. "Okay, there is so much wrong with what you said that I don't even know where to begin."

"Come," Garahk said in vrix, waving the group on. "I would not beg my *daiya's* wrath by remaining in mud any longer."

They followed him through an opening in the temple wall and into a corridor lit by low-burning blue-green fires. As they moved through the temple's interior, Urkot made several comments regarding the stonework and materials, resulting in a good-natured argument between him and Garahk about the skill of thornskull stoneshapers.

Urkot pointed out that he'd spent most of his life under-ground, surrounded by stone, which Rekosh amended by saying it simply meant Urkot's skull was full of rocks and thus he was very familiar with them. Garahk claimed nothing the shadowstalkers had made could match the glory of this temple; Urkot asked how a thornskull could know that when they spent all their time playing with sticks in the trees.

Ivy imagined it would've gone on like that for some time, but the argument ended abruptly when they entered a large chamber where the worked stone met natural, untouched rock. The air was thick and wet, filled with steam from the large, tiered pools inside. Water flowed down from those pools into a stream that ran into a wide tunnel through which Ivy glimpsed daylight.

"A hot spring?" Will asked incredulously. "These guys have a *hot spring* inside their temple?"

"Here you may make clean," said Garahk, pulling a pouch off his belt. He removed a handful of dried herbs from inside, which he crushed and sprinkled into the water. Their aroma permeated the air the instant they hit the water; it was reminiscent of lavender, but with a minty undertone.

Once Garahk divested himself of his belt and pack and entered the water, everyone else hurried to get in, too, removing their clothing—except for Lacey, Callie, and Ahmya, who left their underclothes on. More than one human remarked that they'd thought they would never have a hot bath again, and everyone let out at least a few contented sighs.

The water was hot, but not unpleasantly so, soothing away the aches and pains of their long, hard journey like nothing else could have. Ivy and her companions luxuriated in it for a while before washing themselves, and then luxuriated in it a whole lot more.

Were it not for Garahk telling them it was time to return, Ivy was sure they all would've remained there until well after nightfall. Her time on this alien world had been full of surprises— every day had brought something new. But this was amongst the most pleasant of those surprises.

The thornskull that emerged from the pools was not the

same as the one who'd entered. Gone was the thick layer of mud Garahk had slathered himself in, replaced by hide so white that it put fresh snow to shame. The black spots and patterns in that white had a glossy sheen, and his many spiky protrusions darkened to black toward their tips. His hair, which had been caked with mud and gathered in a high knot, was now loose, its long, silky white strands run through with streaks of black.

The thornskulls didn't have clothing to replace the soiled jumpsuits, but the large, folded cloths piled nearby served well as towels, and the humans kept those cloths wrapped around themselves after drying their bodies. The vrix rubbed oil from jars lined neatly on a ledge onto their hides as the humans dried.

Though Ivy didn't cling quite as tightly to Ketahn when they crossed the bridge again, she kept her eyes closed until they arrived on the far platform. This time, however, all the bouncing and swaying left her stomach feeling even more uncertain. She spent most of the journey back to Nalaki's den willing herself not to puke.

Fortunately, the cozy interior of Nalaki's den felt grounded enough that Ivy's nausea passed—just in time to eat.

They shared a large meal consisting of fresh meat—cooked for the humans—and fruit with their thornskull hosts, and the conversation was light and friendly. There was no more talk of what would happen, no more talk of Zurvashi or the inevitable confrontation, no more talk of death and doom. Ivy knew that would come later, but she'd relish every moment before then as much as possible.

After eating, Garahk and Nalaki brought Ivy's tribe to another building. Nalaki explained that the large, low-ceilinged structure was used to store supplies. While everyone had been bathing, she'd had her people clear the place out, bring the tribe's bags and weapons inside, and arrange ten sleeping spaces with fluffed silk, soft furs, and woven blankets.

"But there are twelve of us," Ivy said, tilting her head.

Nalaki chittered. "When Garahk is away, I feel alone. I want only to be with him when he returns—no other. You have journeyed long and far. You have been with your mate, but not only with him. I know what I would want were I you."

Despite everything, that brought some heat to Ivy's cheeks, but she was far more touched by Nalaki's thoughtfulness than embarrassed.

She and Ketahn collected their belongings and followed Nalaki to a nearby platform, this one set a little farther out on a branch, away from the mighty tree trunk. The structure atop it was small, not much larger than a four-person tent, but it too was stuffed with comfortable silks and furs and fragranced with dried flowers—and, most importantly, Ivy and Ketahn fit inside with plenty of room to spare.

Smiling, Ivy turned toward Nalaki. "Thank you."

Nalaki dipped her head and lifted a hand, tapping a knuckle to her headcrest. Ivy mimicked the gesture; she knew from Ketahn and the other vrix that it was a sign of respect and acknowledgement.

She doubted it was a gesture Zurvashi would ever make to anyone.

"I will send for you near sunfall, that we may share words over important matters," Nalaki said. "But for now, take your rest."

When Nalaki was gone and the cloth door had fallen back into place, Ivy said, "She isn't anything like I expected the queen of the thornskulls to be."

Ketahn chittered and shook his head. "She is not," he replied as he placed their bags on the floor and stood their spears against the wall. "Zurvashi has ruled Takarahl since I was a broodling, and I knew there could be none as cruel or arrogant as her...but I did not realize a queen could be so different from her in every way."

"Nalaki doesn't place herself above the others. She treats them as equals. That's why she is *daiya* and not queen."

"And for that she has their respect. Mine also."

Ivy moved toward the small window and lifted the silk curtain, hooking it over the nearby wooden peg to let in the sunlight. She peered outside. The branch upon which they were perched stretched on before her, narrowing as it went, and all around was lush plant life—the thick jungle canopy above, the tops of smaller trees and other large branches below. There were vines and flowers everywhere, and she glimpsed flashes of colorful silk and paint on thornskull structures through the surrounding foliage.

"It's…beautiful here," she said.

Ketahn stepped behind Ivy, hooked an arm around her chest, and cupped the underside of her chin with another hand. Tipping her face up toward him, he looked down at her with bright violet eyes. "Ah, my heartsthread. You speak of beauty out there, yet I see only you, outshining even the sun."

Another of his arms slipped around her, and he settled his big palm over her belly. She didn't resist when he drew her against him; she just leaned into him, letting his warmth and scent wash over her.

"Ketahn? Do…you think we could stay here? After this is all over?"

He made one of those low, thoughtful hums, and it vibrated into her through his chest. "I do not know. Garahk says we are of Kaldarak now. Is this where you would like to make our home?"

"I would like a place where we'd be safe. A place where you, your sister, your friends, and the humans would be accepted— where *we* would be accepted." She turned in his arms to face him fully and raised her hands to cradle his jaw between them. "I think we could be happy here."

"I would be happy anywhere so long as I am with you," he

purred, smoothing back her hair with one of his hands. "There will be time to think on it. Time to choose. But for now, my *nyleea*, all my attention goes to this moment."

Ivy smiled, her eyes searching his as she brushed her thumbs over the hard skin of his cheeks. But despite her hope for a future, a home, for remaining in the haven they'd found here, she could not shake her anxiety and fear of what was to come. She could not shake the fear that everything she loved could be taken in the blink of an eye.

It would destroy her.

Her chest constricted as something aching, deep, and real surged within her, something that no words could truly describe. It squeezed her heart and stole her breath, flooded her with withering heat and frigid cold all at once. She felt the invisible strands that bound her to Ketahn pull taut—and she was more aware than ever of how delicate those strands were. Of just how many outside forces would cut them without a second thought.

She drew Ketahn's head down and pressed her forehead to his. "I won't let Zurvashi take you from me," she said fiercely, voice thick. Tears stung her eyes, but she did not look away from him. "You are mine. My *luveen*, my heartsthread, my everything."

CHAPTER 27

KETAHN WENT STILL. The now-familiar dread in his gut grew impossibly heavier in response to the anguish in Ivy's voice. His mate was terrified of what would come—and so was he. But there was so much more than fear in her tone, in her actions. There was love. And that love sparked a deep warmth in his chest that resonated along his heartsthread and radiated outward, fighting back that dread, fighting back the shadow of the unknown that now more than ever loomed over them.

He would not let even a single moment they had together be wasted.

"I am yours," he rasped, cupping the back of her head in his hand. "Nothing will take me from you. Not the Tangle, not the Eight, not *her*." Turning Ivy's head aside, he brushed his face down her hair, taking in her sweet fragrance, until he reached her neck.

He could not properly kiss her, but he caressed her flesh all the same with tender strokes of his mouth and tongue. A shuddering breath escaped Ivy, and she slipped her fingers into his hair, holding him close as she angled her head to grant him easier access.

Ketahn flicked his tongue beneath her ear. She shivered, her grip on his hair tightening, and her flesh, so responsive, prickled with tiny bumps. Then he moved his mouth back down to the marks upon her shoulder—*his* marks—and trailed his tongue over those, chest rumbling with pride and desire.

"Ketahn," she whispered, pressing her body against him.

His claspers circled her hips and clutched her against his aching slit. His stem was already throbbing and straining to emerge, eager to sink inside his mate's heat.

Ivy turned her face toward him, her lips skimming his cheek before she kissed the base of his mandible. "Claim me, Ketahn." She dropped her hands to his shoulders and curled her fingers, raking her nails down the hard ridges of his chest. "Conquer me. Make me yours, again and again."

Ketahn opened his mouth to graze her shoulder with his teeth, making her shudder again. "I have conquered you, female."

"Prove it. As you did before."

The mating frenzy stirred deep within him. He slid his fingers into her hair and grasped it, muscles trembling with that rising instinct, with that consuming need. But he would not give in yet. *He* would be the one to claim Ivy. He would be the one to mate her, by his will, by his choice.

He was the conqueror.

Lifting his head, he tugged back on her hair, forcing her chin up. Ivy's breath hitched as Ketahn leaned down, his face a thread's width from hers. The tips of his mandible fangs skimmed her cheeks.

"You are mine, Ivy," he growled. "I claim you, now and forever." He caught the cloth wrapped around her body with a lower hand. "You are mine. Body"—he tore the cloth away, throwing it to the floor—"heart, and spirit."

Her body, her soft, alluring human body, molded to his; her

breasts with their pink, hard peaks against his chest, her belly to his abdomen, and her hot sex against his slit. The feel of her urged him to action. The frenzy buzzed in his mind, clawing for control.

But stronger than those urges was her scent—the delicious fragrance that grew stronger with his every breath, that tempted him more than anything else. The scent that made him hunger for a real taste of his mate.

His rear legs were already drawing silk from his spinnerets when he withdrew from Ivy, keeping his hold on her hair but breaking all other contact between their bodies. His hide tingled in her absence, and his slit parted immediately, allowing his stem to burst free.

"My mate desires pleasure?" he asked, cupping her jaw and forcing her gaze to meet his.

Her blue eyes sparkled because of her previous tears, but their color had darkened with need.

"Yes. She desires her male."

Ivy reached for him. Though he longed for her touch, he caught her wrists before her hands reached his hide and raised her arms over her head. He worked the silk strand without conscious thought, wrapping it around her arms, his fingers tying quick, tight knots.

"I have claimed you, human. You will receive"—he fastened the strand to the ceiling and let it take her weight—"only what I give."

Faster than even he could perceive, his hands worked the silk around her thighs and knees, lifting her feet off the floor. Her scent only intensified; with each loop, each knot, her desire flared.

He looked upon his mate. Her skin was flushed, her chest was heaving, and those breasts, so heavy, so sensitive, were angled upward. His gaze trailed lower, over the bump of her belly—where their broodling grew. That deep, powerful instinct stirred in him again; it was pride, possessiveness, protective-ness, *everything*.

She was his in every way. She bore his marks on her body and her spirit, and she had accepted his seed. Yet his hunger for Ivy would never be satisfied, no matter how much of her he had. It was larger than the Tangle, vaster than the star-filled sky that spanned beyond the jungle's boughs.

His eyes dipped lower still. Ivy's legs were spread, baring her sex to him. Her essence glistened on her inner thighs and the petals of her slit, beckoning him, tempting him.

Ketahn's hide felt stretched thin over his muscles and bones as he palmed Ivy's backside with two hands and lifted her. His mandibles spread wide and twitched with anticipation, and his claws pricked her tender flesh. He lowered his face and drew in a deep breath.

Ketahn growled as he exhaled, the sound undulating with his own overwhelming need. Ivy trembled and let out a soft whim-per, raising her hips toward him.

Her desire only heightened his own. He shifted his gaze up, looking over her belly and breasts, to see her staring at him with eyes glossy and lips parted.

His little mate had shown him beauty in more forms than he could ever have imagined. Each time he looked upon her, there was something more to appreciate, a feature to lose himself in. And there was nothing he could lose himself in quite like the lust burning in her eyes now.

But she had demanded a conqueror.

"Beg me, Ivy," he rasped, letting his breath flow over her sex again. "Beg me for pleasure."

"Please." Her lashes fluttered as her head fell aside to rest on her arm. She wrapped her fingers around the silk bindings and strained toward his mouth again. "Touch me, Ketahn."

He dipped his head a little lower and extended his tongue, running it along her inner thigh to sample her essence. He could not contain a trill—and he would not be able to hold himself back much longer. Her scent alone would drive him to madness within a few more heartbeats. "*Beg.*"

"Oh God." Ivy's legs quivered. More of her nectar dripped from her sex. "Please. Please, I need you, Ketahn." Panting softly, she held his gaze. "*Kiss* me."

With a snarl, he lifted her to his face and speared her sex with his tongue to draw her essence straight from its source. Ivy gasped and closed her eyes, head falling back. Ketahn dragged his tongue along her inner walls, thrilling in the way they tightened around it, and then withdrew to take her taste into his mouth.

Before he could even think to do so, his hunger and desire had him lapping at her folds. He licked the dew from her petals, lavished the swollen bud at the apex of her sex, and plunged into her depths again and again, coaxing out more and more of her sweet nectar to slake his unending thirst. She clutched at the strand and rocked her hips to the motions of his tongue, seeking her pleasure in any way she could—and he gave it.

Her moans filled the room. There was no need to keep quiet, no need to hide. Nothing would stop him from hearing the music of her pleasure now.

The movements of her hips grew more frantic as he increased his pace and gave in fully to his hunger. When he flicked his tongue rapidly over that small pleasure nub, her thighs squeezed around his head, and her moans became breathless cries; he drank her flood greedily, pressing her pelvis firm against his face and allowing her no escape despite her writhing and bucking. While she was swept away by her climax, he offered only one word to her, growled directly against her slit.

"Mine."

That declaration shattered what control he'd maintained. The mating frenzy crashed through him.

Rising, he adjusted his hold on her with his lower hands, spread her thighs, and drove into her with a powerful thrust. Her sex was so tight around his stem that his body seized. He released a wordless grunt and pressed his claws against her skin as impossible, irresistible pressure gripped his shaft, and his mind swam in a haze of need and sensation.

It should have been his undoing. It was too much all at once, too strong, but he had to have more. This was beyond a craving, beyond a need. This was everything; *she* was everything.

Ketahn braced his forelegs beneath Ivy, clamped his hands on her hips and his claspers around her thighs, drew back, and drove into her again until his pelvis was flush with hers.

"*Fuck*," Ivy breathed. Her eyes, half-lidded, met his. "Again."

Instinct recognized that not as a plea, but a demand—a challenge. But he was too far gone to care. He lifted her, angled his hips back, and slammed her onto him again, and again, and again. Her wet heat clutched at him, welcomed him, drew on his stem greedily. He snarled, thrusting violently against her, deeper and deeper, unable to get deep enough.

Her breasts bounced, and he covered them with his upper hands, squeezing and teasing her nipples. She arched into his touch, wordlessly begging for more as her head fell back.

The pressure in him built; it grew twofold stronger, threefold, with each pump of his hips. But he needed more, needed more of her—needed her hands on him. He needed her fingertips trailing fire across his hide. Needed the dull bite of her little nails.

One of his upper hands darted over Ivy's head. His claws sliced the strand binding her to the ceiling. Her full weight came down upon him, and he tore the rope away from her arms to free them. To free her. She wrapped her arms around his neck without hesitation, drawing close, her breath mingling with his. And she used her new freedom to move with Ketahn, meeting him thrust for thrust, her nipples grazing his chest.

"You're mine," Ivy rasped, spearing his hair with her fingers and clenching the strands. "My mate. My *luveen*." She moaned, grinding down upon him, her essence coating his stem and slit. She rested her forehead on his headcrest. *"Mine."*

Her lips collided with his mouth, and suddenly, her body locked tight, and her movements faltered. She squeezed her eyes shut and cried out in pleasure.

The clenching of her sex around his stem was beyond anything Ketahn had ever felt, but it was nothing compared to that word coming from her lips with such passion and possessiveness. He roared, hammering her down upon him one last time as his whole body tensed, as his shaft thrummed, about to explode, as the golden radiance of her hair in the sunlight overcame his vision.

The pressure broke. His seed spilled into her, draining him of everything—and then filling him with ecstasy. His tendrils extended within her, fluttering and vibrating, and her convulsions began anew, drawing out even more of his seed.

For those moments, he could not distinguish between their bodies. She was one with him, and he with her.

Mine. Yours. My mate.

My everything.

Ivy's nails bit into his hide as she released muffled cries against his neck, her breath hot on his skin. She whispered words of love, whispered words he didn't understand, and over and again, she told him she loved him, all while holding him tight through the savagery of their pleasure.

And he embraced her, locking her firmly upon him, unwilling to relinquish any part of her. Ivy's sex quivered around his stem, and her sweat-dampened body trembled. Ketahn breathed deep, taking in the fragrance of their mating as he brushed his mouth over the marks upon her shoulder.

Something wet touched his hide and dripped down his back. Ivy sniffled, wracked by a shudder.

He tightened his hold on her, moving a hand to her hair to comb his claws through it slowly. "Ah, my *nyleea*. No more fear. No more sadness."

"Promise you won't let her take you from me," she rasped.

The fury he'd carried for so long sparked deep in his chest. The queen truly had left nothing untainted.

"She will not take me," he rumbled. "When next I encounter Zurvashi, she will meet her end. I weave my words into a bond, my heartsthread."

CHAPTER 28

CALLIE SIGHED and tipped her head back to look up at the gray early morning sky. "Do I have to?"

"Everyone else did," said Cole, tossing another stick into the fire. "Don't *chih ken* out on us now, Callie."

"I really don't understand why the conversation went in this direction. Aren't we supposed to be leaving all that stuff behind us? The past in the past and all that?"

"Yeah, we are," Lacey replied with a grin. "But we also left music, *tee vee*, and *bookz* behind, so our options for entertainment are pretty limited."

"Back to the basics," said Will before taking another bite of meat.

Cole grunted. "Wonder what cavemen did for entertainment."

"Stories." Smiling, Ivy passed Ketahn a steaming piece of roasted meat. "Humans have been telling stories forever, right? Even before we were at the same level of technology as the vrix."

Ketahn nodded his thanks and slipped the food into his mouth. The juices struck his tongue with a burst of flavor, and he made an appreciative trill. The vrix had dried meat to preserve it for as long as anyone could remember, but it had been common to eat kills raw for much of Ketahn's life.

He'd come to enjoy the flavors brought out in meat when it was cooked.

"Yup," said Diego. "The human experience has always been a shared one."

Ivy's gaze lingered on Ketahn. "And how could we have known those experiences would be shared well beyond humans themselves?"

Cole huffed, picked up another stick, and snapped it in two. "It's too damn early in the morning for conversations to get so deep. Callie's not getting out of this. She owes us a story."

Callie pursed her lips and wrinkled her nose. "Sharing a story is one thing, but why does it have to be an embarrassing one?"

"Because those are what will forge the strongest bonds in our little fellowship," said Diego. He'd shaved the hair off his face this morning; it was strange to see him as he'd looked upon first waking those eightdays ago. "We've all been embarrassed at some point in our lives. Sharing some of those moments will help us see each other on a deeper level, to see that we are all flawed, but that we trust each other enough to be flawed."

Will chuckled and shook his head. "Did you say you were a nurse or a *theruh pist*, Diego?"

Diego grinned, displaying his flat, white teeth. A few of the thornskulls sitting with the group tilted their heads; it would take them time to get used to such expressions.

"I'm whatever you need me to be, William," Diego said.

Will dropped his gaze, but not before Ketahn caught the shy look in his eyes, or the upward curve of his lips.

"You don't have to share anything if you don't want to," Ivy said, propping her elbow atop Ketahn's bent right foreleg and leaning her side against it.

Ahmya looked down at the pieces of grass she'd been

fiddling with in her lap; she'd woven them into a long, neat braid with subtle variations in its pattern throughout. "I could tell another of mine instead if you want?"

"Ugh." Callie's shoulders sagged, and she hung her head. "No, you don't have to do that. I'll tell a story. But a quick one, okay?"

"These *hyu-nanz* share many words," said Garahk, who sat to Ketahn's left. "Do they ever make silence?"

Ketahn chittered. "Yes, but it is rare."

Though he didn't understand all the things they'd talked about, Ketahn understood their reason for doing so—fear. They knew the fight with Zurvashi was drawing near. Garahk's Eyes, who fulfilled a role similar to the Queen's Claw, had reported that Zurvashi was camped on the edge of the mire closest to Kaldarak with at least fifty Claws and Fangs.

This conversation was a way for the humans to distract themselves from what would come. A way to forget what they'd spent the last two days preparing for, to ignore all the possible outcomes undoubtedly flitting through their minds.

Callie drew in a breath. "Okay, so sometimes when I was a little kid my parents had to go out of town on work trips, and I would stay at my grandma's house." A gentle smile lifted the corners of her mouth. "I loved it there. She always had these *buhterr kookeez* that came in little *tinz*, and so many fluffy knitted blankets, and she'd always snuggle up with me on the *kowch* and watch nature and *syens* shows. And the smell… It was like, an *old* smell, I guess, but it was a good one. So comforting.

"Anyway, I loved juice as a kid. All kinds of juice. And one day I was at my grandma's, getting ready for *skool*, and I opened the *frij* and there was this purple juice in there. I thought it was *grayp* juice, even though I could clearly see *proon* on the *lay bull*. My brain said it was just some kind of fancy *grayp*.

"I drank four glasses of it. Don't even think I really liked it, but just… I guess I was really thirsty? So everything was fine for a while. I walked to *skool*, played with my friends, expanded my mind. But then right after lunch, it hit me."

"Oh. Oh, no," Lacey breathed, eyes wide.

"Oh, yeah. Right in the middle of practice for a *ree sytull* we were doing."

"In front of everyone?" asked Cole.

Ivy cringed.

Callie laughed and shook her head. "No, thank God. I made it to the bathroom, but…" She cleared her throat. "Let's just say I lost my favorite pair of pants that day. The end."

Cole blew out a heavy breath. "Shit."

"Yes. Literally."

"Ah, fuck, I didn't mean to—"

"Don't worry about it." Callie waved a hand. "It really was shitty all around. But mostly just, you know…down there."

The humans laughed. Their easy laughter seemed the perfect complement to the crackling and popping of the fire, making it somehow warmer and more welcoming. The vrix chittered along, though most understood neither the humor of Callie's story nor the words she'd used to tell it. Even Ketahn lacked enough understanding of human matters to piece together what she hadn't said until the end.

But human laughter was what Diego had once called *kun tay juss*—it spread from individual to individual. He'd said he was speaking with great knowledge on the matter because of his training as a healer, a comment that had produced several chuckles at the time.

Perhaps over the years Ketahn would learn to truly understand such things.

He just had to ensure he and Ivy had those years to spend together.

Ketahn placed a hand on Ivy's shoulder, massaging her tense muscles, and she leaned against him a little more firmly. She covered that hand with her own and gave it a squeeze.

Their first night in Kaldarak, Ketahn and his tribe had met with Nalaki again to form a plan for their stand against Zurvashi. Kaldarak could win this battle against the queen if it came to it, but Nalaki had told Ketahn she had only enough seasoned warriors to match Zurvashi's numbers and no more—not without leaving many of her kind vulnerable in smaller settlements around the Tangle.

The moons had been high by the time they'd solidified their plan. It had seemed that no one was happy about the decisions, but none could argue them. Ketahn in particular had protested the presence of the humans during the encounter. He'd wanted them in Kaldarak, or even better, led far away to hide until Zurvashi was no more. But Ivy and the humans had insisted that the fight belonged to them as much as it did Ketahn.

Zurvashi had killed Ella and all but vowed to destroy the remaining humans.

Though Nalaki hadn't seemed pleased to do so, she'd sided with the humans in that argument. For the thornskulls, anyone willing to fight to defend their kin, their home, was a warrior at heart, and they would not deny the humans their right to battle.

And Ketahn could not deny that the ideas contributed by the humans could well turn the battle in their favor should it come to open warfare. The vrix had been confused by Callie's requests for animal fat, but they had complied. For the next two days, humans, thornskulls, and shadowstalkers had worked together to prepare their chosen place of battle, down on the jungle floor just outside Kaldarak.

Those human ideas did not seem so strange now.

Cole had busied himself, as well, having been inspired after toying with a few sticks that had fallen onto one of the platforms. After a day of tinkering with various tools and pieces of wood, he'd asked Rekosh to weave him a tight, strong silk thread. The day before yesterday, as the sun had been falling, Cole had demonstrated his creation—a bow.

With a strip of flexible wood and a silk string, he'd created a weapon that could launch tiny spears called arrows with considerable speed and force. He said he'd learned *archuree* when he was a child, and that his bow wasn't very good, but the vrix had seen the advantage.

Telok, Cole, and several thornskulls had spent their day yesterday crafting as many of the bows and arrows as they could. Though Ketahn doubted the weapons would be able to slay a vrix—especially one such as Zurvashi—they would allow the humans to inflict damage from a distance should the need arise.

The farther they were from the queen's warriors, the better.

With good fortune, the humans would practice with the weapons today. Only Cole was familiar with their use, and though Will and Lacey showed potential, everyone required time to learn. The same went for the few vrix who'd tried the bows.

The next moment was never a guarantee—even less so now than ever.

"Do you carry fear, Ketahn?" Garahk asked, leaning closer. He bumped Ketahn with his elbow. "Down in your gut?"

Ketahn looked down at Ivy. "Yes."

"Your Blooddrinker Queen gives fear and war. But fear does not make shame."

"It does not. But I do not fear her, regardless."

"No shame, shadowstalker. She gives fear in my gut." Garahk tapped the tip of his leg on the ground. "A warrior is not one without fear."

"But one who acts despite it."

"Yes. You carry wisdom almost as great as mine." Garahk held up a hand, finger and thumb curled with only a tiny distance between them. "A little more wisdom, and we are same."

Ketahn chittered, but his humor faded quickly. "I do not fear her, Garahk. I fear…what she wants to take from me. Fear what I may lose. Do you understand?"

The thornskull's eyes shifted to Ivy, and his mandibles twitched downward. "I know your words, Ketahn. Know them down to my heartsflame."

Ivy squeezed Ketahn's hand again and glanced at him over her shoulder. Though she smiled, he didn't miss the glint of fear in her eyes. How could he when it had been in them for so long now? How could he, when Zurvashi was the one who'd put it there?

He and Ivy had been unsure of whether they should tell Nalaki and Garahk of her state, having had no idea how the thornskulls would react. Would they see it as a terrible omen, as an abomination, a monstrous thing, like Zurvashi undoubtedly would? Would they decide to cast Ketahn's tribe out—or worse, declare that such a broodling could not be allowed to exist?

Yet ultimately, the most important thing to Ketahn was that Ivy and their broodling were safe. For all his rage, all his determination, all his clarity, he could not say what the future would bring. He was certain Zurvashi would come. He was certain she would agree to battle him alone.

Once that battle began, there was no way to know what would happen.

If he could not protect his mate, if his friends or sister could not, *someone* had to. And how could he have asked that of the thornskulls without first telling them that Ivy was carrying a broodling—*his* broodling—inside her?

Nalaki and Garahk had listened closely to Ivy and Ketahn's words. Disbelief had been clear in their eyes, but it had faded, replaced by growing wonderment. When Nalaki had asked to touch Ivy's belly, Ivy had smiled so brightly that Ketahn's hearts ached—and his whole body had tensed at the thought of the female thornskull placing her hands upon his little mate.

But Ivy had agreed. Somehow, Ketahn had kept himself in

place while he'd watched Nalaki's huge hand descend to cover Ivy's belly and the broodling within. Part of his mind recognized what was happening—the bond that was formed between the females in that moment, a bond of motherhood and expectancy, of delight and uncertainty. The rest of his mind demanded he fight the thornskull back because a twitch of her fingers would have been enough to bury her claws deep in Ivy's flesh.

The thornskull *daiya* had been nothing but gentle, however, and with Ivy's permission, had explored a little more. She'd examined Ivy's hands closely, right down to their tiny fingertips; she'd placed a hand on Ivy's shoulder, making her sway, as she studied the human's legs, clearly wondering how such a creature could remain upright. She'd touched Ivy's hair and even woven a few strands into a braid. Afterward, as a show of mutual trust and friendship, Nalaki had brought Ivy to the nest in the corner and allowed her to touch the eggs.

"We vrix and these *hyu-nanz* are meant to be together," Nalaki had said. "If not, why would they be able to communicate with us? Why would they be able to make broodlings with us? I cannot believe anything such as this could happen were it not the will of the Eight, and if it is not their will... I would question their wisdom."

Garahk had hissed at her then.

Nalaki had snapped her mandible fangs and glared at him. "I will share what words I choose, my *luveen*. You see it as well as I, you who are my eyes. It is as Ivy said. These *hyu-nanz* look different, but they are the same as us within."

Last night, while Ivy and the other humans had been cooking their evening meal, Ketahn had gone to speak to Nalaki and Garahk again. He'd obtained their vow. Should anything happen to him and his friends, the thornskulls would protect Ivy. They would care for her and her broodling just as Nalaki had said—as though they were thornskulls themselves, hatched right here in Kaldarak.

Their promise had relieved the weight that had settled over Ketahn. It had been the last such burden he could shed; the rest he would carry alone until the end. Until he slew his foe.

Garahk dipped his chin, indicating the humans sitting on the opposite side of the fire. "They are done sharing stories?"

"Yes," Ivy said, "I think so."

"I would share a story. Will you give it to them with your *hyu-nanz* words?"

Ivy twisted her torso a little more, facing Garahk. "I will."

Ketahn raised his mandibles in a smile and carefully hooked Ivy's hair with his claw, sweeping it behind her ear so he could see her face fully. She appeared almost otherworldly with the fire backing her, its light dancing upon her skin and glimmering in her eyes.

Tilting his head, Garahk shifted his gaze to Ketahn. "It is a story from the war between mine and yours. Will that give insult?"

"No," Ketahn replied.

His response was echoed by his friends and sister. He had no desire to be reminded of those events, of what he'd done and what he'd lost, but the thornskulls looked at things differently. If Ivy truly wanted to make a home here—and Ketahn could see it, could see them finding happiness and peace here—he would have to learn their ways.

He would have to learn to see his past differently. He only hoped that would become easier after Zurvashi was gone.

"This story has risen in my mind many times since I saw yours in the mire," Garahk said, with Ivy translating for the humans. "I would share words of a warrior with great *shar'thai*, a shadowstalker we give honor since the day he was witnessed in battle.

"Yours and mine battled in the mire. Hungry mud sucked at

355

our legs, and eshkens bit at our hides, but we fought hard. You were close to our home, to Kaldarak. Blackfurs fought as one with the mire, and gave great pain and wounds to ours, until our *daiya* came with her warriors. One such warrior was called Okalan ka'Hana, Breaker of the Goldshells. She strode forth without fear to make battle with your blackfurs."

Garahk curled his fingers like he was gripping an invisible shaft and thrust his hand forward. "Her spear struck as lightning, piercing blackfurs as a needle pierces cloth. When it broke, her club struck hard enough to fell trees. She pushed deep into the blackfurs, and only one stood before her. A blackfur who was short but formed as a thornskull—broad and strong."

A low buzz vibrated in Ketahn's chest, and he looked at Urkot, who was leaning forward with his arms on his bent forelegs, watching Garahk warily.

"Okalan swung her club. It shattered upon his headcrest, but the broad one was not felled. His spear sank deep into her gut. Okalan would not be slain by one such as he. She roared and grabbed the blackfur. His strength was great, but hers was greater. Our warriors heard the sound as she tore off his arm. The ripping flesh and snapping bone. The mire water was red with his blood as she threw him aside.

"But the broad one would not take death. He rose from the water and answered Okalan's roar, and his call shook the mire. With his spear stuck in Okalan, he took up his fallen arm and used it to give her death. The mire drank much blood that day, but that fight would not be forgotten by those who witnessed. We named him Three-Arm, Breaker's Bane."

The few other thornskulls who'd joined the group made wordless sounds of agreement and thumped fists against their chests.

"Did he seriously beat a vrix to death with his *arm?*" Callie asked, wide eyes shifting from Ivy to stare at Urkot. "That's crazy."

Urkot chittered. His mandibles twitched with it, and he sat back, slapping the scar on his side. "There is much more glory in your story than in the truth, Garahk."

"Share your words then, Three-Arm," Garahk said with a chitter of his own, gesturing to Urkot. "Give us your story."

"He is not known as a teller of stories." Rekosh tapped the tip of a leg against Urkot's hindquarters. He had a long piece of thread twined between two of his hands, arranged in criss-crossing patterns. "It may be best to leave your words in place, lest the story be ruined for everyone."

Snorting, Urkot bumped Rekosh with a leg, hard enough to make the lean vrix rock. "My arm, my story."

"Then tell it before the jungle grows over us and buries our bones," said Telok.

"Well...there is not much that has not been said."

"Come, Three-Arm," Garahk said, "you must have more words to share."

Urkot huffed and absently brushed his fingers over the scar. Of Ketahn's friends, Urkot carried the most apparent marks from the war on his body—but he'd always seemed the least marked by it in mind and spirit. Ketahn did not doubt Urkot had quietly suffered, but he'd always held firm.

"Very well." Urkot dropped his hand to his foreleg. "The truth of it. The thornsku— Ah, what did you call her?"

"Okalan ka'Hana, Breaker of the Goldshells," Garahk said.

"Okalan. She was already wounded when she reached me. Must have fought through six or seven other Claws before. I do not know if her wounds slowed her, but I wanted it said. When I looked upon her, I saw my death. I am a delver, a stoneshaper, and my place was not amongst warriors. But I was all that remained to defend our flank, so I offered a few words to the Eight"—he quickly made the crossed forearms gesture that would always be incomplete for him—"and charged to meet my doom.

"I hit her first. Buried my spear half a segment in her gut. I did not feel her club. My sight went black, and a great noise filled my skull, but I did not feel it. My only thought was to free my spear. I *needed* it. But it would not come out. I did not understand why, so I kept tugging on it."

"Because your head is hard and thick, but your mind can still be addled by a good blow," said Rekosh.

Urkot chittered. "What few wits I had possessed, Okalan knocked well out of my head. I was confused when she grabbed me. I remember thinking that I was not searching for a mate, but how could I deny a female who was so interested in me?"

The other vrix, thornskulls included, chittered. A few moments later—as Ivy's translation caught up to the story—the humans laughed.

"Then she roared in my face and pulled my arms in opposite directions," Urkot continued. "Your story, Garahk, did not tell enough of this part."

"What does it miss, Three-arm?" Garahk asked.

"That it *hurt*." Urkot's tone—which suggested the answer should have been obvious to all—drew more chittering and laughter. "There is only one worse pain I have endured in all my life."

"And what was that?" asked Ahnset.

"Listening to Rekosh talk every day."

That sparked yet more amusement, even from Rekosh.

For Ketahn to see everyone—his friends, his sister, the humans, and the thornskulls who had once been his enemies—gathered like this filled him with a hope as bright as his mate's smile. If only it all wasn't so delicate. If only it wasn't under threat of being broken.

Without looking up from the thread around his fingers, Rekosh said, "Once every moon cycle or two, Urkot, you manage to put your words together in a way that suggests more than rocks are tumbling in your skull."

"And once every few seasons, you put your words together in a way that suggests more than fluffed silk stuffed in yours," said Telok.

They might have gone on that way as the sun crept toward its midday peak—with Ketahn and Ahnset inevitably joining—but for a question from one of the thornskulls.

"Did you truly slay Okalan with your arm, Three-Arm?"

"No," Urkot replied, lifting his upper left arm to study the scar. "I knew only that I had lost my spear and that Okalan would attack my friends. I picked up the first thing my fingers touched. And I set upon her in blind fury, swinging my arm like a club. She fell before me, into the mire, and began to sink in the mud. That is when I pulled my spear free and drove it into her again. The water was so dark with blood and mud that I could see only her head and shoulders above it."

"Such a victory must have made your *shar'thai* burn bright as the sun," said another of the thornskulls.

"I do not know. I fell atop her and watched the blood spread in the water. I knew much of it was my own. I thought it was time for my long rest. Then Ketahn"—Urkot dipped his chin toward Ketahn and touched a knuckle to his headcrest—"dragged me out of the water and carried me to safety. I remember little of what followed."

Lifting his mandibles, Ketahn chittered softly. "I remember you being very heavy."

"I do not think that has changed."

"Your life for an arm," said Telok, stepping closer to thump Urkot's shoulder. "A small thing to trade in the end."

"And it was my least favorite arm." Urkot patted the gnarled scar again. "Sometimes I still feel it there. Like...a lingering spirit."

"Humans call that *fantum* limb," said Ivy.

"Happens to a lot of *ampyu teez*," Diego added, with Ivy translating what she could. "It's like that part of you having been there is *wi urd* so deep in your *nervuss siztum* that your body can't forget it."

Movement on the edge of Ketahn's vision called his attention. He turned his head to see a pair of mud-covered thornskull males approaching the fire. Garahk turned as well, the hairs on his legs rising.

"Did you carry your arm to Takarahl?" asked one of the other thornskulls.

Urkot grunted, his gaze also flicking toward the approaching males. "I left it where I fell. It is a trophy for Okalan. The piece of me she took and may forever keep."

Cole laughed after Ivy spoke. "Wow. That's...that's fucked up."

Garahk pushed himself upright and turned fully toward the newcomers, striding to meet them.

Ivy tensed, her smile fading, her blunt nails biting Ketahn's hand even as the dread in his gut made itself known again.

Garahk and the two Eyes spoke briefly in hushed tones; though Ketahn could not make out their words, each one solidified the heavy feeling in his belly, each one twisted his insides a little tighter. He should have known that it was impossible to enjoy this taste of peace and camaraderie without receiving some reminder of the truth.

Mandibles twitching, Garahk spun about to face everyone still gathered around the fire. The light in his eyes had taken on a serious, hard glint like Ketahn had not seen in them, a glimpse of the warrior Garahk was in his hearts.

"She's coming," Ivy whispered breathlessly. Her body shuddered against Ketahn's leg.

For a long while, Ketahn had known it would come to this. He had known he would never have the life he wanted with his mate without confronting Zurvashi. Without killing her. But some part of him had hoped for more time—for time to live and love, to spend all these little moments with his mate that would bind their heartsthreads together tighter and tighter.

A low, unhappy buzz emanated from Garahk's chest. "The Blooddrinker Queen strides for Kaldarak."

CHAPTER 29

KALDARAK'S WARRIORS descended from the trees in silence at Garahk's call. During Ketahn's short time here, the thornskulls had been friendly and warm, always eager to speak, to chitter, to hear and share stories. The vrix who now approached seemed different from those who'd welcomed Ketahn's tribe into their village.

The thornskulls were as they'd been seven years ago, when Ketahn and his friends had battled them—fierce warriors willing to die to protect Kaldarak.

Standing with Garahk to his left and Ivy to his right, Ketahn watched as the warriors gathered on the other side of the fire along with the rest of his tribe. They carried spears, clubs, and axes, but more importantly, they all carried a hard light in their eyes.

They were now facing the battle they'd expected to come years ago. The battle for their home.

Ketahn was determined to prevent that battle from occurring. If not for him coming this way, these vrix would not have had to amass their warriors in defense of their land, would not be striding to make war against the queen who'd broken them.

Garahk raised his voice so it carried between the trees. "Kaldarak has made war with many enemies. Ours have lost, ours have won, but always our *shar'thai* shines. War is the way of the Tangle, and so Kaldarak gives no hate for it.

"But the Blooddrinker Queen did not give only war. She gave hate, filled Kaldarak's hearts with it and drank the blood of our kin. She gave death to all. It did not matter if they could not raise spear. Broodlings and elders, growers, shapers, weavers. The mire is forever filled with bones and overflowed with blood. The blood of ours.

"She alone has earned Kaldarak's hate. This is true under sun and sky, under moon and stars, under their eightfold eyes. Now, the Blooddrinker Queen strides for our home to take those who have become ours, just as she took our sisters and brothers, our mothers and fathers, our broodlings, our friends. She has taken much from us already. Too much. Will she take any more?"

The thornskulls answered as one with a powerful *no*, thumping fists against their chests and their weapons on the ground to create an immense sound that swept outward from the group like a storm wind.

"None of ours would shy from giving war," Garahk continued. "Our *shar'thai* is great. We do not fear battle and take only glory from death. But Ketahn tes Ishuun'ani Ir'okari, Spear in Shadows, has offered himself as champion. He will fight, that the rest of ours may be spared new scars. Do you take this champion?"

Again the thornskulls replied as one, this time a *yes*—and with even more thumping and banging accompanying it.

"Spear in Shadows shall fight for Kaldarak. The Blooddrinker Queen will fall to his spear." Garahk turned to face Ketahn. "Yours are mine, shadowstalker, and mine are yours. We are as one."

One of the thornskulls strode around the fire, carrying a

large bowl. The liquid inside was thick and deep red; the paint looked like blood, but smelled of spearblossom flowers.

The thornskull lifted the bowl toward Garahk, who accepted it in his lower hands.

Garahk dipped one of his upper hands into the paint, coating his palm, and then pressed it to Ketahn's shoulder. "We are as one. With this mark, I share my *shar'thai*."

One by one, the other thornskulls stepped forward. Each stopped before Ketahn, dipped a hand into the paint, and touched it to him, leaving a new handprint on his arms, legs, hindquarters, back, or abdomen. Each echoed Garahk's words —*we are as one*.

At the encouragement of a few of the otherwise quiet warriors, Ketahn's tribe walked forward when the thornskulls were done. Rekosh, Urkot, and Telok performed the brief ritual, their hands lingering a little longer, their gazes holding his a little more firmly.

"We stride with you," Telok said.

When Ahnset approached him, she seemed about to speak. But her mandibles twitched downward, and no words came out. A sorrowful light danced in her eyes—regret, loss, resignation. She pressed her big, paint-coated hand to his shoulder and said, "We are as one, broodbrother."

She moved away, and the humans came next, starting with Diego.

"You're going to win this," he said as he placed his hand in the paint. He touched that hand to Ketahn's lower left forearm. "*Ikesh elad iln ul*."

We are as one.

The other humans repeated the words in vrix as they left their marks, some more stumblingly than others, but each also spoke English words to him—words of encouragement, of belief.

"Kill that bitch so we can relax a little, dude," Cole said.

"We have your back," Lacey told Ketahn.

"Whatever happens," said Will, "we're all getting through this."

Callie grinned, though the expression was strained. "She doesn't stand a chance. We'll be celebrating your victory by lunchtime."

"Come back to us safe and whole," Ahmya said as she stood on her toes to leave her mark on Ketahn's neck, which seemed to be one of the few bare spots on his body. "*Ikesh elad iln ul.*"

Last was Ivy, who had lined up with the others as the ritual had proceeded. She stepped up to him with deliberate slowness, her lips parting and shoulders rising and falling with her deep, shaky breaths. But her eyes, so pure and blue, did not leave his. The golden hair framing her face made those eyes even more vibrant.

Ketahn's chest swelled with love, with longing, with a hundred emotions that forced aside his fear. The female he'd taken from the pit all those eightdays ago had changed so much since—but in those changes, she had become more *herself*. More beautiful, more self-assured, more courageous. The strength she'd shown had only grown as she'd endured trial after trial.

Ivy stopped in front of Ketahn, and he instinctively sank lower to bring his face closer to hers.

"You are mine." She dipped a hand into the paint and pressed it over his hearts, which thumped harder beneath her touch. "Hearts." She moved her hand down, placing it just over his slit and making his claspers stir. "Body." Now she coated both hands in paint and lifted them, cupping each side of his face. "Spirit. You and I are as one, Ketahn."

He placed his lower hands on her hips and bent down to touch his headcrest to her forehead. One of his lower hands found the bowl, and he touched it to the paint. "We are as one, my *nyleea.*" Drawing back, Ketahn placed his paint-coated hand on the side of her neck, two fingers and his thumb stretching up to mark her cheek.

They stood that way for many heartbeats, staring into each other's eyes, and Ketahn battled the urge to sweep her into his arms and carry her off into the Tangle the whole time. Her place was at his side, far, far away from Zurvashi and Takarahl. Far away from anything that meant her harm.

"You will come back to me," she said firmly.

"I will, my heartsthread. You have my word. My vow. My promise. For you, I would stand alone against the Eight. I would find a way to cross the blackness between the stars. Nothing will keep me from you."

"We must stride," Garahk said gently. "All must be in place before she comes."

Ketahn knew that was true, but he was reluctant to release his mate. He would return to her, he was certain of it, he would do *anything* to fulfill his vow...but he could not silence that part of his mind that said he was about to stride to his doom.

Ivy drew Ketahn's head down and kissed him, letting her lips linger on his mouth long enough for him to taste a hint of her sweetness. She squeezed her eyes shut, and he caught the faint scent of her tears. When she pulled away, she met his gaze again, her eyes watery but filled with determination, and said, "It's time to go."

His chest rumbled. "I know, my heartsthread. I know."

But it was Ivy who pulled away first, Ivy who had the strength to break the contact between them.

"We need to grab our stuff and get set up," said Cole, who was grouped with the rest of Ketahn's tribe.

Ivy nodded, walking backward a few steps, gaze lingering on Ketahn, before she finally turned around and joined the rest of the tribe. Ketahn's hands, now empty, curled into fists. He already missed the warmth of her touch.

As she walked off, Ivy glanced back over her shoulder. Her

eyes, shimmering with unshed tears, met Ketahn's again. As clearly as though she'd spoken aloud, he heard the message in her gaze.

I love you. Get back to me.

Ketahn's hearts ached more with each of their heavy beats. This would not be the last time he beheld her. It could not be.

And then she was gone, blocked from his sight by the gathered thornskulls. He was suddenly aware of the paint on his hide, already drying, of every place he'd been touched during the thornskull ritual. But only the marks left by Ivy's hands burned like they'd been seared onto him, body and spirit.

You and I are as one, Ketahn.

Garahk thumped Ketahn's foreleg with one of his own. "Come. Let us stride."

"Did you mean to be off without me, my *luveen*?" called a female from nearby.

Ketahn and Garahk turned toward the vrix who'd spoken to find Nalaki approaching. A trill ran through the thornskull warriors at the sight of her, and they parted to allow her through, thumping their chests and clattering their weapons in a quick, strong rhythm.

"Nalaki, my *daiya*, my heartsflame. Why have you come?" Garahk's voice was laced with confusion and concern, but there was a firmness underlying it.

"You know why," she replied, halting before him. She rested the butt of her spear on the ground; the weapon was taller than her.

"Our brood must be tended. We know this. You know this."

Nalaki snapped her fangs. "Do not give harsh words, *luveen*. Spiritspeaker Akoral watches over our eggs."

"I trust none to do so but you, *nyleea*. Who could give more than you, their mother?"

Closing the remaining distance between her and Garahk, Nalaki cupped the back of his head in one big hand and bent down to touch her headcrest to his. "My heartsflame sputters with my every moment away. But I am more than mother to our brood. I am *daiya* to Kaldarak also, and I am a warrior. If Zurvashi means to give us war, I will meet her, as I have before."

"Nalaki…"

"As one, Garahk." She closed her eyes. "As one."

In that moment, Ketahn understood what he was fighting for more than ever. Of course Ivy and the broodling growing inside her came first—they always would. But so much more was at risk. Not just Ketahn's tribe, not just his friends and sister, but Nalaki and Garahk. Their unhatched brood. All the vrix of Takarahl and Kaldarak. All those lives were in Zurvashi's shadow, threatened by her. And if Ketahn failed, how many more would suffer before she was through? After all that had occurred, he would have been a fool to think she'd be satisfied with merely taking him as her own. She'd want to gift her rage to everyone and everything, including Kaldarak.

Nalaki and Garahk withdrew from one another and, side by side, strode toward the place they'd chosen for the battle. Ketahn and the thornskull warriors followed. Despite the instinctual pull to do so, Ketahn did not look back. His tribe, human and vrix both, would be along soon.

Part of him still wished he could send them all away to safety. No one for whom he cared should ever have been walking toward Zurvashi.

Though their destination was only a few hundred segments from their morning fire, the journey seemed much longer. Ketahn felt all the distance he'd crossed to get here, through jungle and mire, felt the weight of all the dangers he and his tribe had faced, felt all they'd seen and done like scars on his spirit. And for all they'd endured in hope of escape, Zurvashi had still come.

Yet all those thoughts fell away as he and the thornskulls reached the prepared grounds. Ketahn stopped beside Nalaki and Garahk and looked down the slope. Well-hidden as they were, he knew where all the humans' clever traps lay. None of Zurvashi's warriors would make it up the slope unscathed.

The thornskulls had questioned such methods. If it came to battle, they wanted to fight Zurvashi only with their strength and skill, as true warriors. But the humans had swayed them by explaining that this battle would not be about honor or glory, but about survival. Kaldarak could win the day, but would not survive the loss of half its warriors in the defense. These traps would protect thornskull lives.

Garahk gestured to one of his warriors, who stepped forward with four barbed spears cradled in his lower arms, their shafts bundled together in a hide sack with a long strap attached.

"As you asked, Spear in Shadows," Garahk said.

Ketahn accepted the bundle and slung it onto his back so the spears lay across his hindquarters. He could tell immediately that they were a little heavier than the spears he'd always used, but that was all right. They'd need the extra weight behind them to pierce Zurvashi's hide.

Nalaki turned to Ketahn. She swung her spear so it rested flat over her upturned palms and held it to him. "You asked for this also."

Near the blunt end of the spear, thin strips of hide were wrapped around the shaft with colorful beads attached that mimicked the rainbow Ketahn had seen in front of Kaldarak's temple that first day. The wood was smooth, dark, and perfectly straight, the silk fastening the head to the shaft tight and precise, and the blackrock honed to strong point.

Ketahn had only requested a war spear sized for a female, not the *daiya's* personal weapon. He met her gaze, his mandibles twitching.

As he closed his hands around the weapon's shaft, Nalaki

said, "My mother carried this weapon against Takarahl, as did I. It thirsts for Zurvashi's blood."

Ketahn tapped a knuckle against his headcrest. "It shall drink well this day."

She chittered softly and bumped his foreleg with hers. "Come. We shall await our guest."

Garahk and Ketahn accompanied the *daiya* as she strode across the clearing, avoiding the many hazards they'd put in place as they descended. They halted just beyond the traps— where the first and hopefully only battle would occur.

Ketahn's mind was still as he waited. Calm draped over him, comfortable as a soft-woven shroud, but beneath it was all his rage, all his frustration, all his desperation. He knew at some point that his tribe had arrived, hearing their hushed voices somewhere behind him, which were followed by the sounds of thornskulls and shadowstalkers climbing to carry several humans to the watch platforms arranged in the trees. He was aware of Ivy's gaze upon him, though he dared not look back at her, and was aware of his sister's approach.

After a long silence, Ahnset asked, "Do you think Korahla will be with the queen?"

Mandibles falling, he glanced at his sister. Her eyes were fixed forward but seemed to be focused on nothing within sight.

"I do not know, broodsister."

"I have wanted nothing more than to see her again since we left," Ahnset said, "and yet now... I dread both her presence and her absence."

What was the truth? What did Ahnset want to hear? Neither of them knew, and no answer would bring comfort. If Korahla was with Zurvashi, she and Ahnset would stand as enemies. If not...it meant Korahla was already dead.

"You will not fight your mate, Ahnset. And she is fine."

"You cannot promise that, Ketahn." A low, unhappy buzz

sounded in her throat. "You do not have to. Just know I stand with you."

Ketahn turned to his sister, hooked a hand around the back of her head, and tugged her down to tip his headcrest against hers. He drew in her familiar scent; it was the first he'd learned upon hatching, even before that of his mother.

"I *will* bring this to an end, Ahnset."

"Vow it will not be yours."

"It will not. I weave my words into a bond, broodsister."

They separated as Telok, Rekosh, and Urkot strode forward to join them. Ketahn tapped a knuckle to his headcrest, meeting each of his friend's gazes, and faced forward again, standing the long war spear on end.

The Tangle was quiet, almost serene, but for the sound of a cool breeze flowing through the leaves overhead. The air smelled of coming rain, and though the sun had risen, the sky remained a gloomy gray.

Half the morning had passed before the first Queen's Claw came into view, high up in the trees. A dark-shrouded thing slinking through the branches, undoubtedly aware of his nearness to Kaldarak; a cautious predator seeking prey too great for it to attack alone.

"No closer," Ketahn called.

The Claw stilled as he was reaching for another branch, his gaze snapping toward Ketahn. "Bold to show yourself, traitor."

"Bold to show yourself, Claw."

Snarling, the Claw glanced beyond Ketahn to the gathered thornskulls. "Betraying your queen once was not enough? Now you join our enemies?"

"*Her* enemies," Nalaki growled.

The Claw's fingers raked the branch, and his mandibles twitched. "You will all suffer for this. Queen Zurvashi is your master—yours and the thornskulls', traitor."

Ketahn raised his forelegs. "Tell her to make haste, then. I have much to accomplish this day after I have slain her."

"I will enjoy watching her slowly pick all of you apart."

The Claw was high up and far off, holding the advantage of height over Ketahn, who stood well within distance of a thrown spear. But Ketahn had tired of waiting. He'd tired of this exchange.

Reaching back, Ketahn tugged a barbed spear from the sack.

From his perch, the Claw chittered. "You are no danger to—"

Ketahn drew his arm up and back and threw the spear hard. The weapon flew in a high arc, its tip angling down as it began its descent.

With a hiss, the Claw darted aside. The spear struck the tree with a dull *thunk* not more than a handspan from where the Claw had been standing. The shaft quivered with the impact.

The Claw stared at the weapon with his mandibles spread and his mouth hanging open.

"Tell Zurvashi she is summoned by Ketahn tes Ishuun'ani Ir'okari, Spear in Shadows." Ketahn hammered a fist against his chest. "She will answer for all she has done."

Cursing, the Claw withdrew, hurrying through the branches without the care he'd displayed during his advance.

Ketahn waited for his dread to resurface, for fear to settle in, for restlessness to spread through his body and sour his gut. But all he had was that calm layered over his seething rage. This was inevitable. It could not be avoided; it could only be won or lost. And some part of him thrilled in fighting back.

He bade that roiling rage wait a little longer. He would gorge it on blood soon enough.

Unlike the Claw who'd come to scout, the queen's main group made no attempt to hide their approach. They sounded like a pack of yatins stomping through the undergrowth, snapping branches and shaking leaves with their heavy steps. The message was clear—even here, beneath the thornskulls' home, Zurvashi neither feared nor respected her old foes.

In response, the thornskulls began thumping and banging—but their rhythm was steady, unified. Not the stomping of wild beasts lusting for blood but the music of a united tribe.

We are as one.

The undergrowth ahead shook and thrashed. Branches broke like bones crunched under a warrior's legs, leaves sighed as though releasing their final breaths. The first drops of rain fell on Ketahn's hide, cold and heavy, just as the plants at the edge of the clearing parted not fifty segments ahead of him.

He felt Ahnset tense beside him. Felt deep growls from Garahk and Telok. Felt the vibrations of the approaching warriors through the ground, in the air.

A gold-clad monster strode into the open, her adornments glittering despite the gloomy sky. But brighter than all that gold were Zurvashi's eyes—blazing amber, they fixated upon Ketahn immediately, and her mandibles spread wide.

She stopped and stood her war spear beside her, rising to her full height. This was not the arrogant, bored creature who passed judgment from the Den of Spirits. This was the warrior queen who'd driven the thornskulls across the mire. This was the beast who'd tried to crush an entire tribe because they had something she'd wanted.

There were no shrouds. Nothing hidden.

This was Zurvashi.

"Little Ketahn," she purred. "We have *much* to discuss."

CHAPTER 30

FANGS EMERGED behind the queen in a broad line, their golden adornments clean and gleaming despite their travels through difficult terrain—though none were as resplendent as Zurvashi herself. Two females Ketahn recognized were at the forefront of the group. Irekah, one of the queen's zealously loyal warriors, and Korahla, who walked with her chin tilted down and her green eyes burning with a grim light.

Korahla's gaze rose, falling upon Ahnset, and her stride faltered.

Ahnset let out a slow, uneven breath beside Ketahn. His heart ached for her.

The Fangs were joined by Claws; the males were all in black shrouds with fur on the shoulders, their barbed spears jutting from the hanging cloth. More of them moved up in the trees, but this spot had been chosen well. None of those branches would lead Zurvashi's Claws any closer to Kaldarak or its defenders.

Zurvashi spread her arms. "Nalaki. I expected you to beg for peace knowing that I was coming. Yet you have arrived with warriors. Is this the full might of Kaldarak?"

Garahk hissed, forelegs rising. "Enough might and more to end you, Blooddrinker."

"So you would have war with Takarahl?"

"War with you," Nalaki said, stepping forward. "For you alone have brought it to us."

Chittering, Zurvashi strode forward. When her warriors moved to follow, she halted them with a wave. "You have taken something of mine. Return it, and I will leave Kaldarak untouched."

"We have nothing that belongs to you," said Nalaki.

"All the Tangle belongs to me," Zurvashi snapped, softening her tone as she continued. "But you have my mate."

Ketahn growled, striding ahead of Nalaki. "I was never yours, Zurvashi, and never will be. If you would conquer me, come try."

Zurvashi took a step closer. "I have conquered you, Ketahn, many times."

"Yet here you stand in the shadow of Kaldarak, come to catch me. You have conquered nothing."

The queen slammed a leg down and curled her fingers, baring her claws. "I have conquered all! The Tangle is mine, you are mine, the lives of every creature here are *mine*. And if Nalaki and her thornskulls mean to stand against me, I will crush them just like your ugly little pet, Ketahn."

His rage burst forth then; he could not look at her hands without seeing them dripping with Ella's blood. But the fires inside him were cold, and his vision was clear—he was not the storm, destroying all in his path without care. He was not Zurvashi.

He was Ketahn. He was Spear in Shadows. He was Ivy's *luveen*, sire to a coming broodling.

He was Zurvashi's end.

"You have much to answer for, Zurvashi," Ketahn said.

Zurvashi's mandibles spread wide, and she opened her

mouth to bare her pointed teeth. "I answer to *no one*. But you, Ketahn, you—"

"Enough words!" he roared, raising his forelegs and spreading his arms. "You have come for me. Take me. Or do you need an army to capture one male?"

Even from such a distance, he could see her fine hairs bristling, could see the faint shimmers rippling through her adornments as they shook with her fury.

"Nalaki, lead your beasts home," Zurvashi said without looking away from Ketahn. "You have no part in this."

"And you have no place here," Nalaki replied. "If you do not wish for war, return to your dark, damp hole."

Now Zurvashi raked her fiery gaze over Nalaki, Garahk, and Ahnset, over Ketahn's tribe and the gathered thornskulls. "Your trees will drink your blood before I am through. All of you. Your little creatures also, Ketahn."

"I will not allow you to harm any of them." Ketahn strode closer to her, all too aware of the nets and spears held by her Claws and Fangs—all too aware that he was entering their range. That he was farther from his friends than from his foes.

Zurvashi advanced too, keeping her warriors in place with another gesture. Fury and desire shone in her eyes. "Do you believe you can protect the rest by facing me alone?"

"I will protect them by slaying you."

"You are unmatched amongst males, little Ketahn. But my Fangs are more than you can overcome."

They stopped with only ten segments left between them. Ketahn stared at her, and in his mind's eye, he saw only more blood. The blood of fallen friends, of brothers and sisters, mothers and sires. Of Ella and all the thornskulls who had died because the queen was fond of a particular shade of purple.

And her scent—her accursed, overpowering scent, carried by the wind—slammed into him, battering his senses, clawing at his instincts. He breathed out heavily through his nose holes, forcing that smell out of his lungs.

His instinct to protect his mate and his broodling would always win out over all else. Always.

"One gesture, and they will be upon you," Zurvashi continued. "You cannot win."

"By your words, you are the one who cannot win. Not without aid." Ketahn clenched his fists, grasping the war spear even tighter. A single throw could end this, but he could not do it with the overly long weapon, and Zurvashi would have too much time to react if he drew a barbed spear from the bundle now.

"There is no warrior among the vrix who can overcome me, fool. None. Not you, not Nalaki or any of her vile beasts." She held her spear with the head angled down, displaying a deceptive lack of care; Ketahn knew she could have it up faster than his eyes could perceive if she wanted to.

"Show me. Show all the Tangle." Ketahn raised his weapon, pointing the head at her throat. "Show your strength or call your Fangs to prove your weakness."

Her mandibles twitched closer together, and the fine hairs on her legs fell before rising again. She growled. "When this is done, you will be mine in every way, little Ketahn."

Turning her spear fully down, she jabbed it into the dirt. With one hand, she grasped the silk wrap that dangled from her belt and tore it away, casting the cloth aside. She swept her bead-and-gold-adorned hair back and tied it into a bundle with a strand of silk.

Irekah stepped forward, breaking the line of Fangs who'd amassed at the edge of the undergrowth. "My queen—"

Zurvashi silenced her with a sharp hiss. She spread her arms wide and rolled them at their shoulders; powerful muscles rippled beneath her hide.

The rain fell a little faster, pelting Ketahn and drumming on the leaves and boughs nearby. Thunder boomed somewhere far off.

Ketahn grasped his war spear in two hands, placing his rear hand close to the shaft's blunt end. Everything else faded away as he focused on the queen. His mandibles opened wide, and his chest rumbled.

Zurvashi took hold of her weapon. Ketahn charged as she pulled it free of the ground.

She snarled, knocking his thrust aside with the shaft of her weapon. The spearhead sliced open her cheek. He was already ducking back when she swung her spear in retaliation. The air itself cried out as her weapon passed just over his head.

Her maddening fragrance was as strong as ever, but it was overtaken by something more enticing—the smell of her blood.

"You will take no more!" Using the length of his weapon to its fullest, Ketahn jabbed at her again and again, faster than thought, allowing her no time to recover between each attack.

Zurvashi growled in frustration and fell back from his onslaught, struggling to defend herself. Her speed was not enough to save her from the bite of Ketahn's spear, yet none of the wounds he inflicted were enough to do anything but spill a few more drops of her blood.

One drop of hers for every one she'd spilled. He would accept nothing less.

She twisted her torso on his next thrust, placing her upper left shoulder directly in the weapon's path. The point punched through her hide and caught against the thick muscle beneath; he'd not put enough force behind it to penetrate any deeper.

But the time it took to pull the spear free—not even a full heartbeat's length—was enough for her to strike.

Zurvashi's spear darted from her right side, striking upward toward Ketahn's head as she knocked his spear farther aside. He dipped backward. The spearhead cut his cheek, crossing the scar she'd left in Takarahl. His left hands flew up to catch the shaft.

Her muscles tensed, and her legs sank into the dirt as she prepared to pull. Ketahn forced her weapon down to the ground, bent his legs, and dropped them onto the shaft with his full weight behind them. The wood snapped, and the upper third of the spear broke away.

Ketahn tried to leap clear of her inevitable strike, but he didn't get clear of her legs. She kicked him in the hindquarters with enough force to flip him backside-over-head. His face hit the ground first.

Ivy called his name, but her voice sounded like it had come from afar—like she'd shouted down from the stars.

The pain of the impact was dull and distant. More immediate was the tingling along his back that resulted from having an enemy behind him. Before his legs swung down, he braced a hand on the ground and shoved hard, flinging his body over in a sloppy flip that sent leaves and clumps of dirt into the air. Spears fell from the sack on his back.

For an instant, he saw the world standing on end. He saw Zurvashi, huge and gold and fiery, swinging her broken spear like a club. The weapon passed his torso with a *whoosh*, close enough for him to feel the disturbed air against his abdomen. Then he crashed down on his back. The shaft of the lone barbed spear remaining in the sack struck his spine hard, and the air burst from his lungs.

No.

Chest and throat ablaze, he sucked in a breath and rolled away. The shaft of Zurvashi's broken spear came down on his left rear leg. Bone crunched, and intense pain jolted through him. Both sensations had faded by the time he'd drawn himself upright.

Somehow, he'd kept hold of his war spear, though the head was in the dirt. Zurvashi lunged at him, arms spread to grab hold. He swept the spear up, spraying dirt and debris into her face.

She snarled and turned her head aside, swinging the stick blindly. Ketahn backed away to avoid the swing. Meaning to thrust his spear at her with full force, he braced his legs behind him. His rear left leg buckled.

Ketahn hissed, his thrust faltering from the unexpected loss of support. It was enough time for Zurvashi to recover—but not before his spear struck her abdomen. Its head sank halfway in; she halted it by clamping a big hand around the shaft.

He tightened his hold on the weapon as his eyes met hers, his mandibles flaring wide. "For Ella!"

Ketahn growled, the sound made as much in rage as in pain; he planted his legs on the ground, causing fresh agony in his wounded leg, and pushed with all his might.

The queen snarled as the spearhead plunged nearly to its widest point. Crimson bubbled from the edges of the wound and trickled over the gold-inlaid leather of her belt. Her body went rigid, hide pulling taut over solid muscle; that quickly, all Ketahn's strength was no longer enough to move her.

He grasped the war spear with both lower hands along with the upper pair, locking his joints in a meaningless attempt to withstand her might.

"All your effort," Zurvashi said, taking a step forward; the spear went no deeper, instead forcing Ketahn back. "All your defiance. All your rage. And it comes to *nothing*."

The spear kept her three segments away from Ketahn. Out of her reach, but not out of danger. But this was meant to be—it always would have ended with him battling her.

Zurvashi advanced another step. The tips of Ketahn's legs slid across the jungle floor and dug gouges in the dirt, and that rear leg screamed again, threatening to give out. The spear shaft crunched in the queen's tightening grasp.

"I learned to make war before you were out of your egg, little

Ketahn." She squeezed the spear harder. The sound of it splintering further was swallowed by thunder rolling across the sky.

She gnashed her mandibles and forced him back another segment. "My greatness was shaped long before you ever held a spear. What are you but a thing for me to do with as I please?"

He released the war spear with his upper right hand just as the shaft shattered in her grip. His fingers caught the lone spear that had remained in the hide sack slung across his back.

Zurvashi knocked the war spear aside, lunging at Ketahn.

"For Ishkal!" He swept the barbed spear up over his shoulder and threw it in one smooth, hard motion. It struck Zurvashi's chest just as the broken shaft of her spear hit Ketahn's exposed right side. Splintered wood pierced his hide and broke against his chest plate. The force of the blow resonated through his every bone. He staggered backward; the queen did the same, the barbed spear jutting from her chest.

Somewhere distant, Ivy called his name again. His heartsthread pulled taut and coursed with fire. He would return to his mate soon. Very soon.

Ketahn's leg struck something long and hard; one of the fallen barbed spears. He hooked it with his leg claws and drew it to his hands. His entire right side throbbed with every movement.

Zurvashi backed away farther, grasping the spear stuck in her chest. Ketahn knew at a glance the wound was not deadly. The spearhead had only lodged itself in the hard bone of her chest without penetrating to the organs inside—not deadly, but painful.

From the edge of his vision, Ketahn spotted the second fallen spear. He kicked it into the air, caught it with his left hand, and advanced.

"For my broodmother," he growled, jabbing with his right spear and striking one of her arms. His left spear lashed out before she could recover, opening a new wound on her abdomen. "For my sire."

His spears struck as fast and often as the rain falling around him. With each blow, he growled the name of someone who'd died because of her. With each blow, more of the queen's blood flowed, running over her gold and leather, over her bits of purple silk, mingling with the rainwater and falling to the ground.

Roaring, she tore the spear free from her chest and swung it at Ketahn. He sank low, driving one of his weapons deep into the uppermost segment of her foreleg. Zurvashi's leg buckled. As she fell forward, she lashed out with a hand.

Ketahn released the lodged weapon and leaned back. Her claws raked across his face, leaving burning trails from just beside his right eyes down to his jaw. He turned his head toward her hand quickly, snapping his mandibles together. Their fangs shredded the flesh of her right hand but did not get a hold.

Zurvashi caught herself on the bent joint of her uninjured foreleg and thrust the spear she'd freed at Ketahn.

He twisted his torso. The spearhead grazed his abdomen. Ketahn slapped his arms down, catching the weapon's shaft between them and his side. Before Zurvashi could pull back, he slammed his foreleg into her extended arm. Bone cracked.

The queen grunted, hand releasing the spear. Mandibles wide, she hissed and threw herself at Ketahn, three arms splayed wide.

Hearts pounding with that cold, deep fury, Ketahn darted aside. Zurvashi just missed him. Her momentum was already carrying her to the ground when he turned with her, stabbing a spear into her lower back just above her hindquarters.

"For all those you have harmed!" He took hold of the spear tucked under his arm, raised it high, and leapt, seeking to drive it down into the back of her neck.

He was only vaguely aware of shouting nearby, of frenzied

movement on the edges of his vision, of others calling his name. During any other battle, he would have seen. He would not have allowed his focus to become so narrow.

A net caught him just before his spear would have hit its mark. The heavy silk strands, weighed with stones, tangled around his limbs and weapon and skewed the angle of his descent.

His spear glanced off the bony ridge between the queen's neck and shoulder and struck the ground. Ketahn came down atop her, landing heavily on his side. He felt the landing jolt through his broken leg, felt the splinters of wood embedded in his side stabbing deeper, felt the heat of blood trickling down his cheek, but none of that meant anything.

No! No, no, no!

Ketahn thrashed to escape the net, attacking the strands with fangs and claws, trying to tear them apart by forcing his arms and legs outward.

Bodies swarmed around him; hands grabbed, claws bit into his hide, and beneath him, the queen shoved herself up.

Ketahn's claws bit back at the vrix grabbing him, but he was too tangled in the net. He roared as they dragged him off Zurvashi. Roared and fought, inflicting as much damage to those around him as possible, and all the while he kept his gaze fixed upon the queen.

His captors slammed him onto the ground. Thick, hard legs came down on his back, arms, and legs, pinning him in place.

"Zurvashi," he growled, twisting his head to bring her into view again.

The queen was standing upright, her shoulders heaving with her ragged breaths. Blood streamed from her many wounds like the runoff from a rainstorm flowing down a cliffside, but her amber eyes were fiery with life. She reached down with two hands, grasping the shaft of the spear jutting from her foreleg, and snapped it off within a handspan of the wound.

"You are without honor!" Nalaki called.

"Honor is for fools," Zurvashi snapped. "I need only strength."

"This battle was between you and Ketahn," Korahla growled from somewhere behind Ketahn.

"He made no challenge. He knew he could not win, and now he will endure his long punishment."

"It was a challenge in spirit, and you—"

"It was no challenge!" Zurvashi roared, stomping a leg on the ground and driving it deep into the dirt. "And you will question your queen no further, *Fang*."

Korahla huffed. "This is not right."

Ivy's voice cut across the air, piercing straight to Ketahn's core. "Ketahn!"

He saw a flash of pale skin and golden hair beyond the queen, and his hearts stuttered. Ivy was standing beside Ahnset and his friends, her eyes wide, wisps of her golden hair blowing in the wind.

Ketahn snarled and bucked, nearly dislodging the vrix holding him down. Ivy wasn't supposed to be this close. She wasn't supposed to be here, especially not now—not when a full battle was unavoidable.

"Hold him steady," Zurvashi commanded, "but ensure he sees."

More weight crashed down on him, ceasing his struggles. His hearts quickened.

Lightning flashed across the gray sky. The immediate thunder shook the ground and made the nearby trees tremble.

The queen turned toward Ivy and the others. There was an echo of that thunder in her voice when she spoke. "Give me the creatures, Nalaki, and those who have betrayed me. Kaldarak may yet survive this day."

Ketahn's claws dug into the dirt, but he could not gain the

purchase necessary to free himself. He had to get to his mate. Had to protect her. "You will not have them."

"I have *you*, little Ketahn. I will kill them."

"They are of Kaldarak." Nalaki stepped forward, standing tall and straight. "You will do them no harm."

The fine hairs on Zurvashi's legs rose. "Korahla."

"My queen?" The Prime Fang's voice was tight and strained, as though she'd spoken through clenched teeth.

"Arrange my Fangs for war. All Kaldarak will be bled dry."

"We do not—"

"Irekah," Zurvashi snarled, "arrange my Fangs for war."

Through the queen's legs, Ketahn saw Ivy. Her eyes met his. So much glittered in their pure blue depths, so much more than he could ever decipher, so much that he yearned to spend his life learning. And now something hardened in those eyes.

The dread in Ketahn's gut hardened along with it.

Ivy curled her hands into fists, one of which was clutched around her little spear, and pressed her lips together.

"*No*," Ketahn rasped. "By the Eight, no."

Ivy walked forward, shrugging off Ahnset's hand when the female vrix reached for her, stopping only when she was ahead of Nalaki.

Ketahn heard his friends and sister speak Ivy's name in question and alarm. She did not reply, and she was no longer looking at Ketahn—she had lifted her gaze to the queen.

"Zurvashi." Ivy's voice, normally soft and sweet, had a hard edge in it as she uttered her words in the vrix tongue. "I, Ivy Foster, challenge you for rule of Takarahl."

Ketahn's hearts ceased beating. His chest constricted, his throat closed, and his fine hairs stood straight up. The world around him fell apart, flooding him with cold beyond anything he'd ever felt, beyond anything Ivy had described from her Earth.

A long, harsh buzz sounded from the queen, and she tilted her head. "You?" She chittered. "You mean to—"

Ivy's eyes narrowed into a glare. "I also challenge you to release my mate."

Zurvashi stiffened and went silent as she stared at Ivy. Finally, she turned and looked back at Ketahn, spreading her mandibles. "This one. *This* is the one you have mated."

No. Broodmother, Hunter, Protector, anyone—no.

CHAPTER 31

"Go back, Ivy," Ketahn rasped in English. "Go back!"

Ivy drew in a deep, shaky breath, clutched her spear a little tighter, and took another step forward. Her legs each weighed a thousand pounds, but that would not stop her. She kept her gaze locked with Zurvashi's; she'd never seen such malice in anyone's eyes.

God, what am I doing?

Exactly what I must do.

"I am his mate," she said, the words coming out strong and smooth, "and he is *mine*."

Some of the humans and vrix behind Ivy called her name and echoed Ketahn's plea for her to withdraw, but she didn't even glance their way. On a primal level, she recognized that she was facing a bloodthirsty beast, a monster, and that looking away from it now would be as good as accepting defeat.

"You chose *this*." The words rumbled from Zurvashi, whose mandibles twitched with the menace of a rattle snake's vibrating tail. "You could have claimed the greatest of our kind, but you chose this ugly little creature that can barely speak. This weak, useless *thing*."

The anger that had sparked in Ivy at the sight of Ketahn being hurt and captured flared again, building into a flame larger and hotter than the bonfire around which she and her friends had sat earlier. It blazed outward from her chest in waves, not nearly strong enough to banish her fear, but she latched onto it all the same.

Ivy thumped the butt of her spear on the ground. "I have claimed him. You will not have him."

"I have him already." Zurvashi waved dismissively. "You are nothing. But I will find pleasure in your death, regardless."

"And I will find relief in yours."

The queen's posture stiffened. "Even from something as pathetic as you, I will not tolerate threats."

Let the real warriors handle this. Ahnset or Telok, Nalaki or Garahk. One of them will overcome her.

But what if they can't? How many of my friends will die? How many of Nalaki's people?

And you think you can, Ivy?

I need to. Ketahn is my mate.

"So answer my challenge, Zurvashi. I am right here." Ivy put her arms out the sides. Rain continued to fall upon her, soaking her hair and running in rivulets down her jumpsuit. "Or do you fear me?"

Zurvashi's eyes narrowed, sharpening her glare, and her injured foreleg scraped across the ground. She chittered. Even to Ivy, it sounded forced, a purposeful display of bravado—or perhaps just an effort to mask the depth of her rage.

"You have been challenged." Ahnset strode up to stand beside Ivy, her heavy steps making the ground shake. "Do you concede victory to Ivy Foster?"

The queen's chittering now was far deeper and more genuine—and more spiteful than anything Ivy had ever heard. "This creature has no right to challenge me." Zurvashi turned to face her warriors, her foreleg nearly buckling as she did so.

"Collect the gold-haired creature. Bring it to me alive. But all I want of that traitor are her fangs, torn from her face."

Several of the female vrix, all clad in gold like Ahnset had once been, stepped out of their formation.

"You have been challenged," said one of the Fangs who also stepped forward. This one was larger than many of the other females.

"You have no place to speak, Korahla," Zurvashi snarled.

Korahla. Ahnset's mate.

Korahla held herself tall, chin raised. Defiant. Strong. She advanced farther. "You have been challenged."

The group of warriors who had moved to obey the queen's command halted, a few visibly confused.

"This creature"—Zurvashi jabbed a long, claw-tipped finger toward Ivy—"is not vrix. It can make no challenge."

"Not the Eight nor Queen Takari proclaimed such." Korahla stomped on the ground, making her gold adornments rattle. "You must answer the challenge."

"Collect the creature," the queen growled.

Korahla and a number of warriors, male and female alike, strode out of their formation, placed themselves ahead of the first group who'd stepped forward, and turned on their comrades with spears raised. Only Korahla remained facing the queen.

Zurvashi curled her fingers to brandish her claws. "More betrayal."

"I will not allow you to deny the very tradition that made you queen." Korahla took her spear in both hands, leveling its head toward Zurvashi. "And I will not allow you to harm my mate."

A soft sound, equally sorrowful and prideful, came from Ahnset.

Korahla's gaze flicked past the queen to land on Ahnset. Only then did Ivy notice that Korahla was wearing a gold band on each of her mandibles—exactly like the one Ahnset had worn before her last journey to Takarahl.

"Your challenge is recognized by the eightfold eyes, Ivy Foster!" Ahnset called.

"No!" Ketahn struggled, but with three female vrix and one male holding him down, his efforts accomplished nothing. "Ivy, no!"

"I do not recognize this challenge," the queen said, snapping her mandible fangs.

The vrix who'd tried to obey her command readied their weapons.

Nalaki chittered. "When your warriors have finished killing each other, mine will gladly end those who remain."

Zurvashi's growl escalated into something closer to a roar as she spun to face Ivy again, halting her warriors with a firm hand gesture. "Your name is not even worthy to be counted amongst those of my slain challengers, worm."

Somehow, Ivy met and held the queen's withering gaze. Somehow, she kept her voice steady. "Maybe not. But you will not need to remember it, Zurvashi, for you will not leave this place. You will not take what is mine."

"The Eight bear witness," intoned Ahnset.

"Our tribe bears witness," said Telok.

"Kaldarak bears witness," said Nalaki.

"Takarahl bears witness," said Korahla.

"And you bear witness, little Ketahn. Watch as I tear your creature apart, one piece at a time." Zurvashi's shoulders rose with a heavy breath. Fresh blood flowed from several of her wounds, immediately diluted by the rain.

"Take my spear, my queen," said one of the Fangs who'd first stepped forward—the one Zurvashi had called Irekah.

Zurvashi walked toward Ivy slowly, completely uncon- cerned by the thornskull army gathered only a few hundred feet away. One of her arms hung at her side, her gait was awkward, and her injured leg nearly faltered with every step. "I need no weapons. My own claws and fangs are more than enough to end this creature."

"Do you understand what you are doing?" Ahnset whispered. "You cannot defeat her as a warrior, Ivy, even with her wounds."

"So I will not defeat her as a warrior. I will defeat her any way I can as a human. As a mate. As a mother-to-be, as a friend." Ivy turned her head and smiled at Ahnset, surprising herself with how genuine the expression was. "As a sister."

An unhappy buzz pulsed from Ahnset. "I cannot help you. No one can. If we do, it will become war. But say the word, sister, and I will battle them all for you."

Ivy extended a trembling hand and settled it on Ahnset's forearm. Ketahn had defeated the queen; Ahnset may well have done the same, given the chance. Especially now with the queen slowed by her wounds. But Ivy? Who the hell was she to attempt this? What could she possibly hope to achieve?

Zurvashi will not have you, my luveen. My heartsthread.

"So you and everyone else may return to their mates, I must do this, Ahnset."

Ahnset huffed. "Eight watch over you, Ivy."

"Kaldarak is behind you," Nalaki said.

"As is your tribe," Rekosh added.

Zurvashi halted after crossing half the distance between herself and Ivy. "You have your challenge, worm. Come and meet your death."

Ivy's hand fell away from Ahnset, immediately settling on her own belly. Her heart clenched and stuttered.

I'm sorry, baby. I know it doesn't make sense, but I have to do this for you.

She felt the presence of her companions behind her—the nearby vrix and the more distant humans, all of whom had come to mean so much to her. All of whom had become her family. Then there were the thornskulls gathered in their battle line just behind the traps, who had accepted Ivy and her tribe despite having so many reasons not to, who had given them a place that could become home.

And before her...

The queen.

If Ivy had thought Ketahn and Ahnset frightening when she'd first glimpsed them, then Zurvashi was utterly nightmarish. Though her immense size and obvious strength were a large part of it, there was more. Ahnset was nearly as big and unbelievably strong, but she didn't exude the same aura.

Zurvashi radiated malevolence. She filled the air with her selfishness, with her ego, with her arrogance—and she carried herself in a way that made it clear she could fulfill any threat she chose to make. This was a being, a *beast*, that saw every other living creature as little more than an insect.

And Ivy had challenged this monster to combat.

Her stomach twisted and sank, making her legs impossibly heavier. This might well have been the dumbest decision of her life. Ahnset was right—Ivy was no warrior. And even if she was, Zurvashi was more than twice her height and at least three or four times her size.

Ivy's gaze fell upon Ketahn again. His eyes were wide and gleaming, his mandibles twitching, and she could almost hear his quick, ragged breaths even from that distance. She'd never seen him so terrified and frenzied. He didn't want her to do this. She didn't want to do it either. Yet she had to. Ketahn had spent all this time protecting Ivy, constantly risking himself to keep her safe, to feed her and shelter her, and she'd felt so helpless through much of that time.

Now Ketahn needed help, and she would not leave him to the whims of fate. She would have her mate back.

Ivy swallowed, her throat dry and raw, and passed her spear to her left hand. She dropped her right hand into the hip pocket of her jumpsuit and closed her fingers around the grip of the flare gun inside. She walked forward.

Zurvashi also advanced. Even her injury-disrupted stride covered the distance faster than Ivy could. "You are like Ketahn, worm. A fool. And you mistake your foolishness for bravery."

The queen seemed larger and larger as she and Ivy drew nearer to one another, and Ivy felt smaller and smaller. Her fingers, damp from rain and sweat, twitched around the flare gun's handle. She'd never used such a tool before—had never fired a gun at all. And now she was relying upon one.

You can do this, Ivy.

Maybe.

God, you'd better pull this off.

"Nothing to say now?" Zurvashi flicked three of her arms outward, spraying blood and water from her hands. "Do you understand? Do you see?" She was only forty feet away now and closing, her gold jewelry clinking as she walked. "You never had any hope of claiming victory, little worm. I hope your screams are as loud and desperate as those of the other creature. What was it called? Ella?"

Ivy clenched her jaw and halted, resting her spear on the ground. Being so close to the queen felt an awful lot like being caught in the path of that tornado with nowhere to go. A spear, a flare gun, a knife, and some traps weren't enough to overcome a force of nature.

She's not a force of nature. She bleeds. She can be killed.

"Is there a part you want me to tear off first?" Zurvashi purred. "I will go slow this time."

Twenty-five feet now, and Ivy couldn't stop her limbs from trembling. She was all too aware of how quickly a vrix could close such a distance.

Only have one shot.

Ivy's nostrils flared as she drew in a steadying breath. "Are you angry to know a worm like me will be the one to end you?"

Zurvashi growled. She put up no defense as she approached, again demonstrating just how unthreatening Ivy was to her.

Ivy tugged the flare gun out of her pocket; it snagged on the material briefly, making her chest seize with panic and allowing the queen to draw a few feet closer.

Raising her shaking hand, Ivy pointed the flare gun at the queen.

Zurvashi stopped and tilted her head. There was only ten feet between them now—a tiny distance for a creature her size. "What have I to fear from anything so small and—"

Ivy pulled the trigger.

The flare gun went off with a heavy thump. A flash of light hit the surrounding rain, making it glow red, and the flare struck Zurvashi in the face. Ivy slitted her eyes against the sudden brightness, turning her head away—but she could still see from the corner of her eye.

Sparks and flames, all in that intense, hellish red, hissed and spat as Zurvashi screamed and reeled backward, her hands flying up to beat at the fire. She growled and snarled in pain and fury. Smoke curled into the air over her, and the stench of burning flesh mingled with the smell of the storm.

Oh, my God. Oh...

Ivy could only stare, horrified and disbelieving, at what she'd done.

This isn't over, Ivy. It's not that easy.

She forced her frozen legs into motion just as the queen swatted the still-burning flare off her face. Ivy backed away with the flare gun raised, though she knew it needed to be reloaded if she was to fire it again.

Zurvashi lowered her hands, and Ivy gasped. Half the queen's face was raw, charred flesh, still smoldering in the rain, and the eyes on that side were ruined. Her other eyes blinked rapidly, and she turned and angled her head as though straining to focus them on something.

Those eyes finally fell upon Ivy.

Spreading her mandibles wide and opening her mouth to release a bestial roar, Zurvashi charged.

Ivy had no time to think. She backpedaled a few steps, the flare gun falling from her numb fingers, and grasped her spear in both hands. Death was racing toward her; all she could hear over the queen's roaring charge was the furious beating of her own heart.

She doesn't get to win. Not ever again.

Tipping her spear to a forty-five-degree angle, Ivy braced its butt on the ground and sank into a wide, low stance.

Zurvashi ran straight onto the spear. The impact of its head piercing her lower abdomen jolted through the shaft. Ivy fell backward, landing hard on her ass. The queen's legs skidded on the damp ground, her injured foreleg buckling and making her drop onto the lowest joint, driving the spear deeper.

The queen filled Ivy's entire field of vision now. Huge, thick limbs, terrifyingly powerful muscles, blood-stained gold. High above, those amber eyes turned downward, still unfocused but ablaze with even more hatred and rage.

"You worm," Zurvashi growled, swinging her arms at Ivy. "You are nothing!"

A claw caught Ivy's left forearm, slicing through the jumpsuit and the flesh beneath. She sucked in a sharp breath. People shouted in the distance, but their voices were muted, distorted, almost ghostly.

Ivy threw herself back and flattened herself on the ground, clamping her right hand over the gash as the fiery pain hit her.

The queen kept swinging wildly, bending lower and lower, forcing more of the spear into her body. Any pain Zurvashi might have felt didn't seem to penetrate her bloodlust. Those huge claws shed drops of blood and water as they cut the air over Ivy, drawing closer and closer.

Had Ivy been able to, she would've pressed herself right

down into the ground. Each *swoosh* of claws was like a fast-swinging pendulum that made her heart skip a beat, and her chest was so tight she could barely draw breath.

Blood streamed down the spear shaft, and the raging queen jerked. More of the weapon disappeared into her body, and those wicked talons came closer still, close enough that Ivy turned her face away to avoid having her nose sliced off by a hair's breadth.

The queen's injured leg was to Ivy's side, its lower segment bent to rest on the ground. The broken shaft of Ketahn's spear jutted from the upper segment of that leg.

"You do not get him," Ivy said through her teeth. Releasing her wound, she hammered her palm up into the broken spear shaft like she was forcing a stuck lever.

Zurvashi snarled as her leg buckled again and her body pitched toward it.

Heels digging into the ground, Ivy scrambled away, narrowly avoiding the queen's falling body. Her heart pounded hard enough to shatter her ribcage, her left hand was cold and tingling, and her forearm was warm and sticky with blood. But she rolled over and got her feet under her, using her hands to balance her first few stumbling steps.

One of the traps was just ahead. She just needed to get Zurvashi over there and—

Pain exploded on Ivy's right thigh, hip, and side. Her feet left the ground, and her body flew forward and to the left. She flipped in the air; she found herself looking up at the dark storm clouds and rustling boughs as lightning arced across the heavens.

Her brain told her that she must've been hit by a truck, that she really should've looked both ways before crossing...

She landed on her right shoulder and rolled, getting a face full of dirt, leaves, and her own wet hair before finally stopping on her back.

Thunder boomed, rattling Ivy to her core. Black spots danced across her vision, and her whole body throbbed with at least a hundred different aches—too much agony to tell what damage had truly been done. She spat the filth from her mouth and sucked in a breath, nearly choking on her dirty hair as she willed her limbs to move. Tears stung her eyes and trickled down her cheeks, lost in the falling rain. She settled a hand upon her belly.

Please be okay, baby. Please, please be okay.

Something large released a strained huff nearby. Leaves and twigs crunched, and a heavy leg came down on the ground. Something dragged behind it, and then there was another step.

Thump, draaaag. Thump, draaaag.

Ivy blinked away her tears and lifted her head, which tried to spin as she was hit with a wave of vertigo.

The queen, a huge, hulking form with one foreleg dragging on the ground, was coming.

CHAPTER 32

KETAHN'S HEARTSTHREAD coiled around both his hearts and squeezed, halting their beating. The breath caught in his lungs, stinging and hot, his every muscle flexed, and all his senses failed save sight.

Ivy was hurt and on the ground. Zurvashi was advancing toward her.

His rage swelled, crashing through him with the force of a flooded river and filling his limbs with fire. He had to get to his mate. Zurvashi would not take his Ivy, would not take his broodling.

He drew in a breath. His fingers curled, sinking deeper into the dirt, and his mandibles spread. His exhalation emerged in a harsh growl as he pushed up with all the might of his fury.

The weight atop him shifted, giving him just enough freedom to spread his legs and use them to drive himself up even harder. The vrix who'd pinned him stumbled away.

His claws caught the strands of the net and shredded them, arms flying outward to tear those strands apart. They were beginning to fall away when the Fangs rushed back to restrain him. Ketahn's claws lashed out at them.

Hide yielded to his blows, and blood flowed from the wounds he inflicted. Big hands grabbed at him, but he kept his body in frenzied motion, giving his enemies no chance to gain a secure hold; they succeeded only in helping tear the broken net away from him.

His injuries pulsed with hot agony, but the pain only pushed him harder, faster. Warm blood mingled with the cool rain on his hide.

Vrix shouted nearby, and he was aware of movement, of bodies approaching. But his focus, despite all his flailing, remained on Ivy—and on Zurvashi, who was only a few segments away from Ketahn's fallen mate.

One of his hands hit something solid dangling from the belt of one of his captors. He clutched the object and tore it free, barely noticing the weight in his hand.

A fanged club, with shards of blackrock jutting from its edges.

He swung the weapon. Flesh squelched and bone cracked beneath the blows he rained upon his enemies, sounds he felt rather than heard. They were blocking him from the only thing that mattered, from the only thing that was his, from the only thing he could not bear to lose.

"Ivy!" he roared as the club struck a Fang's skull and the blackrock teeth lodged deep. "Get up!"

He spun toward his mate only to find a pair of females in his path, both of whom were larger than all the rest—one clad in gold, one with bare hide. The club would not come free, so he released it. His claws thirsted for more blood.

The unadorned female stood her spear upright, aiming its head toward the sky. "Stop, Ketahn."

He lunged at her, prepared to take advantage of her lacking defense, but recognition halted him when she repeated his name.

Ahnset...

"Stand aside," he growled.

"You cannot intervene," Ahnset said firmly. Her shoulders were rising and falling rapidly, her breaths quick and shallow, and her eyes, looking down upon him, were filled with worry and sorrow.

She had been with Ivy and the others. Had she just raced across the clearing to meet him?

It does not matter.

"I will not watch my mate die!" He rushed forward again, and Ahnset stopped him with a hand on his chest.

The other female, Korahla, stepped closer. "If you intervene, the challenge ends. And they"—she tipped her head toward something behind him—"will rush out with you."

Ketahn glanced over his shoulder.

Two groups of the queen's vrix stood facing each other. Irekah was at the center of the group pointed toward the battlefield, Nahkto—a Fang who had been a comrade of Ketahn's during the war—at the center of the group in their path.

His imagination presented him a fleeting but clear image—Ketahn with his injuries racing two dozen healthy Claws and Fangs to reach his mate.

He snarled, his suddenly impotent fury burning his chest and throat and filling him with maddening pressure. His hide itched, and fire crackled just beneath it. "I must go to her."

"If you do, she will die," Korahla said, her voice thick.

"She will die if I do not!"

Zurvashi stopped over Ivy, who was still down on her back, and Ketahn pushed forward again.

Ahnset wrapped her arms around him and held him fast.

He needed to free himself, but the strength lent by his rage was already fading, and he could feel the heavy, angry gazes of the queen's warriors upon him.

Zurvashi bent down and caught hold of Ivy's left arm. Ketahn's mate cried out, clutching at the queen's fingers with her free hand. Undeterred, Zurvashi lifted Ivy off the ground, dangling the human's slight body more than a segment in the air. Blood flowed from between Zurvashi's fingers—Ivy's blood.

Ketahn's heartsthread pulled taut, on the edge of snapping. His leg joints shuddered, threatening to give out, and he remained upright only because of Ahnset's unwavering hold. His entire body trembled in helpless terror as he watched his heartsthread in the grip of that monster. Zurvashi might as well have been holding Ketahn's hearts in her clutches.

"It is not done," Ahnset rasped. "We must have faith in Ivy. She is our hope now."

By your eightfold eyes—or the eyes of any god that will listen—see my mate through this safely.

Or I will tear apart this world and every other to avenge her.

The queen moved Ivy close—almost close enough to take the human's face between her mandibles—and chittered.

That sound reverberated deep into Ketahn, piercing his very spirit. It was the sound of nightmares. It was a sound that would haunt those who heard it until their dying moment.

It was all Zurvashi's hatred, cruelty, and arrogance given voice.

*I*vy clenched her teeth and sucked in a ragged breath through them as her right hand fell away from the queen's fingers. Her pain had found a new focus—her entire left arm. The gash on her forearm burned, her shoulder, forced to support her weight, felt on the verge of being torn from its socket, and the tiniest strengthening of the queen's hold would crush Ivy's bones.

And again, the queen dominated Ivy's vision, spanning from well below her dangling feet to almost two feet over the top of her head. She blinked the rainwater from her eyes.

Zurvashi turned her half-ruined face to direct her working

eyes at Ivy, nearly touching Ivy's throat with the fanged tip of a mandible. The queen's hot breath smelled sickeningly of flowers and blood.

Not going to die here, Ivy.

"More of a fight than I expected," Zurvashi rasped. "For each wound you gave me, I will lengthen your suffering eightfold."

Fighting her instincts, which demanded she grasp the queen's arm to help alleviate the burden on her shoulder, Ivy dropped her right hand to the leg of her jumpsuit.

The queen lifted Ivy higher, putting distance between their faces. Looking slightly down at Zurvashi did not diminish Ivy's fear; she felt like a goldfish dangling over the gaping maw of a hungry cat.

Ivy's fingers found the strap of her leg sheath and followed it to what she sought—the handle of her knife.

"How much pain can you creatures endure?" Zurvashi tilted her head and released a low buzz. "Not nearly enough. Never enough to satisfy me after all you have done."

"And what have I done to you?" Ivy said, the words gritted through her teeth.

"You took what was *mine.*"

"Ketahn chose the better female." Ivy closed her hand around the knife. Her left shoulder wailed; even the small movements caused by her search for the weapon amplified the agonizing strain. She called forth her anger, her loathing, and her protectiveness, using them to tamp down the pain.

"The better female has won, worm," Zurvashi growled, mandibles spreading.

The knife leapt free of its sheath.

"You have not won anything." Ivy swung the knife up.

In her time exploring Ketahn's body, Ivy had discovered spots that were not quite so hard and armor-like. Spots that were softer beneath that leathery hide. His throat, the underside of his jaw, the insides of his joints and under his arms. And the insides of his forearms from wrist to elbow.

The blade hit the underside of Zurvashi's extended forearm and sank deep. The queen hissed in surprise and pain, her grip on Ivy weakening.

Ivy swung her legs up, braced her boots on Zurvashi's chest, and pulled the knife toward the queen's wrist.

The razor-sharp blade sliced through muscle and hide, and hot blood poured over Ivy's hand. The queen's hold broke. For a fraction of a second, Ivy hung by the knife. Then her blood-slick fingers slipped, and Ivy dropped.

Roaring in pain, the queen snatched her arm back, spattering blood all over. Ivy's feet hit the ground. Her legs bent, but she threw her arms out to the sides and caught her balance before she could fall onto her ass again.

Her head spun, and dizziness blurred her vision.

No. Not dying here.

Drawing upon reserves of strength and will Ivy had never known she possessed, she turned and hurried toward the nearest trap. Her legs moved, but they were heavy and clumsy; she struggled to even reach a jog.

The queen snarled behind Ivy. That stomp-drag gait, uneven and labored, began again. Zurvashi was giving chase.

Blood. Bleeding. Need to...

Ivy's vision blurred further. She growled and shook her head hard, clearing it. She dipped a hand into one of her jumpsuit pockets. Her fingers caught the scrap of cloth folded inside. As she pulled it free, the fire starter that had been wrapped within fell out, dropping into her pocket again.

A heavy thump shook the ground behind Ivy. She reflexively glanced backward.

Zurvashi was pushing herself up off the ground, having fallen. Leaves and small twigs clung to her bloody, rain-soaked hide.

Ivy had a thirty-foot lead, and the queen was moving slow, but that was little comfort.

Keeping her feet in motion, Ivy wrapped the cloth around the cut on her forearm. Blood was already blossoming on the white fabric as she bent forward and, using her teeth and her trembling right hand, tied the cloth in place as tight as she could.

Just a little more...and Diego will patch me up.

Just a little more and this is done.

A little more and I'll have Ketahn back.

The ground ahead looked like that of any other part of the jungle—strewn with fallen leaves, twigs, and branches, though it was thicker here. Ivy skirted the edge of that ground, climbing onto a low rise before turning toward the thornskulls who were watching the contest in transfixed silence from upslope.

The queen's pace increased; Zurvashi crashed through the debris on the jungle floor.

Ivy's muscles were on fire, her breath was ragged, and her heart hadn't slowed since word of Zurvashi's approach had reached the early morning bonfire. Her body was desperate for a respite.

Ivy stumbled, her aching legs giving up. She pitched forward, catching herself on hands and knees.

Zurvashi's monstrous growl was pure, cruel glee. Panting, Ivy turned her head toward the queen.

A little farther, you bitch...

Sensing weakness in her prey, Zurvashi put on a burst of speed that was startling due to both her size and the severity of her wounds. "I will feast on your flesh!"

Her leading leg came down on the thick patch of leaves and sank. Her good eyes widened, but her momentum was too great for her to stop.

Zurvashi's huge body crashed through the twigs and leaves,

breaking them away in a cacophony of snapping wood. Her hind legs scraped divots in the ground behind her.

Ivy heard the sound of flesh being punctured amidst all that snapping and thrashing, heard the queen's startled grunt. She took a deep breath, then another, willing her body to stop trembling, willing it to find the strength to move. Finally, she crawled to the edge of the pit to look down upon the queen.

Zurvashi lay at the base of the pit, her hide covered in debris and glistening animal fat. Sharpened stakes had punctured her torso, hindquarters, and two of her arms. But her eyes were already on Ivy, their furious light undiminished.

CHAPTER 33

KETAHN'S BREATH escaped him in a heavy burst. His eyes had not deceived him; what he had just witnessed was true, it was real, but some part of him could not accept it. Some part of him did not believe Zurvashi could be dead.

Everyone stood still and silent, as though afraid to so much as breathe. The air was thick, bristling with uneasy energy that had nothing to do with the storm, an unseen presence that intensified the heavy, sinking feeling in Ketahn's gut.

Zurvashi's growl of pain and fury broke the silence.

"To the queen!" Irekah shouted.

What relief Ketahn might had found vanished as he looked over his shoulder. Irekah and the other Fangs and Claws loyal to Zurvashi charged into Nahkto's group.

At least two dozen more of the queen's warriors remained in their original line, watching warily.

Korahla hissed a curse, and Ahnset released Ketahn. The females raced to join the battle, spears in hand.

Again, Ketahn's instinct demanded he go to Ivy, but he forced himself to turn toward the battling Fangs and Claws. If any of them broke through Korahla's line, they would be free to charge for Zurvashi—for Ivy.

He bent down, retrieved a spear from the Fang he'd killed, and rushed to aid his broodsister and her mate.

The fighting was frenzied; gold-clad Fangs and black-shrouded Claws battled in a chaotic jumble. Ketahn did not hesitate to join. His rage had purpose again, and his spear had fresh targets. Korahla, Ahnset, and Nahkto fought around him, their spears and clubs singing a battle song as they sliced the air and felled their foes.

A Fang charged at Ketahn. Even in the chaos, he recognized Irekah's face, noticed the hateful gleam in her eyes.

He dropped low, well beneath her thrusting spear, and drove the head of his spear up into the underside of her jaw. She sucked in a sharp breath and collapsed over him.

Blood poured onto him as Irekah made strained, choked sounds in her throat. Whether trying to draw breath or to speak it did not matter. A rattling exhalation flowed from her nose holes before she sagged atop him.

Growling, Ketahn heaved her aside.

Ahnset darted past him, slamming into another Fang who'd been about to run her spear through Ketahn. The females fell in a tangle of limbs, but Ahnset came out on top—and stabbed the end of her spear into the other female's neck several times in quick, bloody succession.

Many of the warriors were wounded or dead now, but it was Korahla's fighters—many of whom had fought in the war—who were still standing. The Prime Fang hefted her club, which was dripping with blood and gore, swept her gaze over the battle, and leveled it upon the warriors still hanging back in observation.

"Will you honor the result of the challenge?" she demanded.

Silently, one of the Claws stepped forward, made the sign of the Eight with his arms, and bowed deep. "Yes, Prime Fang."

The rest echoed his words and mimicked his actions.

Korahla's mandibles twitched. She ran a hand up over her face, wiping away blood, and looked at Ketahn and Ahnset. "Go to her. Ensure it is done and your mate...our queen is safe. We will advance soon."

Ketahn barely noticed the pain in his broken leg as he turned and raced across the clearing, only vaguely aware of Ahnset's heavy steps behind him.

The thornskulls had advanced and now stood amidst the traps and around three sides of the pit. They thumped their chests and their weapons in a slow, strong rhythm.

Before them was Ivy, on her knees at the edge of the pit, staring down at Zurvashi—who growled and dragged herself forward, breaking branches and sticks in her path.

Hearts quickening, Ketahn ran faster.

*I*vy let out a shaky exhalation and lowered her hand into her pocket. She doubted her legs would support her if she tried to stand, and her stomach was all fluttery and uncertain. She wasn't sure if it was just the adrenaline high fading or if it was the magnitude of what had happened, of what she'd just done, finally crashing down upon her.

The steady beat created by the thornskulls behind her swept through her body, and somehow it eased her heartrate. She was not done yet, but she was close. So close. Then she could rest.

Zurvashi reached out, buried her claws in the leaves and dirt at the base of the pit, and dragged herself forward. Her hind legs kicked out behind her to give her a boost, but her other limbs seemed unresponsive.

Ivy closed her hand around the fire starter.

"You...cannot win," Zurvashi rasped, her voice choked and thin. "I...have the strength. I...have...the might."

For a moment, Ivy couldn't help but think about the

monsters she'd seen in movies. Those creatures that had almost seemed...immortal. Bloodthirsty killers that could endure unfathomable punishment and continue their terrible work.

How could anything natural sustain such damage and keep moving? How could anything natural *survive* such punishment? Yet here Zurvashi was, body riddled with terrible wounds, her blood pooling on the ground beneath her, and still she drew herself forward. Still, she acted like this wasn't over.

But it would be soon.

Cradling her belly with her left arm, Ivy withdrew the fire starter from her pocket. She activated the device, producing a small, concentrated flame at its end.

"Fire...in the...rain..." Zurvashi chittered. It was a broken sound, still filled with malice but no longer menacing. It had become...pathetic. "Foolish worm."

"You had the strength," Ivy said, "and you used it to take. To take from people, to try to take my mate. But I have something you do not." Pressing her lips together, Ivy extended her arm to hold the fire starter over the pit. "I have a chemist."

She released the tool. It tumbled as it fell, and Zurvashi snarled, clawing her way forward in a sudden, desperate frenzy. Ivy saw the light of that little flame reflected in the queen's amber eyes, four tiny, flickering dots.

The fire starter landed amidst the leaves and branches at the bottom of the pit. With a *whoosh*, the fire flared and spread across the pit, its heat striking Ivy almost immediately. Ivy struggled to her feet and backed away.

The thornskulls quickened their thumping.

As the flames spread over Zurvashi, she thrashed and roared, breaking branches and stakes and sending up burning leaves and ash. Her struggles only intensified the flames. Her blackened, burning form struggled forward a few more feet, spewing a smoky, charred stench into the air.

There was pain in her cries. Pain and fear.

Ivy clutched her belly tighter and clamped her mouth shut, gritting her teeth. She could take relief from this, could be glad that it was finally at an end...but there was no satisfaction in it.

Because I am not like her. I will never be like her.

Zurvashi's hand grasped the edge of the pit. The flesh was largely burned away, revealing the bone beneath, but somehow those fingers curled to sink into the dirt. Ivy backed away another step as the queen pulled herself closer.

A weight settled upon Ivy's shoulder, startling her. She turned, eyes wide, to find Nalaki behind her.

The thornskull *daiya* flicked a glance toward Zurvashi and then looked back at Ivy, drawing her away from the flailing, dying queen. "It is done, Ivy. Only her hatred remains, but it will soon be burned away."

Zurvashi growled. The sound was thin, ragged, savage, and ended in a drawn-out, strained exhalation.

The only sounds that followed it were those of the hungry flames consuming everything in the pit.

"Ivy!"

That voice commanded her attention.

Ketahn. He was running toward her, his gait made awkward by his broken leg, with Ahnset close behind.

Ivy's heart flipped. Tears spilled down her cheeks, and her bottom lip quivered. "Ketahn..."

She raised her arms and had only taken a couple unsteady steps before he was there, snatching her up off the ground and clutching her close. His arms banded around her, one of his big hands engulfing the back of her head, and she embraced him tightly, using all the strength lent by her relief, her elation, her love.

His body trembled against hers, and he released a harsh, shaky breath. But he was solid, he was here, he was alive.

They were alive.

She turned her face toward him and kissed the base of his

mandible, kissed his jaw, kissed his mouth as soft sobs escaped her. "We did it. She's dead."

"You did it," he rasped, fingers curling and claws grazing her scalp. "My foolish, foolish mate. You did it."

Stiffly, hesitantly, he lowered her onto her feet and drew back. His hands were impossibly steady and gentle as he took her left arm and looked down at her hastily bandaged wound, as he cupped her jaw and turned her head to survey the scrapes and bumps she'd taken, as he brushed his fingers over her dirty, tattered jumpsuit to wipe away the leaves and debris clinging to it.

His eyes gleamed with unmasked concern, and his mandibles hung low. An unhappy trill rumbled in his chest. Slowly, he bent down and guided her face up toward his. He scraped his mouth roughly over hers and breathed her in before tipping his headcrest against her forehead and cradling her belly with his lower hands. "My foolish, brave, spirited mate. My queen. You did it."

My queen? He'd never used such an endearment before. Why would he...

Ivy sucked in a sharp breath. "Oh... I challenged..."

I challenged the queen for Takarahl.

And I won.

Shit.

Ketahn straightened and pulled back, opening Ivy's field of view. Ahnset was only a few feet behind him, a bloody spear in hand, and the vrix from Takarahl had gathered close with Korahla at their lead.

"The Eight have witnessed," Ahnset said, "as has our tribe."

"Kaldarak has witnessed," said Nalaki.

"And Takarahl has witnessed." Korahla strode forward, lifting a knuckle to her headcrest and bowing deep. Her eyes were fixed on Ivy. "I am yours, my queen."

The vrix behind her repeated her words and her gesture.

Nalaki thumped her chest. "Ivy *Thoztur*, Slayer of the Blood-drinker Queen, Kaldarak sees you as queen of Takarahl. We welcome peace between yours and mine."

The thornskulls thumped their chests fast and hard to echo their *daiya*.

Ivy turned panicked eyes toward Ketahn, and in English, she whispered. "Ketahn, I don't want this. I can't be a *queen*."

He chittered, mandibles rising in a smile. "I do not want this either. I want my mate all for myself."

"Don't just smile at me then! What do I do?"

His smile only widened. "You are queen. I cannot command you."

"What? Well, I...I...I command you to command me!"

Ketahn chittered harder.

"What does the queen say?" Korahla asked.

Ivy glanced at her and stilled. Ahnset had moved to stand beside Korahla. Even without all those golden adornments and beads, Ahnset was tall, powerful, majestic. But there was so much more to her than that.

Ivy's panic vanished. All that weight slipped away, all that indecision. Zurvashi hadn't been right for the vrix of Takarahl, but Ivy wasn't either.

She stepped forward, meeting Ahnset's gaze and holding it. Every part of Ivy's body hurt, and exhaustion threatened to topple her at any moment, but somehow, she kept her back straight and her shoulders squared.

"I will gladly serve as your Fang, my queen," Ahnset said, sinking closer to Ivy's eye level and dipping her head.

Ivy reached up and placed her fingers beneath Ahnset's chin, raising it. In vrix, she said, "Takarahl would be better served with you as queen."

Ahnset's mandibles twitched, and she tilted her head. "I... Ivy, what are you saying? I...I will not challenge you. Never."

"You do not have to. I am...passing it to you."

"I do not want to rule."

"Which is why I think you will be a great queen." Ivy raised her voice so everyone could hear. "Before all of you and the Eight, I declare Ahnset tes Ishuun'ani Ir'okari queen of Takarahl in my place."

Soft, startled sounds rippled through the vrix on all sides. A few questioned whether it could be done, and it was Korahla who answered.

"If it is the queen's will, then it must be so."

"I will it." Ivy cupped Ahnset's jaw, drawing close and pressing her forehead to the female vrix's headcrest. "Rule with strength, my sister, but also with kindness."

A shiver stole through Ahnset. Her voice was a barely audible rasp when she said, "I am not worthy of this."

"You are more worthy than anyone I know," Ketahn said from behind Ivy. "May your rule be long and peaceful, broodsister."

Ivy released Ahnset and stepped back into her mate's open arms.

"My queen!" the other vrix of Takarahl called in unison.

"My queen," said Korahla to Ahnset, head bowed and knuckle against her headcrest. "I am yours."

Ahnset's stunned gaze lingered on Ivy for a few seconds longer before she turned to Korahla. She closed the distance between them and lifted a hand, taking the gold band on Korahla's right mandible between her forefinger and thumb. Gently, she drew the band off.

"You will always be mine, Korahla." Ahnset slid the band onto her own right mandible. She dipped her head, touching her headcrest to Korahla's. "My mate. My heartsthread."

Ketahn turned Ivy to face him and gathered her up, hugging her against his chest. He nuzzled the side of her neck, one of his mandibles brushing her throat. "I would not have shared you, my heartsthread. Not with anyone."

Ivy smiled and slipped her arm around his neck. "Mmm, that's good to know, because I won't share you either. I won you fair and square."

"What does that mean, Ivy?"

"It means you're mine." She closed her eyes and rested her head on his shoulder. "Now, let's find Diego, because I freaking hurt and I'm feeling woozy."

EPILOGUE

"EVERYTHING IS GOING GREAT HERE." Ivy brushed her palm over her rounded belly, delighting in the intricate patterns woven into the silk of her dress. It'd been a little over three months since they first came to Kaldarak, but she looked as though she were nine months pregnant. "Ketahn started weaving again, and he's been in this heated competition with Rekosh. It drives them crazy that everyone keeps refusing to say which of them is better.

"Cole is like a totally different person. Give that man wood to work with and he'll keep himself occupied for weeks at a time. At least when the thornskulls aren't asking him to go hunting. He's become like the archery master around here."

Ivy chuckled, dropping her gaze to watch her own hand. "And he wasn't just talk. The thornskulls helped us build new dens here in Kaldarak, and the deck Cole built around his was so solid and unique that they've had him helping with all the other platforms. He's really found his place. We're all finding our places. It's hard work, and it's slower for some of us, but Kaldarak is a good place with good people. There's happiness here.

"Ahmya's been learning about the different herbs found around the jungle, and her and Lacey have been working on making gardens up in the trees to grow what we need. Lacey's been pairing with Callie a lot too, coming up with different soaps and mixtures we can put to various uses. Diego, of course, is the village healer, and Will's been learning from him." The corners of Ivy's mouth curled upward. "Those two are so happy together. I'm glad they found each other. We're all really making a life out here.

"Takarahl is a lot better too. Telok, Rekosh, and Urkot just came back from a visit a few days ago. They say the vrix there are happier. No more fear, no more starvation. And you probably already know this, but Ahnset is queen, and she's having a statue of you made to stand in the Den of Spirits. I can't wait until I can go visit it sometime."

Sighing, Ivy lifted her eyes and frowned at the little stone memorial before her. Urkot had helped make the carvings, Cole had added some woodwork, and Ahmya and a few of the others made sure there were always flowers of all colors bunched around it.

In Memory of Ella Lewis. May your dream be forever peaceful.

Ella had lost everything chasing her dream. And this—a piece of stone on a relatively flat part of the hillside near the temple's base, overlooking the waterfall and the pool far below —seemed so insignificant compared to that loss. But when the sun hit just right, the waterfall's mist shimmered with rainbows, and this spot was magical.

"We all wish you were here with us. You would've liked it here." Ivy lifted a hand to wipe gathering tears from her eyes. "I don't know if there was more we could've done, but I know we've all thought about it so much and... And I hope that you found peace. I hope that you're at rest. And I hope that you know you were part of something so much bigger than any of us. We changed this world. We changed the universe.

"We didn't know you for long, but the impact you made on us, on the vrix...on me... That will last forever. This place is our home now. Yours too. And I'll always have a place for you in my heart."

The baby shifted, and Ivy winced at the sharp pang in her pelvis that followed. The pains had come and gone over the last few days, but they'd been especially uncomfortable and consistent today. She took in a deep breath, released it, and rubbed the spot where she'd felt the baby move, waiting until the sensation faded.

Her lips curled into a smile. "Diego thinks I'm due any day now. We're not sure what to expect, but I'm...I'm excited to meet this little one." Ivy chuckled. "And I say one because we're pretty sure that's all that's in here. I'm not going to lie and say I'm not scared. I'm actually terrified. But I...I can't wait. It wasn't something we thought was possible, but here we are, a human and a vrix making life together."

Ivy turned her face toward Ketahn. He sat upon a large rock, basking in the sunlight, with his legs drawn in against his body and his long hair hanging loose around his shoulders. Though he appeared relaxed, Ivy knew he was alert and watching for any signs of danger. He carried new scars from the battle with Zurvashi—as did Ivy—but he was as hauntingly beautiful as ever.

Ketahn's violet eyes met hers, and Ivy's heart quickened. The intensity, desire, and devotion in his gaze was stronger every time he looked upon her.

"I fall deeper in love with him every day," she said, loud enough for him to hear. Her smile softened as Ketahn cocked his head. "I never imagined I'd be this happy when we boarded the *Somnium*. As much as I'd hoped things would get better for me, I think a part of me never really believed they would. But all this... It's beyond my wildest dreams."

Ketahn let out a low rumble. His long legs unfolded, and he

rose languidly from the rock to stride toward her. "I have not yet given you even a small part of all you deserve, my *nyleea*."

Ivy chuckled. "I also never thought my dream lover would be an arachnotaur."

"Vrix."

She grinned. "A sexy spider man."

"Female…"

Laughter bubbled up from within her, cut short by a hiss as she clenched her belly.

Alarm flashed in his eyes, the fine hairs on his legs rose, and he hurried across that last bit of distance, sinking low to lean over her and place his hands on her shoulders. "What is wrong, my heartsthread?"

Ivy shook her head. She took in several deep breaths and waited until the pain ebbed before speaking. "It's okay. I'm okay. It's just the false labor pains Diego mentioned. They're getting a little stronger."

"We should return," he said, brushing a knuckle over her cheek.

"Okay. Can you help me up?"

He settled a pair of hands on her hips and slipped his other palms beneath her arms, easily lifting her off the ground and placing her on her feet. As soon as she was standing, Ketahn placed a hand on her back for support until she found her balance and turned to face him.

It was in that moment that something popped inside her.

Ivy gasped as a gush of warm liquid ran down the insides of her legs and pooled at her feet. "Oh God."

Ketahn's chin dipped, and his mandibles twitched as he looked at the ground. His nose holes flared with a deep inhalation. Voice thick with concern, he said, "Ivy… What is this? What is happening?"

Placing both hands on her belly, she looked up at Ketahn with wide, uncertain eyes. "The baby is coming."

$\mathcal{K}$etahn stared at his mate, trying to make sense of her words. He'd known that humans gave birth rather than laying eggs—he'd known it for a long while. He'd watched Ivy's belly swell over the last few moon cycles as their broodling grew inside her, and she had described the process to him in hopes of helping him know what to expect.

But Ivy and Diego had also made it clear that they didn't really know what to expect themselves.

And even with all that knowledge, even having watched some of that process take place before his eyes, a part of his mind couldn't quite understand that when she said the baby was coming, she meant it was going to come out of her.

Not hatch from an egg, but come *out of her.*

Instinct forced him out of his stupor. He sank low, sweeping an arm behind her legs to lift her off the ground, and cradled her against his chest. His embrace was as tight as he could make it while remaining mindful of her belly, of the broodling, of her state.

Diego had told him there was a chance of losing both Ivy and the broodling, wanting to ensure Ketahn knew the risks. That he understood what could happen.

After all he and Ivy had survived, Ketahn would not lose her now. He could not. This was the little female who'd overcome Zurvashi. She would endure. She *had* to.

He raced back into Kaldarak, barely noticing the bridges swaying beneath him, crossing the pathways and platforms as though he'd lived amongst them for his entire life. She tensed in his arms, her brow pinched with pain.

"Almost there, my *nyleea*," he rasped. His fingers trembled with the effort it took to keep them from curling and pricking her with his claws.

He called for Diego the moment the healer's den was in

423

sight, not slowing his pace to await a response. Within heartbeats, he'd reached the platform. He shoved the silk hanging over the entrance aside and darted into the den.

"Shit! Ketahn!" Diego was beside the bed, frantically shoving his feet into a pair of pants, his bare ass toward Ketahn. Will, shirtless, was standing on the opposite side, holding a blanket over his pelvis.

"Ivy leaked," Ketahn growled. "The broodling comes."

"Leaked?"

"Um...sorry for intruding," Ivy said, flicking a glance between Diego and Will, "but um, my water broke."

"It did not break, it spilled," Ketahn said. "Like a flood."

"Okay, that's an exaggeration, but it doesn't matter. The—" Ivy's words were cut off by a grunt. Her face scrunched up again, and she turned it against Ketahn's chest, digging her blunt nails into his hide.

Will's eyes flared. "The baby's coming?"

Ketahn snarled, fine hairs bristling. "That is what I said!"

"Lay her there," Diego said, pointing toward the raised bed on the opposite side of the den. "Will, we need hot water, and gather up all the spare cloth we have."

"On it," Will said, dropping the blanket, seemingly uncaring about his nakedness as he snatched his pants off the floor and tugged them on, hopping past Ketahn toward the entrance.

Diego strode toward Ivy and halted, spitting a curse. "One sec." He darted to a bowl of water set on a stand near his bed, snatched up one of the soaps Lacey had made, and scrubbed his hands and arms.

Ketahn crossed the den and carefully laid Ivy atop the bed. Her cheeks were red, and a sheen of sweat had formed on her skin. She hooked her hands under her belly and let out a long, trembling breath through rounded lips.

She looked up at Ketahn, and her voice was small when she said, "I'm scared."

"I will not let anything harm you, Ivy." He smoothed her hair back and took one of her hands in his. "This will be a day only for joy."

"You're going to be just fine, Ivy," Diego said as he hurried over. He'd thrown on a white shirt and was drying his hands with a cloth. "Are you sticking around for this, Ketahn?"

Ketahn growled. "I will not leave her."

"Figured as much." Diego opened the container set atop a nearby stand, the one he'd called a medkit. "Hard as it might be, I'm going to need you to do anything I ask you to without question, okay? Whatever your instincts, I need you to listen to me."

"Anything for her. For our broodling."

"All right. Go ahead and get that dress off her unless you're okay with it being ruined. You can put a blanket over her instead."

Ketahn looked at Ivy, and she nodded. He lifted her gently to slide the dress up, and then supported her in a sitting position while he drew the garment off over her head. She lay back again slowly, hissing through her teeth.

Heartsthread twisting and pulling tight, Ketahn took her hand again. Already, this reminded him too much of when she'd been ill—of when he'd been helpless to relieve her suffering.

Will returned soon enough, and Ketahn was vaguely aware of voices outside the den. Humans and vrix spoke out there in hushed tones, but he did not grant their words any attention. Everything he had went to his mate.

The day, which he had declared one only for joy, dragged on. Diego remained calm and controlled. He directed Ivy's breathing, spoke to her encouragingly, soothingly, and gave Will and Ketahn tasks with firmness and surety—though Ketahn's work largely consisted of helping Ivy remain comfortable and at ease.

She maintained calm well on her own, but comfort seemed beyond Ivy's reach. She was in pain, the worst Ketahn had witnessed, and his spirit itself ached at seeing it. He prayed silently to the Eight during his mate's agonized moans and whimpers, begging them to let him take on her suffering, to let him carry the burden of that pain, to spare his female from this.

They did not answer his prayers.

The sun had fallen, plunging Kaldarak into gloom, when Ivy's soft sounds escalated into cries. Will hurriedly arranged several of the strange human lights to illuminate the den, casting Ivy in an unnatural white glow.

"It's time," Diego announced, positioning himself between Ivy's legs.

"I thought it was time when we came," Ketahn said, wiping sweat from his mate's brow.

"It was. But now it's *time* time. Ivy, I want you to grasp your thighs and push on your next *kun trakshun*."

Ivy nodded. Her breaths were heavy, her skin was glistening and overly pale, and there were dark circles under her eyes. With Ketahn's help, she sat up and wrapped her hands around her thighs. The next time her belly tightened, she bared her clenched teeth and pushed.

But for all his mate's pushing, the broodling still did not come.

She pushed again and again, straining a little harder each time, drawing upon deeper and deeper reserves of strength. Her exhaustion was apparent; she could not have had anything left to give. But she pushed again, regardless.

"I see it," Will exclaimed from the other side of the bed. "It's coming. You're doing amazing, Ivy."

Ketahn squeezed her hand. "Almost, my heartsthread."

With a gasp, Ivy turned toward Ketahn and pressed her forehead to his, panting. "I love you."

"You are my heart beating outside my chest, Ivy. You are my reason, my desire, my everything." He cupped the back of her head, holding her firmly against him. "You are strong, female."

They remained that way, sharing breaths, until she was

struck by another contraction. Tearing away from him, she grasped her knees and pushed, her growl growing into a scream.

"That's it, Ivy! Keep pushing!" Diego said. "Almost...almost... Yes!"

A rush of air fled Ivy as she slackened against Ketahn's arm, her head falling back on his shoulder. Diego cradled something in his arms, which he hurriedly wrapped in a silk cloth.

Ivy stared at the bundle with worried eyes. "Is it...?"

A soft, high cry broke the silence that had seized the den after Ivy's words.

Diego looked up at them and grinned before placing the bundle in Ivy's outstretched, waiting arms. "Your baby."

She drew it against her chest and peeled back the silk cloth. Violet eyes blinked up at Ketahn.

Ketahn's hearts stuttered, and his breath hitched as he stared down at the broodling. *His* broodling. Four eyes, their violet as vibrant as Ketahn's, set in a soft-featured, human face. Two little mandibles, and a head topped not by a headcrest but a tuft of black hair streaked with gold. Four arms, six legs, tiny claspers, hindquarters, and black skin with purple and white markings.

The shape of a vrix with the softness of a human. A perfect mix of two worlds that had come together as one.

And it was male. He was male.

Ketahn brushed the pad of a finger over his broodling's belly. The little one squirmed in his mother's arms. A tiny hand caught Ketahn's knuckle, not even large enough to circle it completely, but the grip was firm. Claws tipped the broodling's five fingers.

Ivy traced her fingertips over the broodling's eyebrows. "He's...beautiful."

Warmth bloomed in Ketahn's chest, pulsing soothingly along his heartsthread. He felt that thread weaving itself anew, adding a new, impossibly strong strand that led directly to this tiny, wondrous creature. "He is. Our beautiful broodling."

"Our son."

"You two picked out a name yet?" Will asked, grinning.

Ivy looked up at Ketahn, her eyes shining brighter than the stars on a clear night. She smiled. "Give him a name."

Delicately, Ketahn smoothed his hand over that gold-streaked hair. "Akalahn. Akalahn tes Ivy'ani Ul'okari. Son of the female who freed Takarahl, the once-queen. He who is our hope, our joy, our future."

AUTHOR'S NOTE

Thank you so, so much for following along on this journey with us! You seriously cannot express how grateful we are that you took a chance on this trilogy, especially if you are someone who is deathly afraid of spiders. We know it took a lot for you to look past those creepy parts to see the loving, protective soul that is Ketahn.

We love Ketahn and Ivy, and it was wonderful to tell their story...but it's time to say goodbye—at least for now. We've had so many of you asking: Will Ketahn's friends get their own books?

The answer: Yes! Rekosh, Urkot, and Telok will each be getting a standalone book of their own with their human mates.

Working on this trilogy has been an amazing experience. We loved being able to tell a story at its own pace, allowing us to fully build the world and not rush the relationship or the plot. We definitely plan to do it again sometime in the future.

For those of you interested, we also have a Facebook Reader Group where we post updates and more! We'd love it if you joined us there.

Also, if you enjoyed *Bound*, could you maybe, possibly, perhaps leave a review? Pretty, pretty please? We would be ever so grateful! I mean, we're already incredibly grateful, but it would still be wonderful. :D

Also turn the page for a sneak peek at Rekosh's cover, The Weaver.

USA TODAY BESTSELLING AUTHOR

TIFFANY ROBERTS

THE VRIX BOOK

THE WEAVER

ALSO BY TIFFANY ROBERTS

Fallen from the Stars

Lover from the Waves

ALIENS AMONG US

Taken by the Alien Next Door

Stalked by the Alien Assassin

Claimed by the Alien Bodyguard

STANDALONE TITLES

Claimed by an Alien Warrior

Dustwalker

Yearning For Her

Escaping Wonderland

His Darkest Craving

The Warlock's Kiss

Ice Bound: Short Story

ISLE OF THE FORGOTTEN

Make Me Burn

Make Me Hunger

Make Me Whole

Make Me Yours

VALOS OF SONHADRA COLLABORATION

Tiffany Roberts - Undying

Tiffany Roberts - Unleashed

VENYS NEEDS MEN COLLABORATION

Tiffany Roberts - To Tame a Dragon

Tiffany Roberts – To Love a Dragon

ABOUT THE AUTHOR

Tiffany Roberts is the pseudonym for Tiffany and Robert Freund, a husband and wife writing duo. Tiffany was born and bred in Idaho, and Robert was a native of New York City before moving across the country to be with her. The two have always shared a passion for reading and writing, and it was their dream to combine their mighty powers to create the sorts of books they want to read. They write character driven sci-fi and fantasy romance, creating happily-ever-afters for the alien and unknown.

Sign up for our Newsletter!
Check out our social media sites and more!